The

ELOQUENCE

of

GRIEF

a novel

JANET HUBBARD

THE ELOQUENCE OF GRIEF
By Janet Hubbard
Published by TouchPoint Press
www.touchpointpress.com

Softcover ISBN: 978-1-956851-95-3

Editor: Kimberly Coghlan
Cover Design: Sheri Williams
Cover image © Wayne Ensrud

Library of Congress Control Number: 2024943869

Printed in the United States of America.

To Colette Buret

And to all the women who came forward in the #MeToo Movement, something I never dreamed possible when I started this novel.

PART ONE

What happened on that night would shape the rest of my life. Unbeknown to me, I was about to keep a secret—a devastating, suffocating secret . . . one that I wouldn't breathe a word of to my husband of a decade, one that would silence me for the next 21 years.

—Rowena Chiu, "Opinion," the *New York Times*

RUTH – 1996

1

"Ruth, I'm desperate for a memoir. We're missing the boat on this one."

I swore under my breath. As a literary agent known to be ahead of the latest book trend, I had helped to make Jim Horowitz, the editor on the other end of the line, a name in the business. Along with myself, of course. The sudden memoir craze after Mary Karr's *The Liars Club* and Dave Pelzer's *A Child Called It* became bestsellers had caught me off-guard. Rumors making the rounds in the industry of a memoir written by an Irish schoolteacher to be released in a few months further convinced me that the memoir was here to stay.

My assistant Kathy walked quietly across the room and placed a manila envelope on the growing pile before me. "Listen, Jim," I said into the phone. "I'll find a memoir if I have to write it." He laughed and hung up.

Kathy returned with a cup of coffee. "That last manuscript I put on the pile has a personal letter attached," she said. I picked it up. Round letters, beautifully scripted, the date inscribed in the upper left corner. April 16, 1996. *Dearest Ruthie,* it started. Only two people called me Ruthie—my mother, who was no longer with us, and Moira Rivers. Looking at the ink flow on the page, I assumed she still had the Mont Blanc fountain pen I gave her when she sold her first story to *The Paris Review*.

I consider the enclosed pages a letter I have been writing for a decade. I apologize for the length, but that's what it takes to craft a portion of one's life on paper, I've found. It starts that weekend sixteen years ago when you and Paul were out of town. A phone call from a stranger. A bad decision on my part. A terrible fate awaited me. (My name, Moira, is Greek for fate, remember?)

Memories of the weekend Moira was referring to flooded in. I had gone up to Connecticut with my then-boyfriend Seamus to meet his folks. When I returned to the city, I learned that Moira, a junior editor like me, had called in sick two days in a row and missed the most important appointment of her career. I rushed to her and found her curled up on the sofa in Paul's apartment. I knew he had left for Chicago on business the same day I took the train to Connecticut and was due to return soon.

"I know. I look like the wrath of god," she said when I entered.

"I won't deny it. I wish you had called me when this started. Your cheek is red."

She reached up and touched it. "I was dizzy and fell against the medicine cabinet door."

"Flu?"

"Something like that."

Moira was my best friend. We had been roommates for five years before I met Detective Seamus O'Connell and fell in love. Moira decided to move into a studio apartment. I had never seen this version of her. Averting my gaze. Curled up in a knot. She looked to me like someone in a state of despair, but what did I know? I went into the kitchen, made tea, and brought it to her. She sat up and took a sip. I asked her outright if Paul had dumped her, and she shook her head. Something had happened, though, and I knew it would take all my wiles to wring the truth from her over the next few days. I ran down the list: Your parents? Bad diagnosis? I didn't dare mention depression. I knew her mother had "spells" when Moira was a child and that she worried it could happen to her, too. "You look sad."

"I'm really tired, but I'll be okay. I'm already better now that you're here."

But when she returned to the office, she was detached and began making excuses whenever I suggested a film or dinner. I called my mother, Stella, who loved Moira as much as I did. She advised me to be patient and let Moira tell me what was troubling her when she was ready. So I stood at the sidelines as Moira, in quick succession, announced she was pregnant, was marrying, was moving to Connecticut, and announced the birth of Lyra—and here we were sixteen years later. I had intuited years ago that she was running, but from what? Eventually, her sedate life in the suburbs felt fake to me, and as much as I still loved her, I had started to pull away. What is friendship, after all, without shared confidences? I had put all my energy into my literary agency and was now successful. At the same time, I hadn't created time for relationships. Seamus was long gone. My mother, too.

I returned to the letter.

> Some people manage to exist in the womb of a lie with aplomb. When I signed up to live a lie, I had no idea of the consequences if the truth began to emerge, or, on second thought, perhaps I knew the consequences would be so dire that to speak the truth would cause my life to unravel. What I didn't grasp when I decided to live in the darkness of secrecy, which means living in silence, is the chasm it creates between me and those I love. Secrets divide. I hope after reading the enclosed pages, you will understand. I admit I also need your help. Remember those nightmares I used to have of a wolf chasing me, nipping at my heels? The wolf is once again at my door.
>
> I love you, Moira

I opened my desk drawer and felt behind papers until my fingers wrapped around a chocolate bar that had been there a record length of time, then sat down and pulled Moira's manuscript from the envelope. Time to push away the emotions that threatened to engulf me, the way you push away a cobweb with a broom when entering a long-unused room.

MOIRA'S SECRET:
A MEMOIR - 1979

2

The night of the rape, April 15, 1979, started on a lilting note. Paul Rivers and I were making dinner together in his kitchen on West 72nd Street in Manhattan. In my twenty-eight-year-old purview, I had arrived. Maybe you'd have to have come from a small, nondescript town in the South to feel that way. Come as the only child of a mismatched couple—from the groin of a shamed preacher. Maybe you would have to have filled your library shelves with your journals, reflecting your struggles with writing two hundred short stories over the past decade. You'd have to know about striving to know what I'm saying.

I studied Paul as he stood at the center island, chopping mushrooms. Lanky and boyish at thirty-five, he had inserted himself into my celebration dinner with my best friend, Ruth, at a French bistro on West Fifty-Fifth Street and shared my fifteen seconds of writing fame. I had just sold a story to The *Paris Review*. On top of that, after five years of sharing our deepest secrets, clothing, interests, and occupations, I had also opted to leave Ruth's apartment and move into a place of my own, a tiny studio on West Seventy-Fifth Street near Central Park West. No one could argue with the price, ninety dollars a month. The timing was perfect, for Ruth had announced only yesterday that she was seriously thinking about having her boyfriend Seamus move in with her. We were on the cusp of our third decade, when women of our generation were experiencing a new freedom that permitted us to dream of a lifestyle different from our mothers.

I had noticed Paul the moment he entered the restaurant. The owner greeted him warmly in French and ushered him to the banquette next to Ruth and me. When I glanced over, he gave a slight nod, then pulled papers from his briefcase and began to study them. Ruth lit a cigarette and began talking about the story I had sold and the question it had raised. What kind of mother would protect her son who she knew in her heart had killed someone?

"I knew when I started the story that she would never turn him in," I said. "The story is based on a true event, though I doubt anybody remembers."

"Then she admits she lied on her deathbed. It's a damn fine story." Ruth put out her cigarette, reached into her bag, pulled out a beautifully wrapped gift, and handed it to me. I opened it and gave a little gasp. Inside was a Mont Blanc fountain pen I knew she couldn't afford. "Oh, Ruthie." I reached across the table and grasped her hand.

"You can call yourself a writer now," she said gruffly. "And don't forget, if we can make it in this town . . ."

I joined in chanting the credo of every talented young person we knew. ". . . we can make it anywhere."

The waiter arrived with a bottle of champagne. "Ruth, you've really gone too far."

"I didn't order it." She glanced up at the waiter.

The man sitting beside Ruth on the banquette said, "I couldn't help but overhear your conversation. It's a big deal to sell a story. I hope you don't mind . . ."

"It was a fluke," I said.

"They all say that. May I join you? Paul Rivers. Reporter for *The New York Times*."

I glanced over at Ruth, who acquiesced with her eyes. "Why not?" I said.

He turned out to be a nimble conversationalist, and soon, the three of us were talking as though we were old friends. Paul mentioned his parents' newspaper in Connecticut, and Ruth piped up, saying she couldn't imagine a paper that contained more opposite views from hers on just about everything. Paul had a defensive comeback: "If I shared the views of my parents, I wouldn't be writing for *The Times*."

Bravo, I wanted to say.

He invited us to stay for dinner. His treat. We smiled at each other and accepted. The conversation continued until late in the evening. We lamented the state of the city under Ed Koch, the graffiti everywhere, the drugs threatening to overtake all the parks, and the high crime rate, but we also compared notes on our favorite bands and the books on our shelves.

I gave Paul my phone number, and the next morning he called to ask me out. I soon entered a social vortex that felt way out of my league. Paul's world shifted seamlessly and swiftly from meet-ups with journalists to elegant sit-down dinners on Park Avenue with friends with whom he had grown up, attended boarding. Their feet were planted on the same path when they were toddlers, if not before. Everyone was polite—and vaguely curious. Paul's mother was attractive but a bit like a mannequin, with coiffed shoulder-length black hair that didn't move when she threw her head back with laughter and a manner of speaking that Ruth described as Park Avenue lockjaw. His father was silver-haired, erudite—and charming. He tended to hold a woman's hand a second too long, splay his hand across her back, and then bring her in for a little smooch, acceptable behavior in their vaunted circles.

As we sat in his apartment's kitchen a year into our relationship, I marveled that we had gotten this far. Paul's voice brought me back to the present. "Where are you, on the moon?"

"I was recalling what it felt like to enter your parents' world. Your world, too, of course. It was like landing on the moon."

"I thought I had landed on the moon when I met you. We were in ze leetle French beestro." He started singing like Maurice Chevalier, "I remember it well . . ." He poured more wine into our glasses.

"We should go back. Make it our spot."

"We'll do it when I return. I just learned today that I'm being sent back to Paris for two months."

I was shocked. "When?"

"I leave for Chicago tomorrow morning before the crack of dawn—and return in a week, then I have two days here before taking off for Paris." He put the chicken onto heated plates, and we sat at the round table in his kitchen. He lit the candles. "You're invited to join me there."

"Where? Chicago? Paris?"

"Either or both."

"Paul! I have a job!"

I felt a mental slump when he mentioned Paris. I knew he had left someone behind, a fellow journalist named Katia, when he had completed a three-month apprenticeship there a year ago. I was also aware that she had been in touch with him recently, as she was trying to acquire a visa to work in the United States, and she knew he could help her. When I told my mother about her, she'd advised me to 'strike while the iron was hot,' then added, "You're not getting any younger, I might add." I was twenty-nine.

"Oh, Mama." I had sighed, wondering how she could advise her only child to marry when she had been miserable in her own marriage.

"There's more," Paul said.

"Oh?"

"My father called yesterday. He wants me to consider taking over his newspaper in a year or two."

"You mean move back to Connecticut?"

"That's the idea."

"What'd you tell him?"

"I said I'd have to think about it."

"I see."

"No, you don't." He laughed. "You've already told me you won't leave the city."

"But this doesn't really have to do with me."

He grew serious. "But it does, Moira. Your opinion matters a lot."

"Okay. Connecticut is too far away."

"How about Paris? Oh, too far away. Sorry." His eyes twinkled. He grabbed my hand. "Come on," he said, "I have to be up at four to catch my flight. Your place or mine?"

"Mine. I have to finish typing up the reasons Mr. Cohen should promote me to senior editor."

"You'll get the promotion, Moira. That little publishing house wouldn't survive without you."

I wanted to sort through the mixed feelings running rampant through me, but Paul's humor was intoxicating. He linked his arm in mine on the short walk to my brownstone and stopped every few yards to kiss me.

As we arrived in front of the four-story dilapidated building I called home, he said, "This is a good time to announce we're getting rid of this drab little apartment." I, too, was growing tired of the traipsing back and forth between his luxury apartment and my studio, but I also didn't feel ready to let it go. Sensing my hesitancy, Paul said, "We'll keep it as your writing studio."

That was Paul. A solution for any problem that might arise— and a laissez-faire attitude about life. Everything would work out because, well, why wouldn't it? I, on the other hand, was brought up by a mother who waited for the next shoe to fall—and a father who turned everything over to Jesus the Savior. If something good happened, then Jesus had singled you out, and if something terrible befell you, then Jesus was trying to teach you a lesson. Jesus delivered a severe blow when my father was ousted from his big Baptist church in the city. A woman he was counseling committed suicide. Thereafter, my mother suffered terrible bouts of depression that made her take to her bed, sometimes for weeks. What cheered her was to have me read to her. She eschewed the Bible, but she adored listening to Charles and Mary Lamb's *Tales from Shakespeare;* at the same time, she relished a good mystery like Dashiell Hammett's *The Thin Man.*

It was her entry into the world of the imagination that fed my own. I began writing to entertain Mama and listened carefully when the black woman who worked for her, Neta, started sharing her own stories.

"You make it all sound so easy," I said to Paul. "Move in with me. Come to Paris . . ."

"Even better, you could quit your job and write full-time."

"Tempt me some more." I laughed.

We ran up the two flights of stairs to my apartment. Paul turned up Kiss' song, "I was made for loving you," and crooned along with the lead singer, taking me in his arms with a fervor that made me feel more wanted than I ever had. He sang, "I wanna lay at your feet . . ." and with that, I took him in my arms in a flight of abandonment, both of us hungry for each other.

We lay there after, spent, talking. "I wasn't protected," I said.

"I know." He turned over and looked at me. "Look, Moira, we have a lot to iron out with our careers and all, but I want us to be together . . . forever. We can do it all—make babies, write, travel . . ."

"Wrong order," I said. "Write, maybe travel, maybe marry, maybe have a baby?"

He sighed. "I wish we could stay together tonight, but I have to go home and pack. You want to come back with me?"

"Of course I do! But I also want to be fresh for tomorrow's meeting with Larry Cohen."

"Compromise. Walk me down to the street then?" I slipped into lounge pants and a tee shirt, and sneakers. "My doorman Eddie will have a set of keys for you. Feel free to move in while I'm away."

"I'm already feeling abandoned."

"Don't. I'll be back in a week. And if I go to Paris for two months, I'm guaranteed a promotion when I return."

"Well, in that case . . ."

"You'll have time to devote to your writing. He took my hand, his face serious. "This period abroad will establish me as a journalist. I'll fly you over." I was quiet as we continued moving down the stairs, trying to hide what was starting to feel like neediness. Once on the sidewalk, he put his arms around me. "I love you, Moira." The first time he had uttered the magical words.

"I love you, too."

Something shifted in that moment. Our relationship suddenly felt solid. Like we had a future ahead. I watched him walk down the block, suddenly breaking into a tap-dance Fred-Astaire style, his trench coat flapping behind him. I laughed, resisting the urge to run after him.

3

The telephone jangled at midnight as I sat on the floor working on a presentation for my boss the following morning. *Paul calling to say good night*, I thought and picked up automatically.

"Hey you," I said in a whispery voice.

"Moira? It's Jonathan Starkweather. Erin Charles' friend." When I didn't respond, he said, "Sorry. I'm not Mr. Romeo." His laugh was charming.

I tried to recall what Erin had told me about Jonathan. I had barely been paying attention to a girl eight years younger who was smitten with a guy she met at her college. A dancer with a new company. Cutting-edge stuff. Erotic. Towers of entwined muscular bodies on the poster Erin brought to show me.

"I have a huge favor to ask," Jonathan said. "I stay at my manager's when I'm in the city, but he forgot to leave me a key. Erin is with her parents way the hell out in New Jersey."

I didn't hesitate. "I'm sorry, Jonathan. I have an early morning meeting."

"You won't know I'm there. It's raining."

Ambivalence set in. "Really, I'm sorry."

"Well . . . thanks anyhow."

He hung up. I felt slightly guilty; people always came into the city and crashed with friends. I had just hosted a guy from my hometown, a friend of a friend, and it was no big deal. I went into the bathroom and washed my face, then returned to my studio/bedroom to work. Paul called and said he would only get five hours of sleep, if that. He promised to call once he settled in Chicago and told me he loved me again. "Love you, too," I said. I didn't think to mention the call from Jonathan.

I reached up to turn out the light when the phone rang again. I let it ring a few times, then thought it might be Paul calling back or my friend Ruthie calling from Connecticut. I answered.

"Moira. Jonathan again. Seriously, I've called five friends, and no one answered. I'm a little desperate." Just when I was about to suggest a hotel, he added, "I didn't bring my credit card, and I'm low on cash."

"Alright, then."

"You're a doll. I'll be there in ten minutes."

He didn't ask for my address. I wanted to call Erin in New Hope for a head's up, but I knew her mother was ill. I was annoyed at myself for relenting. I could go to Paul's if Jonathan seemed weird, I told myself. I put on my favorite album, "Blue," by Joni Mitchell. When the buzzer went off, I ran down the stairs to the door. Through the glass door, I saw a man of medium height and strong build peering in, a cocky grin on his face. I opened the door. Reddish-gold curls fell just below his ears, and I gazed into purplish-blue eyes. He wore jeans and a tee shirt, his hair wet from the rain, and he was chewing gum. Relief replaced the minor concern that he might not be a good guy. Nothing threatening. I relaxed.

He followed me up the stairs, saying how grateful he was. "You don't travel with a backpack?" I asked.

"Naw. I'll be out of here tomorrow morning. I can pick up a toothbrush on my way out."

I put my finger to my lips as we entered the small foyer that divided my apartment from my neighbor's—an old woman whose space consisted of a single room filled with clutter. Mozart's *Concerto in C Major* wafted from her stereo but diminished once the door closed. I carefully put the police lock back in place. Entering my apartment, I pointed to the bathroom if he needed it, then led him to the dining area, where there was a daybed. "That's all there is," I said. My room is there," I added, pointing to the doorway leading to my combination living room/bedroom.

He glanced around. "This place is cool," he said.

I turned on the light in my tiny kitchen and asked if he wanted a drink of water before retiring. As I turned to open the refrigerator door, he grabbed me from behind, and I felt a rush of adrenaline coursing through me. I moved quickly enough to break his hold and turned to face him. "Forget it," I said.

He laughed. In a flash, he had me in a chokehold, dragging me into my bedroom and pushing me onto the bed. "You want me," he said. "They all do." I felt his erection through his pants as he climbed on top of me. I reached for the telephone, but he knocked it out of my hand.

When he let go, I jumped up. "Get away from me!" I yelled.

He slapped my face so hard, I reeled backward. The sound of his pants being unzipped brought on another rush of power, and I somehow managed to crawl up, but in a second, he was on me again, his arm across my chest, pinning me down.

I was like a fish caught in a net, pleading with him to stop. His eyes turned slate gray. I opened my mouth to scream, but no sound emerged. He yanked at my lounge pants and succeeded in pulling them down. I tried to keep my legs straight, Barbie-doll style, but he wedged his way in, all the while calling me a cunt, a whore, a slut. Talking, talking. The pain was searing. My mind fragmented, like the pieces of glass in a kaleidoscope. The primordial grunts of the beast on top of me, monosyllabic like the humming and drumming of a rotating fan, faded as I drifted up into the ceiling and beyond. I remembered that Pablo Neruda attacked his maid, who came to clean his toilet. The words from his book, *Memoirs*, appeared in the ether: *"One morning I decided to go for all, and grabbed her by the wrist . . . The encounter was like that of a man and a statue. She kept her eyes open throughout, unmoved."*

What kept me alive was Mitchell's voice singing in my ear, *"I am on a lonely road, and I am traveling, traveling, traveling . . ."*

I turned my head to the right, where the light from my neighbor Irene's window shone like a beacon. The stranger on top of me moaned, hopped off quickly, and went into the kitchen. I instinctively pulled the sheet up over me. He was back in a second, wiping himself with my dish towel.

"You wanted that," he said again. "They all want it. I see them standing outside the dressing room, wanting, wanting. But I take who I want." I refused to look at him. "Erin didn't tell you how I fucked her friend Lucy while Erin was in the other bed, pretending to be asleep?" He looked at me. "I'm here for the night, you know. You invited me. Who would deny it?"

I reached up and touched my neck. "God, did I hurt you?" His voice turned soft and compassionate. Then, "I'm going to check out your fridge. Don't even think about picking up the phone." He whirled into the kitchen. I leaped up and slipped back into the pants. I heard the refrigerator door open, then the sound of the utensil drawer opening and closing. He returned with a can of beer in his hand.

"I need to go to the bathroom," I said. He sipped the beer. "I want to take a shower."

"Go ahead, Moira. I'm not going anywhere."

I rolled off the bed without glancing at him, pulled up my pants, walked to the bathroom, and closed the door behind me. It didn't have a lock. I turned on the shower. I leaned against the sink, trembling. The brownstone was a turn-of-the-century building, and there was a dumbwaiter in my bathroom, which used to be a kitchen. On days when I was home, I heard the building janitor maneuvering the dumbwaiter up and down the five floors, removing trash. I unlocked the door the size of a window to the dumbwaiter and hesitated before the dark, gaping hole. Two hairy ropes acted as a pulley. I grabbed one and pulled, and the elevator lumbered up from the basement. I was relieved to see a pair of slippers left under the sink, and I slipped into them. Once the elevator was level, I stepped onto it and closed the door behind me. It was pitch black inside, and I was three floors up. I pulled hard on the rope in my right hand and felt the elevator descending. After what felt like an eternity, it touched the bottom, and I pushed on the door, and it opened. A dim light burned in the corner of the basement, enough for me to make my way to the back door of the building. I exited, the pounding of my heart drowning out any other sounds. I slogged through puddles as I made my way to the front of the building. Jonathan, I realized, could be on the sidewalk waiting for me. I peered around the corner of the building and, seeing no one, took off at a lope to Columbus Avenue.

The light from a coffee shop beckoned. I entered, shivering uncontrollably. The clock on the wall said two o'clock. Two other patrons were seated in front of the window. A young pimply-faced waiter came to my table. "I need a cup of coffee," I said. "But I don't have any money." He sauntered to the back and spoke to an older man who looked over at me. I saw him fill a mug with dark, steaming liquid. "I can bring the money to you tomorrow," I said. I picked up a newspaper from an empty table and held it up in front of me in case Jonathan passed by.

Paul was still home, but to reach him, I either had to go out the door and run to his apartment or find a phone booth and call him collect. The waiter kept bringing coffee. I sat, numb, unable to think clearly. It occurred to me that Paul wouldn't understand why I let a strange man into my apartment at midnight. He would have to cancel his trip.

The manager approached. "Everything okay, miss?"

I hesitated. *Should I ask him to telephone the police?* Jonathan would tell them his version of the story. He would say that I invited him to stay. The manager poured the rest of the pot of coffee into my cup and returned to his perch. My vagina felt bruised. Sitting was uncomfortable. The next time I glanced at the clock, it was four o'clock. Paul's flight was at six, which meant he would be leaving soon for the airport soon. He offered me his apartment. *I'll go there*, I decided. I stepped out into the light rain and walked south to 72nd Street. The doorman said that Paul left ten minutes ago. His expression conveyed his concern that a love story had gone awry.

"He left a key for me?"

"He did, miss." He handed me the key, and I walked to the elevator. Entering the empty, mirrored elevator, I stared into the reflection—a stranger's eyes, as the elevator swooped me to the tenth floor. I unlocked the door to Paul's apartment and found a note.

> *Darling, I couldn't sleep. I had the urge to go to you at two this morning but know how important your meeting with Larry Cohen is. Good luck, angel. Make yourself at home. See you in a week—an eternity! Love, Paul.*

I climbed into the shower and stood beneath the pelting water for a long time, hoping the hot water would wash it all away: the semen, the horror, the pain, the shame. I scrubbed and scrubbed. I climbed into Paul's bed and fell into a deep sleep. When I emerged from my dream state, I was convinced that the semen of the rapist was an embalming fluid and I was a corpse.

4

Hours passed. The phone rang in Paul's kitchen, and I could hear Ruth's voice, then Paul's, on the answering machine, asking me to pick up as I moved in and out of a recurring nightmare from childhood. A wolf chased me, teeth bared, until I screamed—only the scream was silent. This morning, the wolf's eyes bounced around the room, and I woke up in a cold sweat, sure that Jonathan was in the room.

I stayed awake. It was the next day, and I felt preternaturally calm as I thought about what to do. To report to the police or not to report. I had already taken a hot shower, which I realized too late had destroyed evidence. Maybe on another level, I knew exactly what I was doing. Stories were always being passed around among women about the nightmare of surviving rape, only to have to go through the emergency room ordeal where your body was invaded again as health professionals followed the protocol of examining the victim, seeking evidence, then photographing the most private part of the person, along with any areas that were bruised. This was followed up by interrogation by police, who were looking for any flaw in the victim's story. I couldn't bear the thought of being touched by anyone, nor when I went back over the rape could I be sure I would remember every detail.

What had me reeling was that only hours before, I had experienced transcendent lovemaking with the man I hoped to spend my life with. The aftermath of that experience had left me in a state of bliss, and I thought that perhaps it was being in this space that had made me more vulnerable when Jonathan called asking for a place to stay. My musings emerged from a childhood spent in an evangelical church. Had I done something horrible to someone that God would bring Satan into my life to crush me?

Late afternoon Tuesday, the door buzzer sounded, and the doorman announced that Ruth Schwartz wanted to come up. I climbed out of bed and staggered to the door, wearing a bathrobe. From the peephole, I saw Ruth walking down the corridor with purpose. I unlocked the door and went back to the couch. She entered. "I've been calling your apartment. It finally occurred to me I might find you here."

"I'm sorry."

I followed her into the kitchen, where she placed a grocery bag on the counter. "I brought some soup. We could go to my doctor if you're up for it."

"I don't need to see a doctor."

"I'll make some tea, then." She wore a miniskirt and pumps. Finally, she had a good haircut. Since I had known her, she had complained incessantly about being too fat and short— having too much frizzy hair and oversized breasts. Her lips puckered as her intelligent brown eyes studied me. I couldn't hold her gaze. "You look awful." When I didn't respond, she said, her voice tender now, "I can't go away three days without something happening?" She was subtly checking on her basic hunch that things weren't right in my world. After sharing an apartment with me for five years, she had an uncanny sense of my emotional status. "No bad diagnosis? No getting dumped by Paul?"

I shook my head. "Flu, probably. What about you?"

"Seamus' family, meaning his mother, has reservations about him being with a Jewish girl." She made a face as she got up and went into the kitchen. I watched from the couch as she ladled soup into the bowls and placed one on the table in front of me. "Taste the soup. It's delicious." I did as commanded, and she was right. "There's a girl in the town, I forget her name, Seamus dated her in high school. His mom kept bringing up her name, which is probably why I've repressed it."

I half-listened to her story, and when she stopped speaking for a moment, I knew she was studying me. I couldn't look her in the eye.

She said, "What's going on with you and Paul?"

"He's returning from Chicago in five days, then goes to Paris for two months." I told her about his opportunity to prove himself to the *Times*.

"I'm away from you for three days, and all this happens? You're not okay with him leaving. Is that it?"

It felt as though we were discussing something no longer relevant. As though the past forty-eight hours had wiped away the past year. "It's fine." I knew I sounded snappy. I was, in fact, glad for the reprieve. I would figure out a way to mend the crack in my psyche. I still believed it possible to do that.

Her intuition was in high gear. She knew something had caused my current state. She tended to sound like she was scolding when she was worried. "I wish you had called Larry Cohen to cancel your appointment. He's miffed."

Larry was the top editor at our publishing house. "You think I won't get the promotion now?"

"I'll talk to him. He can't do without you and me both, and he knows it. I'm outta there, which he's not happy about. He'll come around."

I didn't care, but I couldn't tell her that. She went quiet, and maybe for the first time in our friendship, we experienced an awkward silence. My mind kept repeating, *Tell her tell her tell her.* I suddenly wanted to hear her yell, "Fuck, he did that to you?" Hear her at her most pissed off, calling the police. Swearing vengeance on the rapist. On Erin for introducing the guy into my life. Ruth had been my protector since I moved in with her six years ago. "You won't have a chance in hell in this town without me," she had said. "It's a snake pit. Deadly dangerous if you don't know what you're doing."

She was my introduction to New York—and a world of infinite possibility. She seemed to know everything. She knew how to swim away from a shark—and which schools of fish were acceptable. It took a while, but I grew a thicker skin and developed special antennae for dangerous situations. I learned to walk tall, move at a rapid clip, ignore the whistles and catcalls, keep my shoulders back, and look straight ahead. I learned how *not* to look or behave like a victim. Though it could be said that danger lurked at every corner, I developed an invincible attitude that had served me well. Yet, after all that, I blinked wrong and was raped. Why did that make me feel like a failure? Like a slut who would never feel clean again.

I decided to test the waters. "You know, Erin's boyfriend, the dancer, called and was looking for a place to stay Sunday night."

"Good god! That girl has no boundaries. I wouldn't trust anybody she sent my way." An existential crack opened between us in that moment. The raped woman and the un-raped woman.

"Sorry. I know you like her, or you've adopted her, or whatever, but she's troubled. You're a magnet for people like that."

Erin and I had met at a book fair where editors talked to students about job opportunities. She showed me a few poems, and I gave her suggestions about where to send them. She called a few weeks later, and I met her for tea. That was when she told me she was raped at age twelve and had gone through a big court case in New Jersey. The poor girl! What I found disturbing was how disengaged she was when recounting her story. How flat-toned. How unhealed. And how queasy her story had made me feel.

At the same time, I was sympathetic, and she had latched onto me. She invited me to her parents' home in New Jersey for a weekend, and I accepted. Ethan and Sarah Charles were socialists, bohemians, and drunks. Theirs was a rambling house, cobbled with porches on two sides and a kitchen where serious cooking and drinking occurred. The living room was floor-to-ceiling books and record albums.

They were starting a new book on jazz after moderate success with other books. A piano occupied the far corner, and they applauded when I sat down and played a Chopin piece. Sarah played ragtime music and gardened and wrote biographies with her husband. Ethan was a raconteur. They barely had enough to live on, always planning the next book, lost in research and dreams. I found them fascinating.

After a few visits, Erin entered my bedroom and asked me not to sleep with her father. I laughed as though she were a jealous kid sister and told her she was being absurd. But when I told Ruth about it, she said, 'She's sick, Moira. Advise her to get help and run like hell.'

I followed her advice, creating more space between Erin and her family and me. Erin had come to my apartment a month ago demanding to know why I had not returned her calls. For the first time, I wondered if she had intentionally sent Jonathan my way.

Ruth's voice interrupted my reverie. "You said no, didn't you?"

I opened my eyes and saw the look of reprobation. I barely hesitated before answering, "Of course." I would look back and view this as a watershed moment—the moment I decided to once and for all keep it a secret from my best friend.

5

Erin answered on the first ring. I asked her to meet me for lunch. After a brief hesitation, she agreed. I hung up before she could change her mind. I had written only one word in my journal over the past four days. "Raped," plus the date: April 15, 1979. On the next page, I put the date, April 20, 1979: "Tomorrow, I meet with Erin. If she supports me, I will go to the police." Next, I dialed an old friend, Bill Erickson, who was with a small law firm that handled criminal cases. His secretary answered and asked me to wait.

"Moira?"

"Bill, something happened. I need to see you."

"You just got lucky. A client canceled. Can you be here in an hour?"

I rushed to my apartment for clothes. I couldn't believe the anxiety that overcame me when I entered the building. I continued up the stairs and unlocked the door to my apartment. A quick peek in the bathroom and I saw that the dumbwaiter door was wide open. I locked it, then went to my closet and changed. I was trembling.

Bill was on the phone when I was escorted into his office. He motioned for me to take a seat. After hanging up, he turned to me. "Moira. It's good to see you. What's going on?" He sat in his chair across the desk from me.

I told him the story of my rape. He sat quietly, his hands forming a steeple, his eyes never leaving my face.

"I wish you had called me immediately. And gone to the emergency room that morning. You've showered, obviously."

I nodded.

"Without a report from the police or the hospital, you need corroboration of a witness who maybe heard something. I assume you fought. Don't you have an old lady next door who stays awake all night?"

"Irene. She had music blaring. And besides, she's nearly deaf."

"You didn't scream?"

"No. I tried to fight him, but he slapped me. Hard." My eyes filled with tears.

"On the face?"

"Yes. He slapped me, and I froze."

"Okay. Whatever I say is not about blaming you or making you feel worse. I am going to try to deal with facts. Personally, I want to kill the guy, but let's not go there. If we go to the police, will you try for a conviction? If he's arrested, and that's a big *if*, there will be publicity—even I know his name. I saw a small write-up in the paper about his troupe—ask yourself if you can handle that." I remained mute. "If the police understand the attacker had some relationship with you, you can go to headquarters before the district magistrate and swear out a complaint."

"But I didn't have a relationship with him. They'll say I should have known better."

He nodded. "If the district magistrate believes you, he can issue a warrant for his arrest. Of course, Starkweather might countersue." He stopped and looked at me. "You mentioned his girlfriend. She could make it a much stronger case. Will she help?"

"I'm having lunch with her after I leave here. I think so."

"That's your best bet." He paused. "Do you have support? Boyfriend?"

"I haven't told anyone."

"Moira . . ."

"My boyfriend was away when it happened. He's coming back tomorrow."

"If he's worth his salt, he'll be there for you."

"Would you want to know if your girlfriend was raped?"

"It would be hard, but I think yes, I would want to know. To help."

"How would you do that?"

He squirmed in his chair, then got up and paced back and forth. "I'm not sure. I'd go after him legally, though, I hate saying this, but very few rapists are convicted. I would say fewer than one-tenth. And they don't get much time." He stopped and looked at me. "If it were my girlfriend, I think I would pay someone to harm him. I can't believe I'm saying that, but I'd try to make sure he didn't do it again—to anyone."

"I hear women say that if they manage to take the guy to court, they feel like they're on trial."

"I think that's true. The NYPD has the Sex Crimes Unit now. I know an officer there. He says the rape kits will be stacked up a mile high in a decade. They're not out there looking for these jerks."

"When my friend Tom was mugged in Central Park, they went after the perpetrator, and he's in jail. He got justice."

"I get what you're saying. Men get justice, and women don't. If you ask me, there's too much verbiage around this. The new wave of feminists want rape listed as a violent crime, which it is, but it's sexual assault, and the minute the word sexual is introduced, it seems to lessen the impact."

"Men make the laws, and they don't see this as a serious crime; is that it?"

"I'm afraid so. It's tough for lawyers when victims come to us. We know they won't get a fair chance."

"This has changed the trajectory of my life," I said. "I know that already. I am not functioning on the level I was before this happened."

He paused. "I never thought of that. If it makes you feel any better, and it probably won't, but this Jonathan Starkweather is one sick dude. He went to a good school, and he's getting some fame, and he feels entitled." He glanced at the blinking light on his phone. It was time to wrap up our conversation that had no solutions.

"You're busy, Bill. Thank you for your time."

He stood, and I did, too. "You girls need to elect better representatives. Listen, if you want to go after that bastard, I'm your man. But from everything you've said, your only hope is Erin." He walked me to the door. "You should probably get checked for venereal disease. And maybe get a pregnancy check."

The fear that arose in me was excruciating. I nodded.

"Call me if Erin says yes to helping you."

I nodded and exited his office, unable to meet his gaze, though I knew it was sympathetic.

6

Erin sat at a corner table reading the menu. "Hullo," she said, glancing up at me when I approached the table. She was wary. Sullen. I sat quickly and glanced at the menu. "Order whatever you want," I said. She chose *lapin a la moutarde,* and I decided on an omelet.

"How's Paul?" I found her nonchalance unsettling. Anxiety licked at my brain. "Erin, let's cut to the chase. Sunday night, your dream guy Jonathan came to my apartment and raped me."

"He told me you seduced him."

So he had gotten to her first. I sat for a moment staring at her. *She's a victim also,* I thought, *and now unwilling to believe me.* In her case, a man ran from the woods and knocked her off her bicycle. A court case followed, and he was locked up, but the moment he was released, he attacked another girl and murdered her. Her mother and I sat up late one night, and she had cried while describing what the trauma had done to their family.

"Emotionally, she's never recovered," her mother had said. "She was an innocent child, for god's sake. She's very unstable, especially sexually."

"Erin," I said at last. "What else would he say? Do you really think he would admit to it? He told me he got in bed with another friend of yours."

"She had been flirting with him all day." Her tone was petulant. I had an urge to slap her, and two seconds after, I wondered if

Jonathan Starkweather had ever shut her up by hitting her. The waiter arrived with our food, and we grew quiet as he placed our dishes on the table. Erin shifted her attention to her plate, eating painstakingly. I picked up my fork and tried to take a bite of the omelet, but it sat in my mouth like a church wafer.

"Why did you give Jonathan my phone number?"

"The last time I visited you, he asked me for your number in case he wanted to call me." She looked uncertain. "Don't blame me, Moira. You could have told him he couldn't stay."

"I did, but he persisted. I trusted the situation because he was *your* friend. I assumed you wouldn't be with a guy who went around attacking your friends."

Cold reality set in. She was not going to help me. I studied her lank, stringy hair. The poor quality of her skin. Slumped posture. Yet a strong, sexual energy percolated beneath her bookworm demeanor. I suddenly recalled how she had been amazed at this attractive man entering her university library and selecting her, of all people, to take to his bed. He was a senior at an Ivy League school, starting to be known for creating an *avant-garde* dance company. Erin was proud that she had said no to his advances but laughed when she told me how he got his way anyhow. Why was that just coming back to me now? I had barely been paying attention to her the day she stopped by and rambled on and on about him. A girl with a crush.

"He's my knight in shining armor," she said now. "He's been through a lot. He's from a rich, fucked-up family. His brother killed himself." She put her fork down, bemused, and possibly deflated. "What do you want me to do?"

"Go with me to the police. I waited too long, and now I need your help." Words tumbled out of me. "I'm pleading with you, Erin."

"I can't."

I reached over and grasped her wrist. "You mean you won't." People from the adjoining table glanced over at us. She jerked her hand free. "Admit it, Erin. You set me up in his eyes as unattainable. You fed his lust with lies about me. You put your friends in the line of fire."

Her expression told me I was right. She put down her fork. "Okay. He stole your number from my wallet."

I was right. I had been targeted by Jonathan Starkweather. I wasn't completely insane.

"It doesn't bother you that you're with a serial rapist? After what you went through?"

She looked suddenly stricken. "He's a wounded soul."

"He has no soul! And you don't either. Your poor mother." Despair clouded her face.

I hissed, "I will never forgive you." I put cash on the table, quietly got up, and walked out of the restaurant towards home.

7

The fatigue was overwhelming. I woke several times a night, sometimes from a nightmare, usually involving the wolf at the door, and other times from a slight noise or imagined movement. I slept now with a light on. During insomniac hours, I would lie there and wonder how other victims coped with the trauma. I questioned my stability and worried that I would disappear into the world of horrors my mother had succumbed to when I was a child. The black hole of depression. There wasn't a name for it back then, or at least I never heard the word uttered.

I looked up the phone number of the therapist I had seen when my previous relationship fell apart. I dialed it, and a receptionist came on and explained that he had moved out of the city, but she would be happy to recommend someone in his group. She made an appointment for the following week.

Paul called me at work and said he'd be home in time for dinner. On my way home, I stopped by the local grocer and hurried to the apartment to change clothes before he arrived. The phone rang, and it was his mother, Katherine, who, after a few pleasantries, asked me to write down the number of a friend she wanted Paul to speak with about an article for her paper. I opened the drawer to the secretary and pulled out a legal pad. A photo fell out, which I ignored, and after a few more pleasantries, Katherine said she had to run. I picked up the photograph. Paul was standing with a woman, looking up at him with an adoring expression. He returned her gaze, a warm smile on his face, his arm circling her waist. I knew it was Katia.

I put a small lamb roast in the oven and went to shower. When Paul arrived, the table was set, the wine opened, and the roast almost done. I had changed into casual clothes. He kissed me warmly and took off to shower. When he returned to the kitchen, he poured each of us a glass of wine and told me about his week in Chicago.

Removing the roast from the oven, I asked, "What about Paris?"

"It's a go," he said. "But it's going to involve much more traveling than I thought."

"Where to?"

"Russia, for one. Paris will be a base. It's an incredible opportunity." We sat at the table, and he carved the meat into thin slices. "Let's look at a calendar after dinner and figure out when you can take a week to come over."

"Sure."

"I won't know my schedule until I'm there, but I'll do my best to make it happen." I could tell he was excited but was downplaying the whole thing slightly for my benefit. "I'll be back in time for your birthday in June. In fact, I made reservations at a special place for the big day."

"I'm not allowed to guess?"

"Nope. It's a surprise." He sipped his wine. "*Pas mal.*" He held up his glass. "To us."

"To us."

"And a big apology for going on about myself. You're back to normal?"

No, never, I wanted to blurt but said instead, "Almost. I missed my job interview Monday."

He frowned. "You weren't sick when I left you. Remember? I wanted you to come back with me, but you said you had the interview with Cohen."

My story wasn't adding up in his mind, and he was correct. But I wasn't about to tell him what happened, so I said nothing.

He didn't wait for a reply but instead continued speaking. "I hope you'll have some time for your writing while I'm away. That's one benefit, and there must be more . . . let's see . . . no love crazy man disturbing your sleep in the middle of the night, no parties we must attend . . ."

"I'm going to miss you."

"I hope you mean that."

The phone rang, and he jumped up. It was his boss. I put the dishes in the dishwasher. Paul hung up and dialed another number. He was in full-on work mode, which I had gradually adapted to over the past year. He moved at a lightning pace, drank more than usual, and talked rapidly. He exhausted himself. I went into the bedroom when he went to his typewriter. That could take another hour. We had tonight and tomorrow night before he left.

I was in my robe when he entered. "I'm sorry," he said. "I plan to have all the business out of the way so we can have a fine evening tomorrow. Does that work?" He sat on the edge of the bed. "You've been pretty quiet."

"I'm okay."

"I realize I never consulted with you about the Paris job."

"I assumed you didn't want to know my reaction?"

"I knew I wouldn't change my mind if you objected. I'm confessing to being self-centered, in case you don't know."

"Having to do with needing your dad's approval, I would say."

He smiled. "Psychology 101? My brother got out of the rat race. Moved to another country. That left me doing double duty in a way. Not that I mind that much."

"Is your dad sufficiently impressed? That's maybe what you need to let go of."

"My mom expects great things of me, too." He said it jokingly, but I knew he was serious.

"Do you think she approves of me?"

"She doesn't quite know what to make of a southern belle with strong opinions."

"Interesting. She's the most opinionated woman I know. Well, next to Ruthie. Did your mom get to know Katia?"

"Oh, yes. They became fast buddies."

"I saw the photo in the desk. I was looking for a pen."

"It's okay, Love."

"She's working in Paris?"

"She is."

"Will you be working with her?"

"Yes."

"In Russia?"

"I don't know. She and I are friends, Moira. And colleagues. I hope you and I have a future, but I can't do anything about that until I return." I remained mute. "We told each other a week ago that we love each other. Can that be enough for now?"

"Will you promise to tell me if anything changes?"

"Of course. And I'd like to ask the same of you."

I suddenly felt caught in a trap of my own making. He leaned down and kissed me, then crawled into bed with me, his hands racing over my body beneath my nightgown. I would learn later about dissociation and how that act often meant returning to literature in my mind, just as I had done as a child. Just as I was doing now. Again, the words of Pablo Neruda in his memoir published in 1974 after he had assaulted a maid: *One morning, I decided to go for all, and grabbed her by the wrist—the encounter was that of a man and a statue. She kept her eyes open throughout, unmoved.* There was something more, but I couldn't remember.

Paul came quickly and hopped up immediately. "I hate to say it, but I have another hour of work."

I pretended to yawn. "Okay." He reached to turn off the lamp, but I said, "No, please, I'm sleeping with a light on now."

"Oh. Okay. When did that start?"

"I was having nightmares."

He gave me a peck on the cheek. "See you in the morning, Darling."

"Night."

I felt myself dropping into a void where faces swirled around me. I had been reading a New Age book on souls departing the psyche and people going on quests to find and restore them. I sank deeper into the abyss of night and found myself surrounded by hundreds of blinking eyes. I started to run, and in a moment heard panting behind me, someone's breath on my neck. I turned to look, and the wolf was gaining on me, nipping at my heels. I screamed.

Paul's voice woke me. "Moira, come here." He reached out and pulled me to him. "You're safe," he said.

8

The therapist was a square-shaped woman with a gray pageboy, bangs, and big glasses worn down her nose. She could have been sixty or in her forties. The address was on Madison Avenue in an understated building. I wondered immediately upon entering where to sit, as there was a sofa with three cushions, which would put me close to her, or a chair across from her that would give me distance. I chose distance.

"I found your file from a few years ago when my colleague left," she said. "How are you doing?"

"That was three years ago when the man I was seeing went back to his wife after a two-year separation."

"Ouch. And now?"

"I'm okay. Or *was* okay. I like my job, and I'm writing . . . well, not actually writing, but thinking about it."

"Writer's block?"

"No. Well, maybe. I've been through something and have been debating about what to do." I was having a hard time finding my words.

She leaned forward slightly. "Are you comfortable there? Or would you prefer to be on the couch?"

"I'm okay. A friend's boyfriend came into my apartment and raped me."

She didn't blanch or display surprise. "This is really serious, Moira. Did you report it? Go to the emergency room?"

"I didn't call the police. I didn't call my boyfriend or my best friend. I didn't go to the hospital to have a physical exam. I feel like I left my body and haven't returned. It's the strangest sensation."

She jotted down a few words in a notebook, barely glancing down. "Dissociation," she said. "When someone is going through an assault, and they have no way of physically escaping, they *psychologically* escape by dissociating."

"I called his so-called girlfriend, a newish friend of mine. He had already gotten to her and told her I seduced him. His word against mine, and she believes him. Actually, I don't know what she believes. We had lunch, and I confronted her."

"Tell me everything from the beginning."

I did.

When I finished speaking, she said, "Do you know why you relented the second time he called? You were firm, and then you wavered."

"I believed him when he said he had nowhere to go. I figured I could go to my boyfriend's a few blocks away if I felt uncomfortable. It was such a stupid thing to do."

"Please know that I'm your advocate, Moira. I'm not accusing you of anything."

"I regretted relenting, but it was too late. And then, when I saw him, I was put at ease. He looked harmless."

"Are you having symptoms?"

"Insomnia. Nightmares. Flashbacks. His eyes follow me around a room at night. I nearly jump out of my skin if someone comes up behind me. I have fantasies of killing him."

"We're realizing that rape victims have symptoms similar to soldiers in war. The suggested protocol would be for you to enter group therapy. You can continue coming here, of course, and have one-on-ones with me. But I think group would be effective. Many raped women . . . though I may add that this happens to men, too . . . continue to lead normal lives six months after the event."

I noticed that my hands were clutched tightly in my lap. "That's helpful to know."

"A small percentage of women—I think the number is twenty percent but could be higher— end up with elevated fear and anxiety. I think what I might suggest for you is cognitive behavioral intervention. I can suggest someone who can work with you on this therapy that involves thought-stopping, muscle relaxation, controlled breathing, and role-playing. The victim must relive the rape scene and describe it aloud as they imagine it, using present tense and vivid detail, just as you were doing with me. The therapist audio records your storytelling, and you are often asked to listen to it as homework. You are also asked to write about the event and its meaning. Then you reread your trauma account between sessions. After that, a second part of the therapy focuses on your beliefs and the meaning and implication of your trauma."

I suddenly felt nauseous. "I need a little time to think about what I want to do."

"Sure. I have to say I'm impressed that you're here. Most women who come to me have waited at least a year, and often, it's five years. Victims need time to acknowledge what's happened to them. And, of course, most women never report it or seek help."

"They deny and repress. Is that what you mean?"

"Exactly."

"And the perpetrator goes on with his life, continuing to attack women and never receiving justice."

"You could still try, but I agree with the attorney you spoke with. The odds of getting him locked up are almost nil."

I told her that I thought he targeted me.

"It's almost impossible to get a one-profile-fits-all rapist. Yours comes from an Ivy League school. Heading into success. I have my own theory about these men. They probably started in high school. I would guess a dysfunctional family. Narcissistic tendencies, which means deep-down insecurity. No consequences, ever. And no one turns them in, as nothing would happen if they did. It's carte blanche out there for these sickos."

"I can't bear that he will get away with it. He had the darkest energy I have ever imagined. He's a sadist. He couldn't stop talking—telling me that I wanted it—enjoying his control over me."

"The very charismatic Ted Bundy killed scores of women. We don't know what Starkweather is capable of. You escaped. Outsmarted him. It will take time, but you *can* heal. Have you told anyone?"

I shook my head. "You're it. I decided not to tell my family and friends."

"Secrets tend to fester, Moira."

"I grew up in a network of secrets."

"We need to work on this."

I sat in silence.

"Your friend Ruth or your boyfriend might have cared enough to return if they knew you had an emergency. If it had been a car accident, you would have called. Right?"

I was feeling chastised, even though her voice was warm. "This is different. I invited him in. I opened the door."

"You have to stop blaming yourself. My advice is to go to group therapy. You'll hear stories worse than yours, trust me. You're the one who got away."

My chest felt constricted, and it suddenly seemed urgent to get fresh air. "I'm sorry, I have to get out of here."

She seemed to disappear into her own thoughts, and I wondered if her mind was searching through one of her books seeking the protocol for a 'woman about to go off the deep end.' But she quickly said, "Our time is up, anyway. Shall I make an appointment for next week?"

"I guess so."

"If you cancel at the last minute, you have to pay. There's a reason for that."

"You don't have to explain." I wouldn't be back, and I figured she knew it.

9

It was already the end of June. I was off to visit my parents, the flight reservations made weeks ago. I had, with great determination, settled on "repress and deny"—at least for the time being. But I hadn't counted on throwing up three mornings in a row. I raced to the drugstore and bought a home pregnancy test. Positive. Shit. I would be an idiot not to sign up for an abortion. But whose embryo was I aborting? Paul's or Jonathan's? I called an abortion clinic and made an appointment for the following week. I longed for Ruthie all of a sudden and called her. She told me to meet her in a few hours as Seamus was on night duty.

Two weeks ago, we had a come-to-Jesus meeting. Ruth had walked in with a bottle of wine and said we needed to discuss how I had avoided her. She asked if I was angry with her or if she had hurt me unknowingly. I denied that that was the case, mentioning that Seamus and her job took all of her energy, after which she burst into tears, something I had only seen once in all the years I had known her.

"I know what I know," she had said. "You act jittery and come up with a ton of excuses when I ask you to dinner. Maybe you don't like Seamus?"

I felt strong remorse and admitted that I hadn't been myself. "I'm unusually tired," I said, "and nothing feels the same at the office with you gone."

"You might be depressed, Moira. You haven't been yourself since you had the flu."

"I'll be okay. And my pulling away has nothing to do with Seamus, though I will admit I'm surprised you're still together. He's a cop."

She put up her index finger. "Small correction. A detective. Cop sounds derogatory. He was a lit major in college. He's an idealist. He knows how to love a woman."

"Well then."

I dined with them a few nights later and witnessed Seamus' humor and incredible warmth. On the other hand, I received a letter a week from Paul, and sometimes two, mostly written on the fly. All were signed, 'Love, Paul.' His letters were wonderfully phrased, but noncommittal. They could have been stories he filed for *The New York Times*. He wrote about Moscow and a trip to Berlin, where he crossed over to East Berlin and reported on the Berlin Wall. He wrote about his parents visiting for a week and described the three-star restaurants where they dined. He called after a month and said he had set aside a few days for me if I wanted to come. I said I'd try to get the time off. The next time he called, I was certain I was pregnant. I said no to joining him, with apologies about work and a necessary trip to see my parents. He said he missed me, but I knew he didn't understand. A yawning chasm was opening between us.

I had to tell Ruth about the pregnancy. We were in our usual haunt the following week, a coffee shop near her office, when I told her I had decided not to go to Paris. She stared hard at me. "Is that bully Larry insisting you stay? He's your boss, but you deserve a vacation. Paul must be upset."

"It's nothing to do with Larry. I'm not feeling confident that Paul will return to me. I read you one of his letters last week. I think he's vacillating about us."

"Don't get mad, but I've been thinking *you're* the vacillating one."

"Maybe it's a symptom of entering our thirties. Do you ever think about how absurd our world is with zillions of people running around with absolutely no clue why they're here or what to do?"

"Um, no. That's why people have goals."

"Oh! That's what I'm missing." I was being flippant, and she didn't laugh.

"You're going to be a respected writer and win prizes, and I'm going to be your agent, remember?"

"I'm pregnant."

Her mouth literally dropped open. "I know you're famous for your non-sequiturs, but this might be the winner. How far along?"

"I have an appointment next week with my gynecologist."

"You're going to keep it?"

"The appointment?"

She laughed. "No, the baby."

"I'm not sure. It's Paul's, in case you're about to ask."

"Why would I think otherwise? Does he know?"

"Not a clue."

"Shit. What are we going to do?"

I liked that she said 'we.' "Right now, I'm going to fly home to my parents and sleep a lot and eat my mother's fried chicken and decide."

"You're going to tell Adeline? She'll freak out. Guilt you into having it." She was right. "You weren't using birth control?"

"I told you I went off the pill. And the one time I skipped using the diaphragm, this happened." What would she say if I added what had occurred?

"Moira, we've been through a lot. May I be honest here?"

"Go ahead."

"You'd be crazy to have a baby. But let's say you decide to do it. Where does Paul come in?"

"I've already called an abortion clinic. I'm not so young anymore, though, which makes me hesitate. I *do* want to have a family in the future."

"You won't tell him?"

"I must tell him. The abortion coincides with his return. What a mess."

"If you tell him, he'll propose. He's of that ilk. The guy who does the right thing."

"It's the Seventies, not the Fifties. He will say, 'It's your body. Do what you need to do.'"

"He would only say that if he's with Katia."

"Don't think I haven't obsessed over that. They're working together. He didn't hide it."

"You're having dinner on your birthday. Is it a break-up or make-up event?"

"What kind of guy would break up with someone on their birthday? Not his style."

"I wouldn't mention the pregnancy until he's had his say."

"It feels like we're manipulating the scenario. I'll need cue cards."

"We are. I'll be in disguise at the next table, holding the cue cards." It felt good to laugh. "Maybe we should list the pros and cons."

"It's already weighted on the cons side."

"Not necessarily. What if he's planning to propose?"

"I don't know."

"But you moved in with him. That's certainly a step in that direction. The main thing is, do you love him?"

I had loved him desperately on the eve of April 15th, and then I was raped, and the word love felt meaningless.

My silence lasted too long. Ruth said, "Seamus is working all night. You might as well stay here with me tonight."

She cared so much. "Thanks. I'll take you up on that." I slipped into the nightgown she pulled out of a dresser drawer and crawled into her bed.

"I have some chocolate in here, too."

"Okay."

She slid the box out, and we each took two pieces and devoured them. We took turns brushing our teeth, then she set the alarm clock, climbed in, and put her arm around me, and I slept soundly for the first time in two months.

10

Augustus and Adeline were waiting at the gate in Raleigh when I
entered the arrivals area, my mother dressed in bangles, her red
hair gone orange, pouffed into a helmet. Dad lumbered behind her.
Mama had talked about some difficulties he was having when she
visited me six months ago, but I wasn't prepared for the weight loss
and slumped posture. I hugged them, and we traipsed to the
baggage area. I excused myself to go to the ladies' room and
promptly threw up in the toilet. I rinsed out my mouth and rushed
back. Dad was holding my suitcase.

"You're traveling light," Mama said.

"I'm only here for a week."

We climbed into their Chevrolet station wagon. "Off we go," said
Augustus. "Anybody hungry?"

"Not me," I said. "I'm not feeling that great."

"We'll eat when we get home, Augustus." My mother turned to the
back seat to look at me. "You're looking a little peaked. I can fix that."

I smiled at her. "It's great to be out of the city." I glanced out
the window and saw we were passing the street in the expensive
suburb of Raleigh where we lived when Dad was booted out of his
Baptist church. What stuck with me was the humiliation of it, the
rumors that sent my mother spiraling into depression, though the
word was never uttered—my ten-year-old incomprehension of what
caused the uproar in the church that forced my father out. He was
an imposing figure at six-two. He had thick wavy hair, arched

eyebrows, and full lips. I recalled hearing him practicing his sermons in his small study in the rectory. He had a fine baritone voice that he used as an actor would, drawing his audience in with his low pitch, and just when he had them spellbound, bellowing for them to come down the aisle in the name of Jesus.

Augustus pulled off the two-lane road and onto a paved, rural road. I was no longer in the habit of diverting my eyes when we passed the house of Mary Whitehill, the woman my mother called "a tart and temptress" all those years ago. My high school friend Ella told me what people were saying: my father had taken advantage of Mary, who then killed herself. I told my mother the rumor, and she broke into sobs and went to her room. But she didn't deny it, which meant it must be true. After that, a curtain went up between my friends and me. I was fourteen at the time and hated Ella for knowing, and then for divulging such news.

We moved to the small town of Higginsville after the 'disgrace,' as my mother referred to it, where we lost touch with everyone from Raleigh. And soon, Mama rarely emerged from their bedroom, claiming she had a headache. My father slowly retreated into his own inner world and alcohol, managing somehow to deliver a sermon every Sunday at the rural church that lacked the prestige of the Raleigh one. I went to church with him and prayed hard for Adeline to be well enough to be my mother.

I was lonely, the way children are who find themselves taking care of their parents—or who can't rely on their parents to be 'normal.' Who else had a father who practiced his elocution at home and seemed stupefied at dinner—or a mother who refused to come out of her room? That is, until the day I turned sixteen (three years after we moved to Higginsville), when Adeline emerged wearing a red dress and lips to match, with her hair swept up into a bountiful bun, which made her look even taller. She said, "Let it be a lesson to you, Moira. We . . . humans . . . can overcome anything if we rely on the Lord and on the example of Jackie Kennedy."

I didn't know who was more shocked, my father or me. She went on to say that she had been so inspired after watching Jackie

Kennedy give a tour of the White House on television that she thought she could certainly become a good example to the women in Higginsville. Just like that, a new persona was born. Mama went to church meetings and local political meetings. She became a Bible-thumping pastor's wife, going out daily to help those in need. Sometimes she took me with her, and she filled our bookshelves with books by Eudora Welty and Flannery O'Connor, and we read them aloud.

I was thrilled. "You have to figure a way out of this crap hole," she told me one day. "I am here to lead the townspeople to light, but that doesn't mean it's your destiny. You've always got your head stuck in a book. You might as well be a writer."

I took her at her word and began writing stories again, only this time not for her, but for me. Sometimes I read them at dinner. One evening, my father exclaimed, "You took those words in that story out of Mrs. Williams' mouth that day she came and sat right here in this kitchen and told all about her daughter messing around. I don't approve of eavesdropping."

"She's not doing anybody any harm," my mother said. "Where do you think Hemingway got his stories? Almost verbatim from his life."

I graduated valedictorian of my class, and was offered a full scholarship to Dobson College the following fall, a girls' southern college with a reputation for turning out young women writers.

My mother's voice broke my reverie. "We're almost home," she said. A sign, 'Welcome to Higginsville,' caught my eye. I looked out at the rigid little square box houses lined up on either side of the street—their inhabitants conforming to the conservative architecture. I had accompanied my mother to many of them as she took her pies to new mothers and dying grandmothers. Their houses were filled with crafts and artificial scents. They welcomed my mother's social calls and often came to church as a result of her kindness. The church only had one hundred faithful members, but my father exhorted them in his baritone voice every Sunday to mend their ways, the same as he had done to the thousand worshippers in Raleigh.

We pulled into the driveway of a small, three-bedroom ranch-style house. I complimented Adeline on the flower gardens in front. Augustus insisted on taking my suitcase to my room at the end of the narrow hall, and I followed him. "It's good to see you," he said. "Your mama misses you."

My room was exactly as I had left it. Same daffodil yellow bedspread with curtains to match. The quilt my mother had made for me was folded neatly at the bottom of the bed. I opened the door to her room, separate from my father's, and stopped when I saw four 8x10 framed photographs of Jackie Kennedy, now Jackie O, clustered on one wall. By this time, Jackie had gone through her husband's assassination and her marriage to Aristotle Onassis, which was a disaster, but at least, Adeline reckoned, she ended up with a career. And a fortune to boot.

Dad and I returned to the kitchen the color of chicken poop, as Adeline used to say. She stood over a skillet, turning the fried chicken. Feeling nauseous again, I swallowed hard. "Dinner will be ready in half an hour or a little more," Mama said. Dad had sat in front of the small television and turned on the news. Mama placed a glass of iced tea on the table by his chair, next to the bourbon neat he had poured without my noticing. She scowled. "Where'd that come from?"

"It's a celebration, Addy."

Mama walked back into the kitchen, her lips forming a horizontal line. "He insists it's good for his heart."

"Maybe it is."

"Always taking his side," she sniped. Then, within an instant, she switched back to happy mode. Her preternatural cheerfulness was incongruous with her face lined with bitterness. She bustled around a little more, making a lot of noise pulling the plates from the shelf and placing them on the table. "Augustus, come on," she said. She loaded my plate with chicken and mashed potatoes. She had chopped up a head of iceberg lettuce and put it on a salad plate with an orange-bottled dressing smeared across it. I could hear a lawn mower running next door, and children were calling out to each other. Sounds of childhood loneliness.

"Neta is waiting to see you," Mama said.

"I'll walk there tomorrow morning."

"Use the car." Neta lived in the black section of town. She had cared for me when I was a child and Mama was indisposed. She greeted me when I came home from school and asked me about my day. I doubted I ever asked her about her day. She helped me understand that Mama wasn't 'well in the head' but that if I prayed every day for God to make her well, He would.

Mama filled me in on what half the town's population was doing. Augustus went back to his television to watch a game show, and I helped clear the table. I excused myself at nine, pleading fatigue.

Climbing into my childhood bed, I opened my journal and began to write:

> Here, alone in my childhood home, I am aware for the first time of an infinitesimal light I'm harboring in my belly. A light that might be flickering. What if it is my soul returning to me, and I may be about to send it away? Fantastical thinking, but oh, how comforting. I recall how happy Paul and I were the night we ran to my apartment to make love, how thrilling our lovemaking was, and how we declared our love for each other. That exquisite feeling of bliss was smashed to smithereens two hours later, but what if I could hang onto the memory of the before and use it as a source of healing. Maybe, like my mother, I could rebirth myself into light. She became a born-again Christian, but I could be a born-again woman.

I shut off the light and lay there in the dark. Some child part of me wanted to confess the rape to my mother, but I worried that she would end up blaming me, the way she heaped blame on my father for losing the fine life they had created in Raleigh. I was old enough now to see that her posturing covered up her own pain. She had never said more than a few words about her parents' disowning her, sloughing off any of my childhood questions with empty phrases like 'I made my bed, and I had to lie in it.'"

Then just before I left for college, she confessed that she had been pregnant when she married my dad. She had held onto her own secret out of shame. I thought how different it would have been if her parents had accepted her decision. A secret festers, the therapist, what's-her-name had told me.

The radio blaring gospel music jolted me awake the next morning. Coffee gurgled in the percolator. "I've already talked to Linda Martin, and Betty will be by later," Mama said when I sat at the kitchen table. "Everybody wants to see you." She was in Perle Mesta mode. I preferred this to her bringing up my retching during the night. I knew she had heard me because when I exited the bathroom, I saw her door quietly shut. She had been standing there, listening.

She announced she was off with Betty to the nursing home to deliver books and would return for lunch. The morning paper had arrived, and Dad was hidden behind it. I dressed and drove to Neta's, three miles away.

Her face lit up with joy when she saw me at her door, and we embraced. "Look at you, a city girl," she said, laughing and putting her hand over her mouth. I always thought she was trying to cover up the gold buck tooth that was the centerpiece of her face, which made her look exotic. Tall and skinny, with tiny shafts of hair sticking out and watery eyes behind dime-store glasses, she pulled me to her. "Miss Adeline says you have a fine boyfriend up there."

We sat. "I do, though I'm not sure about anything right now. I'm pregnant."

Her eyes widened. "Naw! Does your mama know?"

"I think she's aware. I've been throwing up. I'm repeating her mistake. That's what she'll think. Or maybe it's what I'm thinking. I signed up for an abortion."

She put her hand up to her mouth again. "You don't like the daddy?"

"Neta. A man came to my apartment and attacked me."

She sat still, saying nothing. Then, she reached for my hand, squeezed it, and said, "So you don't know who the baby belongs to."

I nodded.

"You love this man, Paul."

"I was very much in love. I don't know now. I don't feel anything."

"Like your mama."

"What do you mean?"

She grew quiet again. "You're old enough to know. Your mama lost a baby at around four months. It's why she started staying in her room and couldn't come out."

"I never knew that." The silence was comfortable. "I wish I had known. It explains a lot."

"It was a big loss for her."

I looked around the room. Neat. Chairs covered in blankets. An eight-by-ten cheaply framed photograph of John F. Kennedy and beside him one of a white Jesus with long chestnut colored hair and white robes, and on the other side Martin Luther King. And there was the poster I had drawn when I was ten from the Bible verse, Revelations 12:1, which read, "A spectacular sign appeared in the sky, a woman dressed with the Sun, who had the moon under her feet and a victor's crown of twelve stars on her head."

I had painted her skin dark brown and used a lot of yellow to create the sun, moon, and crown. I had painted Neta. She followed my gaze. "Miss Adeline cried when she saw that. She thought you loved me more than her. I told her a child only has one mama, and she can never be replaced."

"I think you saved me, Neta. You know, it's a little late in the game to tell you this, but thank you for always being there for me. I don't think I've ever said that."

"What child does that? You were a good girl. Sad, but good. And you kept me going with your stories."

"What do you mean?"

"I was sad, too. Beaten down by my husband going on a rampage and killing my sister instead of me. He was looking for me but saw her first."

"Why was he so mad?"

"He wasn't right in the head. He was already set up to do bad things long before he met me. Anyhow, your mama was a big support to me when nobody wanted to hire me."

"I can't tell her what happened to me."

Neta reached for my hand and squeezed it. "I cried so hard over my sister dying instead of me, and I lost the baby I was carrying. I don't want that to happen to you."

"You and Mama both lost your babies."

She pointed to a stack of letters secured by a rubber band. "I have all your letters. The last three are full of stories about a man named Paul and how you feel he's the man you want to marry."

"The baby might not be his, don't forget."

"This is some situation, Moira. It really is. I'll say this, things have a way of working out. But you have to be true to yourself and don't listen to others."

The telephone rang. She answered, listened briefly, and said my mother wanted me to come home.

I got up, feeling strangely uplifted. "By the way, what stories did I tell you when I was little?"

"You had a bunch of tales about a fairy who lived in your backyard claiming to belong to me."

"Really?"

"Her name was Henrietta, and she was your best friend. I started to think she was real."

"I remember now. Her thumbs and big toes got switched, and we had to find the right herb to make them go back to normal."

"And she delivered messages to me from my sister in Heaven. Like, 'Neta, don't forget to wave to me when the moon is full.' And there I'd be at night, waving to the moon."

I put my arms around her and rested my head on her shoulder for a few seconds. "Okay, off I go."

The phone was ringing when I walked into Mama's house. She handed it to me.

"Seamus and I have had a big fight," Ruthie said. "A big one. I told him he had to get off the sauce, and on top of the drinking, some girl keeps calling him here."

Dear Ruthie. I had flown home to my mother, but it was Ruthie I needed. Mama waved and was out the door. Augustus hoisted himself up and went outside and started watering the plants.

Ruthie barely gave me a chance to respond. "He called me a flaming feminist and a workaholic. Geez."

"Where is he now?"

"Probably in Connecticut with his mother. Flew the coop."

"Oh, Ruthie."

"What about you? Her voice went to a stage whisper. "Do they know you're pregnant?"

"I think Adeline suspects. She's biding her time to see if I'll come clean. I'll be home in three days and catch you up on everything."

"Oh god! Seamus is at the door. He won't remember what the argument was about."

"Make something up. Tell him it was about a trip to the Caribbean he promised you."

She laughed. "I'll call you tomorrow. Love you."

"Love you back." Dad walked back in, limping slightly. "Can I help you do anything?" I asked.

"Nah. I don't do much anymore. Your mama does it all."

"Does she go to church now?"

"She can't stop going." We laughed.

Adeline entered, removed teacups from the cupboard, and cut into a pie. "The girls will be dropping by in a few minutes. Moira, get the napkins from the drawer."

Dad and I exchanged an amused glance and straightened up to comply with her strict standards for the art of visiting. I was suddenly filled with admiration for her in that moment. Almost nothing had gone her way in life, but she had conjured up an iron will to overcome her circumstances.

After dinner, I announced that I would retire, as I had to catch an early flight.

Mama entered my room, sat on the edge of my bed, and sighed. "I hope you're not pregnant."

"I am."

She stood up, walked to the window, took a Kleenex from her housecoat pocket, and dabbed at her eyes. Her face sagged. "Don't tell your daddy. It's been hard enough that you live in sin." She brightened slightly. "You and Paul are getting married?"

"I'll see him on my birthday. If he puts up a fuss, I'll have an abortion."

Her eyes widened in horror. "Moira! You wouldn't do such a thing! You're living with Paul already. Go ahead and start your family."

"I'm worried he's gone back to Katia."

"He'll be with you if you tell him. He's an honorable man."

"That's your story, Mama. I don't want the same story."

"Life isn't just a story, Moira. God is a tyrant. You might never be able to have another baby."

"You're being a tyrant right now."

"You could give the baby up. I know someone . . ."

"No. Listen, I will tell Paul, and it will be our decision."

She left the room, closing the door quietly behind her. I lay awake, listening to the sounds of the house. The television being clicked off at eleven. My father's ponderous footsteps as he ambled to his bedroom. My mother's chirpy good night to him as she closed her door and locked it. The cuckoo clock going off at three and again at four. I concluded that I didn't want to be a single mom, no matter what. Second, I would not manipulate Paul Rivers into marriage.

I got up at seven. Mama was in the kitchen. "I wanted to say I'm glad your daddy and I didn't have so many choices. We have you. And we have each other, for better or for worse."

Tears dripped off her chin. I put my arms around her. She smelled of liniment and lavender. "Mama, women deserve to have a choice. It's wrong that politicians in suits get to dictate what a woman can and can't do with her body."

"I want you to be happy, Moira. It's all I ever wanted."

"Are you happy, Mama?"

"I get by."

Not good enough, I thought.

My father entered and said, "Adeline, they're not kids, and they can decide their own fate."

Mama and I turned to him in shock. She said, "Augustus, what would your parishioners think if they heard you right now?"

"I don't care what they think." He picked up my suitcase and headed to the car.

Mama said, "Well, I never."

I hugged her and followed my dad.

11

Dr. Sylvia Moss entered the office with a flourish. As my mother would say, she was a handsome woman with her straight posture and thick blond hair worn in a chignon. She held a folder in her hand, which she placed on her antique desk. "You're ten weeks," she said, her red lips parted in a smile. I had been observing the shaft of sunlight falling onto the rich colors of her Oriental rug. Our eyes met, and she frowned slightly. "You're surprised?"

"I don't know what I'm going to do. I'm considering having an abortion."

"You have a choice, of course." Her expression was neutral. Practiced. Abortions had been legalized five years before. "Why don't you list the pros and cons?"

"I'll start with the cons. I'm not sure who the father is." I felt my face turn red.

"I'm sorry, Moira." She glanced at my folder on her desk. "I assumed it to be Paul. We switched you to the diaphragm four months ago. Can you tell me what's going on?" Dr. Moss buzzed her secretary, who stuck her head in the door. "Tea, please," she said. The door closed. She turned her attention back to me, "Do you want to have the baby? If so, we could do an HLA test to determine paternity. "We would need Paul, or whomever, to cooperate."

"It's a blood test?" I asked.

She nodded. "Accuracy has risen to eighty and sometimes ninety percent with the development of PCR."

Her secretary arrived with a tray, and I accepted a cup of tea. Dr. Moss took the other.

"I was raped."

Her hand holding the cup stopped mid-air. She set it down. "Oh god, Moira. Can you tell me what happened?"

I recounted that night and the following days—how the attack followed hours after Paul and I had made love without protection and committed to each other.

"Well, then." She clasped her hands on her desk. "You will *have* to tell Paul. He would no doubt insist on a test. May I assume you are getting psychological counseling?"

"I went once."

"Does anyone know?"

"A lawyer friend. You."

"Moira, it's not too late to talk to the police. The statute of limitations is five years in New York, but your lawyer is right. There has to be some proof. The girl Erin."

"She's out."

The silence was long enough for me to pay attention to the sounds of auto horns below, the music in the reception room, Dr. Moss's breathing. "In this case, I might recommend an abortion," she said, her voice cutting the silence.

"I already have an appointment to discuss it."

"I get the feeling you're really torn. Is it your religion?"

"Aside from my mother telling me God is a tyrant who will rain down punishment on me if I go through with it, no. If it were a perfect world, I would say yes to a baby."

"It will never be a perfect world; you know that."

"I read somewhere that pregnancies are rare after rape."

"That's absurd. Same chance as with a lover. I worry about the emotional aspects. The shock of being so violated can last for years, much longer than people assume. You are brought to the most helpless place a human can endure, and sometimes they don't. You are without will, without power, with another controlling your body. It is also a spiritual assault, one with lasting consequences.

Without testing, I would diagnose you with post-traumatic stress syndrome today. I will reiterate that I recommend therapy—and telling Paul, even if it means the end of the relationship. And, sad to say, I recommend an abortion, even though if you decide to have the baby, I will be here for you one hundred percent. Will you please get back to me once you have decided for sure?

"Yes."

"I can also recommend a therapist."

"Sure." She got up, walked over, and embraced me. I inhaled her wonderful fragrance of rose and jasmine.

"Women are stronger than they know," she said. "But first things first, my dear. Act instead of reacting. And come back to me in a month."

I went out into the cacophonous Manhattan street with new resolve. First things first, as Dr. Moss had said. Ruth was to meet me in two hours at the abortion clinic for a consultation, and we would go from there. I had no idea what to expect from Paul, but I realized I was excited to see him. My last letter to him was sent two days before I visited my parents, when I had just learned of my pregnancy. But, of course, that wasn't mentioned.

I wrote instead about my bumping into mutual friends, about the editing I was doing, and listed the people who had called and left messages for him. I said I was thrilled to be going to a fabulous restaurant. I enclosed my latest short story, one I had written after reading a true story in the newspaper about an American woman who had been an ambulance driver during World War II. She met and fell in love with a Frenchman in the Resistance. He declared his love for her but refused to reveal his last name until the war ended, protecting him and his friends. She waited for him after the war. One day she picked up *Le Monde* to see a photograph of her lover beneath his obituary. She presented herself to his aristocratic family but was shunned. Her body was found a week later washed up along the Seine. (The story was sold later to a small literary magazine.) I signed my letter, 'Love, Moira.'

"Too sad," Paul wrote back. "But eloquent."

Ruth stood like a sentinel in front of the abortion clinic. She led the way into the waiting room, and within moments, I followed the receptionist into a consultation room, where a woman wearing square glasses and a sweet smile greeted me. I explained my ambivalence, and she listened, expressionless. She had heard the same story thousands of times, her face said. She explained the procedure for an abortion and added that she didn't expect any problems. She wanted to know if I would bring someone with me, and I nodded. Then she said, "It is my job to ask you if you are certain this is the right solution for you."

I was suddenly in tears. She plucked a tissue from a box on the table and handed it to me.

"I can tell you that very few who have made the decision to have an abortion have ended up with regret. But this is why we do counseling. If you opt for an abortion, I suggest you talk to a therapist afterward, for closure. They generally recommend group meetings for a while. I'll give you the name of someone." She took my hand. "You can call me here and let me know what you have decided."

I thanked her. A different woman entered and handed me a card, "You have an appointment tomorrow at three. Come half an hour early."

I returned to the waiting room where Ruthie sat reading a magazine. "All set," I told her and handed her the card.

I had vacated Paul's apartment the week before but soon discovered that I could not sleep in my apartment. When I told Ruth a made-up story about someone in my building calling and leaving lewd phone messages, Ruth insisted I stay with her until I could find something else.

We quickly embraced, and I rushed to the hairdresser, then to Ruth's, where I tried on at least four dresses. Nothing worked. I finally selected a short black dress and pumps. Paul was waiting at the bar. He got up and gave me a kiss and a warm embrace. It felt as if he had never left.

"You look marvelous," he said. So did he. His hair was longer, and he had lost a little weight, but otherwise, he was the same. He kept his arm around me and led me to the bar where his pal Ed sat nursing a martini.

"A glass of Sancerre," Paul said to the bartender.

"Make that club soda," I said.

He stopped to see if I was serious. "Really?" Not waiting for an answer, he sipped his gin fizz. I exchanged a brief hug with Ed.

"Carol's late," he said. "Sorry for butting in on you, but a quick drink and we'll be gone. I had some papers for Paul to sign."

"How are you?"

"I'm fine. Carol's miserable. She can't believe the weight gain already."

"She's pregnant again?" This was number two.

He rolled his eyes. "Due in October. We haven't seen you in a while."

Ed was Paul's oldest friend from elementary and boarding school. A hedge fund guy on Wall Street, he was arrogant and known to be tough. I sat on a bar stool with Paul standing behind me. Drinkers were filing in, Carol among them. Kisses all around, and then turning to me, she said, "I haven't seen you in ages, Moira. Did you hear our news?" She made a face. "I'm not ready to do this again."

"No choice now," Ed said.

"No choice ever." She laughed but without humor. "I'll change that. There *is* a choice, but my husband doesn't like the idea of ending a pregnancy."

"I'm hoping for a football team," Ed said, missing the point, turning to the bartender and ordering another drink.

Paul raced off to the restroom. While Ed yakked with the bartender, Carol and I were standing at the bar. Carol leaned over and said, "That French reporter Paul was so smitten with before he met you is in town. Ed and I are hosting her and a few others tomorrow night. Paul begged off. I think Ed's got a crush on her."

My knees felt wobbly from the shock. "Oh." I smiled, "You're talking about Katia. That's an old story."

"Really? I think she's going to be staying in town for at least a few months."

Paul came up behind me. "I'll pay the tab and tell them we're taking off," he whispered in my ear. We said our goodbyes, and he hailed a taxi outside the restaurant. Once on our way, he said, "I know I'm acting edgy. Sorry."

"You've only just arrived. You probably have jet lag."

"I'm trying to think where we left off. It feels like it's been eons and, simultaneously, a few hours."

I didn't like thinking about the last time we made love in his apartment, when the only way I could go through it was to conjure up Neruda's words. He hadn't noticed, as he had been so busy preparing for his journey.

"We promised each other we'd tell if we changed our minds about each other," he said. He launched into a story about his last night in Moscow, and then the taxi stopped at our destination.

At the North Tower of the World Trade Center, we boarded the elevator to the 107th floor. Paul wanted to stop first at the Hors d'Oeuvrie, a lounge overlooking the harbor and the Statue of Liberty.

"Fifty-eight seconds up," Paul said as we stepped off. He ordered a martini, and I asked for a *kir*. I had come here a year before with Ruth and our mothers, but we hadn't dined. Paul said, "I think the Twin Towers will become the most iconic structure in the city. It's symbolic of moving forward. From here, you can almost feel the city entering a new whirlwind of capital. We're starting a new decade soon and can put the Seventies behind us."

I knew what he was referring to: the Seventies of high crime, filth, and drugs.

"The Financial District is starting to thrive, Koch has cut taxes . . ."

"You've lived abroad and are returning with new eyes, Paul. And let's admit it, sitting here on top of the world—or as on top as you can get without being in an airplane, gives that sensation. Even Ruth is feeling slightly hopeful."

He laughed. "I'm glad to be home. You look well." He glanced at his watch. "We should head downstairs to dinner. It took a lot of pull to get these reservations two months ago. The waitlist is six months. Do you believe it?" On the way down, he gave me a sheepish smile. "I know I'm babbling, but I want to write an article about this place, representing the American economic power that's happening. The change that's occurring in front of our eyes."

We entered the main restaurant. What I noticed first were the floor-to-ceiling windows. Next, the red carpet and walls. Waiters in white jackets. The pristine white tablecloths with a small vase containing a daisy on every table. Because it was June, the sun wouldn't set until nine. The vista from our window table faced north, where it was said you could see ninety miles to Connecticut—and I believed it. Looking down, Manhattan was a toy town. The sky was a palette of pale colors, the sun only beginning to fade.

"I shall never forget this moment," I said to Paul. "One day, I'll write about my most memorable birthday."

"I'd forgotten how much I like making you happy."

We studied the menu. We both ordered the duck, and he requested a vintage bottle of Bordeaux. Now he turned his attention to me. "Working at the Paris Bureau was like living a dream. I want to return, but not until they offer me bureau chief."

I laughed. "And when do you expect that to happen?"

"Five years."

"And in the meantime?"

His face grew serious. "I want to write more feature articles. Do more investigative journalism. Travel more."

Exactly what Katia did.

He broke the silence that followed. "Are you finding time to write?"

"Some. Not enough. Never enough."

"Maybe because you were busy writing to me. I saved your letters. They're literary." I sipped the vintage wine, which had been discreetly opened and placed in front of us. "But you didn't come to Paris. I was hurt."

"I felt that leaving would jeopardize my job. I got the promotion and was overwhelmed."

"I can't put my finger on it, Moira, but something feels different. We feel different."

"I'm different. I'm pregnant." I had a half-memory of promising Ruth not to bring up the pregnancy until I knew what he was up to.

Paul's left eye twitched. He was too shocked to speak at first. "How far along?"

"Two months. I hadn't planned to drop this on you this evening, or maybe ever. I don't want you to feel obligated in any way."

"Why shouldn't I be?"

"We were reckless that night in my apartment."

"I haven't forgotten." He reached over and took my hand.

"My mother thinks that my father married her only because she was pregnant. And then her parents disowned her. I've never liked my origin story."

"It was that era. Your parents would never do that to you."

"I think yours would hesitate to welcome me into the fold. My forefathers didn't come over on the Mayflower, though my mother swears she's from Scottish royalty."

"This is about us, Moira, not them. Why do you care what they think?"

"Because over the past year, I have seen how they exercise a lot of control over you."

"Okay then. What do you want, Moira? Do you want to have a baby?"

I had the sensation of being in a space capsule hurtling through the universe, and the odd part was, it was exhilarating. After two months of battling depression, feeling horribly alone, learning I was pregnant, and thinking about how to get revenge one day against Jonathan, I realized I could trade it all for a life of comfort. I could shape-shift into wife and mother.

"Under the right circumstances, yes."

"What if I said I want to marry you and have a family?"

It was exactly as I had predicted. But then he surprised me. He reached into his pocket and extracted a tiny robin's egg blue package. Tiffany. He opened the box and took out an engagement ring.

"Will you marry me, Moira Dean?"

I would look back later and know that the ring changed everything. Hope springs eternal, as my mother used to say. An outcome that I had not considered since the rape happened—a safety net that millions opted for on a daily basis—marriage. Two people facing the world together. The ring, proof of his intention before meeting up with me again.

"Yes." He slid the ring onto my finger and squeezed my hand. He signaled to the waiter, who arrived as if on cue with a half-bottle of champagne on ice. He poured each of us a glass of champagne. "To us," he said. Our glasses clinked. "And to our baby." I took a small sip and smiled at him, already worrying that I had done exactly what I had said I would not do—announced that I was pregnant.

I could tell Paul was slightly drunk. "Where will we marry? When?"

There was no turning back. I was going for safety. Security. And with all my heart, I hoped for love. I knew, sitting there looking at him, that he was the man who made me believe in love. (Yes, I was late to the game.) I could still see him walking away, giving his Fred Astaire dance and the urge I had to run after him.

"City Hall?"

He laughed. "My mother will never accept that. My parents' house in Connecticut, okay?"

"As long as it's a small wedding. And soon. I don't want to be eight months pregnant."

"I'll tell them tomorrow." He stood and took my hand. "Ready?"

We boarded the elevator, and in one big whoosh, we were on the ground floor. A taxi ride home, both of us tired. I found a nightgown I had left behind hanging on the back of the bathroom door and slipped into it. I saw the desire in his eyes. I climbed in next to him. I closed my eyes, only to see Jonathan's face appear before me.

"I'm sorry," I lied to Paul. "I feel nauseous." I got out of bed.

"Poor you," he said. "I'm still in a different time zone. Have to sleep."

I waited long enough for him to go to sleep, then went into the living room to the large window that overlooked 72nd Street and watched the activity below. People rushed around as though it were noon. Car horns blared. I had intuited in a flash this evening that my future survival depended on my ability to shift into a new role that would leave my rapist in the distant past. My father preached about two Gods, one of great compassion and one of wrath. I was rusty at prayer, but I reached out to the God of compassion, asking that my baby be gifted with a joyous destiny. I thought of destiny as different from fate. Fate happened to you; we created our destiny.

12

Within two days of Paul proposing, Katherine Rivers invited us to Connecticut to plan our wedding. As though reading my mind, Paul suggested that he thought we'd be smart to let the studio go. I went up and unlocked the apartment door and entered. Everything remained exactly as it was that night. The record in the stereo player. (I had been listening to Joni Mitchell's "Blue" album.) The towel the rapist had used, tossed onto the floor. The empty beer can, crushed and thrown against the wall. A Juicy Fruit chewing gum wrapper on the kitchen counter. The rumpled bedding. I stripped the sheets off the daybed, and a folded paper landed on the floor. I picked it up. My apartment was a forensics crime site, yet no amount of evidence that this man entered my apartment and attacked me could be used against him.

The doorbell buzzed, and I ran down to let Ruth in. "I can't believe you're letting this place go. It's so cheap." She followed me up the stairs, stopping on the second landing to breathe. She suddenly looked at my hand. "What the fuck! He proposed?"

"To my surprise."

"Which came first, the ring or the pregnancy announcement?"

We entered the apartment. "What difference does it make? I think I told him I'm pregnant, and then, voila, he pulled out the ring."

She turned and looked at it up close. "Beautiful. Classy. Very Paul." She let go of my hand, and we sat at the table. "Everything's going so fast. I guess a pregnancy does that. Creates a sense of urgency."

"I've been thinking a lot about human decision-making. Whether you're a planner or a spontaneous decision-maker, is the outcome so different? Let's say I make Decision A, marry and have a baby, so am I to wonder if I should have made Decision B for the rest of my life? Not have married and had an abortion? You see where I'm going? It's the proverbial fork in the road. Ambivalence is exhausting and solves nothing."

She nodded. "The main thing is if you're happy you're going to be an instant wife and mom?"

"The only really happy period I've known was living with you. So, am I happy? I don't think I'll know for a while. I worry about whether or not I'll be able to carve out time for my writing."

"I worry about that, too. On a selfish note, I'll get to experience what it's like to have a baby vicariously."

We were interrupted by Paul coming in with movers. He looked handsome. A kiss for me and one for Ruth. "You two might have to step out for a few minutes while they take out the bigger pieces. It won't take long."

We descended the stairs and stood on the sidewalk, soaking up the sun. "Speaking of moving fast," Ruth said with a laugh. "Do you think Paul called the movers from France to have them on alert? What if you had said no?"

My neighbor Irene approached, and I gave her a quick embrace. "You've been missing in action," she said in a thick Russian accent.

"I thought you knew I was living at Paul's."

I tried to swallow my guilt for leaving that night and only returning once when she wasn't in. No note. No nothing. What must she have been thinking?

"I saw the gentleman's photograph in the paper last week—the one who came to your apartment last April. I remember him because he knocked on my door and asked if you were there. I said no. He said you ran away."

I acted confused. "I don't know who you're talking about." I didn't dare glance in Ruth's direction. "I'm getting married to Paul." We stepped aside as the movers made a fuss hauling out the daybed, stacking it against the gate for the trash people to take. "You met Paul. Are you referring to him?"

Her eyes were insistent. "It wasn't him," she said. "This one had a bad aura around him. I was worried about you."

"Oh, gosh," I said, interrupting her. "You're mistaken. It might have been Eileen in the apartment below you." I was aware of how nervously I was behaving. Ruth followed me back up the stairs. When we entered the apartment, she said, "What was all that about?"

"She's losing it. I have her niece's number. I think I should call her to let her know."

"You know you can tell me if you cheated on Paul."

I brought a box from the hallway and set it in front of the bookshelves. "You think I wouldn't tell you? I tell you everything."

"Sometimes I've had to wring the truth from you." She began pulling books from the shelves and boxing them. She dropped a book, and a letter fell out. I picked it up. The letter was from *The Paris Review* accepting my story. I stuck it back in the book. Ruth noticed. "Send me your stories once you have four or five. Or I'm happy to read them as you write them."

"I'm in a creative rut." I felt suddenly sad. I hadn't started a story since the rape and wondered if writer's block was another side effect of the trauma. I switched the subject. "Paul and I are going up to talk to his mom about the wedding. Will you be my maid of honor?"

"Of course."

"And the godmother to my child?"

"I'm thrilled to be asked," replied Moria.

"And my best friend forever?"

"That's the plan."

I held up my pinkie finger, and she encircled it with hers.

13

"Your parents are coming, and no one else from your hometown?" Paul's mother sat with her pen ticking off names. Glancing over her shoulder, I noticed our wedding date—August 15th—circled in red. Paul and I were gathered with his parents to finish the details of the wedding that Katherine had organized. We were to marry in the Episcopal Church in the town of Halifax, and the reception would take place on the Rivers' stately, rolling lawn, where today the peonies were in bloom.

Paul's father, Lewis, sat by the pool sipping a martini. "Moira, I want to talk to you," he said from across the pool.

"Go ahead, Darling," Paul said. "Mom and I will finish up the details."

"Wait a second," Paul's mother said. "You have your friend Ruth Schwartz on the guest list. Does she have a partner?"

"Yes. Seamus O'Connell."

"Stella is Ruth's mother?"

I nodded. "They should all sit together." I'd added a few friends from the office, too., all of them now aware of my pregnancy.

I joined Paul's father poolside after pouring a glass of lemonade. "You know," he said, rocking back, "with a new family member coming aboard, it might be a good time to talk about Paul's future. You might not be aware that I have offered Paul ownership of the paper whenever he wants it. I'm not ready to retire yet, but I'd like to start thinking about it."

I tried not to look as annoyed as I felt. "I can't imagine us leaving New York. I've been made senior editor at my company, and Paul has been sent abroad and hopes to be again."

"I'm not talking right away," he said quickly. "Maybe in five years . . ."

"That's the distant future to us."

"I don't understand why you're opposed, Moira. We have a good life here."

"It has a lot to do with my career, Mr. Rivers."

He waved his hand. "Call me Calvin. Listen, you're entering motherhood. In five years, surely there will be more little Rivers floating around." He sipped his cocktail. "Hey, not a bad pun."

"David isn't interested in being a part of your company?"

"He couldn't possibly run a newspaper. Besides, he's run off to Australia." Beneath the genteel surface ran a man used to controlling everything around him, I realized. "I want you to know I will be putting shares from the company in the baby's name when he arrives."

"That's generous of you."

I looked over at Paul, who I knew was pleased to see me conversing with his dad. Paul's mother glanced up and, noticing me, said, "Moira, are you ready to go look for a dress?"

"You mean a caftan?"

Katherine laughed. "The right dress will hide everything. I have the perfect designer in mind. Shall we plan to leave in half an hour?" She went into the house.

Paul ambled over to where his father and I were sitting. "Mom always wanted a daughter," Paul said to me, "someone to buy dresses for."

His father smiled. "As for your wedding, she and I eloped, something she always regretted. This is fun for her. I made up for it by taking her to Paris for two weeks on our honeymoon." He stood and started to walk away, then turned back to us. "By the way, your honeymoon's on me. You can go anywhere in the world."

Paul's mother waved from the door. She was in shopping attire, a summer pantsuit, the latest style. I felt Paul and his father's eyes on me as I moved across the lawn to join her. I wished my mother were here. No designer dresses for her; she would take me to a second-hand shop to find a "frock."

On the other hand, Mama's idol was Jackie O, and she might just advise me to go for the finest. I had a toe-hold in Jackie's world now. Katherine met her weeks ago at a gallery opening, which placed my future mother-in-law in another stratosphere in Adeline's eyes.

That night, Paul and I climbed into his childhood bed. "You and Mom had fun?"

"She selected two dresses. Both expensive."

"Thanks for playing along. You're not having second thoughts, are you?" He put his arm around me.

I smiled at him. "No. Your father told me he had offered you the newspaper and wanted to know what I thought. I was honest. The only thing I've been insistent about is that we call Manhattan home."

"We don't have to think about all that now, Darling. Dad's healthy and doing a great job running the paper solo." He reached over and pulled me close, nuzzling my neck. He was immediately turned on. "I won't last long tonight," he whispered.

I felt nothing.

"Oh! God! Moira, I love you," he whispered.

I was frozen. I recalled that I couldn't keep my hands off him when we first met.

He began kissing my shoulder, my chest, my breasts.

I couldn't breathe.

My hands reached up instinctively to create a barrier between his body and mine. "Paul. Wait."

He was on top of me, his face contorted with passion. With a big thrust and a moan, he was inside me.

I turned my head to the side. I was split in two. Again.

"Moira!" he shouted when he ejaculated.

Moira. Moira. I heard my name echoing in the distance.

Paul rolled off me. "Sorry," he said. "I didn't hurt you, did I?"

"It's okay," I whispered. "Crazy hormones."

"Love you," he said, turning on his side.

I put my face against his back and placed my leg over his.

In my dream, fluid ran out of me and onto the ground until it formed a river, and the river kept rising until I felt myself drowning. But then, a fair-haired child suddenly appeared. She was standing on an island, the waters swirling around her, and I reached my hand up, and she pulled me ashore.

14

I awoke at dawn on my wedding day. The first thing my eyes alighted on was my wedding dress, a confection of ivory-colored silk taffeta designed to cover the slight bulge of my tummy. Sunlight blanketed me as I lay there, listening to Katherine giving orders below. I got up and went to the window to watch the wedding staff running around on the lawn, adjusting the chairs, rearranging flowers, and trimming the hedge once more. Katherine had ended up with one hundred and fifty acceptances.

My father stood on the sideline, observing. Before they arrived, he and my mother had no idea of the wealth I was marrying into. I saw the look of awe on my mother's face the night before when we drove through the estate gates. The rehearsal dinner was at the country club, and Paul wrote a check for it in advance to not embarrass my parents.

After too much wine the night before, my mother said to me under her breath, "This is how I imagined Jackie Kennedy's wedding." In her mind, my wedding symbolized lifelong security for me. "Oh, I know her daddy ended up not walking her down the aisle. There was a lot of speculation about that, but I have no doubt the man was three sheets to the wind."

"And how is my father this morning?"

"Meaning, is he like Black Jack Bouvier? I made sure that wouldn't happen."

The ceremony wasn't until four. Adeline entered my room and announced that she and Augustus were off to tour the town. A maid entered with a cup of coffee. I slipped into shorts and a tee-shirt and went down to call Ruth, who was at Seamus' parents. I was told she had gone shopping.

Katherine told me to help myself to anything in the kitchen and announced she had to rush to town. "Paul is with his dad at the office," she said. "They should be back by one."

Seeing my parents in the unfamiliar setting made me realize why I felt like an outlier. Paul would feel the same were we to move to Higginsville. The fish-out-of-water syndrome. I couldn't imagine sharing a confidence with Katherine, but I was fascinated by how she moved in society. She didn't let on if she had any objection to my marrying Paul, yet after my parents arrived, she couldn't curtail her natural condescension. My mother wanted to know every detail about her meeting with Jackie Kennedy. Katherine obliged, but it wasn't enough for Mama. "What about Maurice?" she wanted to know. "Are they in love?"

Katherine looked haughty when she said, "I doubt that that question ever occurred to them."

"Huh. I told Moira, don't marry unless you feel head over heels in love."

I watched Paul artfully try to distract his mother from her little interrogation.

"How quaint," I heard her say when my father explained that he was the pastor at a small southern Baptist church in a town where most people were farmers.

I flinched when I heard him quoting from the book of Psalms: "Blessed are the poor for they shall inherit the earth."

Katherine couldn't keep the scorn from her voice when she said, "Oh, please, writing a check to help the poor seems far more effective than offering them platitudes."

"I beg to disagree. I don't just give a sermon on Sunday. I visit the sick and bury the dead."

"Let's say we're equal in our abilities, Augustus. You save the souls of the poor, and I save the lives."

"I haven't seen any poor people to save here," he said, his eyes twinkling. "Your job is easy."

She waltzed off, and I touched my father's arm. "Touché, Dad."

"She's not going to be easy, Honey. But in all fairness, neither is your mother."

I caught sight of Ruth rounding the corner of the house and beckoned to her to join us. My father said he thought he would amble up and take a rest. Ruth and I wandered to the pool, and one of the staff magically appeared with lemonade. "I'll be sunburned in five minutes," I said. "I can't have a red lobster face during the ceremony."

She laughed. "You nervous?"

"I think something is wrong with me. I feel fine." I looked over at her. "What did you come down to tell me?"

"Nothing I want to discuss on my best friend's wedding day."

"If you don't tell me, I'll be obsessing walking down the aisle."

"I had a talk with Seamus' mother, who said she worries about him. She hates that he's been assigned to the city's most dangerous area. The South Bronx."

"What about him? Is he upset about it?"

"Not especially. He likes the guys he's teamed with. But it's a cauldron of drugs, shootings, and robberies. Name it."

"Is this *you* being worried, or his mother?"

"She told me after Vietnam, he had PTSD bad, but it's still not listed in the Statistic Manual of Mental Disorders. She said his drinking started when he got back."

"You're taking on a lot."

"Seamus is the only man I've ever loved. It's frightening how much I love him. I think this degree of love might not be healthy."

I had felt that way about Paul before the rape. Not since. I wondered if my new level of detachment was permanent; if so, it was like losing one of the senses. I didn't know I was crying until a tear roamed down my cheek.

"Moira, what the hell? If you think you're making a mistake, we can call it off." She leaped up, ran over to one of the tables set for the wedding, returned with a carefully folded linen napkin, and handed it to me.

"I can't use this."

She pressed the napkin into my hand. "Blow."

I did. She whipped it out of my hand and tossed it aside. As if on cue, we began to laugh hysterically. "You're having bridal jitters; that's all," she said. "Plus, you're a hormonal volcano."

We didn't see Katherine until she was upon us. "I've been looking for you," she said to me. "I don't know what to do with your parents. Can you take charge?"

"Of course."

She turned and strutted away.

"Fuck her."

"Ruthie!"

15

A knock at the door, and our mothers suddenly filled the doorway, big smiles on their faces, one towering over the other. "Are you the cleaning ladies?" Ruth asked.

They giggled. "We're here to dress the bride."

Katherine walked up behind them, and excusing herself, made her way into the room. "We need all of you to come down for photographs in the garden within the hour," she said, and then, she studied my mother's navy linen suit that had seen better days. "Do you want the maid to press your outfit?"

"I'm fine. No one will be looking at me."

Stella, looking sedate in a beige linen dress, her frizzy white hair pulled back in a ponytail, said, "Nor me, thank God."

Beautiful in a floating silk number and stilettos, Katherine strutted out into the hall, closing the door behind her.

Stella said, "Katherine looks ten years younger and a whole lot richer than us, Adeline." She reached up and took the dress down. She whirled it around on the hanger. "Who paid for this?"

"Katherine."

"Be careful, Moira. Don't let her take charge of everything. It's hard once a pattern is set."

Mama said, "I think she does it so you barely know it's happening. Right, Moira?" I smiled. "That's the way money works," Mama said. "We don't see Katherine out there moving chairs or arranging the food. There is an army of people doing the work.

Then, as if by magic, there's a band, caterers, and half the town of Halifax celebrating you."

"I don't blame you now for letting her do it all," Stella said. "You being pregnant and all. But Adeline is right about later on."

"You mean after the baby comes, right?" Ruth had joined the conversation. Both women said yes at the same time. "Moira doesn't have to be under anyone's control. What prevents that is making your own money." When no one replied, she continued, "Of course, salaries in publishing are abysmal. Too many women go into publishing because it's respectable, but many are wealthy enough from inheritance to not have to worry whether they make decent money. Art galleries are the same."

The three of them slipped the dress over my head and zipped me up. "You're a princess, Moira," Mama said. "Jackie didn't have anything over you in the looks department, I have to say." She turned to Stella. "I would never have predicted Moira would turn out so pretty, judging from how she looked in high school."

Stella frowned. "Looks aren't everything, you know, Adeline. I'd give intelligence a higher rating."

Ruth snorted. "That's because you have an ugly daughter with a high I.Q."

Stella looked indignant. "I had the most beautiful daughter on the block. Maybe in the city."

"First impressions are important," said Adeline. "You can't see intelligence."

Ruth barked, "Enough already. I'm going to the bathroom, and when I return, I want the subject to have changed."

Adeline waited for the door to close, then said, "You can have both. Look at Jackie Kennedy. Her looks got her two unfaithful men, both full of charisma, though the Greek way too short for my taste. Her intelligence got her Maurice."

Stella whispered, "Ruth's coming. I just heard the toilet flush."

We were self-consciously silent as Ruth entered the room; then Adeline said to her, "Moira was telling me about your young man. Next thing we know, it'll be you walking down the aisle."

"I hope she'll take her time," Stella said to Adeline. "He's in a dangerous profession. And I got the hint that his parents wouldn't be crazy about him marrying a Jew."

"I'm right here, Mom," Ruth said. "You can include me in the conversation. We're still not on a happy topic."

Stella and Adeline shrugged at each other. "Our girls are touchy today," Stella said. "I wonder how many brides are truly happy on their wedding day."

"Moira's happy, aren't you, honey?" Mama asked.

I no longer knew whether to attribute my feelings of continuing dissociation and anxiety to the pregnancy or to the assault. I continued to sleep with a light on. I was plagued by insomnia. The flashbacks were terrifying. Perhaps worst of all, there was no one to talk to.

"I was excited on my wedding day," Adeline rattled on to break the silence. "August and I ran off and left my parents in a tizzy. I look back and think we were idiots." Her face suddenly drooped. "My mother never forgave me."

Stella rescued us from following Mama down that slippery slope. "Being in love is an idiotic state," she said, smiling. "I'm still in love with my husband, though he is long gone."

Ruth adjusted my veil. "You're a vision, alright," she said. "Ready?"

"I love you," I said to my best friend.

"Love you more." She took my hand, and we descended the stairs, our mothers behind us. We walked across the beautifully manicured lawn, where my father stepped out, and I took his arm. Ruth and our mothers walked ahead, and the mothers sat on the front row while Ruth stood next to the minister. Paul and his six buddies from boarding school and Yale stood horizontally on the other side of the minister, their eyes following me down the aisle, my arm looped into my dad's.

Paul reached out and took my hand.

"You look fantastic," he whispered.

My father stepped back, and the Episcopal rector married us. We kissed and turned to the guests, who applauded. In that moment, I felt a wall of support around me, a wall that Jonathan Starkweather would never be able to penetrate, and for the first time in months, I felt myself relax.

My parents were models of decorum at the reception. Seamus, too. I watched Ruth and him dancing and wished with all my heart that they could make it work.

Seamus cut in, took my hand, and led me to the floor. "I hope you're going to end up liking this town. A good place to raise a kid."

"I'm sure it will be okay. I'm going to miss Ruthie. I already do."

"We'll be coming up more often with my folks one town over."

"I hope you two stick together. I've never seen Ruth in love. It suits her."

He grinned and said, "Neither of us knows much about sticking together as a couple, but I'm going to give it my best shot."

I watched Paul cross the floor towards me. He was the star of the show. Handsome, socially at ease, charming. He led me in a waltz, then turned to his mother, who walked into his arms with a smile. My father put his arm around me, and I was surprised to feel his strength— and his grace.

"I didn't know you could waltz," I said.

He smiled. "Your mother taught me. My parents thought dancing was a sin."

Paul cut in. I could feel everyone's eyes on us. "They are watching Cinderella at the ball," he said, smiling.

"I was just thinking all eyes were on Prince Charming." He pulled me in closer and kissed me on the lips.

The photographer Katherine hired moved in closer, the camera clicking until she ran out of film.

16

We left for our honeymoon in Hawaii on September first, and two days later, Paul's father suffered a massive heart attack. We boarded a flight back to New York the next morning, and Paul went directly to Connecticut while I took a taxi to the apartment. The phone rang at six the following morning. Through sobs, Paul told me that his father had died. I repacked our suitcases and headed for Penn Station. His brother David met me at the door. Paul and his mother were meeting with lawyers, so I walked down to the pond and sat on a bench. It seemed soon to be discussing business, but perhaps there was so much at stake that it couldn't be put off. Frederick Paul Rivers had struck me as the type of man who would have all his affairs in order. I looked up at the house that Paul had grown up in. One of the more elegant houses in a town known for its stately residences.

Paul caught site of me from the porch and ambled down. I got up to meet him. "Paul, I'm so sorry." He held me in a long embrace.

"He's only sixty . . . *was* sixty," he said, tears in his eyes. "Do you want to come up to see Mom?"

"Of course. I was told you weren't to be disturbed."

He sat for a minute. "Someone has to take over the newspaper immediately. My mother thinks I'm the only one who can do it." He gave me a rueful smile, and I tried to keep my face neutral. "I'm going to see if I can jump in for a month. My father had been talking to one of Ed's and my friends, Gordon Chambers, about buying the paper, but my mother hates the idea."

My stomach turned flip-flops. "I know your father didn't think David savvy enough as a businessman, but he's here. You could talk?"

Paul snorted. "David can't wait to get back to Australia."

Katherine stood on the porch watching us approach, looking chic in slacks and a silk blouse. I went to her, and we embraced. Before I could offer condolences, she asked, "How are you feeling, Moira?" She glanced at my stomach. "Thank God the baby will bring solace to all of us."

Someone arrived to ask her about funeral arrangements, and she disappeared. I saw Paul's friend Ed had already arrived. Paul went in with his mother and told us to wait. Ed gave me a perfunctory hug. "Quite a shock, huh."

"Completely. He played several rounds of tennis with Paul before we left. He was fit."

"This puts a shitload of responsibility onto Paul."

"He just told me he might have to act as interim editor until someone is hired."

"Oh, you mean Gordon Chambers? He would only be interested in purchasing it, and I don't think he can swing it right now."

My heart sank. "That's terrible news."

"What's so wrong with this place? If I had an offer like this . . ."

"Ed, Paul and I are finally at a place in our careers where we can see a bright future ahead."

"I hear you. But the baby is going to change that, no matter what they say. Carol went through the same thing."

"But it's her second. She has an impressive job at the bank."

"She just resigned."

"I need to work, Ed."

His eyebrows lifted, and he glanced around the estate as if to say, give me a break. I excused myself and went to Paul's bedroom full of tennis trophies and sailboat racing awards. How could I explain that my job in New York was my lifeline—and that even though I wasn't seeing as much of Ruth as I wanted to, she remained my anchor? Why was it so hard for men to understand that work fed women as much as it did them, even if we made half their salaries? Exhausted, I stretched out on the bed. Paul entered, giving me a wan smile. I put my arm around him when he lay down beside me.

"Mom said Dad was worried about the paper. Revenues are down. She said he was despondent after he talked to you. After you nixed the notion of us coming back here."

Now I was to be made a scapegoat. "Paul, I was honest with him."

"You're okay with my stepping in to help Mom for a month, though, right? My boss said I can send in articles from here."

What could I say? "It's fine. I'm sure the perfect person will step in."

The interim month-long editorship turned into six weeks, then eight. I only went up to Connecticut on weekends, where Paul and I stayed in his room at his mother's. I was tired of the commute and tired of being exhausted. Katherine, ever polite, made increasing demands on Paul. She had him meet with her lawyer to settle the estate. I was surprised that Paul and David would not inherit directly from their father. The money was tied up in a trust and in the company. His mother held the purse strings. Paul was reaching the point where he either had to return to work in New York or let the position go. I had finished editing a book that was predicted to become a *New York Times* bestseller. I received a raise. Not having Ruth in the office was strange, but we still met up for lunch two or three times a week. Her obsession with her new agency and the two books she had just sold kept her mind off me, which was a relief in one sense, and a disappointment in another.

One evening when we met for coffee, she said, "Paul's mother is winning."

"What do you mean?"

"Moira, take off the blinders. He's living with his mother, who is determined he will take over the newspaper."

"But he promised we'd stay here."

"In his defense, he also didn't know his dad would die."

"I don't know who I am without my job, Ruth. I'm going to throw away everything I've worked for?"

"Katherine will dangle something amazing in front of you to help you to change your mind."

"Like?"

"How about a big new house?"

"Oh, stop, Ruthie. You're scaring me. I can ask for a leave of absence until after the baby comes, then decide."

"Good luck with Larry saying yes to that. Your best option is to go freelance. Or write a novel. Hint. Hint."

"I envy you sometimes. Your path is straightforward."

"Seamus has started yammering about a baby. He can't understand a woman not wanting to have children. I get him halfway sober, and now, he wants a baby."

She glanced at her watch and said she had to go meet a client. We stood, embracing quickly and agreeing to a dinner soon with Seamus and Paul. I was lost in thought as I started walking uptown, working out how to argue my case for staying in the city.

Then, I turned a corner, and there he was—Jonathan Starkweather—rocked back on his heels, his curly hair tossed about by the breeze. He was talking to a girl in her early twenties, I guessed. He was more muscular than I remembered him being. I froze, shocked by the degree of fear I felt, followed by the sensation of wanting to harm him, to rip his face off. He glanced in my direction, but there wasn't a trace of recognition. The injustice of him being unassailable increased my fury.

They are everywhere, I thought. *Rapists as ubiquitous as cockroaches. All of them running free.* I despised him.

Once locked inside the apartment, I tried to take a short nap to relieve the fear that continued humming throughout my body. The baby kicked non-stop until I got up.

Paul came home a few hours later. He sat me down and said we had to talk. He wanted to move to Halifax. I cried. I accused him of breaking a promise. He argued. He cajoled. He cried. He said his mother was offering us a beautiful house in Halifax. We could temporarily keep our apartment; after all, his mother owned it. Nothing had to be done until the baby arrived and we were settled. This was exactly as Ruth had predicted.

In the end, I capitulated. It was another hurdle for me to overcome when I realized that seeing Jonathan that day had rattled me enough to agree to leave the city.

Three weeks later, we took up residence in a four-bedroom gingerbread house with a sweeping lawn in Halifax, Connecticut. We were three miles from what everyone in Halifax called the Rivers estate. The move had unfolded similarly to my wedding. Katherine found the house and brought in her decorator. I stayed in the city working, packing, and getting up my nerve to tell Larry Cohen I was leaving. He offered to take me to lunch when I asked him if we could meet.

He was stunned. "What are you going to do up in the hinterlands?"

"We still have an apartment here," I said. "I'd like to come and work part-time after the baby is born." I worried I sounded vulnerable—needy.

He leaned into me and placed his hand over mine. "We can stay in touch about that. You know, I was attracted to you from the moment I laid eyes on you—the day you entered the office. Ruth is my witness. I think we can make an arrangement."

I recoiled. The fucker was coming onto me. I slid my hand out from beneath his. "I'm interested in a freelance contract, Larry."

He laughed. "Women have gotten to be so sensitive these days." His face grew dark. "Don't burn bridges, Moira. You might need me one of these days."

He was right, which made me furious, but I kept my mouth shut. In a few moments, I said I had to go.

At the door, he leaned in to hug me, but I pulled away. "Good luck, Moira." I knew in my gut that I wouldn't hear from him again.

I told Paul about Larry's behavior, and he made light of it. "I thought when you first told me about him that he had fallen for you," he said. "In fact, I suspected you and he had a thing going after I met him."

"You never said anything. What made you think that?"

"That week I was in Chicago and you wouldn't pick up the phone."

"Is that why you went back to Katia in France?"

He grimaced. "No." He hesitated. "How did we get here from discussing Larry Cohen??"

"You accused me of sleeping with him."

"Okay, okay. I believe you."

"And Katia? Dare I ask?"

"All professional." He looked relieved when the telephone rang.

I went to bed in an uneasy state. Something had happened that weekend, and Paul sensed it. The trust factor between us was already being challenged. I felt there was more to the Katia story than I knew, and I also understood the topic was verboten. Unable to sleep, I got up, poured a glass of milk, and sat down with my journal. The face of Jonathan Starkweather popped up, and this time, I picked up my pen and wrote, *My dearest Ruthie.* I had found a key to my creativity. I would write to Ruth in the form of a journal.

A week later, Paul and I drove to our new home in Connecticut. Paul turned the radio on. Barbra Streisand was singing her big hit song, "Woman in Love." After it ended, Paul said, "Wait until you see the final touches my mother did to our house." He reached over, took my hand, and squeezed it. "I must admit I'm excited about taking over the paper."

"I'm glad you're happy. You're home."

"So are you."

"It may feel like home one day, but right now, I'm a stranger."

"The baby will keep you occupied."

"Paul, you are parroting your mother."

"Sorry. I'm nervous. I get it that this isn't fair to you." When I didn't reply, he said, "My mother wants to send this woman, Stephanie, over to meet you. She's a garden genius, as well as a health guru to a lot of the women here in town."

"Maybe she can have my baby for me."

He laughed uneasily. "Mom is hosting a small gathering this Saturday night. She wants to make sure you meet people."

I nodded, then looked out the window as we drove through our new neighborhood, houses with immense lawns in front and three-car garages attached. "What do all these people do?" I asked.

Paul laughed. "Oh, they're doctors, young lawyers, financiers, professors at the local college. People like us."

The gingerbread house was decorated in classic Katherine style. Chintz. Sitting areas. Beautiful rugs. The nursery all pale colors and soft lights. Paul took my hand. "I have a surprise." He took my hand, and we exited the back French doors and walked to a tiny building in the back yard that reminded me of a bird house.

"Close your eyes," he said. I heard a door open, and we entered a warm space. "Open your eyes."

I blinked and looked around. I was in a womb of creativity. A beautiful antique desk sat in the middle of the room with wooden walls, a chair before it. My IBM electric typewriter sat on the desk. A leather-bound diary, its pages bare, lay open.

Paul closed the door to keep the chill out. "I wanted to surprise you." Seeing the hope in his eyes, I reached for his hand, and he pulled me in close to him. "It's all going to work out," he said.

"This studio is a dream come true, Paul. I want to believe you." I put my hands on his face and kissed him on the lips. The next thing I knew, we were making love on the oriental rug, my big belly making us laugh hysterically. He was gentle, loving, and thrilled that I was responsive. As was I.

A week passed. Two weeks. I missed Ruth—and my work at the publishing house—the daily grind. I called Ruth to invite her for a visit, but she said there was no way she could come anytime soon with her agency in high gear. I was silent.

"Moira," she said, sounding defensive, "I told you and Seamus both that this agency would take all of me. It feels like you're a million miles away. Why don't you come down and spend a night next week? I'll take you to dinner."

"Can't. It's Thanksgiving, and then Christmas is coming. And I'm huge."

"I'll come when the baby is born. The minute you tell me to."

We hung up. I felt envious. She would succeed in bringing her dream to fruition. Any hope I had of writing a novel that would land on a best-seller list had vanished. I was no longer recognizable to myself.

Paul went down to the city and returned with a letter for me. "It was in our mailbox," he said. I recognized the microscopic handwriting. I read:

Dear Moira,

It has been eight months since you told me about Jonathan. I didn't hear back from you after I wrote you that my mother died a month later. I told her everything. Her eyes looked feral (maybe the morphine). She told me that if I didn't go to you and beg forgiveness for my betrayal of you, she would ban me from her consciousness until she was gone. In one fell swoop, I lost my mother, Jonathan, and you. He disappeared, and my mother never spoke to me after that day. She turned her back, facing the wall—on me, my dad, and my sister. I feel like I am in some ancient Greek drama. I am writing poems about my mother now. I am willing to talk.

In peace,

Erin

I wrote her back and mailed it the next day:

Erin,

I am sorry to hear about your mother. Please do not write me again. I have left the city and started a new life. It is too late now to make amends.

Moira

17

December was a turning point. It was as if my tormenter had wearied of me and moved on. The nightmares became less frequent, and the constant motion of the baby excited me. Paul and I selected a handsome tree for our living room.

When I returned from a shopping trip into town, Katherine was standing with her maid, attaching ornaments to a high branch. "Oh, I wanted to surprise you," she said.

"My mother just sent me a box full of ornaments from my childhood."

"I thought the white lights combined with silver ornaments looked elegant."

"Thanks, Katherine. Maybe I can combine them."

She motioned to her maid that it was time to go. "I'm trying to help, Moira. I know it's not easy to move to a new place and not know anyone."

"You've gone beyond. I'm sorry. I'm missing my old life."

"It's that time of year." She hesitated. "I've been thinking. Why don't you create a column for my newspaper?"

"What would I write about?"

"Oh, it will come. Send me a few samples of your work when you have a moment."

"Thanks. I will."

"And by the way, I'm considering renting the apartment on 72ⁿᵈ Street to someone I know." She avoided eye contact. "Not now, of course. Eventually. You and Paul can always use mine." I knew my face registered shock. Before I could respond, she said she was due at the hairdresser.

When Paul arrived an hour later, I told him about our exchange. He smiled. "Mother thought that you would make more friends here without the apartment as a crutch."

"Paul, she owns us! She owns this house. And what used to be our apartment."

"She's trying to help out until we accumulate some money. I can't ask her to support this house *and* the apartment."

"I never wanted this house."

"She's been at loose ends since Dad died."

"She's replaced him with you."

He quickly gulped down a glass of orange juice and left. I called Katherine and said I'd like to come by her house. She said she was busy planning a dinner. "It won't take long," I said.

I entered her palatial kitchen, where several women were working. Katherine led the way to the terrace, and we sat.

"I'm upset about the apartment being rented," I started. "You understand that I was opposed to leaving New York."

"But you're having a baby. You won't be going to the city. It's a temporary arrangement, Moira."

"You had babies. And ran a newspaper. And kept an apartment in the city."

"Well, my husband had dealings in the city."

"As does Paul. You were in the society pages weekly, Katherine. Your boys were in boarding school."

She suddenly laughed. "Moira, I didn't know you were so feisty. What is it you want, Dear?"

"We only plan to stay here until you feel comfortable that the paper is thriving. I want to be assured that the apartment on 72nd will be ours when we return—and will *not* be sold."

"You're suggesting I let it sit empty?"

"No. You have already rented it behind our backs. I want the rent to run no longer than two years, and then, you will consider letting us buy it from you."

"And what if I refuse?"

"I will find an apartment to rent and take the baby there."

"But you have no money."

"I will work. Just as you did."

"Alright. But if the paper begins to falter, I want the right to re-negotiate this arrangement."

"Of course."

Paul was waiting when I got home. "Let's go to the city for the weekend," he said. "I need to clear out some of my stuff before Mom's tenant moves in." He reached into his pocket and handed me an envelope. Inside were tickets to the Jerome Robbins ballet created for Mikhail Baryshnikov and Patricia McBride, featuring fourteen dancers. The tickets were Katherine's way of making peace.

Once we entered the apartment, I knew I had been right to fight for it. High-ceilinged with southern light pouring in, a spacious living room, one large bedroom, one small bedroom, and two baths. We would never find another like it for the price. Paul and I packed up his desk and removed a few clothes from the closet.

Afterward, we met Ruthie and Seamus for a drink. Seamus, dressed in leather jacket and jeans, said he would be going on duty in an hour. He ordered soda water. Ruthie confided in me when we went to the bathroom that he had attended two AA meetings, and she was feeling encouraged. "Only five percent stick, though," she added. "And he's an adrenal junkie, which I figure is why he uses alcohol to calm his nerves."

Seamus was in great spirits. He said he didn't think it would be a problem to stay off the booze. He talked about how he came to rely on it once he was home from Vietnam and suffering from PTSD. He had thought about becoming a teacher, but his father and grandfather had been cops, and he decided to finish his education and take that route. "The problem is I'm an arrest machine out in the Bronx," he said. "You can't imagine the depravity I deal with. But hey, I get to retire at forty if I want. Five more years." He kept his arm around Ruthie, as she watched him with adoring eyes.

"You made detective in five years, which is unusual." I wondered how Paul knew that.

"I've been lucky so far," Seamus said. "You know the 41st Precinct is called Fort Apache. The worst of the worst. I've dodged a lot of bullets." I was surprised by how open Seamus was with us.

"I might want to write a series on the police force," Paul said. "New York City's the worst it's ever been as far as crime is concerned."

"I guess there's been enough time since the Serpico debacle. Mayor Koch might go for it if you offer a positive outlook."

Ruth was excited about two new acquisitions, and Paul told them about his work for the paper. "It's a good chance we'll be back in the city in a couple of years," he said. "I'm making changes at the paper that require me to be on board, but it's not a lifetime assignment." He told them how I had negotiated the apartment deal with his mother, and they laughed. It felt strange to be out of the professional loop, to sit quietly while they discussed their careers.

Seamus said he had to take off, and we disbanded. Paul took my hand, and off we went to Lincoln Center for the ballet. I was transported to another sphere watching Baryshnikov dance to Prokofiev's Violin Concerto No. 1 in D. Baryshnikov was dancing a dream; when the ballerina came onstage, I wasn't sure if she was a vision or a woman. Paul thought of the Dreamer's role as a quest. There was no particular story, but more a reflection of the music, the male dancer dancing his thoughts. I thought how elevated Baryshnikov was in this piece, in contrast to what I had read—that Jonathan Starkweather's style of dance went from playful to primal and often segued into violent themes.

On Christmas Eve, Paul and I walked holding hands through the snow to the midnight service at the Episcopal Church. Katherine accompanied us. Hundreds of candles lit up the sanctuary, the aroma of spruce filled the space, and sacred song reverberated around us. I felt a wave of peace wash over me. Paul's hand closed over mine. When we got home, Paul and I placed our favorite children's book, *Good-Night, Moon*, under the tree. I drifted off to sleep, only to be awoken in the middle of the night with the image of Jonathan looming over me. He was back—and with a vengeance. I could barely get out of bed the following morning. The next night was worse. I dreamt about Erin, who kept trying to tell me something, and I told her to speak up, but she disappeared into a fog.

I awoke at four to an internal earthquake. I was in labor. Within moments, Paul and I were on the way to the hospital. The contractions were intense and went on for hours. The doctor and Paul stayed at my side, encouraging me, putting a cold cloth on my forehead, and counting contractions. As the baby's head emerged from my womb, I felt split in two. Again. I screamed. I heard the baby cry.

"You have a daughter," the doctor said, placing her face down on my belly.

She stopped crying. Paul raised the hospital bed slightly while the nurse put a blanket around her. Hair tinted reddish-gold. Translucent skin. Her eyes fluttered open, and in a flash, Jonathan's eyes were interlocked with mine.

"Take her," I said to Paul.

He bent down and lifted her into his arms, asking, "What's wrong? She's beautiful. She's perfect." He looked from the baby to me. "What happened?"

"Give me a minute, okay? I'm overwhelmed."

"Well, sure." He looked concerned.

The nurse told Paul to give her a few minutes to examine me, and he stepped away with our new baby in his arms.

"I'm Nancy," she said. "Sometimes it's a shock to see them the first time. To realize that you are responsible for something so tiny." She was smiling.

"It is a shock."

"I don't tell everyone this, but I will you. From this moment, until she turns one, the most important influence in her life will be the expression on her mother's face. A psychic told me this once, and I believe it's true. I've had four, and I kept that in mind, and I have good kids."

She motioned to Paul, and he walked over, and I put my arms up to take her. Nancy helped me put her to my breast, and she latched on instantly. Her eyelids fluttered open again, and this time, I didn't turn away, but neither could I deny what was in front of me. I didn't need a DNA test. A mother knows. I knew Jonathan Starkweather was her biological dad.

"I see a lot of babies," Nancy said, smiling, "but this one might be the prettiest."

Later, I lay on my side staring at the tiny miracle before me and thought that though she was conceived in darkness, she exuded pure light. I understood something in that moment: I would need to quell the darkness in me for her to shine. I climbed out of bed and picked her up, and this time, when her eyes sought mine, our eyes engaged, and I felt a love that I could only describe as pure. All-encompassing. And vast.

Paul said, "Of the twenty names on our list, what do you think?"

"Lyra Ruth?" We had both liked the sound of Lyra, Greek for the first stringed instrument—one that was said to reproduce the music of the sphere.

"Fine by me. We'll call our next one Katherine."

The hospital released us the following day, and Katherine was waiting at our front door, holding out her arms for the baby. Snow was falling, and Paul announced that he had to go to the office.

"The refrigerator is stocked," Katherine said, "and I'm happy to send Anna over to clean or run errands." She sat down with Lyra in her arms, studying her. "She has the shape of your face and your nose," she told me. "Maybe Paul's mouth." Lyra opened her eyes, and Katherine cooed at her. "But whose eyes, I wonder?"

When Lyra started to fuss, Katherine handed her back to me and said she was off.

I put Lyra to my breast. It was my first time alone with her. I recalled reading that women who bore children conceived in rape were allowed to let the infants die of exposure in medieval societies. Women in some cultures, even today, were forced to marry the man who forced himself on them. I kissed the top of my baby's head, cheek, and eyelids. It occurred to me that if I had gone to the police that night and told Paul and Ruth about the attack, I would not be holding this glorious being in my arms.

"You're my precious little secret," I whispered to her.

18

My parents arrived two weeks later. Adeline fell in love with Lyra at first glance. She was thrilled with our house. With Paul. It was close to being her perfect world. She announced that she was setting up shop in the kitchen. My father ensconced himself in the little den with the television. After a week, Paul offered to rent them a house nearby if they wanted to stay long-term. They were moved by his generosity but said they were not prepared to leave their home yet.

Mama sat watching me nurse Lyra one morning. "I really want to do right by her. Make up for the way I was with you."

I was surprised that she would refer to her years of depression at all. "You weren't well, Mama, but hey, I survived."

Mama's features went askew, and I regretted the remark. "But life is about so much more than surviving, Moira."

Surviving my sad childhood was nothing compared to surviving a rape, I thought. I knew there were millions of us in that club who would likely never speak to each other. Too many blaming themselves, just like me. And too many mothers looking the other way as their husbands abused their daughters. Too many men in offices, holding power over the girls and women working for them.

"You're wearing your sad look," she said. "You remind me of my mother."

"I wish you and Daddy would move up here."

"It won't happen as long as he's alive. He's not one for change."

"He doesn't look well."

"He's given back a little." I almost laughed at the expression that meant one's health was declining, recalling Ruth's puzzlement when I used it the first time with her. "Go see him. I'll unpack our things."

I picked up the baby and went downstairs. My father was dozing in front of the television. I stepped in, and his eyes opened. "A long trip, huh?"

"It wasn't too bad." I sat beside him, and he gently touched Lyra's head. "She's a little angel," he said.

I got up and turned the television off.

"You look like you've lost more weight, Daddy. Maybe you should see a doctor while you're here."

"I have a doctor, Honey. Not to worry. I hardly touch the liquor these days." He looked around the room and smiled. "This is some place you have here. Are you happy?"

"I'm getting there. I still feel like a stranger here. But I felt like a stranger in Higginsville, too. I didn't have many friends."

"What about New York?"

"It's where I was happiest. In New York, you move in a sea of strangers, and I liked that sensation of being a cog in the machine. Ruth was my anchor, and eventually, I felt I was in a community. I miss it. Maybe the same way Mama missed Raleigh when you had to move."

"Your mama had some problems for a while."

"I remember there was a scandal in the church." Here it was, the elephant in the room. The downfall. The topic we had never discussed.

"The girl . . . the woman . . . who committed suicide, you mean? She was young and confused. She confessed to me about seeing a married man, and she worried about God striking her down. She finally told me his name, and it turned out, he was a deacon in my church." He shook his head as if he still couldn't believe it. "I counseled her as I would have anyone. I told her that most men who fell in love in this way never left their wives and that she was being used. This upset her, as you can imagine. I gave her the name of a psychiatrist to call, but she said she wanted me to continue counseling her. It wasn't long before she tried to break it off with the deacon, which made him furious. He started the rumor that he had seen her kissing me when she left my office."

"Was it true?"

"She may have reached up and given me a peck on the cheek. In retrospect, I know she was deeply troubled."

"And why was Mama so affected?"

"Adeline heard the rumor about Marianne and me. That was the woman's name." He looked at me with sorrowful eyes. " I'm sorry, Honey. We're opening a big can of worms, but after all this time, you are due an explanation."

"It's time. Go on."

"I finally had Adeline convinced I was innocent, but then Marianne committed suicide, and everyone wagged their fingers at me."

"Mama, too?"

"She didn't blame me, but she had a hard time. The deacon . . . Nate Smith, his name was . . . made sure I got fired. An awful man."

"Whatever happened to him?"

"He got hit by a train about ten years ago. Driving drunk." The baby stirred, and I changed her position. "It's a sad story, but long over."

"A case of poetic justice, wouldn't you say?"

"I tried hard not to be glad he got his just desserts, but I didn't succeed."

I thought about Jonathan Starkweather. I didn't know what it would feel like to *not* wish him dead. Tortured. His throat slit. Sexually assaulted in prison.

We heard the front door open, then Adeline's voice, speaking to Katherine. They saw us and walked in. Katherine, lean, polished, elegant in her fur coat and hat, two facelifts so far, and Adeline, a shabby wool coat and her hair coming loose from its bun. My father stood when the two women entered the room, and, bowing slightly, he excused himself.

"He's not feeling well," my mother confided to Katherine, who nodded sympathetically.

Lyra whimpered, and my mother reached for her. Katherine showed disapproval. "I always let mine cry before picking them up."

"I only had the one," Adeline said. "And I hardly put her down until she was two. Both our kids turned out fine, so maybe there's no wrong or right way."

"I would have given anything for a girl," Katherine said, suddenly looking wistful.

"I lost my second baby," Mama said. "The boy I had longed for."

It was the first time Mama had ever mentioned it in front of me. I was sure Neta had told her about our conversation.

Katherine sat down, looking relaxed. "Do you and Paul plan to have another?" she asked me.

"Absolutely. I never liked being an only child."

"I didn't know that," Adeline said, her lips turned down. "I couldn't have handled two, which is why God took my boy. Augustus agreed." She darted a glance in Katherine's direction, and said by way of explanation, "My nerves." Then, "My own mama was an anxious woman. I only saw my parents once after Moira was born."

I felt myself sinking into the sofa. "Why on earth not?" Katherine asked.

"They disowned me for having a shotgun wedding. Then when they tried to reconcile, I wouldn't have it."

"Life's too short," Katherine said. "But I can see how it happens. I'm recently widowed, as you know, Adeline. We're always left with regrets."

I wondered what Katherine's might be.

Ruth visited two days later with her mother, Stella, who rushed over and embraced my mother. They were staying with Seamus' family in Roxbury, one town over. "What a house," Ruth said, then when we were in the kitchen, she whispered, "What do you do here all day?"

"I have a baby."

"Who takes up three inches of room. You don't get lost? The house is so big."

Ruth could always get a laugh out of me. "Here, say hello to your namesake." I put Lyra into her outstretched arms. "Meet Lyra Ruth Rivers."

"A good writer's name," Stella said. We laughed.

Ruth walked around with Lyra, whose eyes fluttered open. "I've just changed my mind," Ruth said, then, "just kidding. On the other hand, Seamus is doing great. If that continues, who knows?"

Ruth handed Lyra over to Stella when I told her I wanted to show her something. We slipped into our jackets and walked out to the studio. Ruth entered and stood still, as though she were stunned.

"If Paul Rivers could come up with this, he ought to leave the newspaper business and become an architect."

I laughed. "I agree." Shelves filled with books and framed photographs. A couple of prints on the wall. A colorful rug. "It's where Lyra and I hang out."

She glanced over at my desk. "So. You are writing."

"Another short story. I'm journaling a lot and thinking about writing an essay column for the newspaper. Katherine's idea."

"I just sold a southern manuscript. A family saga. I wish you'd write a novel."

"The journal jottings might shape into something. I'm also considering putting together a small class of writing students. The woman who does the gardening here has become a friend of sorts, and she said she knows several women who might want to join."

"As long as they don't treat it like a hobby. Then it's a waste of time. What are these women like out here?"

"All married. Some bored. All but one with a kid or two. Two working, one in reception at the country club. I would go crazy if I thought this would last forever, but we promised Katherine two years. That, I can do." I reached up and turned the light off, and Ruth looped her arm in mine. "Back to Seamus and having a baby. Really?"

"If he's been sober two years, I'll say yes. I love the man nearly to death, Moira. If anything happens to us, God help me, I don't ever want to care this much again."

Stella and my parents were waiting in the hall, on their way out to dine at the club with Katherine, who had invited them at the last minute. Paul was working late. My father had built a fire in the fireplace in the library, and Lyra was asleep in her cradle. I opened a bottle of champagne, and Ruth and I sat together on the sofa in front of the fire. We would also dine there.

"Is Katherine still working at the newspaper office daily?"

I laughed. "Oh, yes. She's in charge. Our own Katherine Graham. At least that's how she sees herself."

"So. Moira. Are you happy?"

"Funny. My dad just asked me that. I'll quote Virginia Woolf: Nothing thicker than a knife's blade separates happiness from melancholy."

Ruth nodded. "Obviously, melancholy won in Woolf's case. Remember the year we were obsessed with her? The story in her *Moments of Being* of her half-brother George Duckworth abusing her still haunts me."

"Both her brothers molested her. It could have contributed to her later suicide."

Ruth had picked Lyra up and held her as she slept. "How will you keep this little one safe?" she asked. "Every mother must worry."

"Girls have to be taught very young to speak up and speak out."

Ruth sighed. "There's no literature out there about any of it. Seamus told me the other day that they're dealing with a shitload of rapes. It's rampant."

I had to change the topic before I exploded. Lyra came to my rescue when she started to cry. Ruth handed her to me, and I put her to my breast.

Ruth, though, was wound up. "As for girls," she continued, "You're right about speaking out. Stella had a way of extracting everything from me when I came home from school. She would query me about every minute of the day. And lecture me about how to spot a pervert. I'm not sure that was helpful."

"My mother was the opposite. Boys were nuisances, and evil could be eradicated by prayer. You didn't talk about sex or things that happened. I have only recently learned the truth about the debacle in my father's church that brought such shame to him."

"Let me guess. It wasn't at all as you had been led to believe," Ruth said.

"There was so much gossip. My father refused to defend himself, and he paid dearly for that."

Ruth sat up straight. "That would never be me. I would fight to the death if someone accused me wrongfully. And I hope you would, too."

"What I learned from my dad's experience is that people don't necessarily want the truth. Or justice. They bend the story to accommodate their notions of right and wrong."

"But they have to be set straight." She got up and went to the window. "I just heard a car pull in. I need to get Stella home." I joined her, and she put her arm around me. "I miss you. Know that. Also know that my goal is the same as it was. I'm going to make a lot of money and then hope to do good with it. I have Stella to take care of for now."

"What does that mean?"

"I wasn't sure I'd tell you. She was just diagnosed with breast cancer."

"Oh, shit. That's the worst news imaginable. Oh, Ruthie."

She had moved in front of the fire, and I watched her. So beautiful standing with the flames coiling up behind her. "They caught it early. She's ready to fight for herself for a change. Her attention has always been on anyone but herself."

"I wish I could help. I hate being so far away."

"It's okay. She's got her friends in Queens, and she and the local rabbi are close. And I've got Seamus."

"Bring her up here more often. I think she likes it."

"Don't let her know I told you."

My parents walked in with Stella. They were all smiles and ready to continue, but Ruth insisted she get her mom home. I saw them out, then returned to the library where my mother sat looking into the fire. "Your daddy went on to bed," she said.

"I'll make tea. Lyra's been sleeping almost the entire time."

She picked the baby up and followed me into the kitchen. "Katherine seemed surprised at dinner that we're planning to stay for three weeks. I think she was implying that we might wear out our welcome."

"No chance of that. How was it?"

"Dinner was delicious. Paul stopped in at the end and will be right along. Katherine talked quite a lot about a friend of hers named Russell, who is joining the newspaper staff. Divorced. The way his name kept coming up, I had a hunch something might be going on between them."

"I met him at Paul's dad's funeral. Katherine hasn't said a word to us."

"I had the idea she brought it up to me with the expectation that I would tell you and you would tell Paul. People do that, you know."

"I don't think Paul would have any objection to his mother starting a new relationship."

"I imagine one day Paul's going to have to cut the apron strings. You two have a good life, but she didn't hesitate to say that it's because of her."

I couldn't hide my annoyance. "She won't come around much while you're here. Maybe I'll have you and Daddy move in permanently."

Mama laughed, and I did, too.

19

As much as women go through life denying they are turning into their mothers, at some point, there is a reality check. I turned out to be as obsessed with Diana, Princess of Wales, as my mother was with Jackie Kennedy. Diana was twenty when she became engaged to Prince Charles, and the women in my writing class were all caught up in the courtship. It led us into a conversation about feminism. I was in the process of leading my writers on a journey of what it was like to be a woman today. I had grown up in a sexist, racist environment in the South, I told them, and it distressed me to see how little change had taken place. My education on feminism had come through Ruth, but even more through Stella. When I first arrived in New York in 1974, I thought that Ruth and her mother Stella had invented the term "feminist." Stella had worked hard to pass the ERA in 1971, and though it failed, change was starting to occur. Sexism and sexual harassment were still the norm in offices, as was the cover-up. Women didn't dare speak up, though, in our publishing house, Ruth had become a feminist guru. She had met Gloria Steinem and Grace Paley and knew Betty Friedan through Stella.

A decade later, women were still struggling with the same issues. Priscilla had brought up the recent announcement by Diana's uncle declaring her a virgin. Another rumor in the papers was that she had spent two nights with Prince Charles on the train where he had seduced other sweet lasses, but Diana had objected strenuously to the insinuation that she had been one of them.

"It's obscene," I said to Paul later that night. "It's 1981, for god's sake. She's a sacrificial virgin."

"I can tell when you've been with Ruth," he said, smiling. "It's always been that way with British royalty, Moira. I think Diana's virginity, the proof of her desirable youth and innocence, is central to the fairy tale glamour of her myth."

"Remember in *The Metamorphoses*, the Roman poet Ovid wrote of the hunter coming up on the goddess virgin Diana bathing, and she transformed him into a deer for the unwelcome intrusion, and his dogs attacked him. Our Diana might have another side to her."

"Should I warn Charles?"

I laughed. "Absolutely."

Paul surprised me when he wondered aloud if the whole royal wedding wasn't a set-up. "It's known that Philip pushed the marriage on Charles," he said.

"I don't consider him much of a catch. In my mind, he's a fuddy-duddy."

Paul laughed. "You and your writers are still planning a wedding party?"

"Absolutely."

"Dyed-in-the-wool feminists are succumbing to the charm of a fairy tale wedding?" he teased.

"You can take care of all the problems of the world while we take a break."

"Come writers and critics, who prophesize with your pens, And keep your eyes wide open, the chance won't come again," Paul said, quoting Bob Dylan.

It was turning out to be a good summer. Mama had been spot-on about Katherine's new love interest, Russell Wentworth. Newly divorced, the rumor was that he hadn't managed his finances well. Without consulting Paul, Katherine had given him the role of assistant publisher at the paper. He leaned strongly to the right, which was a problem for Paul, who was a liberal. Russell's idol, we were to learn, was Ronald Reagan, predicted to win the next election. Paul had worked for Jimmy Carter's campaign, while Russell had contributed to Reagan. But whatever antagonism existed between them had quelled for the time being. Paul worked ungodly hours, but he felt it was what his father had intended. The paper had been in Katherine's family for many generations, but it was Paul's father who had taken over and given it a national reputation with prize-winning feature articles. Paul's goal was to continue in this vein.

I was getting to know Stephanie, the gardener Katherine had sent to help me. She dropped by frequently, and I'd emerge from my studio to work alongside her in the gardens. To my surprise, she joined my writing class.

"I've been talking to the girls," she said, "and it looks like all of us can come to the wedding party." The girls were the women in writing class, and the wedding party was gathering to watch Diana marry Prince Charles. "We'll have to be up at the crack of dawn. Everyone's saying she's too young," Stephanie said. "But I married at eighteen. And Diana believes this to be her destiny. If karma put her on this path, then what can she do?"

Stephanie was not only a gardener but the local New Age guru. The mother of three, she was an herbalist and self-proclaimed healer and taught classes in visualization. Early on, I had made it clear that I would not be following her down the rose-tinted path she had created for herself, and she accepted it. Occasionally, though, I would indulge her in a conversation like the one we were having now. She knew she had me at the mention of Diana.

"We enter a path because we choose it," I said. "And sometimes the choice turns out to be wrong."

"There is no right or wrong," Stephanie argued. "Even if it feels wrong, I believe we are exactly where we are meant to be."

What if you are violently ripped off your path I wanted to ask, but I stayed mum instead. What did Stephanie know, anyway?

Six women showed up before dawn on July twenty-ninth. Paul had taken Lyra to his mother's the night before. Stephanie arrived early to prepare tea, and I had purchased a bag of scones and other treats. We were among the seven hundred and fifty million wedding observers, I was to learn later. A number too vast to imagine.

I had come to know a lot about the women gathered around me from their writing. And in teaching them to speak their truth, I was aware of how much I hid my own truth. But not so much from myself anymore. I had filled many notebooks and kept them all under lock and key in file drawers. I didn't worry. Paul was the least prying person I had ever known.

When Diana began her long walk down the aisle, her father beside her, the music soaring, I opened a bottle of champagne to the group's astonishment. "We're barely awake," Stephanie said, laughing.

"There's coffee on the tray," I said. "And orange juice. We can make a mimosa."

Everyone agreed. We toasted the new couple and each other. By the end of the wedding, Stephanie had downed a second glass, which surprised me. Bonnie brought up again that Diana and Charles had seen each other only twelve times since their engagement.

Stephanie suddenly blurted, apropos of nothing, "Bert and I got pregnant in high school. He got drunk and had his way with me. Then bingo, I was a mother."

We all went silent.

Priscilla said in a chipper voice, "You have three wonderful children now." She turned to me. "Moira, Stephanie told me you and Paul were trying for another."

Stephanie almost shouted. "When did I say that?"

"It's okay," I said. "There was a period when we talked about it, but no more!" My laugh sounded too high-pitched.

Priscilla chirped in a raspy voice, "I think we're all drunk, and it's your fault, Moira Rivers. We should skedaddle."

"Who says skedaddle in this town?" Bonnie asked, laughing. They started gathering up their things.

After they left, I sat alone, mesmerized, listening to commentators give their take on the grand affair. When it was over, I went to my studio and wrote an essay on Princess Diana's bouquet. I told how every royal bride carries a bouquet that includes myrtle, an evergreen woody shrub considered the flower of love and marriage. Diana's bouquet, weighing in at four pounds, also contained gardenias, stephanotis, Earl Mountbatten roses, freesia, veronica, and the de rigueur myrtle, a great weight for a young woman to carry, not to mention the tiara that I read she had worn all morning, which gave her a headache. I wondered in my column if she had the strength to carry the expectations of so many. If anyone in the castle would be there for her if she found herself struggling.

I gave it to Paul, who said he'd take it in for tomorrow's paper. Of course, I was writing about myself, but plenty of other women related to what I was saying. The proof was that the newspaper received over a dozen letters in the mail after it was published, most of them positive. Maybe it was Stephanie, or I had learned it on my own, but I knew plants were sentient. Paul said later, "Who would have thought our women readers wanted to read about a princess's bouquet? I think you're on to something."

I thought I was, too.

PART TWO

If we had to say what writing is, we would define it essentially as an act of courage.

—Cynthia Ozick

20

It occurred to me one day that I had been right to marry. I had picked the best hiding place in the world, where I existed in a society ruled by politeness and good manners, where it was rude to pry, and where keeping up appearances was crucial to one's well-being. Paul fell back into familiar patterns in the suburban landscape he had grown up in—commuting to the office, drinks after at the country club, and a few hours of golf or tennis whenever he could fit it in. I opted to be at home with Lyra after her preschool activities ended; she made it easy to opt out of Katherine's and her friends' numerous invitations. A strange contentment settled over me. My determination to repress and deny the trauma was effective for now. I still dreaded nighttime when nightmares of being chased drove me from my bed, my body drenched in sweat. I spent the morning hours when Lyra was at school in the studio or in the garden with Stephanie, who was a great source of information on planting by the moon, astrology, and other topics related to New Age philosophy. Sometimes I thought she had set herself up as a guru, especially to vulnerable women, rather than dealing with some of her own issues. I maintained a good boundary, even when depending on her for advice.

Katherine came over one day and offered me a handsome salary for my column. "We're getting good feedback," she said. "But don't go extreme on us."

"What would those parameters be?"

"Not too much New Age. Stephanie's driving me crazy now when she comes to the garden, talking about this guru or that one and telling me how to eat."

I laughed. "Some of it is quite interesting, but she overloads me too."

Stephanie was, per usual, on her way to someplace else, when she stopped by one morning. "You know your audience," she said. "Sophisticated women with careers."

"And ladies who lunch?"

She laughed again. "Welcome aboard, my dear."

I thought about it and decided to write a gardening column called "Moira's Notes on Gardening." Gardening was a fine metaphor for discussions on life and death, nature, and meditation, perhaps—topics that had little to do with day-to-day domestic life, but the bigger issues women faced.

Ruth called once a week to check in, but eventually, the calls became more sporadic. When she and Seamus came up to stay with his parents, she would arrive with fabulous gifts for Lyra. It was as if we all had settled into a rhythm.

Ronald Reagan was elected president in 1980, to Ruth's and my consternation—and re-elected in 1984. The movie star president who could seemingly do no wrong. Paul had begun a series of articles about AIDS that blamed the government—and the president—for ignoring the crisis killing thousands of young gay men. I remained an avid follower of Princess Diana and wrote a tirade against Prince Charles when he started his affair with Camilla in 1985, but Katherine refused to print it. "It won't go over with our readers," she said.

"But you told me I could choose my topics."

Her lips settled into a horizontal line, a harbinger of stubbornness and displeasure. "Alright, Moira, why don't you write something about Prince Charles, who is transforming his Highgrove estate into a gardening paradise?" I knew it felt safe. I went to the library and researched the prince, but also learned from a friend of Paul's that Prince Charles was known to talk to his plants and, in fact, had been quite open about it, which I presented in a very positive light. But I also painted a picture of how a man twelve years older than his beautiful bride spent an extraordinary amount of time tending to his gardens, where he was nurtured and adored by several aristocratic gardening women in their sixties, while Princess Diana was ignored. I acquired more fans and didn't hear a word from Katherine.

Jonathan Starkweather seemed to have been relegated to the past until Lyra started dancing to any music that Paul played. Even I could see that the grace she exuded was extraordinary for a four-year-old. Katherine had also noticed and offered to give her dance lessons. "All the little girls go to Miss Riley's," she said.

"But not at age four," I said. Paul took his mother's side, insisting it could be fun for her. I won but knew it was temporary, for I couldn't justify my objections. How could I say that I was worried that if she became a dancer, there also existed the possibility that her biological father would find her? Some of my anxiety was fed by the new practice of putting missing children's photographs on milk cartons. I learned it was a campaign started by the National Child Safety Council. Each time I saw a face, I thought of Lyra. What would I do? Everyone thought it a great idea, as it took a while for news to spread, especially nationally. The faces fascinated Lyra. While eating her cereal one morning, she asked, "What's his name?" pointing to the photograph of a little boy on the carton.

I picked it up. "Michael."

"I want to put my picture beside his."

"No, you don't."

"Why, Mommy?"

"Because his mother can't find him."

"I could be an invisible fairy looking for the lost kids. And I would find them and take them home."

My eyes stung. "Why don't you go find your daddy?" He took her out for an adventure every Saturday, usually to the local diner, and on Sundays, they played tennis. She ran upstairs as he entered the kitchen through the back door. He poured a cup of coffee and sat down.

"I wonder why we haven't gotten pregnant again," he said out of the blue.

"I figure if it's meant to happen, it will."

"That sounds like Stephanie talking," he said teasingly. Then, hesitant, he said, "We could think about seeing a fertility doctor."

"Let's wait a while." I had also been concerned that nothing had happened.

Ed and Carol came to dinner a few evenings later, and she announced her third pregnancy. That night, Paul and I made love with renewed passion. I desperately wanted to have Paul's baby. I began listening to Stephanie's advice about diet and tricks for getting pregnant.

My writing took on new fervor. I started one short story after another, but my voice seemed dull compared to the earlier days when I didn't think about it. Six women arrived on Thursday nights. I stated from the beginning that we were not a social club, which I found a waste of time, but I wanted to offer them a way to consider the more interior aspects of their lives. They struggled, but after a few weeks, they came up with more interesting stories. I was writing some of my own childhood stories. In one exercise, I realized how frightened I was when my mother went through her spells after she and my father were forced to move. Looking back now, I realized she had no idea how to cope with the trauma of my father being kicked out of the church—and the years of ostracism that followed.

It was a Black woman, Neta, who showed up to work one day in our home, who saved me, with her deep sense of caring. I described her grounding presence for my writing class:

> *I entered my house in Higginsville one afternoon after school when I was six, and a tall black woman stood at the kitchen sink. Seeing maids in my friends' houses was perfectly normal, but it was new for our house. She looked old and young at the same time.*

"Yo' mama's in bed," she said, turning to look at me. "I'm going to help out here for a while."

"What's your name?"

"Neta. And what's yours?"

"I'm Moira."

"That's a different name for around here."

"It's from the Greek myths. It means destiny or fate."

"You don't say." She shook the water off her hands and dried them with a towel. "I'll be here every day when you come from school. Why don't you put your books away, and I'll fix you something to eat? She pulled out a box of Vanilla wafers and started spreading peanut butter on them.

"Can we sit outside?" I asked.

"Sure." She sat on a blanket and shelled butter beans and talked.

It was heaven to be with an adult interested in what I had to say. And I couldn't get enough of her stories. Over the next months, I learned that Neta's ex-husband, who had gone on a shooting rampage, had killed her sister. He was looking for Neta but found her sister instead.

"Where is he now?" I asked. "In a lunatic asylum. He'll never see the light of day again."

"Do you think he's sorry?"

"I can't answer that."

"Do you miss your sister?"

"Every day. It never goes away."

"I miss my mother."

"The real her is hiding in there somewhere in the darkness. You watch and see. She'll find her way back."

When my mother did just that (probably due to medication), I thought Neta a sorceress. By the time my mother emerged with a new outlook on the world, we had all come to rely on Neta for advice and solace. When I overheard Adeline complaining about my father's secret drinking, Neta reminded her that he would find his way out, same as she did. But, I asked her, "Why do people go into the dark?" This was when I was eleven.

"Think of the critters that prefer the dark," she said. "Owls, for example. And think about how wise they are sittin' on a limb blinking and blinking. People, though, are meant to experience light. They fall into darkness by accident."

"Like into depression?"

"Uh-huh." She began clearing the dishes.

I studied her. "You are dark on the outside but all light inside," I said.

She stopped and looked at me. "Now, where did that come from?" I could see she was pleased. "Young girl like *you shouldn't be thinking about all that. You got plenty of time ahead for those things."*

With our constant dialoguing, I went from being a sad and worried child to looking forward to rushing home from school to tell Neta about my day. By age twelve, I began dreaming of becoming a writer between reading to my mother from books 'way beyond my years' in her words and recording Neta's stories. This continued until I graduated from high school as class valedictorian and was accepted into a girls' college known for its writing program.

My students encouraged me to stick with the memoir. And as I dislodged more of my stories from the past, they began to do the same. I came to know them from their stories and not their self-designed personas, coiffed hair, and designer clothes. One woman wrote a story about a newly married woman cheating on her husband. I suspected that the story was about her and was true, but I had taught them to consider every story a work of fiction and not to interrogate the author as to the truth or falseness of the story. This brought up the topic of secrets, and eventually, we segued back to Princess Diana.

Laura, the most serious writer among the students, said, "My sister has attended social events with Diana and the prince. The rumor is they are going to divorce."

I wished Katherine were here listening. This was exactly what women were thinking about Diana.

"She should expose him," one of the women said.

"Or not," said Priscilla, who wrote the story about having an affair on her husband. "These things usually play out. It shouldn't be such a big deal. Besides, royals always had affairs."

Bonnie, a short and perky blond, said, "You all know W.H. Auden's poem, 'At Last the Secret is Out'? The one with the opening: *At last the secret is out, as it always must come in the end . . .?*"

"People always look for the scandalous and hidden aspects of others. It's human nature," Stephanie said.

I picked up the tray of empty glasses. "You're treating secrets as invariably harmful. My mother ignored the bad and focused on becoming the person she chose to be. There were things we never talked about. It's what she wanted."

"A friend who works with the dying says it's shocking how many deathbed confessions she's heard," said Priscilla. "People mostly talk about their regrets. And a lot of it has to do with love. They wish they had not ended certain relationships."

Stephanie said, "I think it must be suffocating to carry a secret for years. There has to be a ripple effect."

"Sometimes that person is protecting others," I said, knowing I sounded defensive.

Stephanie persisted. "But those others have an inner knowing. An unconscious knowing. My mother was adopted but didn't know until she was fifty. She hasn't spoken to her adoptive parents since she found out."

"Why?" I asked.

"Because her life would have been different had she known the secret around her adoption. She says that had she known, she could have decided whether or not to accept her birth parents. She didn't like being kept in the dark. One needs, she said, to know one's heritage, no matter what."

The discussion ended on that note. After they had gone home, I thought how the stories I had continued to tell myself after the rape were delusional. Everything I thought and wrote had to do with self-protection. Stephanie had poked a hole in my armor, and I didn't like it. I wrote in my journal:

If my writing is ever to resonate with others as it once did, it will have to come from a place of truth. This would mean revising my inner storytelling.

21

Ruth called on a spring day in 1985. "It's Seamus," she said breathlessly, hiccupping a sob. "He was shot last night. You'll see it on the news."

"What? Is he . . . ?"

"He's alive. Busted his femur and some other stuff. It's pretty serious."

"I'll come tomorrow."

It so happened that Katherine was driving down to the city and offered to pick up Lyra and me. "You can stay with me," she said. Katherine had continued renting our apartment, and we had not fought it, as our plans to return to the city had not come to fruition. We felt we had no right to hold her to the former agreement, as we continued to stay in Halifax.

Lyra was thrilled to be going to see Ruthie and Stella. She asked a hundred questions about Seamus but finally fell asleep in the car. Katherine waited for her to go silent, then said she wanted me to know she was considering Russell Wentworth's marriage proposal. "He's going to buy into the newspaper," she added. Sensing my alarm, she said, "Maybe it's the shot in the arm we need."

Paul hadn't mentioned it. "Is the paper in trouble?"

"We're struggling like so many are. People are switching to television for news. But don't look so worried. It's okay."

"Have you told Paul that Russell proposed?"

"I thought I'd do a test run with you."

"I imagine Paul and Russell at loggerheads politically."

She smiled. "I'm going to persuade Russell to come more to the center. He's very opposed to the Reagan-bashing Paul has been doing lately."

Paul was not going to like this news. "We want you to be happy, of course," I said.

"But?"

"But Paul has worked so hard to improve the paper, giving it a national rather than regional flavor. He has added sophistication in several departments. And it has paid off, hasn't it?"

"Oh, Paul is a romantic like his father. He sees the paper as a living, breathing creation. It assumes human qualities in his mind." She added, "Please don't say anything to him, right now." I nodded.

Lyra and I went to Ruth's office after leaving our suitcase at Katherine's. Ruth swept Lyra up in her arms and kissed her. Lyra asked if she had a gift for her, and before I could correct her rudeness, Ruth had opened a cabinet and pulled out three books and a doll.

"All for you!" she said, and Lyra danced around the room. "Why don't you go see Seamus now," Ruth said to me, "and I'll keep Lyra here; then we can go to my apartment and have dinner with Stella."

"How is Stella doing?"

"Her cancer has metastasized, but they have a new drug, and she'll be placed on a clinical trial. Fingers crossed."

"This is unbearable news."

Ruth's phone rang constantly, but Lyra wasn't fazed. She had curled up on the sofa and was looking at her books. I got up, gave them a wave, and walked to the hospital.

Seamus lay flat on the bed, his leg elevated, his eyes closed. "Seamus?" His eyes blinked open.

"Hey, Moira. Thanks for coming."

"My god, I saw it on the news after Ruth called. A close call for you, huh?"

"Too close."

"What happened?"

"A woman on the wrong street too late at night. The guy, a drug dealer, forced her to go to his lair up on 124th Street. When we were at the door, he shot through it and got me. My partner killed him."

"What happened to her?"

"He raped her, the bastard, and I'm sure he would have killed her if we hadn't rushed in. The guy was brought in months ago for assaulting a woman, but he was back on the street in no time. Nothing happens to these guys, and it pisses me off."

"It isn't generally known what that kind of violence does to a woman. To be at the mercy of someone, alone in a room, and your body and soul desecrated." Suddenly embarrassed by how he studied me, I quickly changed the subject. "And here you are. Prognosis?"

"Not that great. I might end up with a gimp leg." He tapped his forehead. "It's what inside here that's the trouble."

"What do you mean?"

"I finally got an official PTSD diagnosis. You don't ever want to have it. I get flashbacks to the fighting in Vietnam. I have insomnia. I won't bore you with the rest of it."

I wished I could tell him I understood all of it.

He asked me to roll his bed up slightly, and I did. I also poured a glass of water and handed it to him. "You know, I just told Ruth last week that living in the city is getting old. I admire what you and Paul have up there in the country. I grew up in the next town over, for god's sake."

"You'd consider moving?"

"We both know Ruth's not a country girl."

I laughed. "Far from it."

He sighed. "Her business is crazy busy. And her mom . . . you know."

"She just told me. Paul is fine up in Connecticut. I'm not."

"I thought you were adjusting pretty well."

I didn't say anything.

He broke the silence. "How's that little Tinkerbell of yours?"

"She's a happy and spoiled five-year-old."

"Nothing wrong with that. You and Paul aren't going for more?"

"Hoping." I glanced at my watch. "I need to go help Ruth and Stella with dinner. She said she'd see you later. Let me know if you come up to Connecticut to recuperate."

"Will do. I have a lot of rehab to do here before I go anywhere. Thanks for coming."

"*Ciao.* See you soon." He extended his hand, and I encircled it with mine. "Ruth doesn't want to lose you, Seamus. I know that. She is deeply in love with you."

"And I love her."

"You could ask her to marry you."

"In this state?"

"I'm going to leave you with that thought." I left.

Ruth was in the middle of cooking dinner when I arrived. Stella, looking frail, was reading a book to Lyra. I offered to help Ruth, but she insisted I visit with her mom instead. Lyra ran off to the kitchen to join "Roof."

I sat next to Stella. "Ruth says the cancer's back."

She nodded. "I don't think I can beat it, but don't tell Ruthie I said that. She wants me to fight it and beat it, and it all sounds violent to me. I'm at peace, Moira."

My eyes welled with tears. "I can't imagine us without you."

"You must promise me you'll be there for Ruth when I go. She'll take it hard."

"You know I will."

"How are you doing, Moira, way up there in the 'burbs?"

"Starting to feel irrelevant in the life we've created."

"I felt that way when Ruth was about the same age as Lyra," she said. "I was in the city, but anyplace becomes stagnant when we're wanting something that feels unattainable. I started attending classes again and became a radical for feminist causes . . . or, as my husband used to say, all causes." She laughed. "It kept me out of trouble."

"What were some of your causes?"

"Civil rights. Women's voting rights. I've worked alongside Bella Abzug for years. You remember, in 1977, Jimmy Carter appointed her head of the National Commission on the Observance of International Women's Year? She's unstoppable in her work for women and women's rights."

"And so are you. Don't be modest."

"I try. I advise my young women friends who tell me they're depressed to do something for others. Act, don't react, I say."

"I don't do enough."

"You're raising a kid and writing and teaching writing to women. You're good. Are you and Paul planning to have another baby?"

I had grown sick of the question. "Yes, though it's not happening. Neither is the writing, to be honest. Not in the way I had hoped."

I could hear Lyra chatting away with Ruth in the kitchen. I suddenly had the urge to cry.

Stella reached for my hand. "It seems to me, Moira, that each of us has a big lesson to learn in this life. Mine was selflessness. Maybe I went to an extreme with all my volunteering, but I like what I learned from it. Ruth's will be patience. Notice I use the future tense. She's not there yet, but I think she'll make it." She put her hand out and grabbed mine. "Yours is honesty. Politeness is necessary in a marriage, but so is truth. Maybe I'm out of line, but I think you and Paul tend to dance around your problems, not face them head-on. This could be happening in your writing."

Stella had just spelled out exactly what I was feeling. "Something happened six years ago that hit me hard. I feel like I've lost my voice, in life and in my writing."

"Ruth knew something happened and asked me what to do. I told her to be patient . . . there's that word again . . . that you would tell her when you were ready."

I reached my arm up and brushed away the tears.

Stella squeezed my hand. "You might be ready."

Ruth came to tell us dinner was ready. She stopped abruptly at the sight of us. "What the hell's going on with you two?"

Stella raised her hand. "Truth to power!"

Turning back to the kitchen, Ruth laughed and said, "You're both nutcases! Come to dinner."

22

Journal Entry: December 1986

It is the day after Christmas, and my mother is visiting. She is in the kitchen making a cake, with Lyra as her sous chef. My little girl will be six years old tomorrow. Paul has just come home and turned on the radio. Tchaikovsky's "The Nutcracker" is playing. Suddenly, Lyra is dancing all over the room. Paul stands there, mesmerized. I watch, and suddenly the rapist—I resist calling him by his name—is there in front of me. He will never leave, I think. A sense of despair washes over me.

My mother leans over and says, "Time for dance school, it looks like."

"Don't be silly," I say in a huffy tone. A hot flame courses through my veins. The anger that is constantly being tamped down. I feel it in my stories that aren't selling. It's real. I have lost my voice. I repeatedly tell my students that readers know when the story isn't genuine. The work reeks of shallowness.

Paul turns the music up. My mother encourages Lyra, clapping her large, sturdy hands together. Paul is laughing. I must leave the room. I must escape. I jump up, but Paul grabs my arm. "I wonder who has the dancing genes," he says. "It isn't me." An innocent remark. I march to the stereo and shut off the music.

"Hey, Mommy! I was dancing!" Lyra's face is a mini-storm waiting to erupt.

"But Lyra," I say, "It's almost time for dinner."

They stand frozen, my husband, my mother, my little girl. Lyra comes at me and kicks my leg. She stomps her foot. "I don't have to stop! Right, Daddy?"

He walks over and starts the music again. "A few more minutes won't hurt."

I hear my mother speaking. "Moira," she says.

Moira!. Moira! Moira!. Someone is calling me from a distance, but I can't answer. Something has come over me.

Lyra is crying now, and she throws one of her children's books at me.

"Stop!" *I yell suddenly.*

Paul takes my arm again. "What's gotten into you?" *My hand finds his face. I slap him hard, and he draws back, shocked. Lyra runs to him, then turns her gaze on me and yells,* "You're a mean mommy!"

My mother marches into the kitchen, and I flee to my studio. I am shaking, crying, unnerved. I throw the journal on my desk across the room and sit in the dark. I am a monster. I can see it in my family's eyes. An hour later, I walk across the yard to the house. Paul is putting Lyra to bed. He is reading Madeleine. "There were twelve little girls . . ."

I hear Lyra call out to me. Mommy! And Paul shushing her.

"But I want to see her," *she complains.*

I continue down the hall to the guest room and sit in a chair, lights out. I hear Paul go into our bedroom and close the door. I know I should apologize, but I don't know what to say. I wait until I hear my mother's sluggish footsteps go by the door, then walk into the hall after she closes her door. She has created a trail of sadness. I don't want to do this to my daughter.

I quickly enter the bathroom to wash my face and go stealthily into Lyra's room. She stirs when I sit beside her, her eyelids flutter, and she is quiet. I curl up beside her. "I'm sorry, my darling girl, for being a mean mother."

"I love you more than the highest mountain," *she whispers.*

"The deepest ocean," *I say. I fall into a deep sleep.*

Paul is gone when I get up the next morning. My mother makes breakfast for Lyra and keeps glancing over at me, sitting at the island sipping coffee. Ruth and Stella are coming for Lyra's birthday party, which we had decided to hold on the 28th instead of the 26th. Lyra jumps up, leaps onto my lap, and kisses me, then runs off.

"What if I had kept you from your books?" *Adeline asks me.*

"I can't imagine."

"Remember reading 'The Secret Garden,' and then your daddy trying to create one for you out of our nasty old backyard?"

"I do. I took my dolls out there, dressed in the clothes you made for them."

I hesitate before blurting out, "Mama, I'm living in a secret world that is lonely and dark."

She sighed, "I think more women than we know exist in a knot of secrets. I did; that's for sure. It's hard seeing so much *anger in you, honey. I'm willing to listen when you're ready to talk."*

"Maybe I'll be ready soon."

She decides to stick her long, bony foot out. 'I think y'all should have another baby.'"

A strong "Yoo-hoo!" announced Ruth's entrance. I rushed to embrace her, but Lyra beat me to her.

"Wait till you see what I brought you, Lyra Ruth," Ruth said.

Stella came behind her, and I wrapped her in my arms. I took them to their rooms.

They had just come down to the den when Paul walked in and embraced them each. "Good to see you," he said, not glancing in my direction as he went upstairs.

In a moment, I heard the shower running.

Ruth announced she had brought no work, as she intended to devote time to her godchild. While Adeline played a board game with Lyra, Ruth and I headed into the kitchen. We sipped coffee at the small round table in the breakfast nook, our heads close together, our voices low.

"I hate Stella being so sick," she said, her head drooping, tears falling off her cheeks.

I teared up, too. "She looks better than I expected. Don't lose hope. Is Seamus pitching in?"

She swallowed hard. "It's over. He fell off the wagon. He couldn't handle having a limp. But it's more than that. I hung in with him as long as I could, but it was too much with him refusing to get psychological help and going on benders every few weeks. Basically, I told him to leave. Last I heard from one of his buddies, he's a detective up here in Roxbury. He left New York—and me— behind and went home."

"What about his leg? He never proposed?"

She looked surprised. "Nope. Why?"

"I suggested when I saw him in the hospital that he ask you to marry him."

"That was to the point. And?"

"He didn't respond."

"It's all about what he calls his deformity. He has a permanent limp. Can't he just feel lucky to be alive?" She sighed. "I wanted him out of the Bronx, but I didn't think he'd go to Connecticut. I'm devastated. He's my soul mate. Stella agrees."

"Then swallow your pride and call him."

"Moira, my life is in Manhattan. I can't give that up. I'm supporting Stella and me and paying my niece's tuition at Harvard."

"Still. He's not that far away."

"So?"

"You could commute."

"He has to get sober. And if he does, he might call me. Or not." She motioned for me to follow her outside, where she lit a cigarette. "This is next on my list, giving up this awful habit. I've got to quit, but if I do, I know I'll add ten pounds." Her lips formed a perfect O, and she blew out a smoke ring. "What about you? Doing okay?"

"What about me? Aging suburban housewife who slapped her husband on the face and feels like she's about to be arrested for domestic abuse."

"I could tell something was up when he came in. You don't have to worry. The only time authorities pay attention to that is when there's been a murder. Or if a woman happens to shoot her abuser—trust me, they'll make sure she gets time. What's the problem?"

I felt stupid saying I didn't want my child to dance, so I said instead, "Parenting."

"This is how you get when you're not writing."

"Remember when we read Barbara Gordon's book *I'm Dancing as Fast as I Can*?"

"Vaguely. Why?"

"It's one of the scariest books I've ever read about mental illness. She was in a terribly abusive relationship and ended up in a mental institution after overdosing on tranquilizers."

"What's that got to do with anything?"

"I feel wobbly, as the English say. Mentally unstable. I wonder how much of me is like my mother." I was speaking in a whisper. "I've thought a lot lately about entering therapy, but what if I get the wrong therapist? Barbara Gordon went through twenty therapists."

"I remember the book now. But the boyfriend was a monster, and Paul is anything but. You're depressed? There're new drugs."

"One guy in the book says neuroses are really lies. Lies, lies, and more lies."

Ruth shrugged. "That simplifies the whole thing. I wish someone would write a book without a linear account of mental illness."

"I've thought about that, too. Autobiographical, but more literary maybe."

Adeline appeared in the doorway. "You've got to give up those cigarettes," she said to Ruth.

"Next week, Adeline."

We returned to the house, and Lyra ran into the kitchen, held out her arms, and said, "Mommy, we didn't finish last night. I love you higher than the highest mountain!"

I embraced her. "I love you deeper than the deepest sea!"

"I love you wider than the . . . Sahara!"

I laughed. "I love you beyond the stars."

She jumped into my lap. "Beyond infinity!"

Ruth laughed. "What kid knows the word infinity? It's unnatural."

Adeline stood in the doorway, her arm around Stella, unable to mask her pride. "They've been playing that little game since she was two."

Paul walked in and scooped Lyra up. I gave him a nervous glance and saw that his expression was neutral. He told Ruth to get her coat and that he would take her on a little tour of Halifax with all the outdoor decorations. Lyra ran to catch up with Ruth.

Paul stopped in the doorway when I said his name. "I'm sorry. I don't know what came over me."

"Forgiven."

"I hate the dancing."

"You'll have to learn to like it then. My mother is giving her dance lessons as a birthday present. The card is under the tree, and I'm not removing it."

I turned and started basting the turkey.

23

Lyra had been dancing for four years when she entered third grade in 1988. She stood out for her comportment as much as her open smile and sparkling lapis-lazuli eyes. The eyes that unnerved me at her birth were now hers, not his. Watching her was inspirational. As her passion grew, I began to write with more fervor than I had in years. I ended up selling a children's story about a girl who danced with such verve and speed that her toes touched the moon, and from that moment, she carried a special light around her. Ruth called, laughing. "This is the only time I regret not selling children's books." The book, with illustrations by a friend I had met at Lyra's ballet class, made me a momentary star at the little ballet company in our town after it was published.

Harboring myself in a vortex of creativity, I began typing the many pages of notes from my journals and saw, as though I was studying a graph, the past decade's dips and swirls and peaks. Sometimes while reading my diaries, I thought I was reading about a fictional character that straddled two lives, the secret one and the one who moved in the present. My studio was sacrosanct. Paul rarely entered, but one day he rushed in to tell me he was going to stay in the city overnight, then stopped in surprise. "You've gone New Age on me," he said, looking around at the library of self-help books, amulets, and art.

I laughed. "Blame Stephanie. She's a never-ending fount of knowledge on self-healing."

He looked puzzled. "What are you trying to heal, my love?"

I was caught off-guard. I shrugged. "Old scars."

"Oh, from childhood. It's probably what made you a writer." I was glad to see him. We rarely created time to sit and be. He pulled a book off the shelf. "Visualizing having a baby? I thought we'd let that go."

"I've wanted another baby all along."

He was quiet a moment, and then he reached for me. We were rolling on the floor within seconds, making love like teenagers. A rare moment of abandonment. We laughed after and held each other for a long time. "I love this room" he said.

"You never come to the studio," I whispered. "Did you want to tell me something?"

He smiled. "Whatever it was can wait. I plan to visit much more often."

Paul came home earlier than usual the following night, obviously in a good mood as he entered the kitchen and kissed me. Lyra sat reading a book, and he joined her, putting his arm around her. I watched them out of the corner of my eye.

When she closed the book, she said, "Daddy, I want to show you my new dance."

She put a CD in the player and waited for a second. It was the score from "Sleeping Beauty" that Paul had bought her. I walked over and sat beside him, and he reached for my hand. It was the first time that I thought she was a prodigy.

Lyra ran to us when it was over. "I loved it," Paul said. "I love you. Now bring your books, and let's do homework."

Lyra ran upstairs and returned with a homemade card, all the block letters in various colors, with hand-drawn hearts forming the border. "I made this for you, Mommy."

I read it

> *My love for you is higher than the highest mountain.*
> *Mine for you is deeper than the deepest ocean.*
> *Mine for you is wider than the Sahara Desert.*
> *I love you to the moon. To infinity.*

"Oh, Lyra, I will frame it," I said, gathering her in my arms. "Who helped with the spelling?"

"Daddy."

Once Paul was asleep that night, I felt a rare contentment. We would have another baby; I was sure of it.

Katherine and Russell went off and married, Katherine for the first time saying she didn't want a grand event. I was secretly pleased because it augured well for Paul's and my future. There wasn't room at the newspaper for both Paul and Russ. They were gone several weeks, putting Paul in charge at the paper. He took advantage of the opportunity to write more in-depth articles. He was more enthusiastic than I had seen him in a long time, constantly rushing around, managing staff, and writing. My carefully arranged life, to my surprise, was working. I would do nothing to jeopardize the status quo. I could even go so far as to admit to becoming complacent.

24

It was 1992. Paul was dressing to go into the city, and his mother, Russell, Ruthie, and I would join him the following day at the Hilton Hotel where he would receive an award. His series of articles championing AIDS victims had been published internationally. The first cases had been diagnosed in 1981. By 1985, one hundred thousand cases had been reported. Rock Hudson's death that year brought renewed focus on the disease. It was now a pandemic.

Out of the blue, Paul said, "You know, Katia will be there. She's receiving an award with me."

The first shudder of apprehension I'd experienced in a while. "Oh? For what?"

"Her stories on AIDS in Africa."

"She's not in Paris?"

His jaw tightened. "No. She's been in New York several months on some project. I forget what." He was in a hurry. And nervous. "Do you know where my new blue tie is?" I went to his closet and put my hand right on it. "I have to run, or I'll be late, Moira. Here's a number at the hotel where you can reach me. I'll see you there." A quick kiss, and he was gone.

Furious, I pulled a low-cut, black number that I hadn't worn in two years from my closet. The phone rang, and I picked up. "Is Mr. Rivers there, please? I'm calling from Patmos Laboratories."

"No, but I'm his wife. May I help?"

The voice was that of a young woman. "Let him know that his semen analysis report results are in. He can pick it up at his convenience."

"Sure. Thank you." She hung up. He hadn't told me that Katia was in town, nor had he told me he was getting a sperm test. What the hell!

I hailed a taxi to the hotel where the awards ceremony would take place. The first person I saw was Ed, who reeked of alcohol. "Paul said to tell you he'd see you after. You're sitting with Carole and me. Your friend Ruth can join us."

"Where will Paul be?"

"Up on the dais. Good to see you."

He handed me a glass of white wine. Carole rushed up to say hello. "How's Lyra?" she asked.

"Dreaming of being a professional ballerina," I said. "She's ten now. And your kids?"

"Good, all four of them. We're moving up to Halifax. Did Paul tell you? It's too expensive here." Waiters arrived at our table with plates of food.

Ruth slid into her seat, hugged me, and nodded hello to Ed and Carole. "Are Katherine and Russell coming?" she asked.

"They're at the table over there," Ed said, pointing.

"Who're the empty places for here?" Ruth asked.

"Katia and Paul," said Ed.

Ruth leaned over to me. "Katia?"

"He told me yesterday."

A barrel-chested man marched up to the mike to deliver a welcome speech. Paul looked handsome in his dark suit and the tie I had given him. He leaned over to the woman beside him to whisper something, and she looked up at him with a radiant smile. Katia was more beautiful than I'd imagined her. She stood up to say a few words. Tall, slender, with a raspy voice and a French accent. *Is this what it's like to realize your husband is having an affair*, I wondered. I gulped my wine, and Ed ordered another. Katia introduced Paul. She praised his work in her adorable French accent, and mentioned to more applause that he was the first to call out the American government's denial of the crisis. "And he did all this from a newspaper in Halifax, Connecticut," she added.

Paul walked up to the podium amidst much applause. He turned to thank Katia and said her work on AIDS had been a great influence on him. He launched immediately into what had gone wrong with finding a cure for AIDS. He called on President Bush and the pharmaceutical companies to find a cure. At the end of his talk, he said, "If it was our community in this room dealing with this awful illness, we would have come up with a cure. But the disease is wiping out a large percentage of the homosexual community. Are we going to continue to ignore what is going on?" The applause was thunderous.

A few minutes later, Katia was given a special award for a series she had written on AIDS victims in Africa. They walked down from the podium and came to our table, stopping along the way to accept congratulations from their colleagues.

I stood, and Paul gave me a quick embrace. "Meet Katia," he said.

We shook hands, and she said, "I've heard so much about you."

I introduced Ruth; then Paul and Katia went around the table to take the two available seats. Paul started talking to Ed, and Katia spoke to Carole, asking how the children were. It was obvious they were friends. Katherine and Russell came over and congratulated Paul and Katia, then Katherine asked her if everything was okay at the apartment.

"It's perfect," Katia said. "I love the Upper West Side."

Ruth, who rarely drank alcohol, whispered, "Give me a sip of your wine. You okay?"

"No. Weak in the knees."

Ruth turned to Katia. "Where are you living?"

"I'm in Paul's mother's apartment on West 72nd Street. It's a temporary arrangement until I can find my own place." She stood and lifted her jacket from the chair. "I'm sorry, but work calls. Paul, will you stop by the office tomorrow?"

"I don't think so." He gave me a shifty glance." I'm going back to Halifax."

"Next week then. Congratulations." After exchanging the traditional French kiss on each cheek, she did the same with Ed. She looked at Ruth and me. "It was good to meet you both. Let me know if I can be of assistance if Lyra is accepted into the American Ballet summer camp."

We watched her disappear into the crowd. It was obvious to me that Paul had drunk too much. "Ruthie," he said, his words slurred. "A long time ago, Moira asked me to get an update on Seamus, and I did." Ruth looked frozen in place. "He married, and they have a kid named Sadie. He's gone into forensic psychology, and the word on the street is he's good at his job."

Ruth, looking annoyed, got up and said she was late for a meeting. Why had Paul brought that up now? Was he deflecting our attention?

Paul and I decided to walk to his mother's apartment on Park Avenue South. He kept trying to put his arm around me, but I brushed him off. His words were slurred when he asked, "Are you mad at me?"

We ran across the street to beat the light. Once in his mother's apartment, I let loose. "I had no idea Katia was living in New York, in what is supposed to be our apartment."

He went directly to the bar and poured a scotch. "For god's sake, my mother rented the apartment to her. I had no say in it whatsoever."

"You never do. If you had ever learned to speak up, you wouldn't be her little patsy." I passed the desk piled with mail and remembered the call that came in earlier. "Patmos Laboratory has completed your semen analysis."

I could tell I had caught him off-guard, but he covered it well. "I told you we should get tested. I went ahead."

I felt panic seeping in.

It felt like everything was happening behind my back. Katia and the apartment. The lab test. "Paul, I have no interest in another baby. I want a career again. Listen. We've been talking about Lyra coming here summers to dance. Any newspaper would take you today, including the *New York Times*. I can get work. Ruth told me a week ago that she's about to hire an editor for her clients."

"I'm too drunk to talk about this."

"Things are bad at the newspaper with Russ. This is our chance, Paul. We can start the process. It will take time; I know that."

He hadn't taken his eyes off me. "You're serious."

"This has been on my mind for a while. I will speak to Katherine tomorrow, but Katia needs to get out of the apartment. We're reclaiming it."

He suddenly laughed. "Moira Rivers. I've never seen you like this."

"What? Fighting for my marriage? My family? My life?"

"Okay, okay. Let's talk tomorrow."

I went into the bedroom and closed the door. Paul getting tested was proof that he *did* hope for another baby. I was forty, but it wasn't out of the question. We were both desperate for change— a baby, a move, something to get us out of our rut.

25

I was up early the next morning with something akin to hope stirring inside me. Since moving to Halifax, I had sometimes felt caught in a secret web, struggling, but unable to break the strands that had me so tightly bound. I had created the web, and now, I yearned to be out. I went into the kitchen, where Katherine sat sipping coffee. She greeted me warily, I thought. I was cheerful as I poured a cup of coffee and told her that Paul and I had a great talk about our future.

"And?" she asked.

I giggled. "New baby. New home. And, there's more."

Her coffee mug was held aloft, the only giveaway that she was shocked.

"I'm trying to catch an early train home," I said, "We'll talk later."

Paul stayed in the city another day, saying he had business to attend to, and I took the train back alone. Stephanie came, and we worked in the garden. She was focused on an area of the yard that refused to produce anything. "The soil must have the wrong pH balance," she said. "I'm going to test it and see if I can fix it." She rattled on, and I half-listened. "That happened to me once. My husband and I wanted another baby, but nothing happened in two years. It was like the issue we have with this soil in a way." She babbled on. "Then, just when we decided to let it go, bingo. New baby." She stopped digging and turned to me. "How was the big event in the city?"

"Paul was fantastic. But the French journalist he was in love with before me was also there. She's been living in his mother's apartment unbeknownst to me." I had never been so open with Stephanie.

"Don't let jealousy gain control," she said. "It's probably an emotional affair, meaning the man doesn't consider it legit until they engage in sex. It drives a spouse crazy because the cheater is guilt-free, yet that is far from the case."

"But I *am* jealous."

"You and Paul need to talk. He really has to sever ties."

"You think?"

"I've experienced it. From my own observation, Paul isn't trying to leave his marriage. There's a new therapist in town. Her name is Abigail Levy, and I'm hearing good things about her." When I didn't respond, she said, "Didn't you tell me six months ago you and Paul were hoping to have another baby?"

"Nothing's happened."

"Funny that I should bring the subject up this morning. You could check in with a fertility specialist. Bonnie did, and they were successful."

"So which therapy do I do first? Mental or fertility?"

Stephanie suddenly laughed, and I did, too.

Paul arrived on the 4:00 train, and I was there to meet him. I told him Lyra was at Grandma Beezie's, the name she had bestowed on Katherine as a toddler. Since Russell and Katherine had married, Lyra resisted staying there, claiming that Russell was too grumpy. Tonight, though, she had been promised a pizza and movie night, which she found irresistible.

I took a chilled bottle of wine from the fridge and slid jazz singer Joe Williams into the CD player. "Wow! What's this about?" Paul asked. He looked wan. He poured a glass of wine. "Hair of the dog," he said, sitting.

"Cheers," I said, raising my glass.

His face grew serious. "I apologize for the nonsense about Katia and Mom's apartment. I thought I had told you she was there."

"Paul. You hate conflict, so you said nothing. I called Katherine this morning, and she said Katia will be leaving in two weeks. I was serious last night. Let's move back to the city and go from there."

"But my mother . . ."

Ruthie had been right all along. Paul could not cut the apron strings. "I'm going to start seeing a therapist that Stephanie recommended. Care to join me?"

"God, Moira. What's come over you?"

"The possibility of change. A baby, maybe."

"Too much time has passed. Lyra's enough."

"But last night, you were all about a baby. Please don't tell me you don't remember. I thought about it and want to try."

"I was drunk. No baby. Period."

I stopped the CD. The silence was thunderous. "Then, at the very least, I want to move back to the city." I went into the kitchen, served our plates, and put them on the table.

At dinner, he said, "I am seriously considering the idea of moving back to Manhattan, but I can't commit now."

"I don't think I can stay here."

"I get that."

I went upstairs and confronted myself in the mirror. My husband had rejected my attempt to seduce him for the first time. Paul was not himself and, in fact, seemed suddenly depressed. I wondered if it had to do with Katia, or maybe he and Russell were fighting at the paper again. My thoughts drifted to Ruthie, who admitted she was miffed that Paul had chosen an awkward moment to tell her about Seamus, then admonished me for initiating Paul's search to find Seamus without telling her first. I apologized.

A primal sob from the bedroom made me freeze, my hairbrush suspended mid-air. I don't know how long I stood there, too afraid to open the door. I cracked it and peered into the bedroom. Paul was bent double on the bed, groaning. I rushed to him, thinking he was having a heart attack. He began to sob, great heaving sobs that wracked his body.

"Paul . . ." I had never seen anyone in that much pain. "What is it?" I sat beside him, placing my hand on his shoulder. "I'm going to call the doctor."

He waved me away. "Go!" he said. "Need to be alone." He crawled up and walked across the floor.

"Paul . . ."

"Moira . . . never mind. Please leave me alone." He walked out of the room.

I lay there in terror for what seemed like a long time, listening to Miles Davis on saxophone wafting up the stairs. I got up my courage and went downstairs. Paul had built a fire and sat staring into it. He was holding a glass of brandy.

"Paul?"

He spoke in a soft voice. "I'll come to bed soon, Moira. Don't worry about me. I'm not in a good place."

I went back upstairs and waited. He came to bed at four. I heard him sigh, and then he crawled under the covers. I reached for his hand, but he didn't squeeze mine in return. "I love you," I whispered. No response.

As a child, I assumed that love, like everything else, was an endless commodity. As dysfunctional as my parents were, I felt loved, and I loved them. In high school, I signed birthday cards to friends, "Love you forever," which, in my mind, stretched to infinity, the magical word. I would sing a mantra to Lyra, "Love is all there is." I adored my baby and assured myself over and over that our love for her would make up for her patrimony. I could still conjure up my heart overflowing with a vision of the future with Paul the first time he told me he loved me.

Still, the consequences of the rape—the stress of carrying a secret that, if revealed, could bring havoc—the hypervigilance, the nightmares, the never-ending grief of having lost something undefinable—they were ever with me. After reading everything I could find on the subject, I understood that Jonathan had targeted me from the moment Erin started talking to him about me. He was a serial rapist, and each time he "conquered" a woman, he congratulated himself. He was able to hold power over women, either through coaxing, which is what had happened with Erin, or if that didn't work, through overpowering them. He was white, educated, and a dancer women were attracted to. Not the man who ran from an alley and attacked. I had said no to him staying, which had whetted his appetite for dominance. He had fantasized about overtaking me, bringing Erin's Wonder Woman down a peg. I had no chance once he entered my door. I had at least come to understand that. It was not my fault.

Paul was my safety net. He had been steadfast. Kind. A good provider, as my mother had said. He adored Lyra with all his heart. I lay there, watching him sleep. The love I felt for him had built in increments over the decade. I loved him more profoundly in this moment than I ever had. I wanted to lift him out of whatever pain had overcome him. Maybe his life needed healing as much as mine, and I hadn't noticed.

His clock went off, and as he shut it off and climbed out of bed, I pretended to be asleep. Half an hour later, I heard his car leave the driveway. I got up, made coffee, and thought about Paul's breakdown and what I could only think was an outpouring of grief. But over what? My thoughts segued to Katia and what I had witnessed in New York between them. I wandered to my studio and randomly pulled one of my many journals from the shelf. It was the description of our wedding. I didn't know whose baby I was carrying at the time. I had made a survival decision, and for Paul, getting married had been the right thing to do. Not a great foundation for spending the rest of one's life with someone. Paul would never tell me if he regretted choosing me over Katia. Last night felt like a warning. I wrote in my journal: *It's time for change. We are at a crossroads.*

Stephanie called and invited me to go with her to see the new film her friends were raving about, "Thelma and Louise." We agreed to meet up that very night. The Moira who entered the theater was not the same Moira who emerged after the movie ended.

26

"I feel like I'm going crazy."

"Tell me why."

I felt nestled in a large room that exuded warmth—an Oriental
rug covering the floor, a burnished wood desk, maybe mahogany,
and Chinese artwork on the walls. Dr. Abigail Levy was a petite,
attractive woman dressed in a pants suit. I guessed her to be in her
fifties. Her whole being seemed tuned into me, her body leaning
towards me, her eyes unwavering.

In a voice I barely recognized as my own, the story of my rape
and its aftermath tumbled out of me. The helplessness I had
experienced during the rape. The decision to keep it a secret. The
incredible losses that followed. My hard-earned autonomy. My
relationship with Paul. The guilt. Self-blame. Feeling out of control.
The horror of peering into my baby's eyes and knowing the truth.
The determination to raise this child well and to maintain a credible
(authentic) life. The obsessive writing. The feeling that I had lost
my writing voice. Everything I read of mine felt like sipping weak
tea.

The fingernails of my right fingers dug into the palm of my left
hand, an old trick to ward off tears. "Why did you decide to seek
help now?"

"I saw *Thelma and Louise*."

She sat up straight. "I adore that film. I was expecting a light-
hearted female buddy picture but got two women settling some

scores instead." Then, as if acknowledging that she might have crossed a boundary, she said, "And?"

"It gives me hope that a film like that got produced." Scenes still played out in my mind. Two women on the lam after one shot a dude who attempted to rape her friend and everything escalating from there.

"It must have been hard for you to see Thelma in the parking lot with the rapist."

"It was excruciating. But then Louise shot him, and something in that moment became exhilarating."

"Why do you think Louise shot the guy Harlan?"

"Because he was about to sexually assault her best friend."

"I think it was a case of Louise having PTSD. There are hints that she had something similar happen. I think Louise shoots him because she knows he isn't sorry. She also knew they didn't have a chance if she reported killing the guy. Who would believe them?" She smiled. "Then the ending! What did you think when they drove off the cliff?"

"To me, it was like they were flying. Pure liberation. I'll never forget it."

"You can fly again, Moira."

"It's been over ten years. My writing. My marriage. I have not healed."

"This is a common complaint I get."

"Our marriage started off with a lie. Or lies."

"But don't blame everything on the secret you carry. Neither of you is fulfilled right now. Your plan to spend the next couple of years creating a life in the city sounds viable. Exciting. And sadly, it sounds as if, for the last time, you both must let go of having another child."

"I have the horrible thought that Paul knows now Lyra isn't his biological child. He has been different since the Patmos Labs results came in."

"You can ask him."

"Then he will know everything."

"My point exactly. It's time. I think the wolf in your dreams will vanish once this is out. How close is the wolf now?"

"Nipping at my heels."

"But you manage to get away. Do you think you will want your daughter to know what happened to you one day?"

"I don't know. A woman I learned of from a friend also had a daughter from a rape years ago, and she died, and her secret died with her."

"It didn't die with her because, well, after all, you know about it. And if you know, then others also knew, right?"

I squirmed in my chair, aware of how attached I felt to a story that now felt wrong somehow. "Okay, I get where you're going with this. The mother might have been afraid that her daughter would abandon her for lying to her for years. She could have been protecting herself."

Levy nodded.

"I count the people who know. The doctor I saw in New York. The therapist I saw in New York. You. I regret ever going to Erin Charles. It's odd. She sends a Christmas card each year, but I never open them."

"Because?"

"Because I still blame her. And it feels stalky."

"She tried to make amends. I would think it requires a lot of energy to keep so many people at bay. Including your friend Ruth." She glanced down at her notes. "What did it feel like to lose your voice, Moira?"

"Being silenced is its own hell. Not speaking out exacerbates the grief and guilt. I write about what it's like to be silenced allegorically, but I am not close to describing the hollowness. Maybe I can say my voice has come back, but it's hoarse. That's what I'm feeling now."

"Ironically, a hoarse voice in France is called *le loup,* the wolf."

"Okay," I said. "We have something to work towards. I can go with that."

"We understand more about rape now, Moira. "It will be an enormous amount of work, but I think we can get you to a place of peace. And acceptance."

I nodded, feeling a tiny wave of relief flood over me. And gratitude for the woman sitting before me, her face full of compassion. She glanced at her watch. "I'm so sorry. Our hour is up. Same time next week?"

"Sure."

Not long after meeting with Dr. Levy, I opened Paul's desk drawer in our den, searching for a pen. I saw an envelope from Patmos Laboratories. I pulled out the sheet of paper tucked inside and read. Paul had azoospermia. No sperm. The doctors would be happy to consult with him about options.

I sat for a long time in the quiet of our house, shocked, saddened, frightened. It didn't say absolutely that he was incapable of having a baby. Or, did it? This explained his meltdown. But why hadn't he told me the results? Did he suspect that Lyra wasn't his? And if that were the case, would he have gone for a DNA test? Paternity testing hadn't been common until 1988, and many mistakes were made, but still.

Curiously, his behavior had been more sanguine since the night he broke down. Sometimes I thought it a bit much, and then I knew why: his transition from the extremely busy journalist often on the road to at-home husband and dad reminded me of the overnight transformation of my mother after years of having "nerves," which was the way her condition was described to me.

I mentioned a baby again, and Paul refused to discuss it, and in fact, he got in his car and drove off.

I went back to Dr. Levy, and she opened up the space for me to grieve. I realized that my desire for another baby had been a constant, a tiny beacon that guided me through hundreds of days, but it was not to be. She also counseled me again to consider telling Paul the truth. When I left Dr. Levy's office, I went home and wrote in my journal:

Another chapter finished. A new one beginning.

PART THREE

The more still, more patient and more open we are when we are sad, so much the deeper and so much the more unswervingly does the new go into us, so much the better do we make it ours, so much the more will be our destiny . . ."

—Rilke, "Rilke on How Great Sadnesses Transform Us . . . ,"
The Marginalian

27

Lyra would be turning thirteen on December 26, 1993. She was growing more independent and fiercely determined to become a great ballerina. She had been accepted into the summer program at the American School of Ballet, a feat that we celebrated but also carried anxiety about. To my surprise, Paul began negotiating with his mother about the apartment on 72nd Street in Manhattan. But Katherine was resistant, and I knew it was because she wanted to keep her son in Connecticut, ostensibly running her newspaper, but being forced to capitulate more and more to Russell, who was determined to take over as editor-in-chief.

I saw Dr. Levy every two weeks for six months and then signed off, feeling that the heaviness that had started to weigh me down was lifting. We covered a lot of territory, and now, I wanted to see if I could fly on my own. My writing felt more flowing, and I combined what I now called my memoir writing with short fiction. It helped to address all of it to my beloved Ruthie.

Paul and Lyra and I were settled into the suburban lifestyle that I had dreaded all those years ago, though I managed to avoid the bridge games and tennis matches and engaged more with my fellow gardeners, and yes, writers. The women who had continued with the writing classes had gone from being "the girls" to the women to the writers, and I regarded them as such. The wolf in my dreams was aging, too, and didn't intrude as much, though I felt him sometimes lurking in the corner.

Paul bussed me on the cheek when he came home and mixed a cocktail before dinner for each of us. More and more of our attention focused on Lyra, and I realized that she would become our catalyst for change. Paul confided in me one day that he had a couple of job interviews in the city but wasn't telling his mother. Unfortunately, Katherine still had a financial hold on us, as she owned our home and the apartment in New York and was the one who handed out bonuses and raises. We looked great to the casual observer, but we were not wealthy at all. I wanted to remedy this situation, but my short stories didn't bring in much income, nor did the teaching. It was my gardening column in the paper that I was getting noticed for. A small publisher in New York approached me about a possible book in the future, and I was thrilled. I also used gardening in my teaching, pointing out that a book, like a garden, was about having a vision and emphasizing how both needed constant tending. What I realized with the column was that I was becoming more honest.

Stephanie came once a week in the winter months, and we sketched out my beds and decided what we wanted to change. We also kept adding smaller gardens around the property. The small barren plot she had put a lot of love into suddenly flourished, and I wrote about that, too. How achieving balance, whether through testing or through perseverance or other methods, was always a fine goal. Gardening catalogs were stacked up all over my studio. It was Stephanie who told me that Priscilla and her husband had divorced and that Priscilla was contemplating a move to Philadelphia.

"Whatever happened to that woman Mickey she was accusing of breaking up her marriage?" I asked.

Stephanie shrugged. "I'm not sure that's true. Her husband had his foot out the door years ago." For all her goodness, Stephanie was unquestionably a gossip. She talked again about the woman named Mickey, the femme fatale as it were, who was in town, creating a bit of a stir with her good looks and devil-may-care attitude. I was vaguely curious.

Bill Clinton had been elected president in November of 1992, and for the first time in a long while, Paul was caught up in something that bordered on passion. He wrote articles about Clinton and went to meetings in the city. I, too, got caught up in politics, and for months at night, we turned on the television to hear Clinton deliver another speech in his voice that had gone hoarse from so much time persuading the country that he should be their president. We were excited that he won, and Paul became a stronger member of the Democratic party in Hartford.

My missing link was Ruth. Her agency was one of the most successful in the city. During the Clinton campaign, she called more than usual. She reported that Stella had worked non-stop for Clinton's campaign from her bed. I drove down to see Stella and was surprised to see how frail she was; at the same time, her eyes had the same old vitality.

"It's politics that's kept her goin'," Ruthie said. "Political pressure infuses her with life."

Ruth had taken a month off to stay with her mother. It felt like old times. Ruth went into work for a day while I was there, and I made Stella's famous chicken soup while she sat in a chair overseeing it.

We sat down at the table for lunch. "I wish you could have brought Lyra," she said.

"We'll be bringing her down here for the summer."

"I won't be here."

"Oh, come on, Stella. Where's your fighting spirit?"

"I'm tired. I'm ready to go."

I was shocked to hear her speak like this. My eyes filled with tears.

"Ruth needs you," she said. "She needs to get out of the city more." She asked me to help her to her bed, and I did. She said, "I'm glad you came. If I'm speaking in non-sequiturs, it's the medicine." I nodded. "Did you ever hear what happened to that cop Seamus?"

"Seamus?" Why on earth was she bringing up such a long-dead topic, I wondered. "Yes, I remember."

"She was with others, but he was her true love."

"It's been over a decade, Stella."

"I know. I had a dream about him. He was standing alone on a beach, wearing a trench coat. It was clear as a bell. I want you to find him for her."

Her eyes closed, and she drifted off to sleep. I placed my hand over hers and sat there for a long time, thinking about Ruth, Seamus, Paul, and me during the golden year of 1978 when we were young, happy, and in love. Stella was always around, inviting us to rallies and protests and cooking for us non-stop.

Then our beloved Stella died. I took the train down and stayed with Ruth for three days. She was inconsolable. She rarely drank, but the night after the funeral, she got drunk. It wasn't pretty. She blurted out that it was lonely at the top, just like everyone said.

"I should have had a baby," she said, then in the next breath added, "I didn't mean that." She talked about Stella and how she had devoted her life to helping others, and she, Ruth, had done nothing in years. "I'm a failure," she said. "I need a goddamn book I believe in. I need Seamus. I need something in my life but fucking regret." She put her head down and sobbed. She passed out finally, and I held her in my arms as she had done with me when I so desperately needed a human touch. She snored and talked in her sleep, and I didn't sleep a wink.

The following morning, we had coffee.

"Did I rant about Seamus?" she asked sheepishly. I nodded. "Well, fuck him," she said. "Besides, Paul was right. He's married and has a kid. Just like you."

"One of the last things Stella said to me was to find Seamus. She saw him in a dream, and he was on a beach, looking lonely, I think."

"Oh, god. Stella is still directing things. Well, this time, I'll rebel and say no. His parents are thrilled, I'm sure. They never liked me." She hesitated. "How are you and Paul doing? I was so opposed to your decision to move up there and live a cookie-cutter life. No regrets?"

"I have regrets, but I won't talk about them. Sometimes I read about you and wish I had stayed on track with my career the way you did. Marriage is imprisonment for a writer. Unless you're a male writer. They tend to find devoted muses who clean up their messes and feed them. Name a woman author who has that. I feel awful saying this because I have been given so much more freedom and time than most women. I lost momentum when I got pregnant, I guess."

I sounded weak, I realized—and spoiled.

"You transferred all that creative energy onto Lyra, maybe?"

"Maybe. Or maybe I'm not a writer."

"I'll admit I thought you'd have a book by now. All those southern gothic tales."

"Sorry."

"Don't be. I'm trapped, too. I live in a bubble of success, and now with Stella gone, I'm wondering how I ended up so alone."

"We have each other."

"Do we?"

"What do you mean, do we?"

"You don't share much with me anymore, Moira. The surface stuff, sure . . ."

"It's hard with a family to find time."

"You know how I hate cliches."

I nodded, and tears dripped down. "I'm sorry."

She put her arms around me. "There's nothing to be sorry about. I'm just looking for the Moira I used to know."

As I boarded the train home, I decided to send her my pages.

Paul's and Russell's uneasy relationship came to a head when Paul poured his heart into the Clinton campaign. He didn't hide his enthusiasm in his writing and swayed many to vote for Clinton. When Russell objected, Paul told him that if he continued to put him down among friends and colleagues, he would be forced to leave the paper. Katherine was caught in the middle and constantly saying they were running out of money—that people generally were not supporting newspapers like they used to, but we knew Russell was running through a lot of money and making bad decisions.

"The apartment is there for us," Paul said one day out of the blue. "Mother said we can rent, but not for another year."

"I hope I'm not too old to get a job in publishing."

"Moira, I have no doubt that Ruth will get you in wherever you want to be. Besides, you're forty-one. Not sixty."

To our surprise, my parents decided to fly up for Christmas and Lyra's thirteenth birthday. I had taken Lyra to visit them annually, usually in the summer, but they hadn't returned to Connecticut in two years. My mother and I continued our habit of speaking on the phone every Sunday, but I realized I missed her physical presence.

One afternoon after they arrived, I watched Lyra, wearing a leotard and skirt tied at her tiny waist, make slithery moves over to her grandmother. "This is my charmed snake dance, Granny." Light streamed in from the kitchen window, creating a halo around her golden curls.

"Well, you just slither on around to that stool and get ready to help make your birthday cake," my mother said, her southern accent as thick as mud. She was different with Lyra than she had been with me. Lyra hopped onto a stool and began sifting flour. I recalled being in our kitchen as a little girl, my eyes at countertop level, observing Mama's big hands making pies. Lyra had six friends coming over and was excited.

"Once the cake's in the oven, run up and get dressed," Mama directed her.

I prepared games for the kids and ran up to shower. Paul arrived just as I was coming down and presented Lyra with an envelope. In it were three round-trip tickets to Paris. She and I danced around.

"I promised you a visit there a long time ago and never made good on it," he said. I put my arms around him and kissed him.

Daddy was in his usual spot in front of the television. "Let's go sit," said Mama. She told me Daddy had cancer, but he didn't want me to know. "He wanted to come," Mama said, "But I think it's to say goodbye." I began to cry, and she said she thought it better to be honest. "I'm tired of acting like everything's fine when it's not." Another sea change for Adeline. "Look at Jackie. She married Onassis, probably looking for security." Her voice dropped to a whisper, "She stole him from her sister, you know." Then she returned to normal pitch: "She spent a million and a half in her first year of marriage. I would have, too, if I'd been married to him. But he was always in love with the opera singer Maria Callas. Just like your Diana and her prince who always loved Camilla. Diana's upbringing makes yours look like a picnic, by the way."

"Charles and Diana are getting divorced. It's all turning into a tragedy."

"We don't know the ending yet. She may become who she truly, truly is with him out of the picture. I feel for her boys, but they'll be okay. And so will she."

I nodded, only slightly skeptical. I desperately wanted Princess Diana to succeed. She had her own inner demons, which she had been public about. The world was changing, especially for women, and she had contributed to more openness, and the woman was full of courage.

Adeline was in philosophical mode. "It was when Jackie settled down with Maurice that I started feeling a sense of contentment, too. Your daddy and I have reached a good place after all these years. I told him last year I'm sorry for believing the rumors about him way back when."

"What'd he say?"

"He said, 'Oh, Adeline, it's too late for all that now. I'm at peace with it all.'"

Paul came rushing in, a bouquet of flowers in his hand. "The guests will be here in half an hour."

Lyra danced through the living room, and Mama said, "Honey, you know dancing is fun, but one day you'll be old like me, and then what?"

I could tell this was a new concept for my daughter. "Old people dance."

"What do you love about it?" my mother asked.

"I tell stories with my eyes and hands." She skipped out again.

Mama turned to me. "You always have the worry that if something happens to this one, what would you do? That's the bad part about having an only child."

"I hope you weren't thinking like that when I was growing up."

"Of course I was. And don't tell me it doesn't enter your mind."

"Would you believe me if I say I obsess over that very question?"

"You wouldn't be my daughter if you didn't."

"Didn't what?" my father asked, entering the room, with Paul following behind him.

"Oh, Augustus, how did you hear that when you didn't hear me when I asked you to get back in time to slice the ham?"

"What ham?"

My mother made a face, and we burst into laughter.

I felt a sense of being a part of something bigger, watching Paul engage with my father, my mother smiling with real joy.

The doorbell rang, and Katherine entered. "Beezie!" Lyra yelled, dancing across the room to give Paul's mother a hug. Russell was behind her, and he leaned down and kissed Lyra on top of the head. She was our center, our little Lyra. And I felt deeply grateful for her life.

We're dysfunctional as hell, I thought, *but we do exist in a circle of love.*

28

Moira's Garden: by Moira Rivers

A weekly column for *The Halifax Inquirer*, June 15, 1994.

> Today I look out onto a meadow blanketed with snow.
> As I step out of my studio and walk to the pond, the world
> is still, and silent. I return to light a fire in the woodstove,
> in this small space where I spend hours in solitude. Push-
> pinned to the wall is a map of the perennial beds I have
> nurtured for years. When I am not working in the garden, I
> am writing. Kafka said, "Writing is utter solitude, the
> descent into the cold abyss of yourself."
>
> I first started writing when I was a young girl to
> assuage the loneliness that would overcome me when
> Mama lapsed into depression. It is frightening to see one's
> mother in that state, but she had taught me to read at an
> early age, and that magical world of imagination. was her
> gift to me.
>
> My friend Stephanie and I are planning a large bed of
> white blossoms, inspired by the wide expanse of snow I
> observed daily over the past winter. I am imagining a
> combination of white lilac, lily of the valley, white peony,
> ivory echinacea white phlox, and an abundance of white
> roses. Did you know that white roses as a symbol
> represent purity, but also secrecy and silence? They are the
> favorite flower of Princess Diana, who after years of being
> silenced, has emerged with some shocking revelations. I
> think of the numbers of women who have been silenced,
> who have not had a voice, as I plan this white "garden
> room."
>
> I will dedicate it to the many women who feel silenced,
> and/or who have no voice. I am thinking about them as I
> read the story of Philomela, as told by Ovid. Philomela is

*raped by her sister's husband, King Tereus. When she
threatens to tell, he cuts out her tongue, rapes her again,
and locks her in a room. Philomela weaves the story into a
tapestry and sends it to her sister, Procne, and they seek
revenge. Procne kills their son and serves his dismembered
body to the king. Philomela next appears with the son's
head on a platter. Then the two sisters flee and are
transformed into songbirds, Philomena into a nightingale
and Procne into a swallow. The furious king turns into a
hoopoe, a bird that was later considered "unclean" in the
Bible.*

*Princess Diana refuses to be silenced by her husband
and the royal family. She is criticized for airing the 'dirty
laundry.' Will she succumb to vanity, or will she become a
voice for those who suffer? I don't know, but I shall plant
white roses in her honor—and in honor of Jackie Kennedy,
who died on May 19th, who had finally found peace as an
editor and a cultural preservationist, and a mother of two
loving children.*

*And for one other woman who we can imagine never
found peace living with O.J. Simpson. She and her friend
Ron Goldman were murdered yesterday, and the alleged
killer is none other than her famous husband. Whether he
will be found guilty or not, there were calls to the police
reporting domestic abuse, a topic rarely visited, but the
cause of too many deaths in this country. For Nicole, I am
planting the only red rose in my otherwise white garden.
Three women. Two white roses and one red.*

Writing the Philomena essay was the first hint to myself that I
might be preparing to step out of the secret world I inhabited.
Maybe one day I would tell my story. What would it be like if the
victim of rape wasn't blamed and shamed? If one woman spoke
up—someone famous, or someone nationally admired—I had no
doubt that the floodgates would open.

Paul came home later that night and said we needed to talk. He
made a Manhattan for each of us and started the conversation by
saying how much he supported my essay on Philomena.

"And?"

"My mother is opposed to printing it." He began to speak rapidly, which was almost like a nervous tic. "I think it might be Russell, but Mom won't say."

"What did *she* say, exactly?"

"She questions if women are being silenced. And she questions if women want to read about that."

"You're referring to rape. The Philomena story is a well-known myth, Paul. I studied it in college." I hesitated. "It was your mother who suggested I write a column for her paper, and my answer was predicated on my right to choose the subject matter."

"Right." His glass was empty. "But adding in Nicole Simpson upset her. And she didn't think Jackie Kennedy needed to be there either. How do they fit into the silence theme?"

"Nicole was silenced by brutality. By fear. And she ended up being murdered by her husband."

"That isn't proven."

"Paul, O.J. did it. She had called the cops on him before."

"There will be a trial."

"I'm keeping her in the essay. I like the red rose. And I will compromise and take Jackie out if your mom insists. But the more I think about it, she was a silenced woman. JFK had numerous affairs, and she had to remain silent."

"Maybe it was in her interest to do so?"

Paul and I had maintained our silence, too. Wasn't that what I was writing about? "You could be right, Paul. Maybe all silence is about self-interest."

"That wasn't what I meant."

"Shall I talk to Katherine, then?"

He was quick to answer. "No, no. I can manage it. Don't worry, it'll be published."

I raised my glass. "Thanks."

He scooted off to pour another cocktail. I felt a half-second of elation. A tiny moment of empowerment.

And then something so extraordinary happened that the change I had anticipated for the past few years began to unfold at a more rapid clip. Lyra was sent to dance in the International Competition for Artists of the Ballet in Moscow, *the* competition for ballerinas. Katherine happily forked over the money, and Paul flew with Lyra to Russia, who danced pieces from "Raymonda" and "Esmeralda." She received not only glowing reviews, but five-thousand dollars for winning the silver medal. Paul had taken the opportunity to write a story about the competition, which he sold to *The New York Times*. Lyra having a permanent place with the American Ballet School was assured, and we leapt into planning a move to the city. This time Katherine was on board.

29

My little gang of writing students arrived at the front door. It was 1995, and I had an ARC of a memoir Ruth had sent me by a woman named Mary Karr. *The Liar's Club.* Ruth fumed because she hadn't gotten her hands on it first but explained that she nor anyone else was prepared for the readers' interest in a memoir about a girl growing up in an abusive family in an east Texas industrial town. I read it in one sitting and was struck by the voice, the poetry of the writing, and the mixture of violence and humor. It was stunning and already making a huge impact on writers, as though it gave permission for all things hidden to be exposed. My warning to writers would be to explain that writing a life was an art form and required as much talent and training as a novel.

By now Paul and Lyra knew to make themselves scarce. I had come to relish these get-togethers. Stephanie's eyes met mine, and she said, "I brought the woman Mickey I've been telling you about for a year. I hope it's okay."

I glanced over at the woman she was referring to—around my age, I guessed, platinum hair flouncing around a tanned face, staring blue eyes, striking—and turned back to Stephanie, "You should have called to ask, but for one night, it's fine."

I was protective of the little club I had nurtured into a cohesive writing group that met bi-monthly. Priscilla, who was back after divorcing and wrote endlessly about her ex; Bonnie, who had talent and had started submitting short stories to various publications;

Stephanie, who wrote superficially because she was afraid to go too deep; Sigrid, whose writing was stuck in childhood; and Darlene, our oldest member who had a great wry sense of humor, and liked writing saccharine stories.

Stephanie was quick to respond. "Oh, she was curious . . . and very persuasive . . . and so we'll just call her a visitor. It's one evening." We followed the others into the big den, and Stephanie whispered into my ear. "She's into guns. And men." She snickered, and I started to dread the evening.

I took my usual seat in a leather club chair and they gathered round. I had never seen Priscilla so long-faced, sitting glumly in the corner and casting arrows in Mickey's direction. The woman she accused of stealing her husband. "We have a visitor," I started. "Will you introduce yourself, please?"

We looked in Mickey's direction, and she turned her electric blue eyes on us. "I'm Mickey Olivetti." She was all in black. Good figure. Taller than me. On the voluptuous side. Red nails. Her skin coarse. "I'm one of those who doesn't think writing can be taught, but I'm willing to change my mind. I read a story of Moira's years ago, and it stayed with me. I'm also a fan of her so-called gardening columns that usually have some hidden message. The last one about women being silenced was brave, I thought. That's all I have to say."

"You didn't tell us about you," Darlene said.

A shadow flitted across Mickey's face and was replaced with a wide smile. "I don't share that information randomly."

She knew how to hold the floor. To be in the spotlight.

"Okay. The reason I came tonight," she continued, "is because I read Moira's essay about Philomena and thought, hey, I relate to that. A woman with balls wrote that, I said to myself." I saw the women exchange glances out of the corners of their eyes. "And," she said, snapping her fingers, "Just like that, I thought, I've found somebody to mentor my writing."

"You have to be invited in," sniffed the long-suffering Priscilla.

Some kind of silent warfare was underway, I realized. I felt loyal to Priscilla, but at the same time, I felt flattered that Mickey had actually read my columns and stories. I had smiled over the reference to my column, for Paul told me that the paper had received more letters responding to it than any other writing over the past five years, most of them positive. I had tapped into something universal.

"What have you written?" Bonnie asked Mickey in a stiff voice.

"A novel where I'm the protagonist. All fiction is autobiography, right? I'm still figuring it out."

I jumped in to change the subject. "I'm excited to announce that I have a copy of 'The Artist's Way,'" I said. "And now that I've had a chance to go over it, I think everyone should buy a copy." The book had just been released in paperback, and the author, Julia Cameron, offered two main tenets for artists, which I felt I had been doing for a decade: write three pages in longhand daily and make a date with yourself to write for a certain length of time each week. It skyrocketed to success.

"How long will we do this?" Bonnie asked.

"It goes for twelve weeks."

Everyone seemed enthusiastic. We then opened our notebooks, and instead of offering a prompt, I said, "Let's write for ten minutes on whatever comes to mind. It will get us started with "The Artist's Way."

The room grew quiet except for the motion of pencils and pens across paper. I wrote,

> It feels surprisingly good that a stranger entered and knows my work. That doesn't happen every day. She came tonight because she knows my writing. I see the way she observes the room we are in. I saw her eyes land on the portrait of me that was painted just prior to the rape.
>
> The artist, Wayne Ensrud, was a friend whose mentor was Kokoshka. In a small studio on Jane Street in the West Village, he poured each of us a glass of white wine and turned up the music of Schubert. I

watched him transform from easy-going, charming friend into a vortex of shifting images as he stared at me a long time without blinking, then dipped his brush into the palette and began to paint, all physicality, his body moving to and fro, never taking his eyes off me, his subject. I had been amused by his request to paint me, and of course a little honored, and had shown up in casual attire, which had dismayed him slightly, as he was used to women arriving in their finest. "We'll have to make do," he had said.

About mid-way through that first sitting, I felt such a wave of emotion that I didn't know if I could continue. He was a friend, not a lover, and yet, I had never felt so seen. It was like lovemaking, when all defenses are down and vulnerability is profound. I stirred, but his stare kept me there, unable to move. I felt tears sliding down my cheeks, but I didn't know why. It was as though he had abducted my essence and put it on the canvas. I knew the session had ended when he put his brush down and walked lightly over to me and kissed me on the eyes. Lightly. Lovingly. It was like awakening from a dream. Soon we were as before, going for a drink, laughing about this or that.

I glanced at the portrait again, and caught the sadness in my eyes that today seemed to auger my future. Ensrud had been prescient, I thought, either that or the sadness around my childhood and my mother's mental fragility had been triggered by the music of Schubert.

Mickey looked from the painting to me, her eyes interlocking with mine.

I said, "Time's up." Bonnie raised her hand to read about an exchange with her maid that morning that had left her feeling sad and helpless. Then Mickey raised her hand to read. She pulled reading cat glasses from her pocket, and began.

"I have a great desire to be who I am not. Nothing that I have done to date is who I am. I have married, but marriage tells me nothing about me. I have had jobs, some interesting, some boring, but all the while, I am performing tasks of the job I have taken on, working robotically as it were; surprisingly, I am usually judged to be successful. I stop and look around. The dominant feature of this room is a portrait of a woman. A woman who for a brief moment allowed herself to be exposed. It is that rawness that captivates, and holds the attention. That invites speculation."

The women looked spellbound.

"That's it," she said. "All I had time for."

Stephanie said, "That's called being in the moment. How many times have we all sat here and not really noticed Moira's portrait?"

Bonnie's face was serious. "Portraits are interesting. I read once that a portrait represents both the artist and the subject. We can all look at the portrait and form our own interpretation. We project ourselves onto it."

The conversation ambled on until I called a break.

The group seemed relieved, as they stood and stretched. I went into the kitchen and was followed by Priscilla. "I can barely stand to be in the room with that woman," she said. "If she's allowed back, I'm out of here."

"I'm sorry. We still have to vote. Maybe the others will agree with you."

"She was a major catalyst in my marriage ending. Larry was bowled over by her, and though I can't prove they had an affair, she was all over him."

"Does Stephanie know?"

"Yes. She told me she was bringing her and thought it could be a lesson in letting go."

Oh god, I thought. "Don't worry, Priscilla," I assured her. "We have to vote on a new member, and besides, she hasn't asked to join."

I gave her a quick embrace of reassurance as we went back into the den. I announced that we'd resume class in five minutes. Mickey was at my side in an instant. "Hey," she said. "I got Steph to bring me so I could meet you. I was serious. I think you're the real deal."

"Meaning?"

"A writer. You're probably more of a role model than a teacher for these women."

"I don't know how to take that."

"Take it any way you want. It's not a class I need. I need an agent. I understand you're good friends with Ruth Schwartz."

I grew immediately wary, as I often did when aspiring writers approached me with a manuscript for Ruth. I also had a hard time with people presenting as writers whose goal was to sell before they'd written the book. She continued speaking, "I sent Ruth pages of the manuscript I'm working on, but she rejected it. Or her secretary did. I've been reworking it, and I thought you could get it to her personally."

"Ruth and I are friends, but I would have to read it in order to recommend it. I'm a bit overwhelmed these days." I was going all chitty-chatty. That shadow flickered across her face again, and as quickly as before, vanished. "I mean, I could maybe help . . ."

She smiled. "It's no big deal. Maybe down the road you can read it and see what you think. I'll get it to you." She looked around. "Some place you got here."

The next thing I knew, I was telling her about the artist who had painted my portrait. And then about Lyra. She was an intense listener. Out of the corner of my eye, I caught the look of disapproval on Priscilla's face. I would vote against Mickey joining our group.

Stephanie shouted for everybody to reassemble.

I switched the topic to John Cheever, the writer who had so perfectly created the landscape in fiction that I had moved into and come to absorb. I had come across his daughter Susan's book, *Home Before Dark: A Personal Memoir* of John Cheever, published in 1985, in my studio and realized that some of my attitude about him had come from that, and not from his short stories, many of which had appeared in *The New Yorker*. I was intrigued by the affairs he had with women and men, but more, how he maintained a secret life that eventually drove him to drink himself to death. I recalled a teacher in college quoting him, "The constants that I look for are a love of light and a determination to trace some moral chain of being."

He was, in essence, a moralist. His daughter had quoted extensively from his journals, which, at the time, had set off a firestorm of controversy. Those opposed to their publication hated him being exposed. He came across as vindictive, especially to his wife, who didn't offer up her body to him on a regular basis; sarcastic, and puny, a term Adeline would use to describe a man with no balls.

What I had disliked about some of his characters when I was reading him in college was their privilege, their discussions about lawn parties and boarding schools and country club socials. Their settings were the rolling lawns across which "the morning light is as gold as money, and the lovely houses that appeared in the affluent towns of Connecticut and New York." At the same time, the reader would learn that many of his characters were practically doomed to alcoholism or adultery. There was an almost unanimous disappointment among them, as though what they had been brought up to expect was not coming their way, which left them in some kind of existential crisis that made them feel alienated, or as Michiko Kakutani, the critic who wrote Cheever's obituary for *The New York Times* wrote, deprived of grace. This had contributed to my resistance to suburbia, and still did.

His daughter's decision to employ his journals was a little shocking to me, and yet, his son Ben was quoted as saying that his father's theory was that "a piece of writing can be useful to readers and make them feel less lonely, less disappointed in themselves."

Oh, how I loved that. I read the statement to the writers gathered around me and also asked for any commentary on Cheever's life and stories, as they had been assigned to read at least one of his stories. Bonnie said, "His characters, to me, don't have the courage of Hemingway's. Many of them are corrupted, confused, alone."

Stephanie joined in. "I felt compassion for him. His struggle to hide his homosexuality is what must have led to his alcoholism."

Priscilla said, "I think he was an imposter. He was not of the manor born and in fact was ashamed of his past."

I had referred to myself as an imposter when I moved to Halifax with Paul. My Lily Pulitzer dresses were no different than Cheever's Brooks Brother suits. Maybe Cheever was like me in that he found a hiding place in Ossining, New York. Only I stayed tucked into my studio, sending out a story or two a year, while he sent out hundreds and they were all published. He became a giant in the publishing world.

Mickey next launched into her defense of him, touching on separating the artist from the actions of the author, and judging the writing, not the man. She didn't stop there, though, but went on a diatribe about our town and the people who inhabited it. "We live in John Cheever country," she said. "Nothing has changed. He managed to impersonate the upper middle class well enough to become accepted, though of course it helped that his poor wife's father was the dean of Yale Medical School. He was a prodigious snob, a guy who never went to college, and dropped out of high school."

"You're contradicting yourself," Bonnie said. "You support him in one breath and malign him in the next."

"I support the writer," she said, "but not the man."

I stepped in quickly. "What about a piece of writing making a reader feel less lonely or less disappointed in themselves?"

Stephanie said, "Moira's columns in the newspaper do that for me. They make me feel less lonely."

Oh, god, Stephanie, I wanted to say. *Lay off.*

The evening came to a close, and I realized I was exhausted. Stephanie was the last to gather up her materials, and as she got to the door, she said, "Mickey's amazing, huh? Her insights into you were fabulous."

Amazing and fabulous, my two least favorite words. Still, after Stephanie left, I poured another glass of wine and dialed the radio to the classical station. I studied the me in the portrait, and liked how Ensrud had captured my vulnerability. I had let him in. Trusted him. And though he was known as a bon vivant, a charismatic womanizer in fact, he held me in another space from that sitting on, treating me as he might a sister. And then, as was true with many friends, we lost touch with each other when I moved.

I thought about Mickey's intense focus on me and the portrait all evening and felt a tiny cautionary flag go up.

30

An entirely different side of Mickey was presented on October fourth. The day of Stephanie's birthday party was upon us, and I was about to back out, but Paul and Lyra insisted we all go. I went upstairs and slipped into a lemon yellow dress that Katherine had bought for me on a recent shopping trip.

"Great outfit," Paul said. Lyra walked in wearing a short dress that exposed slender, long legs. Her height, five-and-a-half feet, was perfect for a ballerina. I ran through the criteria in my mind: barely any breasts or hips, pronounced collarbone and elongated neck. Glossy golden hair flowed halfway down her back, her skin was like porcelain, and the eyes that had always haunted me from the time she was born seemed violet today.

"I'm going to be with the two most beautiful girls at the party," Paul teased. The three of us arrived in a festive mood. Stephanie and Phil's large indoor porch swarmed with people that spilled out onto the lawn. They had taken an anniversary trip to Spain and were so enamored of the culture that they had created a Spanish theme for the party. Music blasted from an outdoor speaker and a few people were dancing the salsa. We passed a table filled with an array of exotic looking dishes. The day was unusually warm. Paul took off across the yard to meet up with his pals. I waved to Ed and Carol, who beckoned me over. Lyra disappeared into the crowd. I stood alone for a moment, amused by Stephanie's decorations.

I noticed a woman across the lawn decked out in a décolleté red top with lipstick to match and a long black skirt, platinum tresses billowing around her face. She was surrounded by a small crowd. I walked over to Mickey.

When flamenco music filled the atmosphere, she stood listening for a moment, then began to dance with such verve that I stood mesmerized. Her eyes, black with mascara and liner, closed, and her red lips parted as she became one with the music, stomping her feet and picking up the skirt and whirling around. Outrageous.

When the dance ended, I applauded, along with everyone else. She caught my eye and said, "Let's go get a sangria." I followed her, and she ordered the drinks.

Lyra ran up, her eyes full of curiosity. "I'd love to learn to dance like that," she said.

Mickey laughed. "I learned it years ago when I was in Spain. Believe me; I'm an amateur." She focused her attention on Lyra. "You're the talented one. Dancing with the American Ballet is quite an achievement."

"My dream is to go with them full-time when I'm sixteen. I'm fifteen now."

Mickey laughed. She pulled a cigarette from the little purse that hung off her shoulder. Then she scratched around and pulled out a gold lighter and flicked it. "Don't pick up this habit," she said to Lyra, blowing out smoke. "Once you start, you'll never stop."

Lyra noticed a group of friends and waved. "See you later," she said, and ran lightly across the lawn to join them.

"What a beauty she is," Mickey said. "I don't think I ever wanted anything in my life as much as I wanted a daughter. A daughter would have made me feel I was existing in a magical kingdom. Isn't that what it feels like having Lyra? I mean, she even looks like a fairy princess."

I laughed and assumed Mickey had had too much to drink. "That's really romanticizing it," I said. "Lyra and her friends are not princesses. Her room's a wreck, and they lie up there and listen to music that makes me think the singer is mortally wounded."

Mickey laughed, too, but then said, "You received the ultimate gift from the universe. I try not to be bitter and jealous. I feel sometimes that I have nothing to offer the world—that I have done nothing with my life."

"I'm sure that's not true."

"I tried a singing career and was a minor success, then shifted to painting and even sold some of my work, but then my husband and I moved again, and anyhow, it's impossible to find galleries that take representational work."

A few of the guests were making their way over to us, including Stephanie's husband and Paul, who gave me an inquisitive smile, which, in our code language, meant 'Are you having fun?' I smiled back at him.

Within minutes, it was as if Mickey was holding court. I watched her greet each person with her intense interest. I was reminded of how my mother used to say how Jackie O was known to treat each person she was introduced to as though they were the only two in the room, but this was different. It was if Mickey had a flashlight inside her that she could flick on and off at will.

I saw Lyra breeze by, this time with a boy whose hand was entwined in hers. It was disconcerting enough that it took me a minute to return to the group conversation. Mickey was telling a guest I didn't know, a man who looked a little stricken, about the book she was writing. She was doing what I warned my writers against: spilling all the beans about her story. I caught a few words . . . "This issue has to be more in the open . . . oh, yes, the protagonist is based on my own experience . . . you could compare it to *The Liars' Club* . . ."

Paul nudged me and whispered, "Lyra is with a boy."

He might as well have said alien. "I saw her. Let's find out what's going on."

"She's too young, Moira. My god. Fifteen's too young." She and the boy were in chairs sipping a cold drink.

The boy stood up as we approached, and Lyra joined him. "Mom. . . Dad . . . meet Luc. He's a dancer too."

We said hello, and Paul asked him where he danced, and he confidently explained that he was with Lyra's ballet company, but that he hoped to do more modern dance. It turned out his father worked a lot in Europe, and he and his mother and a sibling, a sister, had moved into our area a year ago. Paul and he began speaking French, and I could tell Lyra was impressed. She put her hand on Paul's arm and leaned into him. I turned my attention back to Luc, who had dark, almost black, eyes, and hair pulled back into a ponytail.

Mickey joined us, and the next thing I knew, Luc and she were talking intensely about Twyla Tharp, and Mickey was telling them about what it was like learning flamenco in Spain when she was a teen and how she wished she'd stayed with dance but that it was too late for all that. The kids seemed mesmerized by her like everyone else. The next thing I knew, she'd shifted the topic to writing, and she said to Lyra, "Don't you wonder what your mom's writing about in that studio?"

Lyra shook her head. "Not really." We laughed.

Mickey looked as if she could eat Lyra with a spoon, as my mother used to say.

"You write every day?" Luc asked her.

"Naw. I think I'm a one-book woman. If I sell this one, I might write another." She hesitated, then said, "The big secret about me, Luc, is I win shooting contests all around New England."

"Guns?" She got the reaction she wanted from him. Lyra and I leaned in.

"It's a sport," she said. "And requires the discipline of a dancer. You have to be precise and accurate. And you have to be completely focused." I was losing interest and about to excuse myself to join Stephanie and friends when Mickey said, "I'll tell you what. I'll take you all shooting one day."

"I don't know if my dad will let me," Lyra said. "He writes articles against guns, but not against you and your friends," she added diplomatically. "He thinks there would be a lot less murders if there were fewer guns."

"Fewer murders," I corrected her.

"That's an argument for another day," Mickey said. "Maybe your mother can be the neutral one in the family."

Lyra and Luc took my silence as an opportunity to abandon us.

"I'd love for you to come with me one day, seriously," Mickey said.

"One day."

Her red lips pooched and widened, and her blue eyes were bright. "What a day to be alive," she said. Eyes closed, her face lifted to the sky, she seemed to go into a reverie. She was tall, almost statuesque, with broad shoulders. It was a startling site. Then, "I'm ready for another sangria. And you can meet my husband. He's the guy in the wheelchair, and don't say you haven't seen him."

"I did notice him."

"Tom made a shitload of money in New York," she said, "then poor guy, he got in a car accident." We shifted our gaze over to him, and he lifted his glass. She shot him the bird, and he laughed. "We have a love-hate thing," she said. "I get my angst out at the local shooting range. We're both into guns. We met in Montreal at the '76 Olympics. First time a woman—Margaret Murdock—ever won an Olympic medal in shooting. I was hooked like a lot of others."

"I have to confess I'm terrified of guns. I don't get why women's interest is so high now."

"You don't? You read the papers? Surely you know that O.J. Simpson was acquitted yesterday." How had I missed that news? "The bastard did it, but our justice system is fucked."

"I didn't know."

"Shocking, huh? You nailed him way back in your column. Good on you, Moira."

Mickey poured each of us a sangria, and we walked to where her husband waited. We sat in the two unoccupied chairs beside him. Mickey introduced me, and he and I shook hands. He seemed frailer up close.

"I'm telling Moira about our favorite sport."

He turned petulant. "Speak for yourself. I don't like guns at all, but I like it that I can shoot somebody who enters my house uninvited."

"He'll end up shooting me one day," she said. "And he'll swear on a Bible that he thought he was shooting a burglar."

"Not funny," he said.

"Not meant to be." A man walked up to Tom, and they began talking about the stock market. "Let's go," Mickey said. "You know, Moira, the reason I like your gardening column is because it's not really about gardening, is it? I think a feminist lurks beneath all the flower petals. You're saying to women, 'for fuck's sake, listen up and take charge of your lives. Be like Princess Diana.'"

I was experiencing a light buzz from the second glass of sangria. And I was having fun.

"Say yes you'll come with me to the shooting range."

"You know how to wear me down," I said, laughing. "Okay."

Paul approached and announced dinner. "I need to drag you away," he said to me. "Everybody's asking where you are."

"Next week, then," Mickey said, winking.

"What's she like?" Paul asked as we walked across the lawn.

"Funny. Smart. Persistent. How would you describe her?"

"Magnetic. Narcissistic." He hesitated. "She sure latched onto you."

"Maybe the other way around. I agreed to go with her to her shooting range one day."

"You?"

I laughed. "One day is the operative word."

Ed and Carole stood holding their drinks, looking self-satisfied. Both had put on weight. I was struck by how they had come to resemble each other.

"It's been a while," I said to them.

"Lyra is adorable," Carole said. "Paul said she's going to go pro with the dance."

"She works hard at it. How are your kids?"

Ed gave a hearty laugh. "Overwhelming, but they're good kids, right, Babe?"

Carole laughed. "What do you know?" She turned to me and said in a wifely tone, "He sees them on weekends."

"You're the one who wanted to move to Darien," he said, then turning to me. "You're writing?"

"Trying to. And editing."

"I thought you'd have a Pulitzer by now," Ed said. "Going by where you were fifteen years ago."

I felt the smile freeze on my face. "You're mixing me up with Paul."

"Moira is the best mom in the world," Paul said, trying to defend me but making me feel worse. I thought of all the journals locked in my desk. If anyone talking to me today was handed one of mine to read, they'd malign me the way they did John Cheever and his fake life.

I heard Mickey's contralto voice over the music and saw that another group had gathered around her. *She doesn't give a shit,* I thought, *about what anyone thinks of her.* I couldn't imagine how liberating that must be.

I had another sangria and was relieved when Bonnie from my writers' class bounded over. "This party is like a writer's prompt," she said, which made me laugh. She glanced over at Mickey. "That one there could be a great character to explore."

Darlene from writing class joined us. "Talking about Mickey?" she asked.

"You know her?" Bonnie asked.

"I don't think anyone knows her, but in fact, who knows me? Who knows you?"

Bonnie laughed. "Darlene, stop trying to sound like a philosopher."

Darlene had a shock of white hair and wore a bold red lipstick. "I'm not defending Mickey, but she does seem like the local scapegoat. I actually liked her writing about Moira's portrait."

"I heard she's trying to worm her way into every social group in town, but most have turned her away. She's so full of herself." Bonnie glanced over at Mickey, and I saw that her husband was the one who had just laughed uproariously at something Mickey had said.

I felt Paul's hand on my arm, "We should be heading out. I have to be up early tomorrow."

He called to Lyra, who came running over, slightly breathless. "Can I stay a little longer, please, please?" Luc came up behind her and reached for her hand.

Paul looked over at me. "It's up to your mother."

"How will you get home?"

"Stephanie said she'd drive me home. A bunch of us are staying."

"Dad and I can wait a while longer," I said. "You have to be up early tomorrow."

Her eyes widened as she protested.

Luc said, "I'll make sure she stays out of trouble."

Before I could reply, Paul said, "Well, okay. But curfew is ten o'clock."

She leaned up and kissed him and ran off with Luc, who had stood waiting while we debated. I turned to watch them and saw Mickey out of the corner of my eye, standing alone, weaving slightly, her eyes following Lyra's movements as she glided across the lawn.

31

Mickey called two weeks after the party. "I can pick you up at five."
When I hesitated, she said, "Come on; it won't kill you." A raucous
laugh followed, and then, "Pardon the pun. We'll grab a glass of
wine after."

I almost called her back to cancel, and then thought, what the
hell, I could leave a casserole in the oven for Paul and Lyra and go
do something different. I had to admit I was curious.

I left a note on the kitchen counter for Paul and Lyra and
dashed out when Mickey pulled up. We drove towards Waterbury,
forty-five minutes away and entered a long, shed-like building.
Mickey was dressed in jeans that looked glued to her butt that
displayed her muffin top, a revealing knit top and cowboy boots. A
bombshell.

"Tom and I go to this one because he can shoot from his
wheelchair," she said. " This is the only range that offers that. But
look around. It has a fifty-foot indoor pistol range, twenty-five and
fifty-yard outdoor pistol ranges, and much longer rifle ranges."

Through the glass, I saw the backsides of women and men lined
up in their lanes, wearing headphones and goggles. "It looks
intimidating."

"Nah. It's like any place that's new." She spoke to a couple of
men who called her Lefty. "I won a big women's competition here a
few weeks ago and got the nickname."

"A lot of women are here."

"It's kinda new. Women shooting guns. It's still not easy to get a carry permit. A lot of discrimination. A board has to okay it, and they turn a lot of women down for one excuse or another. I got mine, mainly because of Tom." She pulled two pistols from her bag. "These are 9-millimeter lightweight Glocks, exactly the same, but with different registration numbers. I'm not teaching you with a sissy gun, a .380 many women prefer." She handed me one of hers. "Now we have twin guns. Hang onto it."

It took a few tries for me to understand the feeling of the gun at a tactile level, how much pressure to use when pulling the trigger, for example, but though I didn't hit the center target, which was a heart in a man's chest, I at least wasn't off the paper.

"Look at some of the women walking around here," Mickey said. "Guns transform how they move through space." I thought of Paul's describing Mickey as filled with swagger after Stephanie's party and thought it perfect watching her today.

I tried again, and missed the guy's heart by six inches. I hooted, and Mickey laughed. Mickey aimed her gun and hit the bulls-eye.

"Who you mad at?" a guy asked when we exited our lane.

Mickey stopped a few inches from him and said in a husky voice, "Maybe you're the one who's mad because a woman can outshoot you."

"Don't go taking it personally. I was trying to compliment you."

She suddenly laughed, and I realized she was flirting with him. "In that case, you want to buy me a drink?"

"Can't. I'm married."

She couldn't take her eyes off him. "I'm not asking you to fuck me." She laughed again. "Come on, Moira. Let's get a drink."

He strutted off, and I followed her to the bar next door. I admired her bravado but also felt intimidated by her hostile response to his rejection.

"Were you really going to go for a drink with him?"

"No. I knew what he'd say."

I wasn't sure she was telling the truth.

She ordered a martini, and I asked for a glass of chardonnay. "I was being Louise by the way," she said. "*Thelma and Louise* changed my life."

"You do remind me a bit of Susan Sarandon in that film."

"Let's create code names. My brother and I did that when we were kids. You can be Thelma."

I laughed. "I'm not a Thelma at all! Don't project that onto me, please."

She smiled. "Just do it for kicks. I like it that Louise knew she'd never get justice for shooting that guy. No woman gets justice in this country. Not in the courtrooms anyhow."

She had downed her drink and put up her fingers for another round, but I said no, and she made a face and called for the bill.

"Look at that school mistress Jean Harris shooting her lover and spending eleven years at Bedford Prison. She should have been acquitted."

She was referring to the Scarsdale murder case that kept the country riveted in 1981. The headmistress had gone to her lover's house with a gun and he ended up dead and she was convicted of murder.

"She intended to kill herself," I said.

"He got what he deserved. He was a skank."

"I don't know if anyone deserves to be murdered, Mickey."

"I can name a few right now. I have an obsession with cold cases in this country. You'd be shocked at how many murderers get away with it. Some of them are out there living normal lives."

"That gives me the creeps."

It was time to go. She asked about my writers' group, then before I could respond, she said, "Let's trade, Thelma. You come with me to the shooting range, and I'll come to your class with those stuck-up women."

I laughed in spite of myself.

And just like that, Mickey became a ubiquitous presence in our household with both positive and negative effects. I had to assert stronger boundaries as she was wont to appear at any hour of the day, sometimes with a gift for Lyra, usually something silly, or with a magazine article for Paul that she thought would interest him. She would pop by to ask my opinion on her outfit or get me to go for a hike.

The women in my writing class agreed to her joining us after Stephanie said out loud that we needed a little jolt, perhaps. I was determined to remain neutral. It was routine now for Mickey and me to enter the shooting range and don the required goggles and headphones and line up in separate lanes. I had improved only slightly. I had to admit, though, that I liked going there with Mickey. All types showed up, and the environment was friendly. It was like a club, quite the opposite of the country club where men in bowties and women coiffed to the nth degree spoke politely while slinging arrows in all directions.

Paul and Lyra and I were focused on her dance career, as she was preparing to return to Manhattan for the summer of her fifteenth year to dance with American Ballet. But for the first time, she was completely distracted. Luc was another ubiquitous presence around our house, and Paul and I were adamant that she was not old enough to date, but that they could meet up in group situations or visit her when she was home. Most of their togetherness happened at the local ballet school, and I thought that was why Luc was putting so much energy into dance. We had met his parents a few times at social events, and while not friends, we found them amiable enough.

Eventually Mickey began to wear on us. Paul complained that her constant dropping in was disruptive. "It's also unnatural," he added. "The way she seems to idolize Lyra."

I had noticed it, too. I agreed to speak to her, but it turned out I didn't have to broach the subject because she did while we were sitting out on my terrace one evening at my house. She was smoking more than usual. Out of the blue, she said, "Tom wants to move again."

"Where?"

"Maybe back into Manhattan. He has no friends here. And now he's jealous of you. Actually, he said *I'm* jealous of you."

"Why?"

"Oh, let me count the ways. The perfect family. The perfect child. The writing."

She was slurring her words, and I thought she had drunk too much vodka. I had recently sold a story to yet another small literary magazine, which had garnered a little attention. Mickey had been coming to my writers' group, but to my surprise, she contributed very little, in contrast to Stephanie's recommendation that she might "jolt" us a bit. In fact, I found her deferential. As the months passed, I realized how she melted into whatever group she was in: she was the fireball at Stephanie's party, the tough draw at the gun range, and the quiet scholar at writing class.

I didn't think Tom had said anything but that the booze had given her permission to say what was on her mind. I also wondered if it was Tom who was suggesting a move to Manhattan. Mickey had entered our house unobtrusively a few weeks ago, and I knew she had overheard Paul and me discussing the possibility of moving back to Manhattan in another year or so. I hadn't even mentioned it to Ruthie, as so much would have to fall into place, including Paul being re-hired by *The New York Times*. It was that statement more than the jealousy remark that had set me off.

She lit another cigarette. I decided to ignore the perfect family statement. "You've never liked it here, have you?" I asked her.

"I'm realizing I've never been happy anywhere, Moira. I was a miserable kid. I was made miserable, and I've been writing about it. But how will a story like that go over with your little group of writers who tell stories of a pet dog, or how they discovered true love?"

"That's not fair. Why do you think their lives are so different from yours?"

"Because they didn't have to survive incest."

"I'm sorry to hear that, Mickey."

She stood up suddenly. "I don't need sympathy. I'd better get home before Tom comes barreling in, which he threatened to do the next time I'm late for dinner."

I felt weighted down by her announcement. "Are you and he doing okay?"

"Is any marriage okay when the woman is *damaged goods*? He's my third and last husband. I'll be honest. He needs my care, and I need his cash. He was in some shady dealings in the past, and I could blackmail him if I wanted to."

"Oh, Mickey." We heard a car drive in, and Mickey jumped up to leave but stumbled in the threshold of the back door.

Paul stood beside his car, observing us as we came out. "Hey," he said to Mickey. "Why don't I give you a lift home? You can pick up your car tomorrow."

"I'm fine," Mickey said, slamming her car door and backing up too rapidly.

Paul shook his head. "She's drunk. She shouldn't be driving." He turned to me and gave me a buss on the cheek. "Did you manage to talk to her about her camping out here?"

I nodded, but of course I hadn't said anything. "She understood."

It wasn't exactly a lie, I thought. But I couldn't bring myself to tell him all that she had revealed. Maybe it was too close to the bones of my own deeply buried secret. I thought again about the weight of it and understood what it would feel like for my family were I to reveal my own truth.

"Good." He put his arm around me. "But hey, the night is ours. I need a martini."

32

Summer was upon us, and we prepared to commute back and forth to the city, as Lyra was attending her fourth summer at the School for American Ballet. We loved having the apartment on 72ⁿᵈ Street. Paul was still working at the newspaper in Halifax and had also taken on some freelance articles for the *Times*. The train ride to the city was three and a half hours, and he had learned to write while traveling. I walked with Lyra to her classroom and sometimes had the opportunity to observe her. I had become her biggest advocate and was in constant awe of the combination of physicality and intellect required to dance. She and I read the stories of the ballets and often went to the library to find more material about the subjects she was dancing. At night, we would curl up and do homework, and when we were lucky, we'd meet up with Ruth. On rare occasions when the three of us were together, we'd ride our bicycles through Central Park. Paul went back and forth between Halifax and the city.

Was I happy? No. Nothing had prepared me for what I perceived as Ruthie's emotional abandonment. She showed up when she could over the summer, but those times were infrequent, and when we were together, nothing intimate came up. Ever since she had gotten drunk after Stella died and let out all her grief over the loss of her mother and the loss of Seamus, she had not shared much of anything about her life. I blamed myself, for once back in the city, the nightmares started again, and I lived in fear of bumping into

Jonathan. The trauma that had existed inside me for sixteen years had affected so many choices, but the decision not to tell Ruth brought the deepest regret. She had never had much tolerance for fake personas, which she could spot instantly, and I was no different.

Over coffee, I told her about Mickey and embellished the story of her dancing flamenco. "Paul described her as swaggery," I said.

Ruth smiled. "That's visual." She sighed. "Sounds like she wants to be seen as a badass. Too bad, Clint Eastwood has dibs on the term. If we hadn't gotten so old, I'd tell you to beware. She wants something." Another day when I was trying to make her laugh by telling her about some of the weirdos at the gun range, she said, "Frankly, I am shocked that you find anything about guns or gun ranges amusing. Guns kill people. And animals."

"They also protect," I said.

"Since when do you need protection, Moira?"

"Oh, forget it. And whose philosophy are you mimicking while we're at it?"

She hesitated before continuing. "I had a manuscript come in a couple of weeks ago that I'd have to file in the self-help category, which, as you know, I'm not too keen on. But I have to say it grabbed me after I read a few paragraphs, one of the author's points being that we're in a pandemic of narcissism."

"So?"

"So. We know so little about them, but they can be two-faced if they get called on their shit, or they feel rejected. They're vindictive. I've had a couple of authors like that, and they're a pain in the ass."

"It's not like you to beat around the bush, Ruthie. I don't even think of Mickey as a close friend."

"But she thinks of you as one. And you talk about her all the time." I almost told Ruth she sounded jealous, but didn't. "I worry that she'll highjack your life. Your writing, your daughter, your status . . ."

"You haven't even met her. I'm sorry I've made her sound so difficult."

"I can't picture your life up there anymore. You haven't mentioned writing in ages."

I felt bad. I hadn't invited Ruth to come for a long weekend like she used to do in over a year.

One day over ice cream, I said, "Paul and I like being back here in the city. Next year will tell us a lot about Lyra's future. We will know if they invite her to join the ballet de corps full-time. Or there's a minute chance that she'll be made a soloist."

"She'll be sixteen. Does this mean you will move back permanently?"

"I think so."

"What would you do?"

"Paul could potentially become a freelance writer or an editor. I could possibly work as an editor."

"Interesting."

Our conversation wound down to too many pauses. I said I had to go, and she stood and said she was meeting friends at a bistro.

"I'm heading out of town for a week," she said, "but I'll see you before you go back to Halifax."

"Sure."

I cried walking back to the apartment. I had kept an emotional distance from everyone, including Ruth, and even Paul, and the payback was the way I was feeling right now. Lonelier than I could ever remember, even in the days when my mother didn't emerge from her dim room for days on end. Something had to change, but what? And how?

One August day after she had returned from another trip, Ruth let loose when we were walking through the park about the O.J. Simpson trial and how it had caused her many sleepless nights. "The fact that he got away with it drives me up the fucking wall," she said. "I can't sleep at night."

I had spent the prior weekend in Halifax and saw Mickey briefly. It struck me now how much the two women sounded alike about the Simpson trial; only I felt it had tipped Mickey over the precipice into a state of insanity. She ranted for an hour after two vodka drinks about how unfair the justice system was. It seemed that she was addressing all men.

"If it had been the other way around," she said, "And O.J.'s wife had killed him, she would be in jail for the rest of her life, no matter what he did to her." She said she'd gone to the shooting range every day since I'd been gone. And she said she'd been writing a lot and thought by the time I got back her book would be ready to send to an agent. "I'm thinking it's time to give it to your buddy Ruth."

Oh no, I thought. "Can we hold off until I'm back in another month, then I can read it and see if it needs editing?"

"I've already had somebody look it over. She loved it."

"Well, then, sure." I hoped she'd forget about it.

The following week I brought Luc back down to the city with me, and Paul joined us a couple of days later for Lyra's final student performance. She was overjoyed to see Luc, and I liked seeing the two of them run in and out of the apartment. Luc's parents had set him up to audition for the ABA, and when he was rejected, I saw a different side of him. He was furious and announced that he had only done it for Lyra, and in fact was better suited to modern dance; on that bitter note, he took the train home.

Lyra was disappointed, too, and feeling guilty over her own success. Ruth was over the moon about Lyra's performance, convinced now that she was destined for greatness as a ballerina. After we went out for drinks, Lyra and Ruth snuggled up to each other and had fun amusing each other. Maybe I had been imagining that Ruth had pulled away. Paul reached for my hand, and I felt a big surge of hope.

That night. Lyra came down to say goodnight. She curled up next to Paul, and he put his arm around her. "Remember when we used to make up stories?" she asked him. "Why do we have to get too old for things?"

"Who said that? You dance stories every day. You tell me one."

She leapt up. "I'll tell you a story in movement. Here goes." Paul glanced over at me and winked. She curled her body over and mussed her hair and walked with bent knees and Paul said, "There was an old woman . . ."

Lyra nodded, then standing straight, whirled around the sofa . . ..

"Who had a beautiful daughter," Paul said.

She frowned and shook her head.

"Who saw a fairy in the woods . . ."

She smiled and nodded. This continued as I sat rapt. Little did I know it was the last moment of my daughter's innocence.

33

Christmas arrived with the usual flurry of activities that go with living in a New England small town. The lighting of the town Christmas tree. Caroling around the neighborhood. The traditional midnight Mass. Paul and I were more focused on Lyra turning sixteen the day after Christmas and on the year ahead than on the holidays. We were now planning a move to the city by August. Lyra would start dancing full-time at the American Ballet School in the fall. She had been accepted into the corps de ballet.

The other path offered to very few young ballerinas was to be given a starring role, which would mean bypassing the corps. Neither was a perfect solution, as once in the corps de ballet, you could be stuck there your entire career, but if you were in a starring part at age sixteen, the responsibility was enormous. Paul and I agreed that we wouldn't have allowed Lyra to come under so much pressure were I not going to be there on a full-time basis. We would do this as a family. It gave us purpose. She would finish school in Connecticut early May, and we would move sometime during the summer.

Katherine and Russell, who had not yet been told of our plans, came for Lyra's party. Paul flew my parents up the day after Christmas, as my father was giving the Christmas sermon at their church. Adeline looked like a giant bauble, with her Christmas red and green sweater and a hat that sparkled. She was overjoyed to be with Lyra, who insisted they make her cake together. My father, a shadow of his old self and sad looking, came off the plane in a wheelchair. We put him in front of the television and rushed about doing last-minute things.

It was the first time Ruth hadn't come to Lyra's birthday celebration, and I missed her more than I could have imagined. She didn't normally celebrate Christmas, unless she was with us and so had decided to give herself a vacation in the Caribbean. She had sent a card to Lyra offering her a trip with her to anywhere in the world that called to her heart. What a godmother! I tried not to let my thoughts lead me down the mineshaft of abandonment. I was writing daily now and figured that by the time I moved to Manhattan, I would have completed my letter to Ruth. Sixteen years of jottings were now congealing into a coherent story.

The doorbell chimed, and when I opened it, I was shocked to see Mickey dressed in her signature red. She said, "I thought I'd bring Lyra's present in person. I just never got around to putting it in the mail."

Tom was in his wheelchair beside her, a perfect foil. He stretched out his hand. "Sorry to barge in," he said. A beautifully wrapped box was in his lap. Mickey ceremoniously handed it to Lyra, who curtsied. Mickey beamed. It was a beautiful sterling silver ballet slipper charm from Tiffany's, and Lyra was visibly enchanted. She handed it to Paul, who put it around her neck. Then she pirouetted over to Mickey and kissed her on the cheek. An unrecognizable emotion came over me, which was either jealousy—or fear.

When I returned to the living room, ten of Lyra's friends had arrived, including Luc, the boy who'd claimed her heart. He came to greet me and then went into the kitchen to say hello to Adeline, who I could tell was impressed.

Mickey and Tom stayed for twenty minutes, then said they had to go. "I've missed you," she said, mournfully, as they stood at the back door. "Can we get together? I have something to tell you."

"Sure. And, thank you for the gift."

"I'd do anything for that kid. I feel like she's part mine."

I wanted to scream, *she's NOT*, but instead, I smiled and waved her out the door.

Across the room, I observed my mother with her arm around Lyra. She had not been a rock in my life as Stella had been for Ruth, encouraging her to forge her own way in the world and to be bold and relentless in her pursuit for what she wanted in life. But Adeline had meant what she said when she declared to me that she wanted to be there for Lyra. And in the process, I thought, she had learned to be there for me.

"I love you, Mama," I said, going over and embracing her.

"What in the world's gotten into you?" she asked. "Of course you do!"

The evening was again a reminder of the importance of family. I sat for a long while holding my father's hand and listening to my mother tell stories about some of the women in our town, which had Paul and Lyra in hysterics. Luc was quiet, though when I had asked him earlier about his plans he had said, "I'm going to be with a modern dance company, but I'm not allowed to talk about it now."

"Oh. Then I'm happy for you." Funny, I thought, Lyra hadn't said anything.

Mama and I spent an hour in the kitchen loading the dishwasher, though she preferred to wash by hand, and so she handed me a towel to dry. "The best discussions in the world happen over the sink," she said.

It was a moment to zero in on the Princess Diana interview with the BBC interviewer Martin Bashir that had happened in November and proved to be scandalous with her revelations of three being in her marriage, and more. I asked Adeline if she had seen it.

"You bet I did. I was on the edge of my seat. I've never heard such talk. A third person in the marriage. Just awful. A divorce will follow, I'm sure of it. No marriage can sustain that, and I'm going to blame Mr. Bashir for the divorce because I smell a skunk. I think she was manipulated."

"That hasn't come out in the news."

"To Diana's credit, the only way anybody in power listens is if they get embarrassed or humiliated. If she had said any of this in private, trust me, Prince Charles would have shut her right down. So, I'm proud of her. But now Prince Charles will have to step up, and it's going to be ugly."

"Our women heroes haven't fared too well. Jackie's gone at sixty-four, and Diana is in a terrible situation."

"I'm not over Jackie's death yet," Mama said. " It hit me hard. She was too young. I'm glad John, Jr. is with Caroline Bessette. I just read that they moved in together. I'm following them very closely. And Diana will find a liberation she's never known, trust me."

I loved our gossipy conversations. Mama shifted from Jackie to Diana to her friend Mabel down south and threw in a few Bible verses all the while barely drawing breath. Ruth had always referred to her as a pain in the ass. One day Adeline overheard her and told her it hurt her feelings.

Ruth had explained she meant it as a compliment. "You tell it like it is," she had said, and Mama liked that.

I said good-night to Mama and tiptoed across the bedroom to quietly slide into bed, trying not to wake Paul.

To my surprise, he turned to me and began kissing me passionately, and I responded in kind. We lay together after our lovemaking, our hands interlocked.

"I'm excited about our future," he said. He leaned over and kissed me, and I curled up close to him.

Soon he was snoring lightly. I observed him as he slept. Paul was handsome. Intelligent. One of the lucky ones on the planet who had suffered little. The death of his father had been hard, but he had coped with it and stood at his mother's side. I could not have imagined a more wonderful father for Lyra.

Three a.m., I got up. Maybe a cup of tea would help me sleep, I thought. I crept downstairs, and there sat Adeline in her robe. "The water's still hot," she said.

"Thanks, Mama. You can't sleep either?"

"I'm lucky to get five hours."

"Like mother, like daughter." I found a chamomile tea bag, poured the hot water over it, and sat down.

"Who's the woman Mickey who stopped by?" Mama asked. " Something about her rubbed me the wrong way. That gift for Lyra was too expensive."

I sighed. "I'm not sure who she is. She has several personas."

"I hope the others are more attractive than the one I saw tonight. She's really that close to Lyra?"

"I didn't think so." I sipped the tea and wondered how much to reveal. "I have to admit I felt jealous."

"You and I should probably have had a bunch of kids. But I guess God had other plans for us."

The silence was comfortable. I said, "Ruth mentioned something last summer that's on my mind. How a person who is a narcissist can try to appropriate your life. Ruth called it high-jacking. It makes me think of Mickey."

"Says it like it is. Meaning somebody wants to be you, right?"

"I think so, though why anybody would want that from me is beyond me."

"I disagree. On the exterior, you have what many women want. Affluence. Looks. The only thing I give your Aunt Bella credit for, by the way." I laughed. "You have a daughter who's about to be a star, which I find scary as hell." She hesitated. "And yes, I said hell. Good word. Probably because I wasn't allowed to use it."

"Well, Mickey might have succeeded a little in hijacking my life, but she won't hijack Lyra's. I'm backing out of this friendship."

"Be stealthy about it."

"Why?"

"I don't think she brooks opposition very well."

"Well said, Mama."

Mama was in chatty mode. "I got a postcard from Ruth a while back. She's what you call a solid friend."

"I know. I miss her."

"You didn't have a falling out, did you?"

"No. We'll be close again when I'm in the city."

"You're putting a lot of stock into a move to the city. It can't cure marriage, friendship problems . . ."

"I know. But it's a new start."

She yawned. "We'd better get to bed. It'll be daylight soon."

We climbed the stairs together.

PART FOUR

I understand the fear of breaking a long-held silence . . . But if there is any hope for justice, we must speak truth to that power. We must tell anyone and everyone who will listen. And those who will not listen must be made to hear.

—From *The Reckonings: Essays* by Lacy M. Johnson, 2018

34

The cherry trees, for which Connecticut was famous, were awash in blossoms mid-April of 1996 on the anniversary of my rape. The Montmorency tree that Stephanie and I had planted in my white garden to celebrate Lyra's birth filled the air with its sweet fragrance. It was one of those days when tears lie beneath the surface. When grief supersedes hope. The dormant pool of sadness that had taken residence in me sixteen years ago had stirred again, proof that my efforts at willing it to unhappen had failed. This happened every year in April, the anniversary. I knew now, though, that the melancholy would pass. I accepted it.

I was in my favorite wicker chair in the reading corner of the kitchen, the Sunday *New York Times* beside me. I could hear Paul whistling upstairs, a sign of tenuous hope that the early-morning lovemaking might have eased some of the tension that wove in and out of our relationship.

Multiple hues of gray outside the kitchen window created a Corot-type landscape, mimicking my interior landscape. Where nothing was transparent. Where thoughts blew around like pieces of debris. My handiwork beyond the French door leading to the back yard was evident now as the irises waved in the breeze, and color popped up in other areas. I made note of the rose bushes surrounding the wraparound porch that would transform into a riot of color in another month to six weeks and shifted my gaze to the large carved-out perennial beds in the distance that had taken years of planning. Hyacinths were inching up out of the ground close to the porch. It had been an unusually warm winter.

Paul, in tennis shorts revealing long legs, rushed past. "I'm off for bagels. Back soon."

I smiled up at him, then picked up the *New York Times,* turning first to the Arts & Leisure section, as was my habit. Lyra had taken to clipping articles about dance, and if I didn't read this section first, I might be greeted with half-pages.

A color photograph took up half a page. A man flanked by a woman on either side stared out at me, blue eyes looking serious. I recognized him instantly, the impact of staring into his eyes so shocking that I thought I might be having a seizure.

"Morning, Mom."

I whirled around, snapping closed the paper as though it was burning my hands. Lyra pirouetted across the kitchen floor. She kissed me lightly on top of my head, then went to the refrigerator, removed the container of orange juice, and proceeded to fill a glass. I watched her dancer body automatically go into second position, her hair piled mischievously on top of her head and secured with a chopstick, her fathomless blue eyes as she turned and looked at me. My hands were shaking.

"You okay?" she asked.

"A headache building. I'm going to take something." I stood, clutching the paper.

"Mom."

I turned back to her. When had she become nubile? I had given her the sex talk back in the fall and told her not to hesitate to ask me for birth control when she felt she needed it. Paul had been aghast, but I reminded him that girls were sexually active earlier these days, and I wanted her to understand about protection. I took the opportunity to tell her that it could be a burden to start having sex so young and that she would no doubt be happier if she waited until after high school. Because of dance and her slender figure, she had not been menstruating very long.

She had asked me then, " How old were you the first time you had sex?"

I replied, "Seventeen. A boy in my church."

"That's forever away!" Her voice brought me back to the present. "May I have a quick look at the *Arts & Leisure* section before you take it away?"

Waiting two beats, I said, "After I'm done." My voice sounded strange. Disembodied.

She frowned. "Mom, you're acting weird."

"I didn't sleep much."

It was a sufficient-enough answer to cause the anxiety in her eyes to diminish. "I promise not to clip anything until you've finished," she said, slipping into sneakers.

"Okay."

I left the paper on the table and started up the stairs, holding tightly to the banister. My heart thrummed with such force that I put my hand there to try to calm it. I crawled onto the bed, curled in a fetal position. *The wolf is here*, I thought.

In a few seconds or hours, I didn't know which, I heard a car horn beep and the back door slam. Paul's and Lyra's Sunday daily ritual was in effect. Coffee, bagels, tennis, Episcopal service at five. Check, check, check.

Footsteps on the stairs. Paul's cheerful, nervous voice. "We're off." When I didn't respond, he said, "Our daughter said you were acting weird. Does that mean she's being a weird teenager?"

"I have a migraine."

"What can I do?" He closed the curtains, and the room darkened. "Pills?"

"I'm all set. Go on with Lyra. I'll be okay by the time you return."

The door closed softly behind him. All was silent except for the shriek of blue jays. What if I had told Paul, I wondered. What if I had fucking told him the night he returned from that business trip sixteen years ago? My secret had backfired, the distance between the people I loved so desperately widening when I thought it would be the opposite. As for Lyra, we were so intricately bound that I thought if she stopped breathing, I would, too. I held onto the secret for her, didn't I? What would I have said to her? You were conceived in violence. You will be an open wound for the rest of your life, my darling. Sighing, I got up. I had to destroy the newspaper.

Entering the kitchen, I saw that the paper was spread open to the photograph of Jonathan Starkweather. Circled in red. Lyra had not only seen the article, but she was intrigued. I poured another cup of coffee and began to read. It was worse than I feared. Jonathan's controversial dance troupe was shifting its base to a town a few miles away in Connecticut, where the founders started the company. They were adding an educational component and welcoming young students. I took the paper to my studio and buried it in a filing cabinet drawer, stuffing it down into a dark interior the way I had stuffed the rape into a deep cavern of my psyche. I pounded the desk with my fist. This was unfair! What God, if God existed, would bring a monster back into my life, threatening not only me, but my daughter and my marriage?

Slipping into rubber boots, I marched out the back door to the gardening shed and picked up a shovel, then walked to the perennial bed closest to the house and stabbed the ground with it.

35

It took a couple of days for me to stop the panic that threatened to derail me. I worried about what his arrival would do to me, but that was nothing compared to the worry I felt for Lyra. The secret was choking me now. I had to take action.

I went into my studio and put all the typed pages into a manilla envelope. I took my time and filled the Mont Blanc pen that Ruthie had given me when I sold my first story. The evening I met Paul. I sat down and wrote a letter to my dearest friend, Ruth. I wrote her address on the manilla envelope. The time had come. Next, I called Abigail Levy, who told me she had a cancellation and that I could come to her at three. These two actions had calmed me enough to appear normal to Paul and Lyra.

Just being in the room with Abigail brought a sense of peace. She was relaxed and had on her listening face. I started with an apology for dropping out, but she stopped me.

"You are here now; that is what matters, Moira." She smiled, "What brought you back?"

"I'm falling apart."

"Because?"

"Jonathan Starkweather, the man who . . ."

"I know who he is."

"He and his board are moving their company to our county. He's going to be staying in the next town over."

I saw the alarm on her face, but she covered it immediately. "When?"

"They're planning an opening night event late summer." I pulled the newspaper article out and showed it to her. I put my finger on the section circled in red, and explained that morning. My voice was shaking.

"Okay, Moira. Let's think *actions* and not *reactions*."

"I sent my pages to Ruth this morning."

I told her about how I felt Ruth pulling away from me and how, now, all of a sudden, I didn't think I could manage without her.

"Bravo for sending her your story. What about Paul?"

"I'm waiting for Ruthie."

"But you're taking action. Your biggest fear right now in this room?"

"Jonathan will take Lyra from me. He'll learn her identity and claim her." When she didn't respond, I said, "It's as though my secret has developed a life of its own and that offshoots are spiraling out from it and I can't contain them. I want to gather them up and stuff them back into the container, but I don't know where to begin."

"Explain."

"Jonathan coming here of all places. Lyra's boyfriend saying he's going with a modern dance company. I have an awful feeling it's Jonathan's company."

"But nothing has happened yet. Besides, it is rare for a rapist to want to claim an offspring."

"You're right. Nothing yet. I was jumping into the future."

"Anything else?"

"My friend Mickey called me yesterday and said she thought she might apply to work for Portobello. That freaked me out."

"The article created a bit of a stir in town, right?"

I nodded. "You're right. It's normal for Mickey to want to connect. She's bored a lot of the time."

"Why have these worries if she's a friend?"

"A sixth sense. She has this kind of obsession with Lyra. She talks about how she always wanted a daughter. She has a fantasy about what it would be like, and now, she's fixated on Lyra. She gave her an absurdly expensive necklace for her birthday."

"And how does Lyra feel about her?'

"Oh, at first she didn't like her, but now she likes the attention. She's sixteen, after all."

"She's going to have a great deal of this projection and fandom in her future, you know. I think you will have to prepare yourself for it."

"I know. The truth is, we won't be here by the time Jonathan arrives. We will have moved to Manhattan."

"That may, or may not be, a solution. You know that."

"This was the plan before the article came out. No confrontation if we're not here."

Abigail's face was neutral when she replied. "And maybe no confrontation if you *are* here. See what I mean? Your imagination has these forces coming at you, but nothing has occurred so far. Do you worry about becoming complacent?"

"Yes."

"There will be more articles coming out on Jonathan Starkweather and his arrival. Ruth will know, and that will shift things. You hope to have her support."

"Why would she not support me?"

"The possibility exists that she will feel betrayed. You lied to her."

"She will understand."

Abigail was frowning. "And, of course, Paul must know soon. Ruth will know, after all. What Portobello's move here is doing is forcing your hand, wouldn't you say? That might be where the source of your panic lies."

"Yes."

"You and Paul can decide when to tell Lyra. I don't usually do this, but I think as hard as the truth is, both you and Paul will find relief in the telling."

"I agree."

"I have not seen your pages, but my hunch is you have managed to transcend the incident of the attack and carry the story into the universal. Women will need to come forward in large numbers to create a voice that is listened to. Yours might be one of them."

"Maybe one day."

"Continue writing, Moira."

"You mentioned antidepressants last year."

"I can prescribe a low dose of Prozac. But if I do, you need to commit to checking in once a week, at least until we know we have found a balance."

"Agreed."

I left her office fortified. But in the depths of my being, I felt a tremble, the tiniest seismic shift in my solar plexus.

36

RUTH

36

Consider me a Greek chorus of one. So. I'm reading the pages Moira sent me. I knew something had happened that weekend in 1979. I should have guessed. That little lady in her apartment building describing a man who knocked on her door looking for Moira. But Moira had been adamant that the old lady had the wrong woman. Moira was right. If she had told me back then, I would have gone after Jonathan Starkweather, and when I finished with him, I'd have gone after that rat-faced girl, Erin. I would have tried to get my best friend justice one way or another, even if it meant hiring somebody to break Jonathan's knees. I felt pretty invincible back then.

At the same time, had it been me he targeted I wouldn't have stood a chance either. Not once he was in the apartment. He was too strong. What I couldn't let go of was the rape was premeditated. The little fucker—the college grad, the dancer, the sociopath—got his jollies by assaulting women. Pedophiles rarely made it through the prison system because it was the one crime that inmates thought intolerable. *Why couldn't they extend that compassion to women?* I wondered.

Because of men. They clung to the fantasy of the ravishment of women by men, the Scarlett O'Hara from *Gone with the Wind.* What would never get fed to men in a hundred years was that most of them were lousy lovers, meaning they were selfish as hell. I had slept with enough men to know that plenty of them had no idea what to do with a woman. But women played the game, too, pretending to have an orgasm or pretending to like being molested by their partner.

Back to the assault on Moira. Erin Charles was an accessory to the crime. And now her book was being released by a reputable publishing house about her own rape when she was twelve, an innocent girl bicycling home on a country lane. I read it in one sitting. And there, on page 76, was the apology. To her friends, the women her boyfriend, Jonathan Starkweather, attacked. After which she moved on. She claimed she never saw him again after Moira confronted her. I have my doubts.

At least, I thought, change is happening in the publishing industry, and for that, I wanted to shout Erin's praises. A famous publishing house had published a book about rape. I wanted the world to understand how damaging it was to the psyche. I wanted women to step forward and get help. I wanted film producers to stop romanticizing it. It would become my cause, in the name of my mother. She was a witness to my close call with a boy.

I could summon the memory in a half second. I was fourteen. A virgin. I went to visit my friend Esther. I knocked and entered and called her name. Her brother Antonio ran down the stairs, and said, "She's in her room. Come on up."

I hesitated, but when I got to the landing, he pulled me into his room and locked the door. He started kissing me, then pushed me down on his bed, but then, Esther pounded on the door, and he jumped off me.

"Look who's here," he said, as I tried to pull my clothes together.

"Ruth?" she asked, wide eyed.

I pushed past them both and ran down the stairs. When I got home, I told my mother, who marched over to the house and let loose a stream of invectives that shattered the neighborhood. We never spoke to anyone in that family again, and the next year, they moved away.

Stella said at dinner that night, "There is evil in this world, and you got a taste of it. I am going to pursue this and get justice for you." My father's solution was to sign me up for karate every Thursday night.

I picked up the last of Moira's pages, which was her euphemism for manuscript. It wasn't finished, but I was a pro, and it had the markings of success.

I went back to the night of Moira's rape again. How unusual that both Paul and I were out of town on the same weekend. Alone, Moira created a cocktail of self-blame and self-punishment, shame, fear, and rage.

As I finished her manuscript, I began to cry. Hard. I opened my dresser drawer and pulled out the stash of photographs. Moira and me on the Staten Island ferry. Us on the Ferris wheel on Coney Island. Moira lying on a couch in our apartment as she edited a book—feet up, big smile. Holding hands with Paul and walking in Central Park. The four of us in front of our favorite restaurant in the village. How handsome Seamus was. Big brown crinkly eyes. Broad-shouldered. I looked pretty good, too. I recalled our last argument. He wanted kids. I wanted success. Jesus.

I got up and dug around for a chocolate bar and ate it. I called Moira the next morning and announced. "I'm coming up."

"Oh, Ruthie. I need you."

I stopped at Zabar's and picked up some staples—bagels, cream cheeses, and smoked salmon. On the bus, I took out my notebook, and wrote, *I feel like I'm on a mission to change the direction of a hurricane, but where is the eye of the storm?*

I was aware that I needed Moira. After Stella's death, I couldn't seem to ward off the loneliness that hovered over me like a cloud. The therapist I went to said it was part of the grief process, and that I needed time. It was grief, but not just for Stella. I realize now that grief covers a lot of emotional territory. I grieved Seamus, and later, I grieved Moira. I, too, had pulled away, finding her life with husband and child something to envy, all the while being snarky about it. As for Jonathan Starkweather, who I started this writing about, I wasn't done with that. Nothing got my goat more than somebody getting away with something. And that asshole thought he had.

Moira was waiting on the train station platform. Make-up free and dressed in jeans and T-shirt. Gorgeous. I grabbed my weekend bag and stepped out of the train and into her arms, opened wide.

"It's been forever," she whispered. Lyra rushed up and hugged me. She seemed so grown up. Lithe and luminescent. She reached up and pushed the hair away from her face, and I saw pure innocence.

Halifax was a still a charming town. The inn at the corner, the central square, the small shops. I could see why Moira felt safe here. But safety, like most things, is an illusion. Moira clicked a button, and the trunk of a BMW popped open. And when she turned on the car, Alanis Morrissette's "Jagged Little Pill" came on the radio. We drove down a street lined with elm trees and forsythia until we reached the gingerbread house that sat on a knoll. "It's like a house in a fairy tale," I said.

"Fairytales can be little horror stories," Moira replied.

"I thought the underlying message was to teach kids how to overcome obstacles."

It was good to see her laugh. The house was warm and elegant. I had liked it from the first time I saw it. High ceilings, wainscoting, a lot of chintz, gorgeous sun porch. And outside, gardens creating a paradise. Lyra ran up to ask Moira if she could go hang out with friends, and Moira gave her a kiss and told her to be back in two hours.

Moira built a fire then took a bottle of white wine from the refrigerator. It was just five o'clock. I had never understood the appeal of alcohol. I didn't know if it was because my parents didn't drink, or maybe I never had more than a glass with dinner. But what the hell. I held out my glass.

"The story is wrenching. I'm so sorry, Moira."

"I regretted not telling you right off. But once the secret was locked in, I built my life around it. To confide in anyone was more than I could bear. I worried about losing Lyra and Paul."

"You've been walking a tightrope. I get it. But I won't deny that you hurt me with your lack of trust."

"I'm sorry, Ruthie. Deeply."

That was all I needed. I shifted into professional mode. "Your writing is powerful. I hope you know that. It has the potential to become a book."

"It's not just my story, Ruthie. I can't risk harming my family, and I doubt anyone wants to read about rape, anyhow".

"I still wonder if anyone wants to read about rape."

"It's not about rape, Moira. It's about love."

"Thank you."

We sat in comfortable silence for a moment. Then I remembered Erin's book. "You must know that your old friend, Erin, has a book coming out. I got an advance copy." I reached into my tote bag and handed it to her.

She sat reading the jacket copy, then turned to me. "Is it any good?"

"I hate to say it, but yes. I put a bookmark on the apology page."

She read the paragraph and looked up. " This could have saved me back then. Just her acknowledging what happened would have given me courage. Her so-called apology has come too late to make a difference. Did you know the statute of limitations for a rapist in New York is five years?"

"I had an idea, Moira. What if we had a private investigator tail Jonathan Starkweather? It turns out he's had a couple of complaints filed against him, one a dancer who left his company. She's twenty-two now. Of course he's denied it. But these things eventually come out."

"How did you find that out?"

"I have a friend in the dance world. I've just gotten started with my own investigation, by the way. Have you told Paul?"

"I'm going to."

"I'll stand by you."

"I worry that he won't believe me."

"A risk you have to take. I hope he doesn't come up with what my friend Donna's boyfriend said when she told him about her rape. He wondered if it really was impossible to break away from a guy who weighed 80 pounds more than she did. She dumped him, needless to say."

"You know, Ruthie, before that night, I was a happy, confident woman."

"I was there. You must hate his guts."

"I hate what happened to me. I wish he could be arrested and go through the shame, fear, and depression that I've experienced."

"Moira, you don't know what will be unleashed if you ever allow this book to appear. You could open the door for many women to follow and open up about their experiences."

She said, "I'm not ready yet. But I do know I can't continue showing a fake and happy life anymore."

She got up and thumbed through her collection of CD's and slipped one into the player. Leonard Cohen came on singing from his 1992 album, *The Future:* "There is a crack in everything . . . That's where the light gets in . . . do not dwell on what has passed away, or what is yet to be."

I went to her, and we embraced each other, our hearts beating against each other. We were crying too hard to speak.

37

The following morning, I lay in bed listening to the sounds of Moira's house. A door closing. Lyra running down the stairs and shouting goodbye. The telephone ringing and Moira answering in a cheerful voice. I put on a robe and went downstairs.

Moira stood looking out the window, a cup of coffee in her hand. "Mickey wants us to go with her to the shooting range."

"Shit. I don't know if I can. You're still doing that?"

"I haven't been in months, but I figured you're going to have to meet her. This is on her territory, and I have to say, different."

"Okay. I'll go. Don't forget I was with a gunslinger once."

She laughed.

A horn blared, and when we peered out Mickey waved from her van. She got out as we approached. She was wearing a white running suit, her hair the length of Moira's but lacking the luster, large dangling earrings attached to her earlobes. A toothy smile with electric blue eyes above it. "I can't believe I'm finally meeting you," she gushed. "I love every book you've sold."

"Thank you."

"I have a manuscript that could top the best seller list. Kind of a *Liars' Club* meets *Bridget Jones' Diary*."

"That's a strange cocktail," I said, and she burst into laughter.

"Hop in," she said. It was like watching a light bulb turning on and off. I sensed she was unstable. Something in the eyes darting about, landing on Moira, then back to me. Needing affirmation.

Before we could pull away, Lyra and Luc drove in, with Luc at the wheel. Lyra got out and came over to the van. "Hey, baby," Mickey said. "How was rehearsal?"

"Fine. Hey, Mom, we just got the news. Luc's going to dance with Jonathan Starkweather's company, Portobello."

Moira barely blinked, but I sensed the shock waves vibrating through her.

"That's nice," she finally said. But I could see her body going into rigor mortis. They waved us off, and Mickey peeled out. Mickey said she was thinking about applying for a job with Portobello, too, then went on about a different topic. Even I was starting to feel nauseous. Too much convergence going on.

"My train is at five," I said to Mickey, and she said, "No problem."

She turned up the song "Imagine" that had taken over the country and lit a Camel Light cigarette. She pulled into a small restaurant that advertised 'best hamburger in town' and parked. I gave Moira a questioning look, but she sat like a zombie. We went inside and placed our orders. Moira said she wasn't hungry, but I ordered her a hamburger.

We went to a table, and I asked Mickey, "When is Portobello opening its doors?"

"I hear they're coming late summer. There's a lot of buzz around it."

"Why?"

"They're cutting edge."

"Used to be."

"What do you mean?"

She lit a cigarette, and I coughed. I hadn't said anything in the car, but I couldn't bear the smoke now that I had quit. She smooshed it in the ashtray. "What I mean is their popularity is waning, which is why they're moving out of the city and started an educational program. The three directors are at odds and the one woman among them has left the company."

"How do you know all this?"

"Curiosity."

"Still, it's quite a coup for this area to have them open up shop here."

"Have you ever been to one of their performances?" I asked.

"Once in person. It was pretty cool the way they formed sculptures with their bodies. I've seen them on TV commercials. You?"

I said, "I saw them in person and thought their themes violent, their nudity boring. I know they had their fan base, but their shock value has diminished."

Moira listened, not touching her hamburger. Mickey didn't seem to notice. I could read Moira's mind. With Luc signing on to dance for Portabella, chances were great that Lyra would at the least be introduced to the company.

Moira spoke softly, "I wouldn't want Lyra anywhere near them."

"I can't believe how negative you two are. I thought the director was hot, and I'm going to try them out. It'll get my mind off my health."

"What's going on?"

"They're doing tests on me."

Moira came to attention. "For what?"

"Cancer. What else?"

"Gosh, Mickey," Moira said, "You hadn't said anything."

"I mentioned it to you a few months ago. Pains in my stomach at night? They said my gall bladder is enlarged, but that's not so uncommon. I'm not that worried."

She waited for Moira to pick up the check and then led us to the gun range that was a concrete one-story building.

We walked into Marv's Gun Shop, which housed an arsenal big enough to take down a whole country. Mickey was high-fiving customers. They ran the socioeconomic gamut from the cliché of women strutting around in big hair and wind suits and men with bellies lopped over their pants to coiffed women reeking of Joy perfume and men in Armani shirts. *Welcome to America,* I thought.

Mickey pulled a Glock .23 from her handbag as she sauntered to the counter to rent a gun and other paraphernalia for me. Shit.

Seamus had carried a gun everywhere, but I was never interested enough to learn about shooting, nor did he ever bring it up. I glanced at Moira who shrugged as if to say, 'Just go along with it.'

The range master, basically the man in charge, came up and spoke to Mickey, then Moira. "You haven't been coming around as much," he said to Moira, who said she'd been spending a lot of time away. He shook hands with me when Mickey introduced us, not hiding the fact that he was assessing me from head to toe, which gave me a second to observe him. Stocky, wide shoulders, crew cut, thin lips that I thought didn't smile much, and eyes I couldn't read.

"It's my first time," I said, "and I'm not sure I want a lesson. I'd rather observe."

"You might as well gear up," he said. "Once your buddies here start shooting, you might change your mind."

I acquiesced and put in ear plugs and slipped on plastic glasses and headphones. Twenty lanes ran parallel, which reminded me of a bowling alley. The spaces allotted for each shooter were separated by plexiglass dividers. Around ten shooters stood in position, several of them women.

The unloaded pistol I held was heavier than I had imagined. I stood next to Moira, and Mickey went into the booth beside us. The target in front of us, which seemed a football field away, was according to Mickey, twenty-five yards. It was the silhouette of a person, the face blank, a red circle in the middle the bull's eye.

"I'll set you up later for ten yards if you want to shoot," she said to me. She stepped forward and shot what I thought must be twenty rounds, all bullets but one hitting the target.

When she stopped, I followed suit and lifted my headphones. "Way to go, Lefty," a familiar said. The voice I still heard in my dreams. Seamus.

I turned and saw him through the divider. He and another guy walked around to where Mickey stood, looking pleased with herself. The guy with him said with a hint of a southern drawl, "It's old Thelma and Louise. How you doing, Louise?"

Mickey looked up at him like a woman in love.

Moira gave a little wave, then looked at me. Seamus followed her gaze. He looked fish-eyed behind the goggles. The shock on his face was almost worth the humiliation I felt standing in this place. He was squinting in disbelief.

I removed the protective glasses and said, "Hello, Seamus."

"What the hell are you doing here?" he asked.

"In this town, or at a gun range?"

Mickey stepped between us. "You two know each other?"

"We used to," I said.

"This woman and I have some catching up to do," he said to Moira and Mickey. Come on."

He took my arm and led me back out into the lobby and out the front door. He smiled, and I felt a whirring in my brain. The twinkling eyes, the dimples.

"You've been living up here all these years?" I asked. "I heard you married."

"Yep. I got married to my high school sweetheart, but she died two years ago."

"The woman your mother preferred over me."

He ignored the retort. "I've got a girl named Sadie who's eight."

"I hadn't heard. I'm sorry."

"Thanks. It's been hard."

"You're an officer?"

"I've upgraded. I'm a . . . you won't believe it . . . a forensic psychologist."

"I'm actually impressed. Not that I know that much about it."

He smiled, and there were the dimples. "It's new enough for people to be skeptical. We get used a lot in the courtroom."

"So give me a profile of Lefty. The short version."

We glanced simultaneously into the building when we heard someone laughing. Mickey and Moira were standing together, and Mickey was talking, her hands gesticulating wildly.

Seamus hesitated, wondering if I was serious. "I wouldn't have put those two together, but what do I know? I knew Moira had moved up this way, but we never connected. I figured she hated me for the way I treated you." I could tell he was being cautious. "Mickey's okay. She drinks too much and runs her mouth when she shouldn't. She's a damn good shot, I'll give her that." He seemed to be debating with himself, then asked, "You married?"

"No. Never had the time. Or the inclination."

He laughed. He walked towards a big pick-up truck. "I'm sorry, but I have to pick up Sadie. You're a big success, I hear."

"Everything's relative."

"What about your mom?"

"She died a while back."

"I'm sorry. A great dame."

"She was."

Moira and Mickey came out of the building. "We need to get you back to the house if we're going to get you on the five o'clock," Moira said.

Mickey smiled up at Seamus. "I've got a competition coming up next week. How about coming with me?" The tension was awkward.

"I can't, Lefty. But good luck."

"I'll give you a raincheck."

He looked at me. "I'll see you around, I guess."

I nodded.

We got into Mickey's van.

She waved at Seamus and said, "Every woman in town wants a piece of him. Including me." I sulked in the back seat. Moira turned to give me a reassuring smile. Mickey rattled on. "What're the chances of that happening? Everything overlapping. What's the word for it?"

"Coincidence," I said.

Moira said, "Or synchronicity." I knew where she was heading. The Jungian definition of synchronicity as divine intervention, or something coming exactly when you need it. That's what she would say about Seamus turning up. But the Portobello overlap would have a darker connotation.

Before I could respond, Mickey said, "Don't get your hopes up over Seamus. Word is he hasn't been out with anyone since his wife died."

Neither Moira nor I spoke.

Mickey dropped us off at Moira's. Paul offered to take me to the train station as Moira had to take Lyra to dance class. Lyra ran up and gave me a hug. "Look, you," I said. "I'll be there for you in New York. Lox and bagels every Sunday, right?"

"I can't wait."

Paul took the opportunity of us being alone to ask me how I thought Moira was doing, and I tried to dodge answering, but then he said, "Something's going on. She's been snapping at Lyra and now doesn't want Luc around."

My chest felt tight with secrets and my own anxiety about bumping into Seamus. I would tell Moira that she could not delay telling Paul everything. Too much seemed to be happening at once: the article in *The New York Times* on Jonathan Starkweather. Luc announcing his plan to join Portobello when they arrived in town. My meeting up with Seamus. Somewhere in the middle of it all sat Mickey, though she had done nothing as far as anyone could see. It wasn't unusual for someone like her to mirror another, in this case, Moira, but it wasn't a crime. The thing that was bothering me on the train home was that this was less about synchronicity and something more negative. I tried to whittle down the collision theory I had studied in chemistry, but it had been too long.

Yet I did perceive that a collision was in the making

38

The telephone was ringing as I entered my apartment. I ran to pick it up.

"You sound out of breath."

"Seamus."

"I timed it just right. I'm coming down for dinner tomorrow night. And I'm hanging up before you tell me not to."

My hand was shaking when I put the phone down. I went back to the hall for my tote bag I had dropped when I heard the phone ringing. I wasn't ready, but what could I do? If I canceled, that might be it.

The following morning, I called my assistant and told her I wasn't coming in and I didn't want to be disturbed. After a five second pause she asked me if I was alright. "I'm great!" I said. Another five second pause before we hung up.

I went to Lord and Taylor's and charged a knee-length blue dress and a pair of earrings. I didn't have time to transform myself, and even if I did, where would I start? I stopped for a pedicure near my apartment building but didn't have the patience to sit while the polish dried. I rushed home and called Moira and told her what was happening, and she said I had to go through with it. She laughed. And yes, she said, she had been despondent and kept reminding herself that she would be gone before Jonathan Starkweather arrived. Or at least she hoped that was the case. Our conversation went on for half an hour, until we circled back around to Seamus coming to the city to see me. I said I'd call her after he left.

When the doorman announced a visitor, I felt like I was having a heart attack as I counted off the seconds: ten waiting for him to board the elevator, ten to zoom up forty-five stories, three to exit the elevator, three to look around for the apartment number. I opened the door. He took long strides to me, lifted me up, and kissed me full on the mouth. Within ten minutes, we were in bed, his fragrance, the heat of his skin familiar to the point that I wanted to cry. I had loved him so long.

"We need to talk," I said as I bustled around the kitchen making coffee the following morning.

"I went to my mom after I saw you and she told me to come and declare myself and start a life. You'll meet Sadie soon. I think you two will hit it off," he said.

"I thought your mother didn't like me."

"I never said that. You made up your mind that an Irish lady could never like a Jewish girl, if I recall correctly."

"Oh. I don't recall you ever being this spontaneous,' I said. "A little out of character."

"My wife Elizabeth's death taught me a lot about living in the moment. She was heroic throughout."

"How are you doing now?"

"I didn't go off the rails after she died the way I did in New York with you. Having Sadie helps. I miss Elizabeth and always will, but she would have encouraged me to start a new life. She knew about you, by the way."

"I regretted kicking you out of my life."

"I deserved it. I was suffering from PTSD. We know a lot more about it now. I'm game to staying quiet about us until we see how this goes."

But it was hard to stay quiet because we soon realized we were deeply in love and willing to make compromises in order to be together. After a month, he introduced me to Sadie, a red-haired ten-year-old with freckles and a serious demeanor, which Seamus said became more serious after her mother fell ill. She called me Ruth when she called me anything. We talked books mostly, as she was well read. Eventually I moved a few of my things in, though I was commuting between New York and Waterbury, Connecticut, where Seamus had a small three-bedroom house. I hoped that in the future he would allow me to purchase a bigger house closer to Moira and Paul.

The summer of '97 was unusually cool, but on August 23rd, the day of Pauls' fiftieth birthday celebration, it climbed to ninety degrees. Seamus and I arrived early in case Moira needed help, but she had hired a caterer and looked unusually beautiful in a white sundress that displayed a perfect tan. She also seemed unruffled. She proudly showed me around the gardens, pointing out her favorite 'English Rose" named Desdemona that was in a bed filled with other roses. A section of the yard was overflowing with daylilies in a myriad of colors, and off in a meadow the sunflowers were beaming. Various boundaries were marked by hedges. The setting was sublime.

It only took me a moment to realize that Moira needed to confide in me. "Ruthie, we might not have another chance to be together before Pauls' dinner. I want you to promise me something."

"Sure. Anything."

"If anything happens to me, I need you to be there for Lyra."

"But you're not going anywhere."

"I don't plan to. I had a dream last night, though, and I can't get it off my mind. I was at a pier. I remember I was supposed to be joining my family on a boat. I walked to the end of the pier and waited. I waited a long time, and I stared out to sea, worried, wondering what had happened. And way in the distance, I saw the lights of the boat, and in seconds, they went out, and all before me was a black void.

"Oh, Moira . . ."

"And I stood there, feeling this incredible abandonment. Feeling utterly alone. I woke up with tears running down my cheeks."

I reached over and embraced her, not knowing what to say. "Maybe it has to do with your resistance to telling Paul about what happened."

"Maybe. Or, maybe the boat is carrying the secret far away to the unknown, and my soul feels unmoored."

"It would take a writer to come up with that one. Sheesh." Moira laughed. "But no matter, I am the godmother to your daughter and will always be there for her. And nothing is going to happen to you because if it did, I probably wouldn't survive, and then Lyra wouldn't have either of us, and that would be a tragedy because we're what every girl needs in this crazy world."

She threw her arms around me. "I had to hear it. She's being a pill, by the way. Stephanie's daughter, Alison, has her driver's license now and is constantly calling and wanting Lyra to join her. On top of that, Alison wants to take a dance class with Portobello when they open their doors."

"What the hell?"

"And Luc is there, too. It's a good thing that Lyra's due in New York next month."

"What's your cowgirl up to?" I asked.

Moira laughed. "Mickey's coming to dinner this evening with Tom. She's been on her best behavior, I have to say. She's mad at the doctors who keep sending her around to various specialists and no one coming up with anything."

"She's probably fine. You seem unusually calm, by the way."

"Blame it on Prozac and wine."

I didn't laugh. "Seriously?"

Paul came bounding towards us, calling Moira's name. "You two disappeared on me. Guests are arriving." He took Moira's hand, "Did I tell you that you have never looked more beautiful?"

"Three times." She smiled up at him, and I agreed with Paul. She had never looked more beautiful, even with all the stress in her life.

Seamus met us halfway up the path to the house and put his arm around me. It was a moment I wanted to memorize: me in love again with the man I had sent away; Moira all in white, holding Paul's hand; Lyra coming towards us and taking her mother's hand.

By nine, the air had cooled a bit. We were gathered out on the terrace at a large round table—Katherine and Russell, Paul and Moira, Ed and Carol, Mickey and Tom, Stephanie and her husband Phil, and Seamus and me. Lyra was there with Luc, and Stephanie's daughter, Alison, sat beside them. An incongruous group, I thought, slightly fascinated because I had learned all their stories from Moira's pages.

Moira toasted Paul, and she and Lyra presented him with a new set of golf clubs. He and Seamus talked a long while about politics, as Paul was caught up in the war in the Balkans and writing essays about it for a couple of magazines.

Katherine said, "Paul and Moira are the ones who have kept our paper going, though not always in the direction Russ and I would have chosen." Everyone laughed. I was sure that even if Moira decided finally not to allow me to sell her manuscript, she still had a novel or two in her.

I noticed out of the corner of my eye Lyra moving over to Mickey and wondered what that was about. Mickey had arrived in a red sundress and stilettos. She had lost weight since I had seen her and tonight looked quite stunning. She was sweet with Seamus and me. A completely different persona than what she had displayed at the gun range. Tom and Seamus talked shop about guns, and later Seamus mentioned that he was impressed with his knowledge. I felt a tiny surge of compassion for Mickey as I watched her with her husband in a wheelchair. He was snappish with her, but she ignored him and continued telling Carole stories that seemed a little too fantastical to be true, but Carol was listening with her full attention, and giggling. Ed was drunk, his eyes glassy, but no one seemed bothered.

Mickey dinged her glass, stood, and beckoned Lyra to join her. Everyone stopped talking and looked up at her.

"I'll get right to the point," she said. "I managed to secure a part-time job with the Portobello Dance Company, helping with their press releases and acting as a Girl Friday."

A quick glance in Moira's direction told me she was unaware of this news.

Mickey continued, "As most of you know, Luc was invited to join the company." A couple of guests applauded lightly. "And . . . ta dum . . . as a surprise, I arranged for Lyra and Luc to share the stage for the last time before she goes to New York. They will dance on Portobello's opening night."

Moira's mouth dropped open. She looked distraught.

Paul was smiling. "Don't keep us in suspense. Will they dance ballet?"

It was obvious to me he didn't have a clue about the dark web forming around him.

"No," Mickey said. "One of the directors, Jonathan Starkweather, will choreograph a contemporary dance for them. The whole town will come out for it. A great welcome for Portobello."

Paul said, "But Lyra doesn't know contemporary dance."

Lyra laughed. "Dad. I can dance modern." Lyra looked across the table at her mother, who had stood, looking like she was carved in granite, her face tormented.

"No!" Moira yelled. "I won't allow it."

Luc stood to face her. "If you're worried about the rumors about him, don't believe them."

"Mommy," Lyra said. "It's one dance. Luc can't do it without me."

Moira's face grew feral. Dangerous. I had never seen the expression before. I looked over at Paul and saw that he was beginning to resemble his friend Ed. No one was sober, I realized, except Seamus and me.

Katherine, ever the controller, said, "Moira, dear, she's right. It's one dance."

Mickey interjected, "For god's sake, Moira. You're being ridiculous . . ."

Everything after that happened in slow motion. Moira raised her right arm, a glass of wine in her hand. She hurled the contents of the glass at Mickey, then threw the glass across the patio.

"NO! she screamed. "I said no!" She pushed away from the table and stormed across the yard into the house.

We all sat stunned. Silent.

Paul's jaw was clenched. "I'll be back," I whispered to Seamus, then went to find Moira. I noticed a light on at the end of the hall and opened the door leading to the attic. Great heaving sobs carried down to me.

"Moira?" I went up. She was curled up on an old sofa. Drunk. I walked over and sat down beside her. "What is it?"

"Ever since that newspaper article with Jonathan's eyes staring out at me, I've barely been able to function. My biggest fear has always been that he will find out about Lyra being his biological child."

"How could he know? You never told Mickey, did you?"

"Oh God no."

"You have to get Paul on board."

"I've been feeling paranoid, as though shadows were dancing behind my back."

"My guess is Mickey was trying to impress Jonathan Starkweather by luring Lyra in to dance with Luc. Nothing more to it than that."

We heard voices below. Paul saying good-night to Lyra, then a door opening and closing. "Paul will be passed out in five minutes," Moira said. "He has to be furious."

I sighed. "He was drunk, too."

"We all drank too much."

"Please don't do anything foolish, Moira," I said. "There is a way out of this."

"All I'll say is there is no way Lyra is going to dance for Portobello." She sighed. "You need to go and be with Seamus."

"Can I tell him what's going on?"

She leaned her head back against the cushion. "Do whatever you want."

I paused before going down the stairs. "There's a chance Seamus can help. His career revolves around profiling people. And he has spent time around Mickey."

"I wish I had never met her."

In the upstairs hallway, I passed Lyra's room, then stopped and went back. She was on her side, holding the little Steiff bear that I had given her on her second birthday. Moonlight splayed across the room, bathing her face in its soft glow. Lyra was theirs, Moira's and Paul's. I had no doubt that the two of them would know how to protect her. The only thing that remained was for her to know the truth.

I crossed the lawn to see my future husband sitting quietly in the moonlight.

"Seamus, I have a story to tell you."

"Now?"

"It can't wait."

"Come here," he said, and I went and sat in his lap.

I talked for an hour.

When I was done, he said, "I'm as guilty as the next cop on the street of not taking women like Moira seriously. I think she'd be forever fucked up if she had gone to the hospital and tried to report it that night. I used to cringe when victims came into the station, pleading for us to find the guy who 'did it.' And we'd tell them to go home and we'd find them. The rape kits stayed on a shelf, and we never pursued the perps. Jonathan may have stopped for a while, but that kind of sickness never goes away."

"We're in an emergency. I'm worried that Moira will do something impulsive."

"Like what?"

"Like confront Jonathan."

"I don't think she will. If my psychology 101 teacher was right, she's still afraid of him. The important thing is for Moira and Paul to stand together. I can have one of my buddies do a check on Starkweather. There's more than one victim, I'm sure of it." He took my hand. "Let's go home. Sadie's asleep in the car."

Once we had tucked her into her bed, Seamus said, "Let's get married today."

"Today?"

He laughed. "That's what I said."

"Okay. I'd better get my beauty rest."

He put his arm around me, and I nestled in.

39

I woke up the day of my wedding in our modest little house and heard Seamus in the kitchen, rustling around. In a few minutes, he entered our room with a mug filled with coffee.

"For my bride," he said, setting it down on the night table, then leaning over to kiss me

"I guess we're not doing the 'bad luck to see the bride before her wedding' thing."

He laughed. "You want a paper bag to put over your head? Or I can make a mask so you can sip your coffee."

"A little late for all that. I love you."

He sat in the wingback chair holding his giant mug of coffee. "I was in the kitchen thinking how lucky I am you walked back into my life. What were the chances of that happening?"

"Low."

A smile flickered across his face and was gone. "Between losing you the first time, and then Elizabeth to cancer, I made up my mind to focus on Sadie and avoid being in another relationship. But that day at the gun range, I turned, and there you were. It was like something was telling me, 'You got some unfinished business here, Seamus.' I know I'm not very eloquent, but what I'm trying to say is it felt like a miracle seeing you."

"Oh, Seamus, for me, too."

A tower of grace moved towards me, and I took the man I loved into my arms, and he picked me up and carried me to our bed. I saved my happy tears for the shower. Or maybe my combo tears. My private moment of grieving the death of my mother and a silent prayer of gratitude to her spirit for pulling the strings that brought Seamus and me back together, and for deepening Moira's and my friendship. None of us were who we were before. Grief had pummeled us, and we were finding our way.

I called Moira, who picked up instantly. "You okay?" I asked.

Her voice was low. "Yes. Paul hasn't come down yet."

"Seamus and I are getting married this afternoon. It's probably too much to ask you to be a witness? We're going to the courthouse in an hour."

"I'm hung over, but of course I'll come. Paul might come, too."

"Sure. We'll have Sadie with us."

I went into the kitchen where Seamus and Sadie sat having breakfast. "Dad told me."

"Are you alright with it?"

"Yep. I knew last week he was going to propose."

I looked over at him, and he winked. "So you knew before I did. Thank you for saying yes."

"Lyra said last night that I should start calling you mom."

"I would be honored, Sadie." She put her hand in mine and asked if she could wear the new blue dress I had bought her. "Let's go find it, then," I said.

Holding her hand made me understand keenly the bond between mothers and daughters. Between Moira and Lyra. Between my mother and me. Her little hand in mine brought another spurt of tears, and I apologized to her.

"I know about tears," she said with a serious face.

Moira and Paul were right on time. Moira explained that Katherine had come for Lyra and would keep her overnight. I was surprised to see Paul, but then remembered he was a dutiful man. He would do the right thing whether he wanted to or not. I could feel leftover tension between them, but I tried to ignore it. Our ceremony lasted twenty minutes, and the five of us walked out. I had warned Seamus that if the opportunity came up for us to sit and talk together about Moira's past, we should take it. But when we suggested going back to our house, Paul said he couldn't, that he had made a plan to go into the city.

Moira showed surprise but didn't say anything. "Another time," she said, giving me a meaningful look.

We embraced, and Moira said she'd like to have a celebratory dinner in our honor the following week, and we said sure. Seamus and Sadie and I got into our car and decided to go to our favorite Italian restaurant for lunch.

Despite my concern about Moira, I was happier than I could ever remember being.

40

MOIRA

40

Paul and I were silent on the way home. I was deep in thought about the morning. The aftermath of my eruption last night.

I had a few moments with Lyra before Katherine picked her up.

"Mom," she had said, "I don't get why you're so upset about me dancing for Portobello."

"I wish I could explain what's going on, but first, I'm going to talk with your dad and then we will decide what is best for you."

"Luc can't do it without me!"

My voice was stern. "It's not going to be your decision."

"Luc said it's about Mr. Starkweather's reputation. That's why you don't want me dancing there."

I kept my voice level. "It's partly about that. And it's also about you going behind my back. I think you knew I'd say no."

"Not true!" But her face showed me it was. I dreaded asking, but had to. "Have you met Mr. Starkweather?"

"Yes. Luc worships him," she said. I knew she was avoiding telling me something. Her eyes darted around the room, then she changed the subject. "Can I meet Alison at the diner? Stephanie's giving her the car for a couple of hours."

I felt I should compromise. "Yes, I'll tell Beezie that you can go out for a hamburger. But you're not to go near Portobello. I mean it, Lyra."

"You're being a control freak, Mom."

I said gently, "I'm being a mother."

We heard the sound of a car horn, and Lyra ran out. I looked out the window and waved to Katherine, who gave a tight smile from her car, but I could see she had no plan to get out and speak to me. Fine.

Paul had come downstairs, put a Miles Davis CD into the player, and sat with his cup of coffee. I told him I was going to stand in as a witness for Ruth's marriage to Seamus in an hour and said he could come along or not.

"I'll go," he had said, and went up to change.

"Paul, we need to talk before we go anywhere."

"I'm furious about last night," Paul had said. "You had too much to drink. You were scary."

I had steeled myself. "Paul, Jonathan Starkweather raped me sixteen years ago. The week you were in Chicago."

His face grew flushed. He was more shocked than I had anticipated. "Jesus, Moira! And you didn't tell me?"

"I didn't tell anyone. I saw a lawyer. I knew I wouldn't stand a chance of being believed."

He was aghast. "You didn't think I'd believe you?"

"I can't explain how irrational I was after it happened," I said. " The shock."

"Moira, this is horrible. That was the week you wouldn't answer my phone calls. I suspected you then of being with somebody behind my back. I thought it was your boss, Larry Cohen."

"And you never felt like asking?"

"I went to France, remember?" he said. "And when I returned, you announced you were pregnant, and I figured at the time you were thinking, who can I bullshit into marrying me? Then, aha! There's gullible Paul who is like a trained seal. He will do what's expected of him. He'll even give up the woman he loves."

It took a moment for Paul's words to sink in. *The woman he loved.* He had bought the ring for Katia, after all. He had honored his promise to take me to Windows on the World, but he had come to say goodbye. I glanced up at him and saw that he regretted his confession.

"The ring wasn't for me?" I demanded.

"That's changing the subject."

"The ring in your pocket was for Katia?" I said.

"But I married you."

"Out of duty." I then slid the ring off my finger and put it on the table.

Then he said, his voice very low, "The next thing you're going to tell me is that Lyra is not mine, right?"

"I think you know. I saw your lab report years ago informing you that your sperm count was at zero."

"Shit, Moira. What a couple of liars we are. Our whole life has been a game of pretend. We should be ashamed of ourselves." He was standing when he said, "For the books, sperm counts can go up and down, and I have clung to the notion that mine was up when Lyra was conceived."

So, he hadn't known all these years as I had suspected.

"But the night you . . ."

"Lost it? Couldn't stop crying? I was devastated that we couldn't conceive again. I know how much you wanted another baby, too. Now I know why."

"Paul, I meant it when I said I loved you on the night before you took off for Chicago. Jonathan Starkweather was Erin's boyfriend. He called and begged me for a place to crash for one night. He assaulted me the minute he entered the apartment."

"You didn't call the police?"

"No. Women knew the hell they would be entering if they did. They didn't call the police or go to the hospital. They kept their mouths shut and they blamed themselves." I started to cry.

"But the pregnancy. Moira, you built a lie. Why?" Paul was staring hard at me.

"I couldn't go through with the abortion."

His eyes narrowed. "You're telling me that Lyra is Jonathan Starkweather's, right?

"She has his eyes. I never did a DNA test."

He threw his glass across the room, and it crashed against the fireplace.

"I'm sorry."

"After all these years, you're sorry. Great." He was pacing like a madman. "I don't think I can continue this charade, Moira. My final interview is in the city today, and I cannot cancel. My future is on the line. I'll come back for Lyra tomorrow. She's fine at my mom's for now."

"What about me?"

"You can have the apartment in the city. I'll figure out something for me."

"You're running away!"

"I'm not. I need a night. I can't take all this in right now." His hands were fists. "I'm sure Ruth knows." I nodded. "And that means Seamus knows?"

"Yes." I had hesitated. "I want us to tell Lyra together."

"No! I'm not ready for her to learn I'm not her dad. Give me some time."

I nodded.

In a barely audible voice, he said, "How do you know Starkweather doesn't know?"

"How would he?"

Paul scowled. "Mickey doesn't know, does she? Don't you find it odd that she went to work for him? And she was luring our daughter there under our very noses?"

"I don't suspect her of that. She knows nothing about what happened to me."

"Get you and Lyra packed up. I'm coming back tomorrow and will load up everything, and we'll move a week early."

I felt a rush of relief. As upset as he was, Paul was in charge. He picked up the keys off the table and went out the back door. The screen door slammed behind him. I was alone. And unburdened of the secret that had kept me so tightly bound up inside for years. And now Paul had to shoulder some of the burden and sort out his feelings. I went up to my room to begin packing up our clothes.

Two things he said were whirring around in my head: he had bought the ring for Katia, not me. And he didn't think he could stay with me now. I wasn't ready to let that happen. I was his wife, and I loved him. I carefully folded his two favorite shirts and placed them in the suitcase. I decided to call Ruth and let her know Paul's reaction, and I would go to Mickey and apologize for blowing up at her. Tomorrow would be the proverbial new day. A new chapter.

41

I called Ruth who said they had just returned from the restaurant. She and Seamus thought they would take a drive up north, perhaps to Vermont, for one night. Unless I needed her. I said no and then told her about Paul's and my discussion. "He says he won't stay with me," I said. "But he's going to get Lyra and me out of here."

"One step at a time. Give him the time he needs."

"I can't stop shaking."

"Don't drink, whatever you do. Can you call Stephanie?"

"Ruthie, I'm fine."

"You're sure?"

"Of course. You'll be back tomorrow."

"Absolutely. And you know you are welcome to my apartment if you need it. I don't think you will. Paul will be there for you. I know it."

We hung up, and the phone rang. I listened to my mother's worried voice. "Moira, honey, it's your daddy. He's got congestive heart failure, the doctor said. It's only a matter of time."

"I'll start making plans for Lyra and me to come down."

I could feel my anxiety level creeping up to new heights. We said goodbye, and I sat in the quiet, my mind racing. I dressed and drove to Mickey's. I had put the Glock and the bullets in a small bag to return to her. Hers was one of the newer houses in a development that was void of any personality. Homes for transients, she liked to say. The facade was Tudor-inspired, similar to the others in the neighborhood.

I rang the doorbell twice. The door swung open, and there she was, dressed in jeans and tee-shirt. I could hear the popular jingle "double your pleasure, double your fun . . ." coming from the television in the background. She yelled at Tom to turn the sound down, never taking her eyes off me.

"Can we have a cup of coffee?" I asked.

"You want to make up after attacking me in front of everybody?"

"I came to apologize."

The door opened wider.

"And to return this." I took the pistol from my bag and handed it to her. She put it on a table, saying nothing. I had only ever been in the foyer, as Mickey always had a reason to meet elsewhere. The interior of the house felt hollow, some of it understandable. Tom had to have wheelchair access to all the downstairs rooms, so no rugs or carpeting, and minimal furniture. But there was more to the sense of emptiness than that. No artwork. A few books scattered about on the dining room table, along with stacks of papers, but no bookshelves.

Tom wheeled himself in, and we exchanged greetings, and he continued on into another room.

Mickey led me into the kitchen, which was large with a round table in the center. "Instant coffee is all I have. Okay?"

I nodded.

She put the kettle on to boil, and we sat down. "I don't have long. I'm due at work in an hour." She lit a cigarette and I waved the smoke away. "The big event is in two nights. Looks like we'll have a good turnout."

"Is Luc dancing solo?"

"It's all worked out. Nobody is indispensable. That's what they said about JFK after he was assassinated."

"Good." The tension ran high. "I wanted to come and say goodbye."

"You're not leaving until next week, right?"

"We're actually going tomorrow."

She looked distressed. "But Lyra said next week."

"Lyra?"

"I saw her with her friend Alison."

"We changed our minds. Paul wanted to get settled right away."

"You know Lyra won't want to miss her boyfriend's dance. Moira, be reasonable."

I was not feeling reasonable. "She'll get over it. I can't wait to have her in school. I don't think Luc is good for her."

"You know, he's the one who got her to dance with him at Portobello. I helped them, but I wasn't the instigator. Once Jonathan saw her on video, he was gung ho."

"What video?"

"From the ballet school here. Luc and his old teacher are friends, naturally."

"Look. I have my reasons for keeping her away from Jonathan Starkweather. He's dangerous."

"Did I ask for a character reference?" She crushed her cigarette in the ashtray. I needed to get out. She continued. "Dangerous is a pretty strong word. The worst thing about him is his temper. He seems to be the type who blows up and then it's over. I overheard him last week talking to the writer Erin Charles on the phone. He was pretty hot under the collar. When he hung up, he said she threatened to name him in public for messing with her friends."

I was shocked.

"I need to go, Mickey."

I heard the wheels of Tom's wheelchair scraping against the floor. I felt like I was in a horror novel.

"He needs new transport," Mickey said. "That creaky sound drives me crazy."

He rolled the wheelchair into the kitchen. "She's telling you about her dancer boss, Moira?" he asked in a raspy voice. "A man with legs, right?"

"Oh, for god's sake, Tom," Mickey said. "Where're you going with this?"

"You're too old for him, Babe."

"Go to hell, Tom."

Was she having a fling with Jonathan? I wondered.

I opened the door, and she stepped outside with me, and said, "I think you're making a mistake not to let Lyra at least see Luc dance tomorrow night. I can make sure she gets there, and Tom and I will drive her home."

I felt nauseous. *Never in a million years*, I thought, but at the same time, I didn't want Mickey getting angry. "I'll let Paul decide, and I'll let you know."

The sudden knowledge that I wasn't carrying the truth alone felt almost exhilarating. Paul would say no and then whisk us away.

"Fine, Thelma," Mickey said. The first sign that I might be back in her good graces. "Where're you off to?"

"More packing. I'm glad we talked."

"I don't know what you've been so nervous about. The Prozac might be sending you off the deep end. There are stories about people killing themselves when on that drug. Or killing others." I regretted telling her. She glanced at the clock. "I have to go to the theater. The kids are used to me bringing sandwiches for them."

"Good luck."

I walked towards my car, knowing that her eyes were boring a hole in my back. I had wanted when she brought up Erin Charles to tell her that Jonathan was a rapist but then decided to keep quiet.

I pulled into the driveway of my home that Katherine planned to sell or rent. It had never been Paul's and mine. We would start paying for the apartment in a month. I looked around and felt clear that I would not be returning to Halifax to live. I had come for a month or two and stayed for sixteen years. It was still early. I would be alone all night.

I desperately wanted to be with Lyra, but I had to wait until tomorrow. She was caught up in saying goodbye to her grandparents, and to her friends. When I called Beezie to see if everything was alright, she told me the girls were driving around, and all was well. She would make sure they were home by nine. I said nothing about us leaving tomorrow. Ruth would be returning tomorrow from Vermont and had promised to go with us to the city. I poured a glass of wine, put a Mozart CD in the player, and turned it up loud. It would take a couple of hours to pack up Lyra's clothes, and then I hoped I could sleep.

42

I walked into Lyra's room, noticed a tote bag on her bed, and was surprised to see it contained her overnight stuff. Pajamas, clothes for tomorrow, toothbrush, her little stuffed bear. I glanced at my watch. It was almost five. She and Alison were going to be at the diner at six. I decided to drive her stuff over there. I wasn't about to call Paul's parents and risk getting an earful. I poured a bit more wine and felt the tension draining. I listened to phone messages. Paul hadn't checked in. I called the apartment in New York and left a message: *Hi. I have us packed for tomorrow. I hope the interview went well. Give me a quick call to let me know?*

It was time to deliver Lyra's tote bag. The air was hot and muggy. A light rain was starting to fall. I turned on the windshield wipers. Slap-slap. I walked into the diner. An elderly couple sat in a booth in the diner. A country singer was wailing, no one I recognized. The owner glanced in my direction. "I'm looking for Lyra and Luc?"

"They were here, but they left for Portobello."

I stood stock still for a second, then rushed to the door. *Damn Lyra.* As I got into my car, Mickey drove up parallel to me. "What are you doing here?" she asked me.

"Lyra forgot her overnight bag. What are you doing?"

"Picking up some sandwiches for the crew."

"I have to find Lyra."

I could tell I was the last person she expected to see. Something was up. "Hold on a minute," she said, "and I'll drive behind you."

I huffed off to the car. Glancing in my rear-view mirror, I observed Mickey's profile. Cigarette smoke poured out of the driver's side window.

A few cars were scattered about in the parking lot in front of the theater. The sky had darkened, and now rain was pelting down. I entered the building, instantly disoriented by the taped rock music blasting from what I thought to be the theater doorway. Dozens of bodies rushed to and fro, their voices struggling to be heard over the din. A girl in a leotard leapt up on the back of a guy who laughingly grabbed her hands and somersaulted her over his head, catching her on her way down.

No one paid any attention to me as I walked towards the door that had a homemade sign attached to it: "QUIET. Rehearsal in Progress." I entered and stopped to allow my eyes to adapt to the dimness. Three performers were onstage writhing around to canned music. Someone sat on the front row of the theater shouting out instructions. "Turn up the music," a man shouted. I felt my way to a seat in the back. "Lyra and Luc!" the man yelled out. "Run through the opening one more time!"

And there she was. My daughter, standing stage left, preparing to enter. Two seconds of quiet, then some form of electronic music containing sound effects that made my skin crawl filled the space. Two masked dancers came onstage.

Lyra stands in a circle of light, in a gauzy costume, looking childlike. Her partner grabs her by the hair, at which point Jonathan cried, "Stop!" and leaps up on the proscenium stage. He still has the physique of an athlete. Tight jeans and tee-shirt. "You have to show more resistance," he says to Lyra. "And then you succumb."

I watch as Jonathan demonstrates, the scene reminiscent of him dragging me into my bedroom. (I now realize, as I write this, that I have shifted to the present tense, just as I did when I first wrote about the rape.) Rape simulation comes to mind. I am taking shallow breaths, gripping the arms of the chair. I can barely hear what he is saying to them over the music. They repeat the scene and continue on. Jonathan then calls a break and tells them to practice the next part. He tells them he has to make a call and will be back in five minutes. He exits.

I expected to find Lyra in the auditorium where spectators sit, watching her boyfriend. I had not prepared myself to see Jonathan, nor to see my daughter in his grip. I wish I hadn't had any wine earlier. My mind feels hyper alert and fuzzy at the same time. I made my way to the stage and walked up to Lyra, who was shocked to see me.

"Get your things. We're leaving."

"Mom! I was going to tell you . . ."

"Don't bother changing. Grab your bag and meet me in the parking lot."

"Ms. Rivers, it's one dance." I turned to look at Luc. It felt like he was taunting me with the line from my dinner party. His face was puffed up in anger.

The stage manager ran up to me and asked, "Is there a problem? You're not supposed to be here, ma'am."

"Lyra," I said. "Get to the car. NOW."

She ran up the aisle of the theater and out the door. I followed, but once in the corridor, I stopped. Lyra had disappeared, and I felt confused about which direction to go in. A swath of light beamed out into the dimly-lit corridor, and I walked towards it. The door to the office was open as I passed by, and I glanced in and saw Jonathan hanging up the phone. Pure impulse led me in. Jonathan's eyes flashed surprise, then anger.

Then, his lips turned up into a mocking smile. "Hello, Moira." His voice low. Soft. Chilling.

Nothing could have prepared me for this moment. I felt suddenly so tightly squeezed into my body that there was no room to breathe.

"I'm taking Lyra out of here." I whirled to exit the room and collided with Mickey.

"Hey guys," she said in her most flamboyant manner, kicking the door closed with her foot. Slam. The music was so loud when she opened the door that I wanted to hold my hands up to cover my ears, but when the door closed, it was like being in a tomb, with the music bouncing against the door. I smelled bourbon.

"What do you want, Mickey?" Jonathan asked, obviously irritated.

"I thought Thelma here might need some backup."

I tried to focus. His curly hair was now streaked with grey. Dance posters covered the walls. One was of Jonathan at around the age he was when he assaulted me. His voice was steely. "Get out. Both of you."

It was then that I saw Mickey had a gun in her hand. A Glock.

Her eyes were focused on Jonathan. "You know what, you bastard? I'm sick of you ordering me around."

His eyes darted back and forth, assessing if he was really in danger. He stared back at Mickey. "Get out. And don't come back."

"Let's go," I said in a pleading voice to Mickey.

"Just a minute." Her jaw was set. Her eyes on fire. "I'll go, but I'll have my say before I go. I know you raped Moira. It's in Erin Charles' book."

I will never know why, but those damn haunting words of Pablo Neruda came back to me. After he had raped the woman he described as a goddess and a wild animal (THAT gave him the right?), he wrote, "She was right to regard me with contempt." Yes, nameless woman, you were right to regard him with contempt.

"She opened her legs, same as you," Jonathan said to Mickey, his face distorted with fury.

Two pops, and I watched him fall backwards onto the raggedy old sofa. Mickey put the pistol into her bag and opened the door. "You coming?" she said to me.

I stood watching a dark circle form on his shirt. Jonathan's eyes slowly closed. No more than five seconds had passed. I staggered out into the hall, closing the door behind me. No Mickey. I moved quickly to the entrance hall ahead, passing people along the way. Then I saw

Lyra bounding towards me. She had been crying. A lot. Her eyes were swollen. "I was in the car, but where did you go, Mom?"

Someone called my name, and I saw Paul taking long strides towards us. "Lyra Rivers," he said, "you're in big trouble. We're going home."

Luc ran up. "Mr. Rivers, it's my fault. I'm sorry."

"Moira," Paul said in a commanding voice. "I'll take Lyra. Meet us at the house." He stopped for a second. "I called my mother, and she was in on this little scheme to have Lyra dance with Luc. I got here as fast as I could." He led her out while Luc stood staring after them. I followed them out, thinking I could call the ambulance. I got into my car and tried to put the key in the ignition, but my hand shook so violently that I couldn't manage. I waited a moment, then tried again, and the engine started. I drove out of the parking lot, my mind veering between a supernatural calm and hysteria. I pulled over and got out of the car and screamed. Once. Twice. I banged the steering wheel with my fists.

I had to talk to Mickey. She opened the door before I could ring the bell. Too casual. "Thelma, what's going on?"

My voice was shaky. Low. "He's dead, Mickey. I saw him die."

"Okay."

"You left the scene of a crime."

"I wasn't going to stand there and wait."

"What're we going to do?"

"*We're* not going to do anything. They don't have the murder weapon. *We're* going to keep our mouths shut. Right?"

Who was *we*?

"But I'm innocent."

"No one's innocent, Moira. Not him. Not me. Not you. What were we going to do? Let him have his way with Lyra?"

"That's not why you shot him. He fired you."

"I shot him because he deserved it."

"But you could go to jail!"

"I'll never do time," she said.

She closed the door.

"What took you so long?" Paul asked, when I walked in the door.

"I had to get some gas. Where's Lyra?"

"Upstairs. And she's not coming down until I tell her she can."

He didn't know. He opened a bottle of red wine and poured each of us a glass. "Calm down, Moira. I'm here."

"Thank you."

"You don't have to thank me."

Lyra came down. "Mom . . ."

"Back to your room." I had never heard Paul so firm. She ran back up and slammed her door. "She can't get away with that kind of deceit, Moira. I picked up a take-out dinner. I'm too tired for any discussion tonight, but I want to say I'm sorry. We're a family, you and Lyra and I, and we will make sure we stay a family."

I wanted to weep. The words I had needed to hear for sixteen years.

Paul grew chatty and distracted. "Speaking of which, my mother might boot me out of the family. I yelled at her for being in on the plan to have Lyra dance at Portobello behind our backs. Mickey got my mother involved after she signed Lyra on for one dance with Luc. Of all people!"

Had he forgotten that he had been gung-ho about Lyra dancing with Luc?

He opened the take-out food. "I'll call Lyra down."

"We need to sit down with her. She doesn't understand why we're so furious."

"I don't want her to know anything about that monster," he said. "Let's let things calm down first." He took a bite of hamburger that he had pulled out of the bag. "Sorry. I haven't eaten in . . . I don't know when. And. Oh. I spoke with an old friend who's a lawyer, and maybe we can do something about Jonathan

Starkweather. We'll find a reason to make him leave town." He shouted up the stairs. Lyra!"

She came down, her face sullen. She turned on the television. "Something's happened," she said. "I just talked to Luc."

And there it was. The News Break. Famous dancer and director from Portobello shot dead. No suspects. Police are investigating. Photos of Jonathan in his youth flashing before us. Vibrant. Handsome. Muscular.

Paul stood rooted, staring at the screen, his hamburger held mid-air. Lyra cried out and ran back to her room. After what seemed like an hour, he turned to me, "Do you know anything about this?"

"Yes."

43

Ruth was at my door the following morning. Alone. Paul had left by the time I woke up, and I sat in the kitchen, sipping coffee. Lyra was asleep upstairs. Paul and I had talked for hours, and I told him everything, then handed him a copy of my pages, which he had put in his briefcase. I had finally taken a sleeping pill. The television was on. The killer had escaped.

I poured a cup of coffee for Ruth, who sat across from me. "Thank God, you're okay!" she said.

"Mickey killed him." I spoke in whispers.

Ruth's mouth was pooched. Her eyes looked stricken. "How do you know?"

We spoke in whispers. "Because I was there."

"Oh, Moira."

Paul rushed in. "I picked up bagels. And I went to the police station and told them we were in the building. They're going to send somebody over." He sat down. "How are you, Moira?"

"Numb. I should get dressed."

I ran upstairs when I heard the doorbell ring. I heard Paul downstairs inviting someone in and then heard Seamus' voice, followed by Ruth explaining that I would be down in a minute. I brushed my hair into a ponytail.

Who was the woman looking at me in the mirror? I was as much a stranger to her as I was to the woman who stared back at me in the elevator that night long ago. Paul called up the stairs, and I yelled, "Coming!" in a little trill that didn't match the face I had just been studying in the glass.

All of a sudden, something that felt akin to elation poured over me, which was shocking in the present context of my life. It felt wrong, and yet, I understood. Jonathan Starkweather could never harm me again. He could not touch Lyra. Or claim her. I knew something in that moment: I was no longer a victim. Maybe I *was* Thelma, and this was what it felt like to fly off that cliff. Maybe I was losing my mind, and if so, so be it.

I moved towards the strange man who stood when I entered the room and shook his hand. "Detective Sawyer," he said, "and this is Detective Norris." Norris had short legs, for her feet barely touched the floor, and she had her notebook at the ready. "Have a seat," Detective Sawyer said. Seamus sat next to Paul on the sofa, and I moved to a hard-backed chair. Ruth came from the kitchen with a cup of coffee for me, which I didn't touch.

I told them about the visit to Mickey's. Going home and realizing Lyra had forgotten her bag. Taking it to the diner, and then to the theater. I noticed Seamus' eyes widen, as did Paul's and Ruthie's, while Detective Sawyer's eyes remained neutral. His assistant didn't look up from her notebook. She was too busy writing.

After it was over, Detective Sawyer said, "Do you own a gun, you or your husband?"

Paul said. "No."

The detective kept looking at me. "I had a gun," I said. "A Glock given to me by Mickey. I returned it to her yesterday."

Detective Sawyer's voice was monotone. Quiet. "Why did you do that?"

"My family and I are moving to Manhattan, and I have no need for it."

"But you had a need before?"

"Well, not a need. But Mickey and I sometimes went to the gun range to practice target shooting."

"To practice?" the detective asked.

"Yes."

"Did you have permission to carry?"

"No. Mickey did, though."

"Thank you for your help, Ms. Rivers."

He turned to Paul. "What brought you to the theater?" Paul explained that he had an important meeting in New York and went down for it, then returned and went to his mother's, to discover that she was in on the ruse to have Lyra dance at Portobello. "I went to the theater to fetch Lyra," he said. "I didn't know Moira was there. I knew nothing about the murder until I saw it on television later that night."

"Ms. Rivers didn't tell you?"

"No."

I interjected. "I was going to, but there wasn't time before our daughter came down and announced it. Her boyfriend had called her."

The detective's attention stayed focused on Paul. "I'll be the lead detective, so if you think of anything, don't hesitate to call. Please don't leave town without my permission, Ms. Rivers."

"What about my husband?" I asked.

"He's free to go and come."

I felt my cheeks redden. "May I ask why I'm not allowed to? I didn't shoot him. I told you what happened."

"Mrs. Olivetti has already called to give a statement. She had just arrived in the parking lot with sandwiches for the crew, but she wasn't in the theater."

Someone must have seen her, I thought.

"That's a lie," Paul said. Seamus gave him a warning look.

The detective said, "We know that your wife here had a big problem with your daughter being in that theater. Several people heard her ordering your daughter to leave. The stage manager described her as unhinged."

"I was not unhinged," I argued.

No one spoke.

The detectives stood to leave, and Seamus followed them out. When he returned, he said, "Moira, it's not looking good."

"What do you mean?"

"I'm afraid Mickey has a foolproof alibi."

"Meaning?"

"Her husband Tom has said he was in the car with her when she went to deliver the sandwiches and that she dropped them off and returned immediately to the car to drive him home."

I felt the anger curling upward. "He wasn't in her car at the diner," I said. "I stopped by their house on my way home after the shooting."

Paul's eyes widened. "You said you stopped to get gas."

"I lied. I had to see Mickey."

"What'd she say?" Seamus asked.

"She told me to keep my mouth shut. I should have listened to her."

"You're not her. I could tell in five seconds if you were lying. Mickey has fooled me more than once."

Ruth had been quiet until now. "So the consummate liar will win? That's what you call justice?"

Seamus said, "We're in the first stage of the investigation. There's a long way to go. And I'm going to do my own research, trust me."

Lyra came down. She had obviously been crying. "Mom, Luc said people are saying awful things about you." She went to Paul and curled up beside him.

"I didn't harm anyone, Lyra. People tend to jump to conclusions."

"Hey, kiddo," Paul said. "Let's get you to bed. I'm going to drive you down to the city tomorrow. Classes start in four days."

"No. I want to stay with Mom."

"Lyra, I need to be here for a bit, but you need to be in school." I couldn't bear to tell her that I could not leave town.

Ruthie said, "I'm going to be in the city, Lyra. Don't worry. Your dad and I will get you settled in. I have two tickets to *Les Misérables* sitting on my desk. One with your name on it."

Lyra sat upright. "Really? For tomorrow night? Well, I guess I can go and come back if I need to, right, Mommy?"

"Of course."

I knew Ruth had no plan to return to the city this week. Nor did she have Broadway tickets. But she would by tomorrow night. Of that, I was certain.

44

I felt heartbroken when Paul and Lyra left for New York while I stood in the driveway waving. But I was also certain in those early days of the investigation that the truth would emerge and that I would be leaving soon to live in Manhattan.

It was early September, and I had spent hours out in the garden, raking, and transplanting. It was now time to prepare for cold weather. We were in limbo with our house. Katherine had put it on the market, but Paul said the asking price was too high. She had stayed away since her altercation with Paul, but on a trip down to the city had picked up Lyra from school and taken her out to dinner. Paul, I knew, was bothered by the distance she had created, but when he learned she was being supportive of Jonathan Starkweather at the country club around her friends, he had delayed trying to patch things up. I could see how she had been won over by the media as far as Jonathan was concerned. He was being presented as a young wunderkind who had transformed the world of modern dance. No mention of the charges pending against him in New York by former young women dancers, nor of the failure of the dance company to pay their taxes. Some writer even dared to compare him to the fabulous dancer, Erick Hawkins, which infuriated me.

Paul and I were hurt, and at the same time determined to become independent. Paul was starting his new job with the *Times* and commuting back and forth. Lyra was living in the school dormitory and calling me daily to beg me to come. Paul had promised to bring her up in a few days. Seamus and Ruth came for dinner, and I complained bitterly about being ordered to stay in Halifax.

"They'll be arresting someone soon, I'm sure," Seamus said. "I'm a little worried about this new prosecutor Bill Short. He's a political newbie and hungry for power and fame."

Ruth asked who the suspects were.

"Sawyer isn't letting me in on the latest updates," Seamus said. "I don't know why. They're looking into a few people. They know about Mickey, but so far, she's not on their radar. Not the way she should be."

"But she did it."

"No proof. And Tom is a friend of Prosecutor Short's."

"Fuck," said Ruth.

Seamus sat back from the table. "I'm going to have to prove that the shooter was left-handed. Starkweather's office is a crime scene, so I have some time to go in and measure. Can you tell me exactly where each of you was, Moira?"

He handed me a sheet of blank paper, and I created a diagram.

He was pleased. "I'll take this in with me and do some measurements. Do you recall if she wore plastic gloves?"

"No. Why?"

"I suspect she shot him with your gun. I'm sure she had on plastic gloves, which means your fingerprints are still on the gun you used."

"Oh god." The old anxiety was creeping in on me. Stomach churning. Eyes burning. Face feeling hot and flushed.

We all grew quiet. Paul said, "They called today and want to talk to Lyra."

"No way!" I said. " Why?"

"Sawyer assured me there would be a female social worker present."

"I need to be there."

Seamus said gently, "I don't think they'll allow that. I'll make the case that she's underage. I think it was an empty threat, Paul."

I couldn't bear another round of injustice. I said, "I am, in fact, not free. Is that correct? If that's the case, I'm going to go and talk to Mickey. She isn't thinking straight. She can't throw me under the bus!"

"I wouldn't advise it," Seamus said. "She's been diagnosed with pancreatic cancer."

"How awful. She knew something was wrong with her. How did you learn that, Seamus?"

"She called me. We used to meet up at the gun range."

Ruth's head swiveled around. "While you two sit there oozing sympathy for her, Mickey has just killed a man in a fit of vengeance. Moira's right. Mickey has thrown her under the fucking bus."

"I have to prove it," Seamus said, obviously frustrated. "It's a tough one."

"Maybe the diagnosis will make her come clean," Ruth said.

"I'm afraid it will do the opposite," Seamus said. "It could send her spiraling into psychopathy."

"Is this what a forensic psychologist does?" Paul asked. "I have no idea."

"I draw up profiles," Seamus said. "Mickey has traits associated with narcissistic personality disorder with some borderline characteristics thrown in. There is an extreme lack of empathy, resentment or rage over perceived rejection, lying about her achievements, a drive to exploit others . . ."

Paul interjected. "But murder?"

Seamus continued. "She saw Moira at the diner and felt confused. My guess is she hadn't told Starkweather that Moira forbade her daughter to dance for him. She was worried about being fired."

"Which is exactly what happened," said Ruth.

"A very bad move in that moment. And he made, in my opinion, the fatal error of accusing her of opening her legs to him in front of Moira. Oh, I forgot to list another characteristic of her disorder: 'bolsters sense of self-worth through sexual exploits.' It was here that she could accuse him of raping Moira, which she learned through Erin Charles' book. I don't know if she assumed it was Moira or if she found out through calling Erin Charles. I'll check that."

Ruth chimed in. Both men were listening keenly. "So it could be said Mickey shot him on Moira's behalf, when, in fact, she shot him for making a fool out of herself."

"I'm talking to the best lawyer in town," Paul said.

I hated where this was going. "We can't afford that."

Paul answered quickly. "Don't worry, we can." He glanced over at Ruth, and I knew she had offered to cover costs.

Dear Ruth. I would never accept it, though.

I turned to Seamus. "You know Mickey pretty well it sounds like. Do you think she'll tell them I shot Jonathan?"

"Yes."

"I'll need to see Lyra. And no more protecting me. We need to work as a team."

We decided to call it an early night. Paul put dishes in the dishwasher, and I put glasses away.

"It doesn't feel normal here without Lyra," he said. "I think we should let New York go. Bring her back here."

I wasn't about to go that route. I said, "You and she are not going to give up what we've worked so hard for. I'm innocent, Paul. We'll somehow prove it. It's going to be okay."

"That's my line." He looked exhausted. "I'm going to bed."

"I'll be up soon. I'll get the lights."

I stayed awake all night, going over old journals, listening to music, thinking how incredibly sweet freedom was. I, of course, had no idea what incarceration felt like.

I decided to hold a writers' class the following night. Stephanie handed me a blue envelope when she entered. "I saw Mickey, and she asked me to give you this." I tucked it into my pocket. "She has pancreatic cancer."

"Seamus told me."

"She's pretty mad at the world right now."

I didn't respond. "Let's talk about this another time, Steph."

"Sure."

I guessed she had been in on the plan to have Lyra dance at Portobello but knew she would be on the defensive if I brought it up. And, I thought, am I going to stop speaking to everyone because I'm suspicious?

Bonnie was normally the quiet one, but she, too, seemed compelled to bring up the murder. "Mr. Starkweather was known for grooming his dancers for sex," she said.

Stephanie was, as expected, offended, and said so. "Innocent until proven guilty, Bonnie."

"Times are changing, Steph," said Bonnie. "I mean, maybe your husband would be in a lot of trouble today for forcing sex on a teenage girl when people didn't bat an eye back then."

I almost slid off my chair. Bonnie was referring to the morning we met up to watch Diana marry Prince Charles and Stephanie slipped and told us what had happened.

Stephanie looked angry for a second, then said, "We married. And it was a long time ago."

I intervened with a writing prompt, and the conversation dulled as my writers pulled out their notebooks. "What does fear look like to you?" I asked. "What is the color of fear? Let's start there."

No one volunteered to read when I asked. A first.

Darlene finally said, "Moira, we're here to give you support. My heart's not in the writing tonight."

I got up and brought bottles of wine out, and we sat together in communion. No one mentioned the murder again, but instead, we talked about our gardens and the new manager of the country club. Sigrid regaled us with stories of growing up in Germany, another surprise of the evening. Maybe, I thought, we never asked her. I felt grateful to them when they got up to leave, and I told them so. We planned our next writing class in a month, and they all embraced me as they left.

I went into the den and pulled out Mickey's letter.

Dear Thelma,

I wanted you to know the detectives came here, and when they asked about your skill set with guns, I laughed and told them you're a lousy shot. I would expect you to do the same for me, if you get the gist of what I'm saying. Tom is friends with the prosecutor, who has the nickname 'executioner.' My hunch is no one will be arrested and it will turn into a cold case if you follow my advice.

You'll be hearing that I've been diagnosed with pancreatic cancer. No prognosis. The doc says I have to quit smoking. Good luck with that, I said. But this will help you understand why I can't help you.

I wrote her back.

Dear Mickey,

I know it is devastating to get a cancer diagnosis. It looks as if both of us have a hellish time ahead. I decided to go for the truth. I am innocent. I trust that justice will prevail. Moira

Truth. Innocence. Trust. Justice. All those power words in one sentence. The words of a martyr. Of a woman who, I would come to realize, had no idea what she was talking about.

The next morning, Stephanie showed up with her garden tools and said we needed to start putting plants to bed. I slipped into my rubber boots and joined her. "Thanks for coming."

"I'm worried. The police were focusing a lot on you when they interviewed me. What's your friendship like with Mickey, they wanted to know. They asked if you had ever lost control with me, and I said no. Never. I hope they don't come back."

"If they do, tell the truth. You have nothing to hide."

Her eyes filled with tears. "I was in on the scheme to get Lyra to dance at Portobello, but not in a big way. Alison wanted to train there, and I thought it would be a way to get to know Mr. Starkweather a little."

"Did that happen?"

"No. I mean we were introduced, but he was busy. I keep wondering if I had stayed out of it, maybe Lyra wouldn't have gone to the theater and you wouldn't have gone in after her."

I said, "Aren't you the one who tried to teach me that everything happens for a reason?"

She gave a little smile. "Yet I introduced you to Mickey, and I don't think she's been good for you."

"How were we to know?"

"I still don't know why you were so adamant about Lyra not dancing at Portobello."

"There's a story behind it. I can't say anything now."

"Okay."

"But I will one day."

"I can wait."

45

"He's gone."

"Mama? What are you talking about?"

"Your daddy died in his sleep," she said. "You need to come right away."

The timing couldn't be worse, I thought. Paul got in touch with Detective Sawyer, and I was granted permission to go. I flew down the following morning. Paul was already in New York and said he and Lyra would come the following day.

My mother's friend Alice was waiting at the airport and drove us straight to my parents' house. Mama rushed to me with open arms and sobbed on my shoulder when I entered the living room. Behind her were a cluster of women from the church, with spray-netted hair and red lipstick. Neta was in the kitchen, at the sink washing dishes, and I rushed to embrace her. Everyone looked old. Obviously, Mama knew nothing about events in Connecticut.

She announced that we needed to go to the funeral home to see him. "I had to pick out the casket without you. I got a medium-priced one. I didn't see the point of getting the deluxe. It's not like we're millionaires."

Slices of pie were placed in front of me, and I selected a lemon chess. The women cooed and said mama and I should have some alone time and they would be back. The pack left. I heard the old clock ding six times. Paul called and said he, Lyra, and Ruth would fly in the following day. I opened the bottle of wine I had brought, ignoring my mother's disapproving look.

"I have some leftover chicken," she said.

I heated it and sat down at the table, and she joined me. She sipped from a glass of iced tea. "Augustus' death was a blessing. He had gotten so he never left the house." She burst into tears and picked up a paper napkin and wiped her eyes. "Poor thing. He never got over that woman killing herself."

"Mama," I said softly. "You need to let that myth go. One of the deacons was having an affair with that woman. Then the deacon accused Dad. Mary is dead. The deacon is dead. And now Daddy is dead."

Her eyes went absurdly wide. "My friend Martha said she saw your daddy's car parked in her driveway just before she died."

"It was the night she confessed to him that she had been having an affair with Deacon Jones."

She scoffed. "Deacon Jones was married to Martha. I don't know what to believe."

Her voice grew plaintive. "I don't know why your daddy didn't tell me all this."

"He said it was a waste of breath. You had made up your mind."

"Well, if you had known your daddy, then you would understand. Women were drawn to him, always calling up and wanting to tell him their problems. He'd come home and go to his study, ignoring my questions about his parishioners. The night of that woman's suicide, he said he was going over there. and I pitched a fit and told him the rumors going around about him and her, and he asked me for the source, and I told him, and he said the truth will come out in the end. I think your daddy secretly blamed me for that woman's death."

It was depressing to think of all those years of blame and inaccuracies and confusion between my parents, with no final reconciliation. Maybe all this shit only happened in small towns, where everyone knew everyone.

Adeline said, "I'm tired of this town. I never wanted to live here. I was forced to be a disgraced preacher's wife."

There was really no way I could point the finger at Adeline, who was a more modernized version of a martyr, one who suffered throughout life and let others know. Wait until she learned I was about to be accused of murder.

I suddenly experienced a moment of serendipity or brilliance or epiphany, I never quite knew how to refer to it. "Mama, why don't you move into New York and help with Lyra?"

"New York City? You must be trying to get rid of me for good."

"Why are you saying such a thing?" I asked.

"Because I'm the type a murderer would go after. Obviously a woman with some cash, and not unattractive by any means . . ." She wasn't joking. Then she added, "And vulnerable."

That was going too far. "Vulnerable? Mom," I said, "You're intimidating, not vulnerable. Say yes, and we'll talk about details tomorrow."

"I thought I just said yes. In a kind of roundabout way. So. Yes. But where will you be?"

"In jail."

"Moira, I'm worried that you're not sane."

"Well, sit down, and I'll explain."

She did, and I did. I told her about Jonathan Starkweather.

She said, "It sounds like he deserved what he got. I don't care about Mickey's motive. He's gone. But you're in a pickle, Moira. I'm proud of you for not lying, but I don't think all those lawyers deal much in truth."

"Well, I might as well bring up one other thing."

"We're supposed to be meeting the preacher."

"We have fifteen minutes."

"Shoot."

I told her the story of Lyra. All of it. This time she cried. She recalled how harsh she was when I told her I was pregnant. I gave her a tissue, and she balled it up in her hand. She was one of those women who look and sound ghastly when they cry.

Then she said, wiping the tears away with her knobby hand, "But maybe I was guided by the Lord because chances are you wouldn't have had a marriage or a baby, had I not threatened you. I mean, we have Lyra, the most precious child in the whole world."

"We do."

"Then everything is okay. I'm going to put on some lipstick, and we'll go." In the car, Mama said, "Did you see Diana and Charles are officially divorcing? The chickens come home to roost I say. Meaning him, of course."

"They'll be better apart, " I said. "She'll have a chance now to become autonomous."

"And he'll be stuck with that horse-faced woman for life."

I surprised us both by laughing, and then I couldn't stop. She looked over at me, alarmed, which made me laugh harder.

"You're hysterical," she said. "They used to lock women up for that."

Oh, my mother, I thought. *Pain in the ass Adeline!*

Paul, Lyra, and Ruth walked out of the airport into an overcast day. I rushed to them, and it was as if nothing had happened. Lyra took my hand, and Paul kissed me. Friends and church members filed in and out of the house for what seemed like hours, placing casseroles and platters of fried chicken on the table. It was obvious that Mama enjoyed the attention. Paul was charming, as always, and she introduced him to everyone as the best son-in-law that ever was. "He's more like a son than a son-in-law," she confided to one of her friends in a *sotto voce* voice, even though I could hear every word. "And look at Lyra," she added, "The spitting image of her daddy."

I shot her a look. She was now going to go overboard to make sure everyone knew this child was his.

"No one has ever accused her of looking like me," Paul said, giving me a look that said, 'You've told her.'

Ruth went with me to the funeral home to say goodbye to my father. His face looked like plastic, and his hands were folded over each other in a gesture of contrition. I held memories of a man with a booming voice at the pulpit and a wounded presence at home. My mother had held on tightly to me, as though I was hers alone. They probably had not had sex since he was accused, and so he spent most of his adult life celibate like a priest, except priests were expected to cheat, and did. No wonder he drank.

Ruth sat quietly in a chair in the back of the room. She joined me in the foyer. "What has struck me on this visit home," I said, "was how my father didn't stand up for himself. He turned to booze instead. I worried about becoming like my mother during the depression years, but I carry Dad's genes too."

"You're doing alright."

"Ha! Katherine thinks I need a psychiatrist. Paul said she had diagnosed me with manic-depressive syndrome after I blew up at the table."

"Female anger isn't tolerated very well in our society," Ruth said. She lowered her voice. "I've learned there are some lawsuits pending against Jonathan Starkweather in New York. One day, it might not be while I'm alive, but one day, women will rise up against men like him." I could see my mother glaring at me with disapproval. I was supposed to be circulating. Ruth saw her, too, and ignored her. "How is the investigation going?"

"I would say it's growing exponentially. I'm back to that feeling of impending doom."

"Just don't use that word exponentially when you're being interrogated, please."

I laughed in spite of the gravity of the warning.

The funeral was a series of Bible readings and hymns played by an obese, white-haired woman who hammered the piano keys. I delivered the eulogy, and Mama whispered "Good job" when I sat beside her after I was done. The little church was packed, which was gratifying. I had already told Paul that I thought we should fly Mama back with us, and he said fine, as though it was already a given, and needed no discussion. It was the right thing to do.

Lyra joined Paul and me in my childhood bedroom after dinner had been served and Ruth retired to the guest room and we had put Mama to bed. "I miss you, Mama," she said. "I don't want to be in the city without you."

"You dad and I have some good news. Adeline is returning with us and will stay in the apartment on 72nd until I can move."

Her eyes brightened, but she also was a little suspicious. "When will that be?"

"It shouldn't be long."

"I know what's going on. You're listed as a suspect in Mr. Starkweather's death. I saw it on the news." She burst into tears. "It's all my fault. If I hadn't gone there, you never would have entered the building."

"You were being your sixteen-year-old self. Of course you wanted to dance with Luc. You don't think I was rebellious in this little town?"

"You were? How?"

"I had a boyfriend whose name was Will. And he and I snuck into the church one night and drank a beer and we were making out when my dad walked up and nearly scared us to death."

"What did he do?"

"Oh, he yelled and told Will to get out, and I can tell you, that boy ran out at lightning speed." Lyra and Paul laughed.

"Were you punished?"

"My dad said God would punish me, but he didn't."

Lyra yawned. "I'm going to bed. I'll see you in the morning."

We kissed her and said goodnight.

Paul climbed into the double bed. "Was that true?"

"All but the part where Daddy beat me black and blue."

"Oh, Moira."

"I didn't date until I went to college. I know it sounds odd, but I was pretty happy here with my books and a few friends. I carried a relentless determination to get away, and I'm glad I did, but I think part of that was Mama's influence. She wanted me to get away." We grew quiet. "I believe women carry too much shame. Sometimes it's incapacitating."

"I understand."

"But you've been free of shame your whole life."

"I know about it from the hundreds of guys I interviewed during the AIDS articles I wrote."

"Daddy suffered a lot from the accusations against him. He was a sinner in most peoples' eyes."

"Is that word still in use?"

"It is here. Everybody's ready to point the finger at somebody else and declare them a sinner. Only the rich people think God has blessed them with so much abundance that the word doesn't apply to them."

Paul laughed. "I don't know how you made it out of here."

"I ran like hell."

I pulled *The Secret Garden* from my bookcase and began thumbing through it. "This book was my childhood home."

"I remember when you read it to Lyra. The French have a term for secret garden, *le jardin secret*, which refers to the sanctity of a person's private life. The inner life that never has to be revealed."

"I hate seeing how people have started thinking they have to reveal everything to anyone who will listen."

"So do you know my innermost thought right now?"

I looked to see if he was teasing, and he was. "No clue."

"Have you ever made love in your childhood room?"

"The sin of all sins? No."

"Well, it's time." He drew me to him.

46

Three days after our return from North Carolina, a police officer arrived at our door in Halifax and issued an arrest warrant to me. Paul had gone into the city to check on Lyra and Adeline, and I had just left my studio and was walking back to our house. He was over six feet tall, paunchy, and bordering on jovial in attitude.

"I sure hate coming here," he said, "but somebody has to do it." He waited while I went upstairs to get my tote bag.

I had been forewarned, but nothing can prepare you for arrest. He drove me to the Roxbury jail. The garage door went up, and he drove in and the door ratcheted down behind us. We were in a high-ceilinged garage space. An officer opened a door across the room and stared out at us. The driver removed the handcuffs and walked me to the door that led to the interior of the jail, stopping to remove his gun and place it in a locker. I was taken to a holding cell.

Seamus arrived and entered the small space. "I called Ruth," he said. "She's picking up Paul, and they're coming straight here." He looked stricken. "I didn't know the arrest was today. I would have warned you."

Someone rattled off the Miranda rights. I was told that anything I said could be held against me. I heard that I had the right to remain silent. I wanted to say I have been silent for sixteen years. I was advised that I could consult with a lawyer, and the rest, I can't remember. A nurse came to talk to me about my health and about medications. A female officer named Karen entered and told me that a judge would set bail via video. "If you pay, you're out of here until trial," she said, "And if you can't pay, you stay."

"For how long?"

"Until your trial comes up, which could be months."

"That doesn't seem fair to people who can't come up with the cash."

She looked at me askance. "Fair? Hah! There's no such thing here."

I thought she might be my age. "What if I refuse bail?"

"You would be considered a nutcase. One of many in here, I might add." She was curious about me, I could tell. "You might not get bail anyhow if they consider you a flight risk. It's up to the district attorney."

"But isn't that the point of setting bail? To guarantee the defendant will show up at trial?"

"Yep. But you're from a rich family. What's a hundred thousand to the rich, right?"

I was stunned. A hundred thousand? Surely, she had made a mistake. I must have looked shocked, for she added, "The DA must think you're a flight risk."

Karen had told me that I would be under suicide watch overnight. A low-wattage light bulb lit the space outside the cell. I thought about bail. The timing couldn't be worse. Paul would clean out our checking account, which still wouldn't come close to covering it, or, depending on the amount the judge posted, if he couldn't come up with it, he would go to his mother. If my understanding was correct, after we posted bail, I would be allowed to go home and basically be under house arrest. But we didn't own a home in Halifax, which was a problem. And Katherine had "our" house up for sale. I was not going to stay at Katherine's. The whole thing suddenly seemed absurd. I was being locked up for murder with no proof because a district attorney had an election coming up.

I wanted to learn more about bail and the American prison system. It had never occurred to me to wonder why people were asked to put up money they didn't have as a guarantee that they would show up for court dates. I smelled a rat. Who was making money off this racket? If I had real courage, I would refuse bail and be like any other woman who is incarcerated because she can't come up with bail.

I looked out to where the CO stood guard. I was in a cage. People peered in, then walked away. I lay down on the thin mattress and dozed. The following morning, I had a court appearance via video. The judge set bail at one hundred and fifty thousand. He explained that in one month there would be a probable cause hearing at the district court, then that would be bound over for indictment at Superior Court. They only meet once a month, he said. He added that the prosecutor presents all charges they think are reasonable to the Grand Jury, which indicts. Or not. I didn't have to show up for that.

I was allowed my journal and was given a flexible plastic object thinner than a straw and about the same weight. I thought it was the refill of a ballpoint pen. I had to ask for it. I had stuck a few notes from Lyra in my diary, including a diary entry of hers I found after the shooting. Yes, I could be accused of snooping. I also had a letter, still unopened, from Lyra.

47

JANE HAMILTON

DATE: *September 25, 1997*

*My mother was arrested and taken to jail because
some lawyer thinks she might have killed Jonathan
Starkweather. My friend Todd said she could go to jail for
life if found guilty. I will never speak to him again. How can
this be happening in our family? Grandma Adeline and I
came up from New York on the train for two nights. She
cried almost the whole time. Her face was a mess. I was
embarrassed, but I didn't say anything. Dad looked beaten
up. He said Mommy is a scapegoat. He dropped Grandma
Adeline off at our house and said for me to come with him
to Grandma Beezie's for a short visit. I overheard him
talking to Beezie and asking her if she had a sixty
thousand dollars available if he needed it for Mommy's
bail, whatever that is. He said he could come up with the
rest, he thought. She said she would have to see, then she
began telling Dad that this scandal could finish off the
newspaper and that she wasn't sure that she wanted to
rescue Moira. She said, "After that outburst at your dinner
I would support her going to McLean." That's a mental
hospital near Boston, Dad told me later. Dad told her that
there was a reason all this happened and that Jonathan
could have harmed me. I'm scared to ask him about that.
There are so many rumors. Jonathan was intense. Two
days before he was shot, he told me to come into his office
while Luc rehearsed. He gave me a coke, and then he sat
there looking at me. He asked me about my dad, what he
was like. I told him he was wonderful. I told him how we
did so many things together and how he understood me
better than anyone. He asked if I had siblings and I said
no and he asked, "Why not?" And I said, 'I don't know, It's
just the way things are.' I was getting weirded out by him.
He looked sad and said he never had kids. He laughed a
little and said, "I had too many women wanting to be with*

me. I couldn't choose; there were so many." I didn't know
what to say. Then he asked me if I knew Mickey very well
and what she was like. I said she's a little crazy, and I told
him how she was always at our house. I told him I thought
I should go find Luc. He asked me if there was any way he
could get me to dance permanently for Portobello. I said,
'No thank you, I want to follow my dream and perform great
roles for American Ballet.' Luc finally stuck his head in the
door, and I said I had to go. I couldn't talk to Mommy about
any of this because I wasn't supposed to be there. Luc said
if she doesn't want me there, then she should tell me why.
My friend Allison knew everything and was trying to help
me. She drove me to meet Luc at the diner, and then I took
off with him to the theater. Then Jonathan was shot and
everything went crazy. It's my fault. I shouldn't have gone
there. If Mommy goes to jail, I will die. Dad said no way
can I go to see her in jail. He said I will be exploited.
Whatever that means. Cameras flashed when Dad and I
left Beezie's driveway, and Dad said Mommy would be
front-page news for a while and we would have to learn to
dodge these people. Luc is being strange. He will stay with
Jonathan's company, as they have another director coming
in, but he hasn't answered my phone calls for two days. I
don't think I can manage without him.

   I sit here with my diary, pen in hand. I see my mother's
face, her expression full of love, turning to me, wanting me
to look at her, to trust her. But I don't know if I can ever
trust anybody again. The only thing I feel good about right
now is dancing.

I wrote in my journal:

   Lyra is too young to be embroiled in our adult messes.
If I were home, I would lie down with her in the evening,
and we would talk about all that was going on, as we have
done many times in the past.
   I opened Lyra's letter, and this is what I read:
   Dearest Mommy, I know you have done nothing wrong
and you will be home in a day or two, or maybe a week.
(That's what Dad says.) New York City with Adeline (My
friends think it's funny I call my grandmother by her real
name.) and not you is hard. She doesn't know her way
around, and she's too nervous. But classes are wonderful.
When I go to the apartment, she is always cooking. I told
her no desserts while I'm in training, and she was shocked.
She says sugar will give me energy. Now she takes her

cookies around with her and gives them to kids in the park and sometimes to the doormen who greet her when she passes. Sometimes I'm embarrassed, but then she is so funny, she makes everyone laugh, and that makes me laugh, too.

Mommy, write to me. Dad said that you will be in New York with me before I know it, but I don't know if he's just trying to make me feel better. I had a meltdown a few nights ago because I wanted you! Dad started yelling because he hates it so much when I cry.

The truth is, I'm scared, but I promise to be brave for you. Love you to Infinity! And beyond! Love, Lyra

I folded the pages and sat quietly, stunned to be in a cell on suicide watch. "What would Diana do?" I whispered aloud. She and Charles were officially divorced as of a month ago, but over the past years, she had become a poster woman for AIDS, walked through fields of land mines, and become a role model of courage for millions of women. Were she me in this moment, I had no doubt that she would use this moment as an opportunity to shine a light on incarcerated women. And it was then I decided to brave up and try to do the same.

RUTH

48

Today they took Moira to jail. Seamus thought the district attorney was acting too quickly. He tried to reassure me. "She'll be out on bail in no time," he said. I heard their house was under contract again. Katherine would have to step in—find a way to stop the sale of their house and allow Moira and Paul to stay on.

I watched until Seamus had driven out of sight, then quickly dressed and took off in my car to Mickey's house. I would say I was coming to see her because I was worried about Moira and thought she could shed some light on what happened.

She came to the door looking disheveled. Worse than disheveled. Gaunt. Thin hair. I knew the look of a newish cancer patient when the docs rolled out the chemotherapy and radiation and assured the patient their chance of recovery is high.

I felt pity for her until she said, "Look at what the cats dragged in." She opened the door wider. "I was just sitting here looking at the news with all the talk about Moira. They're saying she killed Jonathan Starkweather in cold blood." I looked around and saw only space. A sofa against the wall. The walls empty. No books. I followed her into the kitchen that was a wreck. "What's up?" she asked.

"Seamus doesn't think Moira is a good enough shot to hit the target twice."

"He'll have to prove it, then. That's what he gets paid for."

The little shit, I thought.

She added, "She could spend the rest of her life in prison."

I was prepared to argue. "They don't have a weapon, no motive. Everything is circumstantial. Plus Paul knows everybody who's anybody. They won't keep her."

"How about the Pamela Smart case a few years ago? They didn't prove anything about her either, but she's in prison for life with no chance of parole."

"That's because her girlfriend betrayed her by wearing a police mic." I decided I might as well cut to the chase. "I think you're betraying Moira."

She opened a drawer and took out a pack of Marlboro Lights and lit one, leaning her head back with eyes closed. "You have balls, Ruth. I'll give you that," she said in a steely voice, eyes still closed. Then she opened them and said, "I'm going to call Prosecutor Short and tell him you're threatening me. I could be a potential witness, if I live long enough, so that means threatening a witness."

I sent up a prayer that she wouldn't have that opportunity, then felt bad for wishing her dead. I also realized I wasn't doing Moira any favors by being here. I needed to backtrack a little. "I'm here for Moira, Mickey, but I also came because I heard you were pretty sick, and I wanted to say I would try to read your manuscript. I know it means a lot to you."

I waited to be struck by lightning.

She was surprised enough that she was speechless. "Well." It was said emphatically. " I appreciate that. Your secretary gave me the brush-off. I could tell it was a form letter. But I've been working on it." She walked over to a desk, pulled out the pages, and put them on the table. "Sit down."

I did.

"Things have gotten a little out of hand around here, Ruthie."

Oh God no, I thought. *She can't possibly think it's okay to call me by the name only two people in the world were ever allowed to use, and one of them now deceased.* I had on my listening face, but I was actually thinking about some of the stuff Seamus had said about Mickey's behavior, but before that, even I had said to Moira that Mickey was hijacking her life. I knew from Moira that Mickey was from nothing, a great source of shame for her. I had seen people arrive in New York, leaving behind either a sordid life or an empty life, and before long, they had glommed onto people who in their minds were of a higher status and began imitating them. Moira and I were also from humble backgrounds, but we had while young discovered a core of identity that had kept us grounded.

"That's an understatement."

"But it's all fixable. There was a misunderstanding between Moira and me, and that's over. She basically apologized for throwing the wine at me."

"She was terribly upset. Jonathan has . . . had . . . a history."

"So I learned."

We were playing cat 'n mouse, and I thought I was wasting my time, but I would give it one more shot. "Moira told me you really came through in the end."

"I had her back. That's all you need to know."

I wanted to bring up the rape. Lyra. Why she had killed Jonathan. I wanted to grab her around the neck and make her confess. She had me over a barrel. And now I had to walk out with her fucking manuscript. She pushed it towards me.

"Did I tell you it's a memoir?" she asked.

"No." I swooped it up, and said, "I want something in return."

Her eyes narrowed. "A little tit for tat? What?"

"I want you to tell the truth about who killed Jonathan Starkweather when you're called to the stand. If it comes to that."

"Are you trying to say confess? Sure, why not?"

I stormed out and tossed the notebook on the back seat and swore all the way home. Once there, I sat out on the terrace, too worked up to do anything except fume. When I had calmed down and could think a bit more rationally, I went over in my mind the circumstances that led Moira to the theater.

She had told Paul the entire story, and he thought it necessary to go into the city for an interview, but I was sure he needed space to absorb the shocking facts Moira had delivered. Moira saw that

Lyra had not taken her backpack to her grandmother's, so Moira drove off to the diner to deliver it. Here's where it got tricky. My theory was that Mickey showed up at the diner and learned that Moira was furious about Lyra going to the theater and was hellbent on getting her out of there. Mickey followed her. I think she was panicking about what Moira would learn when she entered the theater—Lyra was dancing for Jonathan, which was a nightmare come true, but maybe the worst was learning that Mickey was literally in the bed with Jonathan. It was clear to Moira in those last seconds of Jonathan's life that Mickey had figured out that Lyra was Jonathan's biological daughter and accused him of raping Moira. And then killed him. I wanted to learn how she discovered that information.

Mickey's manuscript was an eyesore. I rammed it onto a shelf with the cookbooks in the kitchen. Seamus and Sadie walked, in and Sadie wanted to show me her latest essay. I told her to run up and do the rest of her homework and I'd read it right after dinner.

"It's about you," she said.

"That makes me nervous."

"You should be." She had the same dimples as her dad when she smiled. God, she was cute.

Seamus looked agitated, so I didn't tell him about my visit with Mickey.

"Moira wants to refuse bail," he said. "Paul told me."

"But she'll die in there. It'll be freezing cold soon."

"She's opposed to the bail system 'on principle.'"

"That's ridiculous. I'll go see her tomorrow."

"Paul said he's scrounging around. He's trying to take out a loan, but they have quite a lot of debt with both of them starting new careers. And Katherine is coming up with excuses not to do it."

"I'll put up the bail, for god's sake."

"You?"

"For my best friend? What else will I do with my money? Build us a house with a swimming pool and tennis court?"

Sadie came down and asked if she could meet a friend for a bike ride, and Seamus said yes.

After she closed the door, I said, "I have a confession. I went to visit Mickey."

Seamus' face grew red. "Shit, Ruth. That's crossing a boundary. I'm the only guy on the force supporting Moira right now."

"I'm sorry. I thought I could talk some sense into her."

"I hope like hell she doesn't report you. The chief is only keeping me on the case because of the forensic psychology. I'm doing detective work on the side."

I was duly humbled. I said, "Do *you* think she killed him?"

He stopped and stared at me. "I think anyone is capable of murder. So, yes, she's a suspect."

"I wanted to kill that smug bitch Mickey a few hours ago."

"Ruth."

"She called me Ruthie."

He smiled in spite of himself. "Even I don't do that."

"I'll stay out of it from now on, Seamus. But a piece of the puzzle needs to be solved. How did Mickey know about Moira's rape?"

He shrugged. "Moira could have slipped and told her."

"She didn't. Add the question to your notes in case you get to interview Mickey again."

"You just said you'd stay out of the investigation."

"I did."

Sadie bounced into the room, and we sat down to dinner. She said she was ready to read her essay, if we wanted to hear it. We said yes. She began,

> After my mom died, I vowed to never laugh again. And I didn't. But then my dad brought someone home who the first day did a pratfall and she swore so loud that I couldn't help it. I burst out laughing; then she started laughing, and this went on a long time. It felt so good. And then this wacky woman became my new mother, and I love her.

I jumped up from my seat and wrapped her in my arms.

MOIRA

49

The lawyer Paul hired, David Long, showed up at ten o'clock at the jail house, and I was escorted into a room to meet with him. He had a brisk manner. We had said hello at numerous parties, and now here we were.

"Paul is coming in half an hour to join us," he said. He smelled of expensive cologne. He wore a suit and carried a briefcase. He had a notepad in his hand. He got himself settled, then looked at me. "Everything said here is confidential. My job is to either prove you innocent, or, we might be able to go for a plea bargain."

"But I *am* innocent."

"So are a lot of people living in prison for the rest of their lives." He continued, "You will need to go through a psychiatric exam. You've been determined non-suicidal, by the way. " He removed a sheaf of papers from the expensive briefcase. "You were the only stranger seen at the theater. They could get you on circumstantial evidence. A young man attending a dinner party you had recently—a dancer at Portobello—said that you threw a glass of wine at a dinner party you were hosting when you learned that Lyra wanted to appear on stage with Mr. Starkweather's company."

Luc.

"There have been accusations against Jonathan Starkweather," I said.

"I'm very aware. I hope to get those women up on the stand, but it's not black and white. It still comes down to he-said she-said."

I already didn't like him. "Let's talk about bail," I said. "The amount is astronomical, and besides, I'm not a flight risk. I have a good reputation in town."

"You don't have a home here. At least I'm under the impression the house you've been inhabiting is for sale."

"I wonder if Mr. Short has anything to do with setting my bail."

He hesitated. "You don't want to go there, Moira. District attorneys have a lot of discretionary powers. But, to answer your question, Mr. Short asked the judge to set bail in your case."

"What do you charge, Dave?"

He leaned back in his chair, comfortable, his legs spread. "I will settle that with Paul. Katherine might help. I doubt that you will be granted a plea bargain, which as you know, means a lesser sentence in return for a confession. The hard part is proving this wasn't premeditated."

"I didn't have a gun."

He frowned. "There's a mix-up, then. Paul said you *did* have a gun."

"I gave it back to Mickey Olivetti."

"I'll check that out."

I thought, *How can this man defend me if doesn't believe I'm innocent?* Now, for sure, I didn't like him. Another frat boy from the seemingly endless pool of Connecticut patrician families. I knew I wasn't being fair, but it was the condescending manner, the way he had of being in charge, the feeling that I wasn't being seen, the dismissive attitude.

Out of the corner of my eye, I saw Paul enter the interview room. "Sorry I'm late," he said, shaking hands with David. He walked over and sat down beside me. His voice went low, as his eyes skirted around the room. "This is a dungeon." He turned to me. "I talked to my mother. I think we can work out the finances. Ruth has offered to pitch in. I did the research on the bail system."

"I don't think this is necessary," Dave said, glancing down at his watch.

Paul hesitated, then said, "Moira asked me to do it. It'll only take a minute, Dave."

He looked at me. "A lot of people in the court system want to end its use, saying that setting unaffordable money bail is unconstitutional. Violates the 14th Amendment. The process is arbitrary and mostly depends on which judge happens to be overseeing a court. The judges routinely assign bail that people can't afford to pay. And, ta-duh, inmates have a higher chance of being convicted because they take plea bargains regardless of whether or not they actually committed a crime."

"Paul, I want to write about this in my column for the paper. Will you get a copy for me?"

"Yes, but write it in the comfort of an apartment I'm looking to rent in Waterbury. Small, but adequate for the two of us. Mom has an offer on our house, which, if it goes through, could help with bail."

I felt an unfamiliar emotion, a mixture of excitement and terror. I felt alive. "I'm going to reject bail, Paul. It would make an important statement. Many poor people who can't afford bail end up rotting in jail. It's not fair."

Dave said, "You will come to regret this. Women who mouth off or who act full of themselves don't fare well in the legal world."

I decided to wait and have Paul tell Dave, but I had just decided to ask for a woman lawyer, if I could. Dave wasn't in my court. Should he ever learn about Jonathan raping me, I was sure he'd secretly blame me.

Dave stood and closed his briefcase. "I'll leave you two for now."

Paul turned back to me. "Moira, I don't get what you're doing."

"I know it sounds insane, but I'm going to stand up for myself. I'm the poster child for wealthy residents, but we can't come up with that kind of money. What must it be like for people who can't even come up with five hundred dollars?"

The guard opened the door and stepped in. Behind him I could see two women trying to see us. "That the new woman?" the bigger one asked in a baritone voice.

His head swiveled around. "Go to your cells," he commanded them.

While his attention was on them, Paul whispered, "What about Lyra . . ."

"She's okay. She's in school, and she's with my mom and you. I don't think I will be here long. I'm innocent."

The guard turned back to us. "Time to go. Sir, time for you to leave."

"Moira, please let us help you." He looked pained. "I'll come tomorrow," he said to me. We hugged quickly, and he was off.

"Follow me," the man with the baritone voice said. I did as bid. "You'll be out of here tomorrow?" the guard asked.

"I've decided to stay."

He stopped and stared at me. "Lady, you out of your mind?"

He handed me over to a female correction officer (CO) who gave me a forest green uniform that reminded me of hospital scrubs. She explained that I'd normally be given orange, which meant high risk, but they didn't have a suit that would fit me. I was taken to a room where only the guard had the key. Four tiny cells in one unit, a toilet in the corner of each cell (no privacy) with a card table and chairs in the middle. No window. Fluorescent light bulbs overhead.

My god, I thought, adjusting my eyes as three women's faces stared up at me.

"I'm Moira," I said.

The old one spoke up. "Muriel." Black, gray wiry hair, tiny. I held out my hand, and she placed her tiny one in it.

"Rhonda." White, obese, chopped hair gone wild, and flip-flops. "I don't shake hands."

I turned my attention to a black woman with dreadlocks. Restless. Pacing. Lighting a cigarette, taking a long drag off it and blowing out the smoke. "Where you think we at? The country club?"

"This here's Kalinda," Muriel said.

"Don't talk for me," Kalinda said to Muriel.

I sat down in the one empty chair. "Nice to meet you," I said. "I'll try not to be in your way."

Kalinda said, "You're a short hauler, so a day or two won't bother us. What they charging you for? Embezzlement?"

"Murder."

She stopped her pacing. "Oh, yeah, I saw it on the TV. You killed that dancer man."

"I actually didn't." I looked over at the empty cell. "Is that mine?"

Rhonda had been listening intently. "It is." She told me the rules. We entered our separate spaces. I peed, then climbed onto the cot, and I lay there staring at the cement wall. I heard them as they shifted their weight, coughed, and snored.

"Night, Bitch," Kalinda said. It had been at least an hour since we had entered our cells.

"What?"

"I said, Night, Bitch."

"Night, Kalinda. Will my flashlight bother you? I have to read before I go to sleep."

"Go for it."

RUTH

50

We were three months into 1997, already and things moved at a snail's pace as far as Moira's trial was going. I had heard of prisoners languishing for years in jails waiting for trial but never believed it. I did now.

Every Friday was set aside for Moira. I commuted between the city and home in Waterbury; Seamus had become a consultant and often traveled back and forth, too, leaving Sadie with his parents when he was away. Paul had rented an apartment near Seamus and me. Adeline and Lyra had only come up to Waterbury once. Katherine had convinced everyone that Lyra needed counseling, and, as it turned out, the therapist felt it would be traumatic for her to see her mother in jail. I saw Adeline once a week in the city, and she seemed to be thriving with her new responsibility for Lyra.

I was initially opposed to Moira's decision to stand up for herself and maybe in the process help others, but after I read her newspaper column about the unfairness of the bail system—which, by the way, was syndicated across the country—I decided to support her. She was initially enthusiastic about exposing a system that didn't work, but now, it had been weeks, and Moira looked tired when she came to the window with the partition separating us.

"I miss my daughter," she said. "I was warned, but I didn't think it would drag on like this."

I had been waiting for this to happen. "The column you wrote garnered a lot of attention, but in an interview, District Attorney Short said it's a way of getting the focus off the murder. Your 'get out of jail free' card is still there if you want it. I've got the cash."

"I'm not sure I'm allowed a second chance at bail. It's up to the judge."

"Do you have what you need?"

"I have the basics. And my cellmates are becoming friends. Their stories are heartbreaking." The guard stuck his head in the door and said five minutes. "A young public defender named Gail Moskowitz has been assigned my case."

My heart sank. "I sure hope she's good. Do you know how absurd this is, that you are on trial for murder? I'm furious over how inept our justice system is."

Moira gave a weak smile. "Paul is thinking about writing a series of articles. We shall see."

"Stella would be proud of you," I said.

"I've thought about her a lot." Her eyes welled with tears. "I try not to obsess over Paul and Lyra and Adeline."

"I keep checking on Lyra through Adeline. I'm not sure that ten-hour days are healthy for a girl her age, but the good part is she doesn't have time to think about anything but dancing."

"Paul feels a million miles away. I know he's working in the city a lot."

"He comes weekly to see you, right?"

"Most weeks. It's hard for him to understand what I'm doing by refusing bail and hiring a public defender."

"He told me when I bumped into him that he is working incredibly hard. He said he will never be in the position of needing his mother again."

"That's healthy. But I wish things were better with Lyra. He told me the last time he came that she refuses to talk about anything that happened around Jonathan. And she has stopped writing to me."

"I'm blaming the therapist Katherine sent her to. I'll see if I can find out more."

"Thanks. You have to go."

"Yep. Love you."

"Same. See you next Friday."

The following morning, I drove to Katherine's house, her yard an oasis of order. Stephanie peered out from behind a hedge and said, "How's Moira?"

Her eyes were big and round. Frightened.

"I just came from the jail. She's okay. Have you seen Lyra?"

I heard my name being called, and Lyra rushed into my arms. Katherine was behind her, wearing a pants suit and sunglasses. "I'm about to take Lyra to an appointment," she said. "How are you, Ruth?" Formal. Polite.

"I'm well. I was hoping to have a moment with Lyra."

Katherine glanced impatiently at her watch. "We can wait fifteen minutes. Would you like to come in for tea?"

"No, thanks. Mind if we take a stroll?"

She turned to Lyra. "You have everything you need?"

Lyra nodded and started walking ahead of me until we were out of sight, then she grabbed my arm. "Have you seen Mommy?"

"I saw her this morning, as a matter of fact. And she asked the same question."

"What's it like there?"

"There's not much good to say about it. I'm only allowed in the visiting section. We have to talk on a phone with a partition between us."

"Are they mean to her?"

I put my arm around her. "Not at all."

"My grandmother Beezie makes me see a psychologist. Dad set it up."

"It's good for you to talk to someone."

"I don't like going. I have Adeline. Beezie said Adeline doesn't know anything about kids. Dad and Beezie won't let me turn on the television or read a paper. They're treating me like I'm a toddler."

"What about Adeline?"

"She's made a list of twenty churches in Manhattan and is trying out each one."

"What about your dad?"

"He comes to the city, but I don't go to the apartment if he's there."

"Why not?"

"I'm trying to work out who I am, and it's better for me if he's not a part of it."

"But he *is* a part of it. He's your dad."

"It's hard to explain."

"How's Luc? Have you seen him?"

Her face fell. "We had a big argument. He thinks my mother killed Jonathan and will get away with it. It's what all of Jonathan's dancers think."

Little bastard, I thought. "That must be hard."

Her eyes filled with tears. "If I could only see Mommy. Beezie says she chose her fate and now has to live with it. She said it's not a good time to decide to become a martyr. Adeline says she's a hero to women all over the country and that laws will change because of her."

"Adeline said that? You know, Lyra Ruth, you're old enough to think for yourself. Ask yourself, would my mother kill someone? The answer is no. What about your ballet school? Do you feel like everyone is gossiping?"

"No. We're too busy. My favorite teacher says that the moment we enter the practice rooms we must drown out the rest of the world. All that exists is dance. I'm good at that."

I glanced up and saw Beezie coming at a lope down the path. "Time for you to go," I said. "Can I take you to dinner next time I'm down?"

"Sure. Love you." She bounced up on tiptoes and gave me a kiss. I wanted to either cry or knock somebody to the ground.

Stephanie came up behind me. "That poor child."

I turned my full attention onto Stephanie. "Are you referring to the fact that her mother is being framed, or is she a poor child because she feels betrayed by her friends?" Stephanie's face froze in hurt and—could it be that she was about to display a tad of anger? "Isn't your daughter dancing at Portobello?" I asked pointblank.

Stephanie gulped. "She is. She's Luc's new partner. She and Luc think it's best not to tell Lyra now."

"You mean Alison is his *girlfriend*?"

"It's pretty new."

"Tell Alison she better do the right thing and tell her best friend. Or I will."

I didn't wait for an answer.

I commuted to New York a few days later and purchased every magazine and newspaper on the stands that mentioned the murder. The tabloids were having a field day. One showed a photograph of Moira and Paul on a sailboat, the breeze blowing their hair around their faces, reminding me of President and Jackie Kennedy in their heyday. Another paper had managed to find a photograph of Paul and Moira at their wedding. There were photographs of Jonathan Starkweather plastered everywhere, most of them taken when he was a young man. Around the time he raped Moira. I studied one of them, seeing an athletic body, intense dark blue eyes, the mouth set in a horizontal line. There must be many more victims. From Erin Charles' book, we knew there were two at a minimum, both friends of hers.

I knew my thoughts had just bought me a one-way ticket to hell, for no matter how hard I tried to feel compassion for Starkweather, there was none. It wasn't that I was glad he was dead—that was going too far—but it was a relief that he was gone. After scanning the articles about Moira and Jonathan—one even had a blown-up photograph of Lyra on the front, taken the year before when she was the lead dancer in a student production of

"Giselle"—I didn't blame Paul and her grandparents for hiding the papers from her. I opened Katherine's paper and a headline in the books section caught my eye, *Erin Charles to Speak at Roxbury Bookstore.*

Erin Charles had a group of mostly women collected around her in the back of the bookstore. I had read her book from cover to cover and begrudgingly acknowledged that the writing was first-rate. But what I suspected back then when she and Moira were friends was confirmed in her book. She was from an alcoholic, dysfunctional family, a victim from an early age. Erin's account of how Starkweather coaxed her into sex sickened me. He was a sly one alright. But so was she—having refused to come to Moira's aid and profiting, all these years later, from her own sordid tale.

I had found Erin unappealing the one time I met her, but by then Moira had taken the young poet under her wing. When Moira started venturing down to the family home in an artistic community in New Jersey and returned raving about the Socialist couple that behaved with wild abandon, I advised her to be careful.

One day I had it and told Moira exactly what I thought. "Erin's parents sound like a couple of genteel drunks who exist in some fantasy world. They'll never finish that book they're working on," then added, "If you want to meet real Socialists, I'll introduce you to the intellectual community on the Upper West Side."

Moira and I were roommates then, and so she would return from Erin's home full of stories about her parents' bohemian lifestyle. They listened to jazz and to recordings of Blaise Cendrars and of course this was accompanied by a lot of drinking, which Moira wasn't immune to. It didn't surprise me when things began to go a bit sour, especially after Erin asked Moira not to sleep with her dad. What became apparent was Erin's jealousy over her parents' infatuation with Moira.

I couldn't imagine what Erin thought about Jonathan's death. She glanced up when I entered the group of enthralled readers waiting to ask the author questions. I could see she felt a hint of recognition when she saw me. She welcomed the group and said that she would read from her book and then take questions from the floor. Her books were piled up on a table beside her, already signed and ready to be purchased. She read the opening, which was poetically written about what it is like to be a girl riding on a country lane in a yellow dress. Even in the moments before all innocence was robbed from her, she recalled the new bra her mother had bought her, the sexy sunglasses. Her audience sat spellbound. I studied her as she read. She hadn't changed all that much. Gangly, long straight hair, dark, expressive eyebrows, a halting speech that smoothed out when reading aloud. After a few paragraphs, she shifted to the story of a masked man running from the woods and assaulting her. No one said anything when she stopped reading and looked out at us.

Finally, a brassy-looking woman with a strident voice said, "They caught the bastard, right?"

"He was arrested and jailed, and when he got out, he killed his next victim."

A straight-laced looking woman raised her hand, and Erin switched her attention to her. "You're fine now, though. Did writing the book help you to heal?"

"It did. I'm also starting a foundation that will assist other victims. There's a flyer on the table that will tell you all about it."

She turned to her left and a woman, obviously the store manager, stepped forward, but not before the woman behind me blurted, "I liked your book a lot, but it was weird to me that you ended up falling for the dancer guy. He was bad news."

She sighed. "I was both promiscuous and vulnerable. This is not uncommon when someone has been sexually violated."

To the point, I thought.

A frizzy-haired young woman said, "I feel for the two friends you didn't believe. That's the biggest problem for those of us who have gone through this." All heads were turned in her direction. "We're not believed." Her voice rose with the last comment; then she burst into tears.

"I feel badly about it," Erin said. "But don't forget I was twenty-one. And, I might add, some victims seek retribution."

Was this in reference to Moira being accused of killing Starkweather?

The bookstore owner jumped in. "So sorry, but the hour is up. We have signed books here."

I made my way to Erin, who had thanked everyone and now was gathering up her sweater and tote bag and, and was headed for the exit. "Erin."

She stopped and turned. "I'm Moira Rivers' friend. Ruth Schwartz." She was taller than I thought. Not a trace of a smile. Still had the wall-eye.

"I thought you looked familiar."

"Congratulations on the publication of your book. It's well-written."

"Thank you." She hesitated before asking, "How's Moira?"

"You have surely heard she's in jail. She's trying to stand up for women by focusing national attention on bail reform."

"I meant personally." She hesitated. "You know, a friend of Moira's called, I forget her name, and she said she had read my book and loved it, and like everyone else, she wanted to know if one of the friends I mentioned was Moira. She told me Moira was doing great and had a daughter, which I already knew."

"Her name is Mickey. Did you tell her Moira was one of the victims?"

"I did."

"She used that information to confront Starkweather."

"Moira didn't kill him, did she?"

"No. But it's pretty clear she will be accused."

Her eyes darted around the room. She was obviously uncomfortable. "Are you accusing me of something?" she asked.

"None of this would be happening if you had come clean when Moira asked you to support her," I said.

"I have regrets," she said. "I even regret the public apology to my friends he harmed. It comes up in every discussion. Readers want to know the names. It's insane."

"Now that it's a hot topic, it strikes me that you would get a lot more book sales if Moira and Starkweather and whoever the other friend is were named."

"No need to be so cynical, Ruth. Every book I sell helps a woman somewhere. You know, Jonathan tried to blame my book for his current misfortunes." She seemed to be debating within herself how much to reveal. "He called me, upset about that same damned paragraph."

"Were you frightened?"

"A little. He said anyone could guess who he was when reading that paragraph."

I suddenly felt hopeful. "Would you be willing to testify on Moira's behalf if she agrees to allowing the public defender to use the rape?"

She had been shifting from one foot to the other and now led us to a table where she could put her briefcase down. "Maybe. Lyra is sixteen. I think it would be a nightmare to learn her biological father's history, but at the same time, I wonder if it wouldn't be better for her to know. I mention this because of what I went through publicly as a raped twelve-year-old. Lyra would, hopefully, have her parents to help her through all the pain of that discovery."

She handed me her card and I walked with her to the parking lot.

"I grew up in an atmosphere of secrets," she said. "And though I was a child when assaulted by a stranger, it was as if I had brought huge shame on our family. Everything that happened after—my brother's drug overdose, my mother's cancer, my father's alcoholism—all seemed somehow related to the rape. It was an amazing release to go public with my story. I felt free for the first time."

She got into her car, and rolled down the window.

"Say hello to Moira. Instead of taking on bail issues, I wish she'd take on women in prison issues. The majority of them have been through abuse. That's proven."

"I will. And I'll tell her you're doing well?"

"Not happy as a lark, okay, that's never been me. I like the mission I have in front of me—to open up dialogue about this awful subject and encourage women victims to do the same. They are terribly resistant."

"Maybe the woman who spoke up tonight was right. No one believes them."

"I have a lot of guilt about Moira. At the same time, I was a very damaged young woman and living in a fantasy world with a man I could project all my longings onto."

We said good-bye, and she drove off. I thought about our conversation all the way home. Why were women so loathe to reveal any verbal or physical assault to their friends, and when they did, why were the friends prone to turn their backs on them? It was bad enough to have men in a constant state of disbelief when it came to women's assault accusations. I wondered if it had something to do with the number of women treated badly by the men they thought they loved, many of them suffering verbal abuse.

Many of us had felt free as little girls, but from adolescence on, girls were put in roles of acquiescence and compliance. The general consensus was that good girls didn't get hurt, only girls who went against the grain. Girls who wanted a career. Who were assertive. Who played the field. The general consensus was that if women didn't take risks, if they stayed under the husband's thumb, they were inviolate.

Seamus listened with interest when I told him of my meet-up with Erin Charles and the questions that came up after I left her. He turned my theories upside down by saying that he thought that if we looked at modern male novelists like Philip Roth, John Updike, and Norman Mailer, we saw misogyny at its height, and should not downplay its effects on the female population.

"And if you want to see a charming sociopath at work, reread Nabokov's *Lolita*," he said.

Sometimes Seamus floored me.

"Moira could make a dent in the female consciousness. And maybe in the male, though I don't know of a man who would read such a book."

"I hope Moira agrees one day to turning her pages into a book."

"She could make a dent in the female consciousness," Seamus said. "And maybe in the male, though I don't know of a man who would read such a book."

"We'll start with two. You and Paul. I have Erin Charles' book here if you want to start there."

"Let's start with getting some rest," he said. "I have a great story to tell you about a man who married a woman who was a literary agent, but whose secret yearning had always been to become a detective, and because of that, she took up interviewing women from various walks of life . . ."

"Who might shed some light on her dear friend who had somehow gotten herself landed in jail and needed a good detective."

We were laughing as we held hands going up the stairs.

MOIRA

51

Moira's Diary entry: November 10, 1995.

I can't believe how settled in I feel here, writing again with
the thin, plastic refill pen that is all we're allowed to use.
Paul puts money in my account, twenty-five a week. I
purchase shampoo and a few other necessities. My
cellmates get less, and I am happy to share what I have.
They, in turn, are more than happy to share their stories of
sex abuse, boyfriend abuse, mother abuse, self-abuse.
Time has slowed down almost to a standstill. The first
month wasn't bad, but thereafter, the time here feels
interminable. Not seeing Lyra is killing me. How could Paul
have agreed to the therapist Katherine found? He came
yesterday, and I tried to convince him that Lyra is seeing
the wrong person. He said his mother is paying, and it's
only every other week, and so it can't be that harmful.

He's back under his mother's control again. Let's turn
it around then, I said to him. Let's be the ones in charge.
He didn't say anything. I saw myself in that moment the
way he must see me: a woman stuck in a cage with no
power. But he is wrong. I feel more powerful here than I've
felt in sixteen years. Maybe ever.

I'm not mad at him. It's hard to change who we are. I
don't know if I love Paul or not. If I am exonerated, I'm not
sure I would go home with him. I would have to fall in love
with him again to be with him. All our cards would have to
be on the table. No more lies.

Public defender Gail Moskowitz came to see me, and I
like her very much. She said it could be six months before
there is a trial, and when I started to cry, she said it could
happen sooner but it was unlikely. She added, "Look on
the bright side. This gives us a chance to do our
homework."

"What about everyone saying it wouldn't go to trial
because there is no weapon," I asked.

"The prosecutor thinks he can nail you with testimonial evidence" was her reply. Gail is new on the job and passionate. She wants to paint a picture of a mother feeling alarmed about her daughter being in the hands of a man who was rumored to be abusing some of his dancers, though she worries that it doesn't make for a strong case. The mother, me, went there to find her daughter and get her away from an alleged predator. She said, *"One person believes it was you he saw in the corridor rushing in the direction of the theater. Let's retrace your footsteps."*

I went over it with her. Yes, I went to the theater and saw Jonathan with his hands on Lyra, choreographing a dance for her. Yes, I was furious with my daughter and also with Jonathan Starkweather.

Gail said, *"You went to his office, right?"* Then, *"This is all confidential, by the way. If I am to help you, I must know everything."*

"Yes. I went to tell him she would not be dancing for Portobello."

"He's known for his temper. Did he get angry?"

Suddenly every second of that scene was flashing before my eyes. Me realizing I was an idiot for confronting him. Him with a smirk indicating he knew about Lyra likely being his biological daughter. Mickey bouncing in. Him making it clear they had sex. Her accusing him of raping me. Then shooting him. Me watching him fall slowly onto the sofa, his eyes closing, the life draining out of him. Me looking down at my hand to make sure I wasn't holding a gun. Me seeing Mickey with the gun in her hand.

"Moira?" Gail was calling me back from my flashback. I began to sob. She reached for my hand. *"Continue when you feel like it. I am here to listen."*

I told her my story, going back sixteen years.

She finally said after I had finished, *"The prosecutor won't want the rape brought up if there is a trial."*

"Neither do I."

"FYI," Gail continued, *"Short doesn't have a stellar reputation with women. One woman he harassed went after him, but she got trampled. We'll go very slowly from here. We need to get it right. I need a night to digest all of this."*

"I'm scared. I'll be dissected like a pig."

She made a face. *"I couldn't bear those labs in high school. We'll go over every angle of this case before we decide anything, Moira. Somehow, we must get proof that Mickey Olivetti is the murderer. I've never come across such an act of betrayal. I can't believe she would let you go to prison. Who is she?"*

I told Gail how we had met. How funny Mickey was. How tragic, too, with a husband in a wheelchair. And how

*powerful she was at the shooting range. I explained how
she insinuated herself into every aspect of my life with me
barely noticing until it was too late. I told Gail that I could
see now that Mickey had always been in the grip of lifelong
rage. And loneliness. I understood that place of loneliness,
I said.*

*Gail stopped jotting down notes. "I have to ask," she
said. " Was there an attraction between you and Mickey?
Sex?"*

*"No sex. But I think we held a fascination for each
other, at least in the beginning. She was different from all
the other women I knew. She was blunt," I said, "and many
times she was right." I explained how in her mind I was
Thelma to her Louise.*

*Gail said, "It's not that hard to see how all of what you
have described escalated into violence."*

*I said, "I have come to understand that when I talk
about Mickey's rage, I am talking about my own. First my
hatred of self for my inaction when Jonathan attacked me."*

*"You froze. It's very common. But you also escaped.
That's not inaction."*

*I was grateful to have the opportunity to explain. I said,
"And I thought after learning that Jonathan was returning
to our county that if I could flee with Lyra to the city before
he arrived, I'd be free. It was incredibly stupid of me to
think that would be the case. He was the damn wolf
breathing down my neck."*

*Gail said, "Which presented a golden opportunity for
Mickey to put two and two together about you and
Jonathan, then act out her own vengeance towards men."*

*I hadn't thought of it that way. I said, " She is clear
that she shot him for me."*

*"I think it's simpler than you make it, Moira. A person
of Mickey's temperament might shoot someone for . . . well,
anything. She went postal."*

*"I believe there's a good chance that Seamus will find
a way to prove it through forensics that I am not the one
who murdered Jonathan Starkweather."*

*Gail was plainly worried. She said, "It's a huge risk
you're taking. I'm really worried. For now, I'm thinking
we'll stick to the facts in front of us. You went into the
theater to get your daughter away from a man you didn't
trust. When you told Jonathan you were taking your
daughter, he was angry, something he's known for, and
behaved in a threatening way."*

She put her notes into her briefcase and stood.

*She said, "I want to say now that I admire you very
much for the life you managed to create after a trauma. If
it helps, I don't think you were wrong to not go to the
hospital or call the police that night. My sister did, and the*

outcome was awful. The perpetrator got away with his heinous crime and my sister . . . well, that's not relevant here."

"What happened?" I asked. "I can take it."

"She is in a mental institution."

"Is that why you became a public defender?"

"Absolutely."

She and I shook hands, and I followed the CO back to my cell. For the first time, it occurred to me that I could be sent to prison for life. I was at a new low. I told my cellmates I wasn't feeling well when dinner arrived. When they returned and we were locked in for the night, they sat at the table and talked in low voices about an inmate who had just been brought in. She had learned that her daughter was molested by a neighbor and she had gone to his house and 'busted' his head in with a brick. He was in the hospital and the police had brought her in for assault.

I sat up. "How old was the daughter?"

"Ten."

"There's no end to it, is there?" I said, lying down on my cot and turning my back on them. On the world.

52

I began to measure time by the turn of a key in the lock of our cell door. Breakfast delivered at six. *Clang.* Follow CO back to cell. *Clang.* Off to art class in a dingy room, escorted by corrections officers. We pass what they call a library, a bin of trashy novels on the floor and shoved into heavily burdened shelves.

I had read Jean Harris's books written in prison, and she despised the COs above all others. I had to agree with her all these years later. 'People with a tiny amount of power will lord that power over others,' I wrote in my journal and underlined it. A subject I wanted to research later on. The art teacher, a woman, was kind, but basically wanted us to color within the lines. I only went twice, preferring to use the quiet time to write.

One day Kalinda said, "What do you write about all the time?"

"My life. And others' lives."

"You ain't got a life. Look where you're at. What's to write about here, locked up in a cell?"

"You three could keep me busy writing for months."

Her look grew suspicious. "Like what?"

"Do you want to hear about you?"

The others laughed. She said, "It better be good."

I rifled through my pages. "Here goes. I only know her as Kalinda. In this place, we are all known by our last names. Jones. Rivers. It's dehumanizing. When the guards enter, they don't look us in the eye. They put trays down on the table and leave, often saying nothing. Like we're robots on another planet. Three of us remain mute when people of authority—usually men—enter. And they pick on Muriel, who I think of as Thumbelina."

"Who's that?"

The others hushed Kalinda, but I said, "She's from a fairy tale by Hans Christian Anderson. A magic fairy gives a peasant woman who longed for a child a tiny grain of corn, which grew into a flower, in which sat the most perfect miniature child. Some bad dudes showed up and brought her down. A life of struggle. Then she finally found her prince."

Muriel laughed softly. "A prince, huh."

I glanced up and was surprised to see I had their attention.

I continued. "Kalinda speaks up in a deep voice to whomever enters. 'Next time you come to see the queen, you better announce yoself," she says.

"There is one young CO who thinks she's funny. He says back to her, 'Sorry, your fucking majesty. I'll do better next time.'

"Then she says to him, 'Thank you, Sir.' And he exits. But there is a nasty guard with a pockmarked face and rheumy eyes, and he doesn't think Kalinda is one bit funny. She doesn't care. She says her thing about the queen, and he says to her, 'In here, you're a slave, you piece of shit.' And she says, 'You need to go home and apologize to your mama for coming outta her the devil. If you talk to the queen like that, and I *am* the queen, it means you talk to your mama the same way. And you will burn in hell for that.' He slams the steel door hard as he can when he leaves, and my ears ring for the next half hour."

Kalinda pounded her fists on her chest, and the others burst out laughing. She carries herself the way Mickey does. Proud. Defiant. And deeply wounded inside.

I continued. "Kalinda has almond-shaped eyes, a lighter brown than her skin. And dreadlocks that sway when she walks. The most beautiful sight in the room are those dreads. I think stories are woven into them. Stories of her culture. The braids are intricate. I think at one time, this girl was loved a lot. The name Kalinda matches her so well that her mother knew she had a prize. That's as far as I got," I said.

The room was silent as the stone that encased us. Kalinda hadn't tapped her fingers once with her nails that stuck out two inches.

Muriel said in a squeaky voice, "Maybe we can write something."

Rhonda interjected, "I can't write words like intricate."

"You don't have to," I said. "That's my voice. That's who I am. Your voice is your own. One of the biggest problems for writers is they lose that original voice. Then they are pretending, and the reader knows."

"What are we going to write about?" Kalinda asked.

I felt a quiver of excitement. "Your name. I'll talk to my friend Ruth and see if she can get the sergeant to give us some paper."

Rhonda said, "Did you write about me? What a big fat slob I am?"

"I did write about you, but fat is the last thing I see."

"Oh. So if I was to write about you, I wouldn't see blond hair and blue eyes, and the grief that rides out in front of you like the cavalry?"

"That probably is what you would see."

My eyes burned with tears. They started arguing amongst themselves to get the spotlight off me as I wormed my way back into my cell, where I lay on my side, facing the wall. They allowed me my dignity.

53

It had been three months since my arrival in Cell Four. One day, Ruth arrived with my mother in tow. The CO escorted me to the usual place, and my mother sat across from me. "Who's doing your hair?" she asked.

I laughed. "What planet are you on?"

"It has the same curl you had when you were a child."

I tried to sound cheerful. "How's my girl doing, Mama?"

"As well as you can expect under the circumstances." I recalled how that expression puzzled me when I was a child. It was a non-answer.

"Is she staying with you or in the dorm?"

"With me in the apartment for now. She's in rehearsals most of the day. She yells at Paul because she can't visit you. I told Paul finally that I didn't want to interfere but Lyra needed to see her mother. She's probably been imagining the worst." Adeline looked around and returned her gaze to me. "Maybe it would be better if she didn't see all this. These people should be ashamed for the looks of this place."

I shrugged. "Mama, it's a possibility that what happened to me sixteen years ago with Jonathan will come out in the trial." I was suddenly sick of making light of it, saying, 'the thing that happened.' I added, "the rape."

"Paul talked to me a little about it. I think she's too young to know about terrible things like that." I knew she couldn't bring herself to say the R word. "And if you two agree that she should know, then it should come from her mama."

I felt the tears sliding down my cheeks. "I ache for her."

"Of course you do. And she likewise. It comes out different. Her last comment was that she wishes she hadn't been born."

"Can you imagine our world without Lyra in it?"

"It would mean the sun had stopped shining." She leaned forward. "Listen, Moira, Deuteronomy, Chapters 18 and 19 says, 'In divine wisdom God determined the need for two witnesses to aid the discovery of truth.' The judges must make a thorough investigation and let the evidence lead where it may."

"Thanks, Mama. By the way, I've started teaching writing to my cell mates."

"I always thought you'd be a fine teacher." She glanced at the CO who motioned that her time was almost up. "Your trial is in a few weeks. You need to do whatever you need to do to get out of here. Maybe even confess and get a lighter sentence."

"I can't do that."

She shifted to a different tactic. She said, "I was thinking about Mickey. Another verse from the Bible came to me the minute I met her: 'Beware of false prophets, which come to you in sheep's clothing, but inwardly they are ravening wolves.' I still find this relevant."

Did Adeline have a sixth sense about what really happened?

She continued, "We die the way we've lived. I'm trying, lord knows, to find some redemption for myself. My mother tried for years to make up with me. I had too much pride."

Mama's tears dripped like rain off a roof. I wondered why I ever thought she was ugly.

"I made your daddy's life hell because I didn't believe him. I lied to you and said I was fine when I wasn't. I forced you into a secret world. And now our baby Lyra is in that world. If you decide to come forth with the truth, I will help in any way I can." She pulled a wadded up Kleenex from her bag and dabbed her nose and eyes. "They say God doesn't give you more than you can handle, but I'm not sure I believe that anymore."

Glancing behind Mama I saw Ruth wave and stop to chat with the sergeant. She had brought enough chocolate chip cookies to the jail staff to have them all on her side.

"I love you, Moira Dean," Mama said. "And I've never said it, but I'm proud of you."

"Now?"

"Now. Before. Always. I hate you being in here, but Ruth helped me to understand that you're making a statement. Then I felt proud of you for that."

"I'm grateful to you, Mama, for everything you're doing for me. For Lyra." Her mouth was starting to tremble, and I could see she was about to start bawling again.

"She's a handful these days. Much sassier than you were. She doesn't want to talk about your . . . situation."

The CO came in looking disgruntled. "Time's up."

Mama stood and gave him a beatific smile, and I saw him smile back. Wonder of wonders.

I was suddenly bereft watching my mother leave. "Tell Lyra I love her." Mama nodded, and walked out the door, turning to give me a wistful wave.

Ruth entered. "Here's the news of the hour. The guard said Adeline used up all the time. I went to see Mickey. She forced her manuscript on me. Surprise, surprise."

"You have it?"

"I rammed it into a bookshelf. The first page tells me it's a misery memoir. I also went to a book reading by Erin Charles. We had a chat after."

"And?"

"She was kind. And willing to help you. Her readers want to know the names of the women she apologizes to in her book. She said she wished she had left that paragraph out."

"I have to be the one to tell Lyra, whether it's made public or not."

Ruthie spoke rapidly. "Seamus will come next Friday in my place. Katherine will be out of town. He will have Lyra."

"Ruthie! Oh, Ruthie . . . my daughter doesn't hate me? Does she know my story?"

"I don't think so. But Paul read your pages and called me. He said he cried through most of it." She paused. "But, he does not want this turned into a book. No way. He's shielding Lyra, of course. But also himself, wouldn't you agree?"

"You mean he's shielding himself from his bruised male ego or his own failure to protect his wife?"

"The former. He would dread having the spotlight turned on his family."

The CO came and stood in the doorway, motioning that it was time for Ruth to leave.

"See you soon," she said. I watched her walk out, stopping to shout up to the guys watching over us. God how I loved her.

54

The girls and I were in a dither the morning I was to see Lyra. I hadn't slept because of the anticipation. We sat around the table. Kalinda told me once more to sit still, then spent an hour trying to style my hair. She painted my lips pale pink and made a line above my lids with her liner. "I don't want to frighten her," I objected.

"You'll scare her if you go out looking the way we see you every day," said Rhonda.

They laughed. Muriel stayed serious. "You keep your talk basic. Don't go on and on about your rapist. You'll be finding something nice to say about him so she won't feel so bad about him being her daddy." The others nodded their heads vigorously in agreement.

"I know Lyra," I said. "The way she thinks. She will want to disappear into a world of imagination where this kind of stuff doesn't exist. Normally I would be there to help her process this information."

"You need to count on Ruthie and Paul." This from Rhonda.

Muriel said, "You have to let Lyra go, so she can figure out who she is without everybody telling her. Your fear has kept her in a protected bubble all her life. The bubble has to burst for everybody at one time or another."

We heard the key in the door that swung open slowly, and the young guard we liked stood there. A good omen for me. "You have a visitor, Ms. Rivers. The most beautiful princess in the world." He glanced across the room. "If the queen says you can go."

Kalinda gave a regal smile and nodded her head. I walked out, not looking back. I sat in the chair and arranged the microphone. My fingernails dug into my palm, my old trick to keep from crying. Seamus entered the tiny visitor's space with Lyra and said, "I'm going to leave you two."

I saw my baby's bottom lip tremble, exactly as my mother's did. "Mommy," she said, " this place is horrible."

"You are seeing the surface, Lyra. I have a queen living in the room with me."

Lyra had never been able to resist a fable. "A real queen?"

"Of course. The guard addresses her as 'your majesty.' I glanced over at our nice CO who nodded, transfixed by the beauty sitting across from me.

"That's funny. What does she look like? More beautiful than Princess Diana?"

"As beautiful in a different way. Her brown skin shines, and she has long dreadlocks. She said that all her life stories were woven into her hair. Every strand a story. Imagine."

I watched Lyra relax. "I'll use that when I'm dancing in a ballet a choreographer Eric has created based on Rapunzel."

I hated leading us back to reality. "Lyra, these visits are kept short. I want you to know that I'm doing well here."

"Your makeup is nice."

"One of my cellmates did it. I'll tell her you like it." I hesitated. "I have to talk to you about something important. My trial will start soon, and everything said will be in the newspapers. One of the reasons they are keeping me is that they think I could have shot Jonathan because of something from the past."

"You knew him?"

"I never knew him, but he was seeing a friend of mine. He used her to prey on me. He came to my apartment and attacked me. I fought him hard but I lost."

"Why?"

"He was psychologically ill. He was a serial rapist."

"I hate that story. Hate it!" Her face was suddenly contorted and turning red.

"I'm sorry I had to tell it to you." I longed to reach out and touch her, but it was impossible with the plexiglass dividing us. "I have learned the destructive power of secrets the hard way, Lyra."

Her voice grew harsh and defensive. "Everybody thinks you killed Jonathan. Luc will never speak to me again. No one will ever want to be with me."

The CO stuck his head in the door and put up two fingers. Lyra's face crumpled. I placed my open hands on the hard plastic partition that divided us. "I'm sorry our story is so sad, Lyra. I'm sorry. Please believe that I am innocent."

She looked at me, her mouth suddenly opened wide in a scream. The microphone was off. I couldn't hear any sound except some inmates talking behind me. I shushed them.

"I'm sorry," I said again.

I watched as Seamus walked in, placed his arm around Lyra as though she were a small child, and led her out. She turned back and put her face up close to the partition.

She mouthed the heartbreaking word. "Mommy!"

My eyes stayed riveted on her until she was out of sight, saying "I love you" over and over, then put my head on the shelf in front of me, the pain so great that I couldn't breathe. When I looked up, she was gone.

The young guard came and said it was time to go. I got up like a robot, putting one foot in front of the other. "I'm sorry, Rivers."

"Don't call me that, please. I'm Moira."

He unlocked the door, and I stumbled into the tiny common room. After the steel door slammed behind me, I let out a wail, a sound so primal that even I was shocked. The sound I wished I'd made when Jonathan Starkweather violated me. The girls staring at me from their chairs around the table became unfrozen enough to catch me when I fell over a chair. They dragged me to my cot.

Lyra, I knew, was gone. Without her, I didn't want to live.

56

I woke up early and propped myself up to write in my journal.

JUNE 1997

Every morning when I wake up and hear my cellmates chattering and arguing, farting and burping, feeling besieged by claustrophobia, I regret my decision to refuse bail. But it was watching my beloved Lyra come undone that tortures me day and night. If I had accepted Ruth's bail money and been locked up at home, would that have been better for my daughter? Did I put my own needs ahead of hers? For the first time, I wish I had entered a guilty plea bargain and swallowed my medicine.

I recalled the child Stephanie told me about who was the offspring of a rapist, only her mother never told her, even upon her deathbed. Stephanie said the girl lived a normal life, whatever that meant. Later I read a story in People Magazine about a Catholic mother from Boston who was sexually assaulted in a back alley by an African-American man, and when the child was born black, she gave her up for adoption. She thought she did what was best for the child. The child found her mother, though, after she had children of her own, and the mother welcomed her. To tell or not to tell? The question that has haunted so many women for years. Perhaps centuries. What did slave women tell their children who were the offspring of their masters who forced themselves on them? What happened to women in countries like Columbia where women, if raped, were forced to marry the man? And closer to home, what about Muriel, who shot her husband in self-defense and has been sitting in the jailhouse for almost a year, awaiting trial. She and I had talked and decided we hated being thought of as victims when we saw ourselves as fighters. I want to write about this.

I heard someone stirring but wanted to write about the girls' behavior last night before they started their gossip about the new inmate Mary, whom they are obsessed with. In their opinion, she had done right by her daughter and now was sitting in jail because she had put a hurting (a Southern expression) on the guy who messed with her child. In our tiny community of four, we wanted justice, even though we knew our chances were slim to none.

Last night, Muriel brought a chair into my cell and reached for my hand. I knew it was her because her own hand was so tiny and scrawny. She said in a low voice, "I have what some call a gift and some call a curse. I can see things. Could from the time I was a child. I see you have spent time in the underworld, Moira. You have been down more than most, but you manage to emerge again into light. You loved your father, but he wasn't there for you. There wasn't much warmth, not much acknowledgment of you. Not much from your mother either, to tell you the truth. You looked for answers in books, but your truth doesn't come from them. It comes from your life. The attack from a stranger sent you spiraling into the deepest part of the underworld, only this time it was much harder to return. You were terrified to go either way. But you made a choice. Now Lyra is where you were, too afraid to choose. Everywhere she turns, she finds herself in a dark forest. She's looking for a light to guide her. You've put your light under a basket. You need to stand tall and be a beacon for her."

"I don't think I can. I really don't know how."

The next thing I knew, someone had placed a cool cloth on my forehead, which had been throbbing. And someone began to massage my feet. I sank into darkness.

"What're you writing?" Kalinda asked. They usually didn't interrupt my morning journaling.

"About the mystery of the healers who came quietly into my cell last night."

"You musta been dreaming."

"What about our writing?" Rhonda asked. "We can't do it without you."

I crawled up off my cot. "Give me a moment. And Rhonda, will you make me a cup of coffee, please?"

"Sure will." I heard the coffee maker hissing. I slipped into a sweater and went to the table. Kalinda sat holding the slender, plastic pen in her giant hand, and I suddenly wanted to laugh but didn't. They drove me crazy, it was true, but when we sat at the table to write, or when I read to them from To Kill a Mockingbird I had found buried under a mound of books tossed into a pile, I felt something come alive in me. Slowly, they began to ask for more. Kalinda wanted to write to her mother, and Rhonda had drawn a picture for her daughter and wanted to add a note. I gave them writing prompts and began to write with them, and through these exercises, they opened up.

"Here's your prompt," I said. "You are eleven. You run outside into the sunshine. The screen door slams behind you."

They held their pens mid-air and then simultaneously began to write. I glanced over at Muriel, whose head was bent over the page, and felt a surge of love. The words she spoke last night caressed me with their tenderness and knowledge. I felt known.

57

Gail came several mornings a week to discuss my case. She had somehow accumulated thousands of pages of testimony and had interviewed twenty-five witnesses. We slowly determined who would be positive witnesses and who would not. Mickey's name came up often, and finally, Gail got in touch with her to tell her that if she refused to come to testify, she would subpoena her. "She didn't like hearing that," Gail said.

Of course Mickey resisted. Anything she said would have to be a lie.

"How is she?" I asked.

Gail hesitated, then said, "Physically, she was a mess. Gaunt. Thin as a pencil. And looks like it hurts to move. But her opinions were strong. She said I should have gotten you off by now. Said the cops are letting the real killer get away." She thought for a moment. "I'm not sure she'll be a good witness for you, Moira. She strikes me as unreliable."

The understatement of the year, I thought. "Someone needs to make her confess," I said.

"I hope that someone arrives soon," Gail said. "She's very sick."

"You mean, like dying?" I asked.

She nodded.

The moment I had dreaded, the moment, as it turned out, that would determine my fate, occurred a few days later. Gail arrived on a special visit, and as soon as we sat, she pulled a stack of newspapers out of her satchel. JONATHAN STARKWEATHER RAPED MOIRA DEAN RIVERS IN 1979 was a typical headline. I had never felt so obscenely exposed. Erin Charles had sent an essay to *The New York Times* about how I had come to her after being raped by her then-boyfriend, and she had refused to help me. She went on to describe the guilt she had carried once she realized that Jonathan was a serial rapist. The focus of the essay was on her suffering. How she had been raped at twelve and had written her book to help other women. It would be unconscionable, she said further on in the article, not to help me now when I was on trial for murdering Jonathan Starkweather.

My first thought was of Lyra. How on earth would she be able to withstand the barrage of public attention this would focus on her?

Gail said, "The prosecutors will have their motive now: revenge. I'm not sure that Ms. Charles is doing you any favors. If we get the wrong jurors, they'll have more sympathy for Jonathan."

We were a week away from the trial. My cellmates knew all about Erin refusing to believe me when I went to her. They also understood that Mickey might be too unreliable to put on the stand. It was Rhonda who said the day before the trial, "You have to remember that every one of us in here is on trial. And millions of other women out there are also watching to see what happens with you."

"That's too much for me to think about."

"Maybe there's a chance they will start speaking up. It could be a revolution."

Kalinda said, "You know, Moira, you being white is probably an advantage. Your trial came up pretty quick."

I disagreed. "I see it as a disadvantage. People like to see privileged people brought down to size. Plus, Prosecutor Short is after fame."

"It's all a crapshoot," Kalinda said. "Take me, for example. I'm probably going to end up in the women's prison the rest of my life.

Or I'll be in here for years, like Muriel. I didn't have the fucking two hundred dollars for bail."

"But you have the self-defense plea, right?" I asked.

"Why do you think I have that when I stuck a kitchen knife in his back?"

"He was beating you unconscious," I said. "And he didn't die. He's out there free while you're in here."

Rhonda laughed, and I turned to her in shock that anything was funny. She shrugged. "I'm looking at the three of you. We're a cell full of men-killers. No wonder the guards hate us. I didn't bother to convert her."

Muriel spoke in a low voice. "I shouldn't have done it. No matter what, it's wrong to kill anybody."

"But he was going to kill you."

"I sometimes wish he had."

We grew silent.

I thought about what I could have had: the powerful lawyer hired by Paul for one, and bail paid by Ruthie. Kalinda was right. It was all there if I had accepted it. But when I talked late one night with Muriel about it, she offered a different perspective. She said, "If you survive this, you will look back and see that you made the choice that would make you whole. You stopped seeing and listening to yourself after you were raped. You started a fake life, and maybe it took something this big to jolt you out of it."

Over the next few days, I felt eaten up with worry. I had no choice but to do what I was told. I was like a robot. I went to meals. And when I returned to my cell, I lay down and closed my eyes. My back had started to hurt all the time. Ruth came weekly, as did Paul in the beginning.

"I have lost all control," I said one day to Ruthie. "I never dreamed it would turn into this. I was thinking a month in detention, not a season in hell."

Ruth said, "Every woman in America has her eye on this trial, Moira."

"I have sacrificed my family. I don't care about the world."

"I hear you," she said. "I'm so sorry."

Paul's expression remained sympathetic as he listened to my second guessing myself since Lyra's visit. I cried while telling him how horrible it was to be unable to touch my own child. Finally, he said, "Moira, I am helpless. Lyra's giving me the silent treatment. Doesn't return my calls. It was the Erin Charles article that sent her spiraling into her own world. Evidently, she has dinner occasionally with my mother, who is paying for the shrink. And of course, she sees Adeline, who is . . . well, Adeline. Adeline now caters to her day and night. The good news is her dancing is better than it's ever been."

"That's where her heart is now."

"Where is your heart, Moira?"

"Broken. Let's not go there."

I met with Gail, and she said everything was set for the trial as she looked at me with worried eyes. Two days later, a knock on the cell door at a non-scheduled time, followed by the key turning, brought all of us into high alert mode. The sergeant stood there looking around. I had noticed that our common area around the table was more orderly than usual. He had a cardboard mailer in his hand. "I'm told you three"—and he looked at my cell mates—"made a special order with your monthly allowance?"

I was sitting on the edge of my bed and saw them all nodding their heads. "I'm going to allow it this time," the sergeant said. "But generally, we can't have you decorating your cells. You know that."

He looked at me, then at them, and left, turning the key in the door. "It's for you," Muriel said. "Open it."

I took it. "What is it, a map for burrowing out of here?"

"We're not giving you false hope, but open it."

I fumbled with the tape and pulled out the life-size poster inside. It was Lyra, dancing in *Nutcracker*. The light in her eyes radiated out into the room. I touched her face with my hands, and fell to my knees. "My baby," I cried over and over. For once, the girls went silent. They stood in a circle, like the giant monuments at Stonehenge. No one touched me, and I felt deeply respected.

"Can we hang it on this wall?" Kalinda asked, and after ten minutes of loud arguing about where, everyone decided on the wall closest to my cell so that I could see her when I was lying down. "She'll be the first thing you see every morning," Kalinda said. She knocked on the door loudly, and the young CO inserted his key from the outside and entered. "We need tape for this poster," Rhonda said in regal queen mode. "We have a princess joining us." He stood there for a moment, looking unsure. "It's allowed," she said. "Now do my bidding."

"You keep talking that crazy talk, and we'll take it away" he said. He slammed the door and locked it behind him. He was back within the hour, tossing the tape onto the table. Finally, the poster was affixed to the wall. It was as though the sun, moon, and every constellation had entered the gray cell.

"We can use her as a prompt for our writing," Rhonda said.

"I don't know how to thank you," I said to them.

We sat at the round table, and without a word, each of us brought out our little notepads and the thin pens. The image of the four of us staring at Lyra on the wall was indelible.

I said, write whatever comes to mind. I started: *"My dearest daughter . . ."*

58

The morning the trial was to start, I awoke in a state of anxiety. Gail had told me that it could be weeks before it was over. Rhonda was snoring loudly. Kalinda sat at the round table, reading an old *People* magazine. Ruth had dropped off my navy suit two days before, which would be brought in soon for me to change into. For months, I had been limited to seeing only a few people. My cellmates, of course, and Gail, Paul every ten days or so as he was working overtime in the city, he said. Ruth on Friday. The idea of going before cameras and crowds was nauseating.

The CO knocked and handed me the street clothes. He said he'd be waiting outside to take me to court, and I thanked him. I dressed quickly.

Rhonda stirred, then sat up. "Maybe your daughter will be there."

"I don't think so."

"She would rather die than be there," Kalinda said.

"Why do you say that?" I asked.

"Her new knowledge that her real dad was a monster. How does that match up when you're fifteen?"

Muriel interjected, "What Kalinda is saying is that somebody has to get the blame for her suddenly fucked-up life." We weren't used to Muriel swearing.

Rhonda was in a surly mood. "The mama always gets the blame, trust me on that one." She grew surly.

Muriel looked over at the poster. "What she didn't say is that they all want the mama in the end. She'll come home to you, don't worry about that."

Kalinda grunted. "I still would keep her away from the trial."

"Why?"

"My mother was on trial for killing my stepdad when I was twelve, and I had to be a witness. I never got over it."

"What happened?"

"She died in prison. Some kind of infection, they said."

"How stupid are you to tell her this now?" Muriel said, butting in.

"Fuck off."

The bailiff knocked and entered. "Ready?"

"Knock 'em dead," Kalinda said when I stood up.

The CO and the bailiff put a taser-like belt that felt like a brace around my waist under the jacket. It was humiliating to stand there having them fiddle with it. "You know I'm not going to run," I said to the CO.

"Doesn't matter," he said. He was finally satisfied. "I have one of these for my dog," he said. "If he barks, he gets zapped."

"I'll try not to bark then," I said, but he didn't pick up on the sarcasm.

I was put in the police cruiser, and once we arrived at the court, the bailiff escorted me to the courtroom through a side door. I noticed a throng of reporters and cameramen in the front. Gail gave me an encouraging look. I could feel every eye on me and only gave a cursory glance at the people who filled the courtroom.

Everyone stood once the judge entered. I guessed the man in charge of my fate to be around sixty, slight in build. The bailiff called the court to order by saying, "Hear ye, hear ye, the court is now in session."

We sat. As the judge gave instructions to the jury, I glanced at their faces. Several kept glancing in my direction. Seven women and five men. Gail had explained that after determining they weren't biased about the case, lawyers asked questions that led potential jurors to offer a hint as to which side they favored. The judge wrapped up his instructions by saying, "The jury is to determine if the government can prove that the defendant, Moira Dean Rivers, murdered Jonathan Starkweather on the eve of September 10, 1995. If the government fails to convince you, then you must acquit."

The prosecutor was handed the burden of proving my guilt. Mr. Short was, in fact, tall, and charismatic. I guessed him to be around fifty. He had dark wavy hair, penetrating hazel eyes, and a narrow Roman nose. Thin lips that revealed straight teeth when he deigned to smile. He was riveting as he spoke to the jurors about the victim, Jonathan Starkweather, who had helped to create a dance company that would become known for its avant-garde performances. After he reached his forties, he decided to return to New England, where he had started out, and focus more on the educational components of the company. He had attracted support from the community and was excited about the future.

"Jonathan Starkweather was struck down in the prime of his life," he said. He turned and fixed his gaze on me for a moment. I blinked as cameras flashed from across the room, and every eye was on me. Short's voice grew somber. "By a woman who is claiming she was defending her daughter, but who was, in fact, seeking revenge on a man who she claims raped her in 1979."

He looked around the courtroom.

"1979, folks. You don't think it would have occurred to her to go to the police after the alleged act? Or during the five-year statute of limitations period? No, she waited until the opportunity arrived when she could get even. This was why she joined a shooting range in the area and practiced hard to become a perfect shot. That was what was going on in her mind—a mind, by the way, perhaps distorted by alcohol and Prozac."

"Objection." Gail's voice rang out loud and clear.

"Sustained."

He continued. "From the evidence that we have before us, Moira Rivers entered the dance studio where her daughter had gone with her boyfriend Luc Lacroix, a new dancer for the company. Lyra Rivers had decided to go against her mother's orders to stay away from the theater and perform one dance for Mr. Starkweather. Moira Rivers, learning of her daughter's whereabouts, marched into the theater to fetch her daughter. She was seen observing her daughter with Mr. Lacroix and the director, but she didn't stay in the theater long. The next time she was spotted was after shots had rung out. A dancer saw her making her way down the hall to the front doors. We are here to prove that she had time to go to Mr. Starkweather's office and shoot him and rush to join her daughter, who was in her car in the parking lot. Her husband showed up then and escorted his family to the parking lot."

He rubbed his hands together, and his voice lowered.

"Let's revisit that night in 1979. Moira Dean invited the victim to spend the night in her small apartment."

He allowed that to sink in. I felt like I was going to throw up. I figured Short must have spoken with Erin Charles.

"It was late at night. What is a woman to expect when she opens the door to a young and handsome dancer?"

Short was smiling.

"It was Manhattan. 1979. The women's revolution was in effect. Women had been demanding their sexual freedom for years. Now let's segue back to today. Mr. Starkweather is dead. This crime has all the hallmarks of premeditated murder. A revenge murder for a crime that was never reported, where the statute of limitations had long run out, and where there was absolutely no proof of anything untoward happening on that night in 1979."

Short sat down at his table dramatically. I didn't return his gaze. Gail stepped forward to present her opening statement. She looked relaxed as she turned to the jury. No histrionics as she told my story in a simple, straightforward manner.

"Moira Dean was raped by Jonathan Starkweather in April of 1979. Many young people allowed friends of friends to crash in their apartments. The victim, Mr. Starkweather, had set out that night to have sex with the defendant. He had forced himself on her friend, who then gave him Moira Dean's phone number. It was a game to him.

"He attacked my client the moment he entered her apartment," Gail said. "And though she struggled mightily, he was far stronger. A fact not well known is that male dancers are equal in strength to football players. Moira escaped the apartment and hid in a coffee shop, traumatized. All women, then and today, are aware of the risks of going to the hospital and reporting the crime. As Mr. Short so blithely stated moments ago, why would a woman resist a handsome dancer? Albeit a stranger who slapped her hard and beat her into submission.

"But boys will be boys is what I believe Mr. Short is referring to. And to make it easier for men on the prowl, rape was considered a misdemeanor in the Seventies. A woman in 1979 had little chance of getting justice, and the same is true in 1996. Overwhelmed by self-blame and fear . . . after all, my client had opened the door to her intruder . . . she decided not to tell. What no one understood or accepted at the time was that many women experience post-traumatic stress syndrome, just as soldiers do on the battlefield. It can last a lifetime. When one finds oneself powerless, when one's body has been taken over by another, and defiled, when all trust is lost, it takes a long time to rebuild, and too often, it doesn't happen.

"The key symptoms are intense anxiety, flashbacks, emotional torment, and a tendency to self-destruct. Moira Rivers was a successful editor in Manhattan, but after that night, her work suffered. Moira tried to seek help, but it wasn't effective. She had been in love with a man, and they married and moved to Connecticut and had a baby. Moira was also a gardener, and she maintained a beautiful house and supported her husband in his work. She taught writing classes. She began going to the shooting range at the encouragement of a new friend and found that she enjoyed the camaraderie common among gun enthusiasts. Like millions of other Americans. Like many of you. It was a step into health for Moira, as a matter of fact, where she was trying something new, and perhaps even empowering herself with her new skills. There was one problem: she remained a terrible shot. Anyone at the range could attest to that."

Gail moved closer to where the jurors sat.

"Consider all aspects of this woman who had endured trauma and who had sought help, who had been a wonderful mother to her daughter and a good and faithful wife."

She stood silently for a moment, as if debating whether or not to say her next sentence.

"Moira Rivers had heard the stories about Jonathan Starkweather grooming young dancers . . ."

"Objection!"

She continued. "Imagine, all you mothers out there, what you would do if you knew your daughter was, at that moment, with him, especially when she had been forbidden to go there? Would you not have rushed to her rescue?"

The judge banged his gavel and called a brief recess.

Gail glanced at her watch and said we had fifteen minutes. I nodded and rested my head against the back of the chair. I said I needed to use the bathroom, and Gail said she would accompany me. The CO stepped forward when I stood, but Gail said everything was okay. She took my arm going up the aisle, and said, "Mickey Olivetti is taking the stand tomorrow."

"Oh no."

"Short is the one bringing her in, hoping she will deliver evidence against you. He subpoenaed her."

"I wish I could see her."

"I had a good talk with Seamus O'Connell. He and his team have proof that the shooter was left-handed. He is pointing the finger at Mickey Olivetti, though the evidence is slight."

"Does she know?"

"Not yet." We were approaching the courtroom. "Listen, Moira, if there is enough proof, I'm asking Seamus to testify as a forensic psychologist. That's where his art lies, though he's a damn good detective. He said his buddy will explain the gun forensics and he'll explain the way Mickey's head works."

"But you won't implicate her, right?"

"Not yet. Tomorrow she will be here as a witness."

We re-entered the courtroom. The prosecutor called up a couple of the dancers who had been in the theater the night Jonathan was shot, and in emotional outbursts, they talked about how much the director had meant to them and how they did not believe him capable of harming anyone. Luc and the boy who came into the office right after Jonathan was shot were to be questioned the following day. It was a relief when the bailiff led me out the side door and took me to jail.

The girls pounced, wanting to know everything. I told them about Mickey, and they chorused back with 'bummer' and 'shit' and 'you're screwed.'

"She might be a star on the stand," Rhonda said.

"I'm sorry, guys. I'm too tired to talk tonight," I said.

I climbed into my prison garb and lay supine on my cot. As I did every night, I looked into the eyes of my daughter and whispered goodnight.

RUTH

59

I sat in the back row of the courtroom that was packed with TV cameramen and still photographers vying for space. I thought of the crowds who turned out to watch Joan of Arc burn. Obviously, the judiciary in Connecticut hadn't learned from the Pamela Smart case in 1991 when reporters and cameras were allowed in the courtroom. That had been a feeding frenzy, too. Television was already proving that people were salivating for personal, i.e., salacious, stories, and it was predicted that new cable companies were being created to feed them. The world was in the process of becoming one giant soap opera.

I studied the backs of the heads of the characters in this drama. Paul's head rose above the others, his hair falling over his shirt collar. He looked straight ahead, only once leaning over to say something to his mother. Even from the back, she looked arrogant, her hair swept up into a French twist, little pearl earrings attached to her earlobes. I guessed when I saw her enter that she had had another facelift. Her husband Russell was by her side, good dog that he was. His rewards for marrying Katherine were sizable: he had attached himself to the Rivers reputation for fine reporting and after only a couple of years managed to dilute it with right wing poorly written editorials and mundane reporting. I thought it probably wasn't a lie that Katherine would have been challenged to come up with the exorbitant bail set for Moira. Readers were canceling subscriptions as they started switching to the World Wide Web when they could get it or could afford a computer. It was the future, no matter what. Mickey's husband, Tom, didn't have the skull shape to make bald look anything but unfortunate. His neck sunk into his suit jacket. Poor man, living in a wheelchair in a house void of all cheer. No one confessed to knowing him. But from what Seamus had confided to me—all the details about the phantom shooter, which is how he referred to Mickey when her name came up (He was that sure!)—Tom was aware of everything and had no doubt planted plenty of false information in his friend Mr. Short's ear.

I had never been so close to the characters in such an event. The truth is that everyone was lying. (Where was Stella with her enormous sense of injustice when I needed her? Oh, right! Guiding things from above, which is what I had told Moira in a moment of sentimentality as I sat across from her for the umpteenth time, trying to cover up my despair with something hopeful.)

Seamus had frightened me a few nights ago when he said, "The prosecutor must prove guilt beyond reasonable doubt. And the public defender can win the case even if there's a twinge of doubt left in the air."

People can't help but love Seamus. I should maybe speak for myself, I thought. He's done some nasty shit in his life, but he's overcome so much. And his psychological evaluations are spot on. I tell him he could be a novelist, which makes him laugh. He has the gift of empathy, sorely lacking in so many of the cops I've come to know. He says almost everybody is interesting if you listen to their stories. I said, welcome to my world.

I watched Mickey walk up to the stand. I knew she hadn't beaten the cancer. But she had done a pretty good job of covering it up. She had a Marilyn Monroe hip shift walk that was effective, judging by the way the men in the room followed her every motion with their eyes. Her bright red suit and makeup were just right. She was the kind of woman men pay attention to even if they know no good will come of it.

I noticed something in her the minute our eyes landed on each other. I didn't know what I was seeing—recklessness, fear, perversity?—but it was enough to keep her in my thoughts longer than she deserved to be there. What's hard for women, I believe, is that if they feel warning signals spring up, they are reluctant to say anything for fear of being judged jealous. I had felt those signals when Moira had introduced me to Erin Charles and again when I met Mickey. I had told Moira to stay away from Charles sixteen years ago, and she hadn't listened, but I had remained silent when I met Mickey, who I thought was a con artist, for lack of a better term.

Good for Gail Moskowitz, I thought, when she was next to the pompous prosecutor, whose ego was about to explode. He was a misogynist who was determined to bring this woman down to her knees one more time. He was part of the reason women didn't dare report rapes. They were intimidated into secrecy. Seamus told me stories that had me hollering in indignation about women brought in, traumatized, and defeated.

I looked down the rows at Moira, who sat in the hot seat, looking almost regal in her composure. Her hair shoulder length, dressed in an elegant pantsuit that I had selected from her closet. I had been wrong to worry that months in jail would finish her off and that she had lost her mind to hire a public defender.

She had decided to fight. She hadn't fought for herself sixteen years ago, but she would fight for herself now, and for Lyra. Her cloak of invisibility had been cast aside. The news reporters couldn't get enough of her, which I thought could be to her detriment. They couldn't get enough of Lyra, either. She was photographed going to her ballet classes, and one photographer had managed to get inside a studio. The photo he published showed a stricken face. I was glad Moira didn't see it.

Seamus learned he would be called up to the stand. He and I had talked at home. He told me how guys at the gun range referred to Moira and Mickey as Thelma and Louise when they entered the building. He described how "Lefty had a swagger and always a cigarette dangling from her red lips, and Moira was so earnest and pretty and maybe fragile looking, when, in fact, she was the strong one. It was all there in her manuscript. One night, I asked Seamus what he thought about Jonathan's murder, hinting that sometimes the victim deserved it.

"The same as I think about all murders," he had said. "It's against the law to murder."

"You have no emotion attached to the Jonathan case?" I persisted.

"I'll admit it's hard to detach from what happened to him," he said. " It upset me to see the body. Mickey nailed him in the balls— and the heart, too. An ugly sight."

My attention reverted to Mickey, now having taken a seat in the witness stand. Prosecutor Short walked toward her, almost jauntily. "You're a sharpshooter, I understand."

She smiled, enjoying the attention. "Do we use that term in the East?" A slight titter from the audience.

He smiled at her, as though she were an amusing child. "You win most of the gun competitions you enter, is that correct?"

"True."

"And you made the shooting range seem enticing enough that your friend Moira Rivers became a regular for a while."

"Correct."

"You were referred to at the gun range as Thelma and Louise? What does that mean?"

She smiled broadly. "It's a movie of two women on the lam after Louise, that's me, shot a guy who was about to assault Thelma, that's Moira, and from then on, they were escaping the law. A road trip to freedom, sort of."

"So you and Ms. Rivers found the gun range entertaining?"

"I can only speak for myself. Yes. It felt empowering. That's what guns do, as I think you know. You feel more powerful with one than without."

"Ms. Rivers has insisted that you were in Mr. Starkweather's office with her the day he was shot."

Mickey had an exaggerated look of confusion. "Me?"

A twitter among her audience, most of them leaning forward in fascination.

"Objection!"

This from Gail Moskowitz.

The judge said overruled, and Mickey said no.

Short said, "But you have said you were in the building. Why were you there?"

"Mr. Starkweather had asked me to order and pick up sandwiches from our local diner for the dancers and the crew. My husband, Tom, said he'd come along for the ride and help if he could. I stopped at the diner a little after six and was surprised to bump into Moira Rivers. She looked stressed and angry and said she was going to find Lyra. Her daughter. She peeled off, and I said to Tom that Moira seemed mad at me, and he asked why, and I said because she thinks I was in on some kind of conspiracy to have her daughter dance at Portobello."

"Weren't you and Ms. Rivers' mother-in-law and some of her friends trying to create a surprise for Moira Rivers and her husband by having young Lyra Rivers dance on opening night at Portobello?"

"Exactly. No malice intended."

God, she was good.

Short glanced down at his notes. "You delivered the sandwiches to a table located where?"

"In the entrance way. And I dashed back out quickly because Tom had decided not to go to the trouble of hauling out his wheelchair just to go in for a few minutes. I don't like to leave him for long."

Bullshit, I thought. Heads turned in Tom's direction, faces full of sympathy.

Mickey sighed. "Anyhow, no one was around, and I left the bags of sandwiches on the table and walked out to my car and drove Tom and me home."

Short let her story sink in.

"I want to touch on Ms. Rivers' shooting ability."

"She's not a sharpshooter; that's for sure." A titter ran through the crowd again. "But if threatened, it's surprising what people can do."

"Meaning?"

"Moira Rivers could protect herself if she needed to."

"Do you think she needed to protect herself against Jonathan Starkweather?"

"I worked for him and never found him to be threatening."

I couldn't believe how she was throwing Moira under the bus. Everything she said was a lie, yet she was gaining support by the minute. I observed Moira, posture perfect in a hard-backed chair, staring straight ahead, as she listened to her former friend betray her in a courtroom. It was a horror show.

Mickey crossed and uncrossed her legs, and shifted in her seat, as Short thanked her for her testimony.

Gail got up and stood directly in front of Mickey. "You and my client had an altercation at her husband's birthday dinner two nights before Starkweather was shot, correct?"

Mickey nodded.

"She threw a glass of wine at you."

Mickey glanced over at Moira and back to Gail. "Yes."

Gail continued. "It was a feather in your cap to facilitate Miss Rivers' appearance at the Portobello Dance Company opening, correct?"

"Well, sure. I was working for the company."

"For Jonathan Starkweather."

"Yes."

"And hadn't Moira Rivers made it clear that she did not want her daughter to dance at Portobello?"

Mickey frowned. "Yes."

"May I suggest that you were being vindictive by continuing to encourage Lyra Rivers to go behind her parents' back and dance for Portobello?"

"Objection." This from Short's corner.

"Overruled. The prosecutor opened the topic."

Mickey appeared disconcerted for the first time. "I was doing my job," she said.

She glared at Gail Moskowitz brazenly.

Gail said, "The night of the murder, the owner of the diner said under testimony that you were parked in his parking lot when Mrs. Rivers went into the restaurant to ask if they had seen her daughter. You were sitting in your car with the lights on and the window down, smoking a cigarette. Ms. Rivers didn't see anyone else in the car."

Mickey was rattled. Her voice went up. "I have my husband as a witness."

Gail was unrelenting. "And did Ms. Rivers give you back the gun you had gifted her with when you started teaching her to shoot?"

"I don't remember." She looked over at Short, as if to ask what was happening.

Gail took her time. She walked in a small circle and then stopped. "Many days, you and Ms. Rivers went to the Downtown Shooting Range. You had a pattern of aiming at the cardboard figures that were the outline of a human and shooting in the heart and the groin. Exactly the locations of the bullets that entered Mr. Starkweather's body. Isn't this true?"

A collective gasp filled the courtroom.

"Objection!" This time Short raised his hand in the air.

Mickey spoke over him. "I think everybody underestimates the fury of women. A lot of women at the shooting range target the man's groin."

"But the heart *and* the groin? Exactly where Jonathan Starkweather was hit."

"I see you're trying to set a trap for me," Mickey said, her voice raspy. She looked up at the judge. "I'm feeling faint."

The judge banged his gavel down on the podium.

Seamus and I met in the corridor, where we could hear people talking about Mickey's performance. Seamus was nervous about the jury accepting his testimony about the shooter being left-handed; he knew the prosecutor had a forensics expert who would testify the opposite. I hadn't realized how many criminals got away scot-free until living with Seamus. How many cold cases were out there? And how many of the people rotting in prison were innocent.

Luc was next up on the stand, but I had to pick up Sadie. Seamus said he would fill me in. "Basically, he doesn't know anything, but he will to try to make Jonathan Starkweather look like a hero. He was his mentor, after all."

Gail Moskowitz, in my mind, was doing a great job. Mickey's alibi was a little wobblier now, and her shooting pattern made an impact on the jury. Still, it seemed to me it would be a miracle if Gail were able to prove Moira innocent.

I thought back to Paul's birthday dinner. One dance, Luc and Lyra had said at Paul's birthday dinner. What's one dance? they had asked. One dance turned out to be a question of life and death, I thought, as I exited the building.

60

From: *The Halifax Courier*

Courtroom Drama Enters Second Week by Jacob Whitten

The trial of Moira Dean Rivers took a different spin as Public Defender Gail Moskowitz brought author Erin Charles to the witness stand, who testified that she, at first, did not believe that her boyfriend of sixteen years ago, Jonathan Starkweather, raped her friend Moira Rivers, but later changed her mind and offered an apology in her book titled, Childhood Lost, released six months ago. "It's an interesting confluence of events," Charles said to a reporter, "A woman raped and sixteen years later allegedly murdering her rapist."

Prosecutor Short put the author through the paces, stating that just because a friend comes to you and tells you she was assaulted does not make it a true story. He also stated that he found it strange that Charles would change her mind after initially believing Jonathan Starkweather when he told her that Rivers had seduced him.

"I was a lot younger then," Charles said in a flat voice, "and too much in love with him to consider the veracity of my friends' accusations. It's in the book."

"And did you stay with Jonathan Rivers after that?" the prosecutor asked.

"I never saw him again. I now see his abandonment as a sign of his guilt."

"But then you were in touch with him just prior to his death, and issuing a threat, correct?"

"Objection," defense attorney Gail Moskowitz said. "She is not the defendant, but here as a witness."

Charles spoke quickly. "He was in fact in touch with me, Mr. Short. He was furious that I had written about him raping my friends in my memoir."

Short said huffily, "Please refrain from adding information without being asked. The prosecutor walked to a table and held up Charles' book as evidence. "Would it be fair to say that by including this story in your book, you were seeking revenge against Jonathan Starkweather for abandoning you all those years ago?"

"No. I didn't state his name. In fact, I was seeking redemption for the way I had treated Moira Dean.

Prosecutor Short hesitated then changed the topic, "You have a new book out, and you are getting a lot of free publicity."

"I am dedicating my life to working on behalf of women who have been sexually assaulted," she retorted.

The unflappable Gail Moskowitz approached the witness stand and spoke to Ms. Charles in a calm voice. "What is the definition of rape to you?"

The witness hesitated. "It is an act of violence where the vagina, the anus, or the mouth are penetrated."

"Do you know why Mr. Starkweather decided to call your friend?"

"I think because I created a fantasy woman in his mind. I admired her writing. I admired many things about her. I kind of worshipped her."

Moskowitz smiled. "You yourself just said you are dedicating your life to working with women victims. You were attacked at age twelve by a man who ran out of the woods. This is actually quite rare. Most are known by their victims. Eighty-four percent, in fact. Often by someone they trust. Moira Dean Rivers trusted you when she said yes to your boyfriend staying overnight at her apartment. Would you agree with that?"

"Yes."

"Yet you already knew after Jonathan Starkweather went after two other friends of yours prior to calling Ms. Rivers that he was not trustworthy."

Her voice rose. "Yes."

Moskowitz remained still, allowing the comment to sink in.

"You were willing to overlook these infringements in order to stay with him. Is that true?"

"At the time, yes."

"Do you agree that perhaps unconsciously you set her up for what happened to her?"

The prosecutor yelled "Objection!"

The judge told Moskowitz to continue.

"She could have said no," Charles said.

"She did say no. Just as in your book, you said no, but according to you, Jonathan Starkweather had his way with you. Jonathan Starkweather felt entitled to do what he wanted to any woman he wanted."

"True."

Short yelled objection again, and this time, the judge agreed with him. Moskowitz said, "I am attempting to establish the character of Jonathan Starkweather," she explained. She sipped from her water glass, creating a small break. Her voice remained calm when she asked the author, "How did you feel when you learned Jonathan Starkweather was murdered?"

"I was full of grief," she said. "Not for him as a person, but more for how everyone around him has suffered. He suffered, too. I'd like to explain if I may."

"Go ahead," Gail said.

Erin paused, then began her story. "I had not spoken to him in sixteen years; then he called me about the paragraph in my book about him. I told him what I told you. Then I told him that Lyra Rivers was a dancer like him, and there was a possibility in my mind that she could be his."

The buzz in the courtroom that followed felt deafening.

Moskowitz dismissed the witness, walked to her seat, and put her arm around Moira, whose head was down and her shoulders slumped.

I wanted to go and lift her up and carry her out of this chasm she had fallen into. That's what I had done in the old days, when we were roommates. I was her protector, her adviser, and her friend. She, in turn, had allowed me to be vulnerable, to feel beautiful, to find joy in the smallest things. We had taught each other to love.

61

The following morning, I rushed out to the mailbox to retrieve the newspaper and see what the reporter had said about Seamus's day in court. Seamus had gone to Mickey with the information he had collected and had come home upset. She hinted that if he kept pursuing his theory that she killed Jonathan, she would kill herself. He told her that he had to do his job.

From: *The Halifax Sentinel.*

Detective Seamus O'Connell Says Portobello Director Killed by Phantom Shooter by Jacob Whitten

The next person to take the witness stand was Detective Seamus O'Connell of the Waterbury, Connecticut, police department, formerly with the NYPD, who testified that two shots were fired, one in the heart and the second in the groin, the first one fatal. He pulled down a screen with photos of the sofa that Starkweather fell back onto and showed a hole buried deep in the frame on the other side of the sofa where the bullet had lodged. The bullet was held up as evidence.

O'Connell admitted that he knew the defendant and had seen her several times at the local shooting range. "She's a bad shot," he said. "If she were taken to the range and tested today, the proof would be there. Also," he said, "The person who shot Starkweather was left-handed. Forensics was able to prove this from the location of the bullet holes in the body of the victim. He offered the theory that someone could have entered the building through a door rarely used next to Starkweather's office, entered the office, shut the door, and shot twice and left the building as surreptitiously as she or he had entered.

Public defender Gail Moskowitz asked if he could name who he thought the perpetrator might be, and he said, "No. But whoever entered the office was angry. And he or she held a gun in their left hand. I would say the shooter was a woman because of the areas of the body she targeted. It's unlikely that a man would have shot another man in the groin."

The defense attorney thanked him and sat down, and this is when Short came in for the kill. Prosecutor Short practically laughed in O'Connell's face at the outrageousness of his theory that a phantom killer had entered the theater and shot Mr. Starkweather and left. He was relentless. "Theories don't add up to much, Detective," the prosecutor said. "That's all conjecture. Plus coming from a forensic psychologist, it sounds like Psychology 101." Then he said, "If what you said about women is true, then I might start wearing a codpiece." The courtroom erupted in laughter, and the judge banged his gavel.

When Detective Eli Sawyer took the stand, he said that the two women, Moira Rivers and Mickey Olivetti, joked often about being Thelma and Louise, and that it was possible they were acting out some fantasy of revenge. The prosecutor laughed boisterously. "You're making this murder into a soap opera. Or maybe an opera is more like it. A dancer accused of a very bad deed. Women with guns. A daughter gone astray. My god, it's all there." He turned to the jury, "I think what Detective Sawyer is implying is that the two women could have been co-conspirators. Only one of them that we know of entered the building."

Gail Moskowitz intervened. "Objection, your honor. This is leading the jury down a false trail."

Short smiled and dismissed Sawyer.

That night, Seamus was in turmoil. "I admit I maybe used too much psychological jargon," he said.

"Oh, Seamus," I said. "Don't second-guess yourself. The jury has a lot to digest."

"I think Gail has to put Moira on the stand," he said. "She has to tell the truth. She saw Mickey shoot Jonathan Starkweather. Two of us on the force have given evidence that the shooter was left-handed and that Moira Rivers is incapable of shooting accurately."

"Short is protecting Mickey," I said.

"And Moira is, too."

"And Short is making a mockery of justice," I added. "Sawyer wasn't good on the stand, but he was trying by coming up with the two women laying out a plan to kill Starkweather."

Seamus started pacing. "We've conducted a search of Mickey's and Tom's house, and no sign of those two pistols. I'm sure she used the gun she gave Moira to shoot Starkweather. I have one more trick up my sleeve. I found an earring when scouring the back parking lot of the theater. I got to see Moira for a minute at the jail yesterday, and when I showed it to her, she said it was Mickey's and she was wearing it the day of the shooting. On the other hand, it isn't strong evidence, as I assumed Mickey probably used that small parking lot every day when she worked there. But when I asked the janitor in the building, he said only Jonathan Starkweather used that parking space. Barely two cars can fit in there. I asked him if Mickey had a key to that door, and he said it had a special lock and the key was kept in Jonathan's office, and an extra one was kept under a plant in the lot in case Jonathan forgot his. We walked out there, and there was no key."

"Gail knows?"

"Yes. She has it. I'm sure she'll put Mickey back on the stand."

Sadie came in, and we all sat down for dinner. I was in a good mood, hope slightly restored. Seamus remained grumpy. His beeper went off at nine just as we were getting Sadie off to bed, and he stepped outside. When I came back down, he was preparing to leave. "She's dead," he said.

"Who?"

"Mickey. Suicide. I have to get over there."

I couldn't wrap my head around it. My first thought was of Moira. Short would double-down on her now.

I turned to my husband, "Seamus, please don't blame yourself."

"She told me what she'd do. I needed to believe her. I gotta go."

Paul called and asked if he could come by. Within the hour, he entered my kitchen with a bottle of wine. "I can't believe it," he kept saying. "Why?

"She already had a death sentence from the doctor. And the evidence was mounting. She had told Seamus she might do herself in."

"Moira is a cooked goose," Paul said." That bitch Mickey could have set her free, Ruth." Tears ran down his cheeks. "I should care about Mickey dying like that, and I do, but she killed Moira at the same time."

"You need to get to Lyra."

"I'm going to the city tomorrow morning. Adeline said she'd make sure Lyra stayed with her in the apartment tonight."

"I'll try to see Moira tomorrow," I said, " but they've tightened the visiting hours since the trial started."

"It's been awful," Paul said. "I have no idea how she is, really." He sipped his wine. "I was thinking the other day that I don't know her well enough to have a clue what she's thinking. It's frightening to live with someone for sixteen years and admit that."

"Even I am struggling to know what she's thinking now."

"I watch her in that chair every day, so elegant, and poised. I dream of us starting over, confiding in each other. I want to tell her I need her."

"I hope you will have the opportunity to say that, Paul."

He had downed one glass and was having another. "How? Through that fucking plastic partition?"

"Seamus will prove her innocent. He won't rest until he does."

Paul drank most of the bottle over two hours. Before leaving, he said, "If Moira is released, I wonder if she'll come back to me."

"It's true, she might not. I think of Mickey now as some kind of a weird catalyst."

"For what?"

"Moira's transformation."

"I don't get it," he said.

"You will see it, Paul. She has been changed by all of this, Paul. She has found an inner strength she never knew she had. If you are in love with the old Moira, I don't think she's there."

His response was weak, perhaps due to the alcohol. "I thought you meant Mickey was a catalyst for Jonathan Starkweather's murder."

I grew impatient. "It's almost beside the point, which woman shot him. We know it was Mickey, but if Moira had been holding the pistol, she may have shot him. Do you know how many women are sitting in jail and prison because they pulled the trigger against an abuser? And do you know how many women have been killed by spouses?"

"The next thing you're going to say is this has to be a book, right? It will mean Moira's

going to be 'that woman' for the rest of her life if it happens."

"She will be anyhow, and she can do it to create change in this world. Trust me."

"But Lyra . . ."

"She will come to see her mother as a hero one day."

"She doesn't today; that's for sure. And I'm an asshole in her eyes too."

"Then somebody needs to set her straight."

62

Adeline had come up to Connecticut with Lyra the day before, but once reporters got wind of it, a battery of trucks with television equipment pulled up in front of the house. I managed to sidestep around and enter through the side door of the apartment building. Lyra was lying on the sofa and didn't get up.

"Hey, kiddo," I whispered.

"Hey." She looked wan. She told me she had a back injury. "Dad made me come up to rest."

I pulled a chair up close to her and sat down. "It might help to go to the trial for a few hours."

"We can't get away from photographers. Dad worries that Mom will fall apart if she sees me in the courtroom. He thinks she's having a hard time coping with Mickey's suicide. I know he's trying to protect me." It all came out in a rush.

"We're still hopeful that the truth will emerge."

"Do you think Mickey killed herself because she couldn't stand to be accused of killing Jonathan?"

"I think there's a good chance that she was starting to feel cornered. And she was quite ill from the cancer."

"Dad said the truth will be buried with her."

I sighed. "I want to know about you," I said.

"I wish I hadn't been born; that's all."

I could feel Adeline listening. My hunch was she did the opposite of Katherine, who was of the stiff upper lip school. Adeline,

I suspected, had started catering to Lyra's every whim, betraying her own anxiety.

"I'm sorry to hear that.

"Adeline!" Lyra called out.

Adeline raced in. "Yes, lovey?"

"May I have a cookie?"

"Of course. And I'll bring some iced tea." She bustled out.

I started speaking again. "Your mother misses you desperately. She's taking a stand for women. For girls. It's not easy."

"Luc said . . . the incident . . . happened a long time ago and it's his story against Mom's. Now it's my story. With no happy ending in sight."

I started to explain. "It's quite rare for women to lie, though men want the world to think the majority of women are false accusers." Something told me I needed to change the conversation, and I did. "I think you should see your mother and have this conversation with her. The public defender can get you in, I'm told."

"Dr. Evans said that would be too upsetting." When I continued to observe her in silence, she said, "I don't want to see my mother, Ruthie. I know you think I should, but . . ."

"I think you should see your mother, yes, but I want you come to the courtroom out of empathy and love, not out of obligation. Everybody's been telling you how to feel, how to judge your mother, how to protect yourself, but only you know what is best for you and for your relationship. "

She lowered her voice. "Dad doesn't know it, but I found Mom's book buried under his papers. I started reading it, and it made me really sad." She started to cry. "I miss her."

I took her hand. We sat in silence. "Here's the deal. I will tell your mom you are healing from an accident. And when you are ready to see her, just call me."

"Luc thinks mom is mentally ill. I know she was taking antidepressants for a while."

"What? That boy needs to shut up."

Her eyes brimmed with tears. "Do you think Jonathan was my father?"

"No, he wasn't. Depositing sperm in a woman against her will does not imply fatherhood. Paul is your father, the man who has nurtured you and adored you every minute of your life."

"Do you think they'll stay together?"

"I saw them when they met. They were madly in love. I believe they still are. My answer is, I hope so."

Adeline entered. "I couldn't help but overhear." She turned to Lyra, "Hope springs eternal, young lady. Let's get you up."

"I'm okay, Adeline." She stood up on her own, and again I was in awe of her grace. "Thanks, Ruthie."

"I'm there for you, Lyra. You are old enough now to understand. Continue reading Moira's pages. It's something you and your dad should be discussing." She walked over to me and put her arms around me.

Adeline and I watched her go up the stairs. "No one's spoken to her like that," Adeline said. She motioned me to follow her. "I have some iced tea in the kitchen and some cookies, of course."

I followed her in. "I didn't say half of what I wanted to say, Adeline." I picked up a cookie and started to nibble.

"I'm not sure I could bear to sit in the courtroom watching Moira. I voted to keep Lyra away. She's a child. How does a child that age understand anything about men harming women?"

"She's sixteen, not six. She can comprehend a lot more than you think. She and Luc may not have engaged in sex, but she's aware. I can promise you that."

Adeline whispered. "It was something my generation didn't talk about. But you're right. We weren't as innocent as we let people think. It's the reason my mother disowned me."

"You know, Adeline, there's a good chance Moira's story about all this will be bought one of these days. We haven't discussed it, but the world is opening up to hearing more from women on this topic."

"I know Moira has written thousands of words about what happened to her. I want you to think twice before you do that." She picked up a sponge and began swiping the countertop with brisk motions. "All this talk from women about speaking out. What does it all mean? Truth can be dangerous."

"At some point, Adeline, you'll have to start looking at the bigger picture. What Moira has written is not a bodice-ripping romance book, but a book that has the potential to change the lives of many. To convince them to tell their stories."

"Think of Lyra."

"I am thinking about her. She's crippled by indecision and fear that's been instilled in her. By the incredible fear of losing her parents permanently."

Adeline said, "And now she's unable to dance."

"Her back will heal when her mind has healed, Adeline."

"She's been fed so many lies, and whether they know it or not, she has that TV on any chance she gets."

"You need to stop kowtowing to her, Adeline. And encourage her to see her mom."

She grew still. "You might be right. She needs to grow up a little and learn that life is full of potholes."

I suppressed the laugh that was making its way up my diaphragm. "You can say that again." I reached over and embraced her.

63

The circus-like atmosphere of the trial continued, as one revelation after another kept the public wanting more. Reporters and photographers lined the streets. The small courtroom was jammed, one portion of it occupied by dancers, judging from their youth and dramatic clothing and make-up, and strong, lithe bodies. As the days passed, one dancer merged into another. Most had witnessed nothing, but made odd statements. Reporters' descriptions of Moira were mystifying: She was angry, haunted, beautiful, malevolent. (That was a good one.)

Moira arrived every day in the same pantsuit. I thought Gail should maybe have coached her to go for the victim look. Even I knew that the public didn't like for a victim to seem self-assured. I was not allowed to see Moira, but I didn't have to. What I did know is this felt like the Moira I lived with for five years, the Moira who knew what she wanted and who was destined to become a known writer.

I didn't know if she had refused to testify or if Gail didn't want her to.

I had sat down and written Moira a long letter detailing my exchange with Lyra and left it with the friendly CO at the jail. He promised he'd get it to her. In the meantime, the prosecutor ratcheted up his attack against Moira, accusing her of being a controlling mother, insinuating that when her daughter disobeyed her and went to the Portobello Dance Studio, she had retaliated by killing the director. Then he had the audacity to bring up Mickey

Olivetti's death, implying that the stress around her former boss' murder might have driven her to suicide. And the jury looked like they were buying it.

A regular at the shooting range, a fifty year old accountant, testified that Mickey had come on to him, then said that he agreed with the dead woman, Ms. Olivetti, that a lot of women fantasize about killing men before Gail could object.

It all boiled down to evidence, as Seamus said. Two days prior, the doctor who had informed Moira that she was pregnant testified that Moira had told her she had been raped and was questioning whether or not to keep the baby. But Moira had not given the doctor the name of her attacker. The lawyer Moira had gone to, an old friend of ours, had died of a heart attack.

There was too much gray area. No murder weapon. No one in the Portobello Theater saw Mickey Olivetti, but they remembered Moira. And every chance Short got, he brought in the suicide of Mickey Olivetti. Nothing, of course, about her general animosity towards men. Or the abuse that she suffered at the hands of her father and brother that might have triggered her rage. It was hard to know which way the jury would go.

I felt guilty over how little time I had spent with Sadie recently since the trial began. It felt like it would never end. I knew Lyra was Sadie's idol; posters of her were plastered all over her bedroom walls.

"When will Moira go home?" she asked me one day.

"We don't know."

We went into the kitchen, and I made hot chocolate. Sadie leaned over me, her hair smelling like berries. Our closeness made me think of Moira and Lyra, who might be separated for many years.

"I know what it's like to have your mother gone," Sadie said. "I feel so much for Lyra. I was angry at mom for dying, but I was mostly terrified because I was so alone."

"I felt that even at my age when my mother died," I said. "Your mom, you know, is a part of this house. But more importantly, she lives within you."

"I know."

For school, Sadie had been handed an assignment—to write an essay about food. She decided to tell the class how to pickle beets. She began browsing through the fifty cookbooks I had stashed in various bookshelves looking for her mother's recipe. I joined her. My eyes landed on a manuscript that had been rammed into the bookcase.

It was Mickey's. I thought I had tossed it. Sadie found her mom's pages, and I glanced in the den to see Sadie writing away, and decided to give her a little more time. I took a seat and debated about opening the damn thing. But since Mickey's death, what harm could come of reading it? I no longer had to worry about giving her false hope.

I skipped Mickey's prologue and started with the first chapter:

> "*The house where I spent my early childhood was like a fairy castle. Lots of carved doors and long hallways. My mother was beautiful. A woman who loved to dance. My father loved women. Period. He couldn't keep his hands off them. I watched him at parties and saw how he copped feels. The women would move away, usually quietly, looking embarrassed. He smiled watching them. He didn't bother me until I had budding breasts. I was ten. It was my birthday. My gift from him was a trip to California. A big deal. That was when he started molesting me.*
>
> *The poor girl*, I thought. I glanced over at Sadie, whose father was so protective. Who would never contemplate touching her in the wrong places. When I stood up, something fell out of the back of the manuscript. I reached down and saw an envelope addressed to Moira Dean Rivers.

I opened it.

> *Dear Moira,*
> *I was looking for my Thelma and knew that I had found her the minute I met you. I don't know how story crawls into us the way it does.*
> *I already know I'm going to shoot myself. I just don't know when. Probably when I know for sure that Seamus can prove that I'm the killer. He's dogged, and this time, he's a man with a mission.*

I have no regrets about Jonathan Starkweather. I know what you're thinking; by not confessing to my crime, I'm sending you to prison for the next twenty-five years. But remember when I told you you needed to trust me more? I wrote the damned confession, but I'd be damned if I'd hand it over for free. The deal was Ruth had to read my manuscript. If not, it would be her fault you went to prison.

One more thing. I love you. Louise loves Thelma. We're in this together. Remember when they head to the cliff? It was liberation! That's how I see Death.

I changed your story, Moira. For the better.

And now, here's the proof you need:

I, Mickey Olivetti, declare that I shot Jonathan Starkweather twice on the eve of September 4, 1995, once in the heart and once in the groin. Perfect aim, of which I am proud. The guns, handprints, are buried in the overgrown cemetery on the outskirts of Halifax. In the northwest corner where Tom will put my ashes.

SIGNED: Meredith (Mickey) Olivetti.

As I tucked Sadie into bed. I understood how after a big shock, people just go about their business as though nothing has happened. It took about an hour, but around midnight, I began to cry. Sloppily. I felt pain in my chest, and my lips trembled. I couldn't sit alone in the living room another minute. Seamus had come in an hour before, and when I said I had to tell him something, he had said, please give me a few hours to sleep first.

I had to wake him up. I went in the bedroom where he was propped up sleeping, still in his clothes. He hadn't slept well in weeks. I went back to the kitchen and listened to him splashing cold water on his face.

"What is it?" he asked. "Did you and Sadie have a spat?"

I handed him the confession and watched him read it.

His eyes grew wide, "My god, Lefty came through."

"What were the chances of me opening this folder?" I asked. "I meant to toss it."

"Why were you looking in that bookcase?"

"I needed your wife's old recipe for pickling beets." He looked perplexed. "I'll explain later. We'd better call Gail Moskowitz."

She picked up on the second ring. She said she needed this for court tomorrow. I told Seamus to go back to bed. I made a pot of decaf coffee and found a piece of a chocolate bar and waited for Gail.

MOIRA

64

It was August 30, 1997, the final day of my trial. The girls rolled out of their bunk, Kalinda grumbling about how she wouldn't do this for her own kids. Rhonda assured me that prison would be a different story from this place.

"It's not that bad once you get used to it," she said. "I mean, it's too many bodies stuffed into one space, but no more than here. You gotta watch your back, though. There are some loonies in there."

"You're acting like my fate is sealed."

"It'll take a miracle if you don't get some time," Rhonda said. "Better to be prepared."

They knew everything about me. The rape, the baby, the lies. I teased them that jail was nothing more than a confessional booth. They were ambivalent about Paul, but all agreed, don't throw him out with the dishwater.

Paul had come the day before, and it had been awkward, us sitting with a partition between us. What could we say? He was heartsick about Lyra, too. I told him about the letter I received from Ruth about Lyra, and he said he felt he had lost control of her. She was detached and surly, and now her back was injured, and she was going through physical therapy. He said he didn't know where to be. What to do. I asked him to spend as much time as he could with her.

The CO put his head in, and we knew we only had a couple of minutes. Paul looked into my eyes. "I need you, Moira," he had said. I felt self-conscious, glancing behind to see if anyone heard. Then, he said, "I think this whole experience has knocked out the walls you put up all those years ago. You are free. I'm the one in chains. Metaphorically speaking, of course."

"Paul, I'm not in any frame of mind to think metaphorically about anything. The fact is, I'm locked up. I'm in fucking jail, and I could be going to prison for the rest of my life. The so-called walls protected me when I needed it. They're a little flimsier, but they're still there."

His eyes widened. The CO arrived and said he had to leave. "It will be devastating if you're sentenced to prison, Moira. I have tried to be there for you. I'm sorry I ever doubted you." All said in a rush.

"Paul. Listen. I had to do this alone. But the truth is I'm not alone. I have a battalion behind me. My cellmates . . ."

"You have me. Please hear me!"

The CO called out, "Time's up!"

Paul stood, looking handsome with his hair swept back. In that moment, I knew something I'd never known before. Paul was the one who was utterly alone. And bereft. Mickey had told me that his writing was off. His drinking worse. I wanted to reach out and pull him to me. I remembered the night he first told me he loved me, how I had followed him to the sidewalk and watched him do his Fred Astaire shuffle as he disappeared out of sight. "Paul . . ." I called after him, but I was once again too late.

I entered the cell. My cellmates were at the round table, cluttered with movie magazines. Fantasies. Lyra's eyes gazing out dominated the space. They waited, expectantly. I had the intention of telling them about what had just transpired with Paul, but I held back. I didn't quite know myself. When I saw him in his aloneness, I had not felt pity, but love. A love deeper than I had ever imagined.

"I need you," he had said.

I knew that later I would go over every word, every expression. I told the girls about Ruth's talk with Lyra and read the letter she sent me. Muriel chimed in, a sly smile on her face, "That girl needed some direction and she got it. I predict your baby will come home to her mama real soon."

My darling girl. She felt far, far away. As though the wicked stepmother had stepped out of a fairy tale and grabbed her. My last image of her was in the jail with her mouth wide open, eyes closed, no sound coming from her. A giant gaping wound.

"Stop giving false hope, Muriel," Kalinda said. She turned back to me. "If you get sentenced to prison, we won't see you again."

"Not true," said Rhonda. "She has to come back to get her stuff."

I felt the first surge of panic in a long time. I looked around at the room that I jokingly referred to as Fog. Everything dull and grey. And yet love had bloomed here. With their faith in me, I had left the cell each morning with a sense of 'I can do this.' When I was led back to our room, they brought out a roll or a hot dog, or something for me. And now my day of reckoning was here. My fate hung in the hands of twelve people who had listened to contradictory stories for weeks.

Ruth had brought me a newspaper article that had as its front page headline, *Who is the real Moira Rivers?* The reporter posed the editorial question: is it correct to call the defendant a victim, or is she an aggressor? The result of weeks of the trial really boiled down to who told the best story and who the jury chose to believe. The truth had nothing to do with anything.

"I'll be back, no matter what," I said. "I will not abandon you. I promise."

The CO arrived, and I put on the despised belt and walked ahead of him to the waiting car with tinted windows. Would I ever feel unshackled again? The trial had been sensationalized beyond my imaginings. I had heard it compared to the Jean Harris trial and also to the Pamela Smart trial in New Hampshire. I would always be the woman tried for murder for killing her attacker from sixteen years ago.

I thought about Mickey. She had been Lyra's age when she learned to shoot guns. She grew fierce. Her father became afraid of her. Tom was also afraid of her. But he also needed her. She took brilliant care of him. She had made herself indispensable to him. The cost of the battle they were waging was terrific, though—

creating a depression in her that would take its toll. I may not have known how to shoot a gun, but I damn well knew how to keep a secret. I know she was impressed that I hadn't ratted on her in the courtroom. That made me happy.

To the world, I would be a hero, or a villain. No in-between. How would I be to myself once this was all over, I wondered. While waiting for the bailiff to accompany me in, I could see through the glass pane in the door that the courtroom was packed. I scanned the crowd. To my astonishment, I saw the women from writing class clustered together on a bench. Dressed in suits and pearls. It was a moving sight. I had the strangest urge to offer them a prompt: *Write for ten minutes about what friendship means to you.*

I was led in the side door and taken to my usual place at the defense table. I sat, and Gail whispered, "We have some good news, finally."

The judge banged his gavel. The bailiff called the court to order; then the judge studied the papers in front of him and said that Gail could submit new evidence to the court. The bailiff walked to our table and took the two packages she handed him, which he gave to the judge who studied it for a few minutes. A pistol was taken from the second package labeled murder weapon. I felt a tiny sliver of hope. Maybe Seamus had found the guns.

The judge spoke to the jury. "New evidence has been admitted that is a confession by the now-deceased Mickey Olivetti that she shot and killed Jonathan Starkweather. Before me is the gun that Ms. Olivetti used to shoot Jonathan Starkweather."

The courtroom exploded. I looked to my right and saw Attorney Short's shocked expression.

The judge had to bang the gavel several times. "I ask the members of the jury to issue a verdict meeting." They stood and exited, and we were told to return in one hour.

Gail said, "It's almost over, Moira." I was led away to a small conference room and Gail followed. "It's going to be okay." she said. "I'll be back for you."

I entered the conference room and heard Lyra's voice before I saw her.

RUTH

65

Lyra had insisted on surprising her mother. For once, I didn't argue. She placed herself in a big office chair with a high back and turned it towards the back wall. I did the same so that Moira wouldn't realize anyone was in the room when she came in. Gail had helped us arrange the ruse. We heard Gail tell Moira she would be back for her. She closed the door.

Lyra spoke. "My love for you is higher than the highest mountain."

The silence was deep. I felt like an eternity had passed when Moira's sweet voice floated across the room. "I love you deeper than the deepest ocean."

Lyra stood and turned to Moira. "Wider than the Sahara Desert. I love you to infinity! Mommy!"

She ran across the room to her mother. I swiveled my chair around. The cry that came from Moira was so deep and guttural, so primal, that it felt like an earthquake was shaking the walls around me, and then I realized it was my own body heaving sobs. I watched the two of them merge, Lyra's shiny golden hair forming a crown over Moira's head.

Lyra was crying, "I'm so sorry, Mommy."

Moira, with her arm around her daughter, turned to me and motioned for me to join them, and I walked over and they wrapped their arms around me. Not a word said. Lyra had a paper in her hand, but there was no time left, as the door opened and an officer called out, "Ms. Rivers! Time to go."

Moira pulled away from us, and walked to the doorway, her head held high, her posture perfect.

"Mommy!" Lyra cried.

She turned back to the room. "I love you, Lyra. All will be well." The door closed behind her.

"What will we do?" Lyra said to me.

"In five minutes, we will go and find Seamus. If Moira is acquitted, you can go with us to take her to a perfect little house we found for her. We won't think about the alternative."

Lyra handed the paper in her hand to me. When Lyra had called me to say she had received a letter and she had to see her mother, I didn't ask much. She arrived on the train, and I picked her up. It was then I asked to see the letter. The writing was barely legible. I scanned down and saw it was from a woman named Muriel.

I read:

> *Dear Lyra, life hurts sometimes. But most of it is damn good. I am in a cell with your mama that she calls "fog" because it is all grey, with no light except you. Your poster is the first thing the four of us see when we wake up and the last thing we see when we close our eyes at night. I can't put together the girl in the poster who makes me want to get up every day and the one who won't see her mother, who, by the way, is not guilty of anything but protecting her daughter. You have a choice: to keep feeling sorry for yourself, or to stand tall like your mama is doing right now. She needs you. That's about it for now, Muriel.*

I folded the paper back up and reached for Lyra's hand, and we walked together out into the corridor, and into the back of the courtroom, where Seamus stood waiting.

MOIRA

66

I took my seat beside Gail. "How'd it go?" she whispered.

"Seeing Lyra makes whatever happens manageable. Thank you."

The jury marched in and the jury forewoman stepped forward. "We, the jury, duly empaneled and sworn to try the issues in the above titled cause, enter the following unanimous verdict: To the charge of second degree murder: we, the jury, all of our number find the defendant, Moira Dean Rivers, not guilty."

Gail leaned over and embraced me. We were suddenly in a maze of flashing lights as the CO tried to escort me out the door, Gail beside me. Seamus approached and said he would use a police car to get me out of there.

Paul pushed through the crowd and put his arms around me. I hugged him back. "Hey, look," he said. "I was just told that you have to be processed out of jail. I'll find out what time you can leave and pick you up and take you home. My mother said she'd make dinner."

How very Paul. How very Katherine. Let's return to normal. I looked over his shoulder and saw Katherine and Russell. She put up a hand to wave, and I waved back.

"This is going to take a while, Paul. I just saw Lyra."

"Really? How come I didn't know?"

"She had to do it on her own. I need to be with her first, okay?"

Paul said, "I agree. He added, "She's guest-starring with the San Francisco Ballet in four days. I'll fly with her out there, and we'll be back in a week."

"No worries."

"I'll call the minute we're back."

Seamus gently took my arm. "We have to get going."

He guided me down the hallway where so many flash bulbs were popping in my face that I couldn't see. He opened the back door, and I climbed in. Lyra was sitting on the floorboard. Ruth peered into the back seat from the passenger seat.

I smiled. "You two are incorrigible."

Ruthie stretched her arm back between the seats, and our hands entwined. Seamus maneuvered the car into the street, while photographers ran up close to the car for one last shot. Seamus swore, and said, "They've already killed one woman today. Isn't that enough?"

"Who?" I asked.

Ruth sighed. "Princess Diana was killed in a car accident in Paris last night. She and her boyfriend. The paparazzi were chasing them."

Lyra crawled up onto the seat and rested her head on my shoulder. The visceral shock from hearing about Diana's death was enormous. The Bible verse I had learned as a child came back to me: *A spectacular sign appeared in the sky, a woman dressed with the Sun, who had the moon under her feet and a victor's crown of twelve stars on her head.* That time, I had painted her with dark skin, and now in my imagination, I saw Princess Diana wearing the victor's crown of twelve stars as she migrated to another sphere.

"You okay?" Ruth asked out of the side of her mouth.

"I will be."

"There's such an outpouring of grief already over the princess," she said.

"A grief so eloquent it will be felt in every corner of the world," said Seamus. "Even I feel it. What a woman."

"You just gave us the title for our book, Seamus," said Ruth. "The eloquence of grief." She turned in her seat to see what I thought, and my expression must have pleased her, for she turned back around and said nothing more until we pulled into the driveway of a beautiful small cottage. "Welcome home," she said.

Thank you so much for reading *The Eloquence of Grief*. If you've enjoyed the book, we would be grateful if you would post a review on the bookseller's website.
Just a few words is all it takes!

Acknowledgments

I want to thank my children Luke and Ramsey Brown for the healing work they provide to so many—Luke as an E.R. doctor, and Ramsey, who teaches self-defense to girls and women through her organization, R.O.A.R.

Years of gratitude to my agent, Kimberley Cameron, who, once she brings you into her literary corral, keeps you close. And many thanks to Sheri Williams, publisher of TouchPoint Press, for making the magic happen with *The Eloquence of Grief.*

The second half of the book thanks to Serene Eastman, Chief Probation/Parole Officer in Belknap Country (N.H.) House of Corrections, and to Keith Grey, Superintendent of Belknap Country House of Corrections. He took me on a tour of the women's jail and the N.H. Women's Prison, which allowed insight into the incarcerated life so many women are living today. Four of my characters were taken directly from the jail and prison.

California attorney Logan McKechnie offered guidance on the American court system, and gave insight into how trials are conducted.

Much gratitude to my friends and readers: Mary Moffroid, Jane Schneider, Peggy Potter, Dana Jinkins, Tina Welling, Pat Harmanci, and special thanks to Valerie Andrews, who helped with editing.

Printed in the USA
CPSIA information can be obtained
at www.ICGtesting.com
CBHW010351260924
14951CB00016B/630